Song of the Highlands
The Cambels

The Fourth Book in The Medieval Highlanders Series

K.E. SAXON

SONG OF THE HIGHLANDS
Copyright © 2014 K.E. Saxon

All rights reserved. No part of this book may be used or reproduced by any means, graphic, electronic, or mechanical including photocopying, recording, taping, or by any information storage retrieval system without the written permission of the author K.E. Saxon, the copyright owner and publisher of this book, except in the case of brief quotations embodied in critical articles or reviews.

This is a work of fiction. Names, characters, places, brands, media, and incidents either are the product of the author's imagination or are used fictitiously. Any resemblance to actual events, locales, organizations, or persons, living or dead, is entirely coincidental and beyond the intent of the publisher. The author acknowledges the trademarked status and trademark owners of various products referenced in its work of fiction, which have been used without permission. The publication/use of these trademarks is not authorized, associated with, or sponsored by the trademark owners.

Cover Photo obtained from Romance Novel Covers
Cover Design created by Angela Waters Graphic Art & Design
Editing Services supplied by:
Valerie Hayward
Bev Katz Rosenbaum
Proofreading Services supplied by Jan Carol

* * * *
ISBN: 1499399057
ISBN-13: 978-1499399059

CONTEMPORARY BOOKS BY K.E. SAXON

Sensual Contemporary Romance
Love Is The Drug
A Stranger's Kiss (novella)
A Heart Is A Home: Christmas in Texas (novella)

Sensual Romantic Comedy/Fantasy Romance
Diamonds and Toads: A Modern Fairy Tale

Contents

Author's Note	*i*
Glossary	*iii*
Part One: A Knight's Quest	*11*
Part Two: A Lady's Journey	*107*
Part Three: A Bond Broken	*231*
Part Four: A Belief Erroneous	*325*
Part Five: A Madman's Lair	*375*
Part Six: A Song Well Sung	*497*
Bonus Material: *Of Us That Trade in Love* (*Morgunn & Gwynlyan*)	*525*

AUTHOR'S NOTE

I would like to start by paraphrasing a portion of my author's note from my Highlands Trilogy: By the time of William the Lion (William I), who ruled Scotland from 1165 to 1214, the feudal systems were more firmly established in the southern region of Scotland, the king had managed to exert his influence and sway in the wilder northern and western regions as well. Mostly through alliances with foreigners to whom he chartered land, or to natives who sought a royal charter for their land in order to secure it for their own offspring.

My vision, therefore, was of a kind of "melting pot." The old ways, not completely abandoned, yet the new coming to be embraced.

This is a work of fiction. Some creative license has been taken with regard to certain aspects of historical accuracy in order to fulfill my vision for the romance, and allow for less confusion to the romance reader.

The Campbells were in the Highlands during this time frame, but were not yet known by the name Cambel (cambeul).

The idea for setting William, King of Scots' court at Scone Abbey actually came from another work of fiction, *The Fair Maid of Perth*, written by Sir Walter Scott, while I was researching *Highland Vengeance*. Within the third paragraph of the first chapter it reads: *"The city was often the residence of our monarchs, who, although they had no palace at Perth, found the Cistercian convent amply sufficient for the reception of their court."* The abbey at Scone was Augustinian, but I loved the idea of using it so much, that I blurred the lines a bit. As well, I want to note, that although I have searched, I have never been able to verify Sir Walter Scott's words with any scholarly account.

The Romans mined copper from Scottish Highlands, set up forts for this purpose, as well as to "tame" the natives.

The idea for Morgana's song weaving a spell on the occupants of the carn (cairn, in modern spelling), comes directly from the section, "Acoustic effects: ancient Scottish megalithic chambers", which I found in the book, *The Quest for the Celtic Key*, by Karen Ralls-MacLeod and Ian Robertson, while doing research for this book. It specifically speculates that sub-sonic vibrations may have altered the mental states of the ancient worshippers, but this sentence alone was enough to set my imagination flying!

Although Schiehallion is not well-forested now, there is archeological evidence that at one time it was. In the 13th century, though much of the ancient forests had been depleted, there were still an estimated 20% standing. Today, there are only an estimated 1%. For those interested in the history of deforestation and afforestation of the Highlands, and Scotland in general, I recommend, *Woods, Forests, and Estates*, by Thomas Hunter; and *Conquering the Highlands: A history of the afforestation of the Scottish uplands*, by Jan Oosthoek.

I hope you can forgive the licenses I've taken and simply enjoy Robert and Morgana's story!

For further scholarly reading, please refer to my research booklist at http://www.kesaxon.com

K.E. Saxon

* * *

GLOSSARY

This glossary is meant merely as an aid to the reader of this story, and in no way is intended to be used as an authoritative guide to the spoken language represented. The glossary contains pronunciations of classical Latin, Old Norse, and Scottish Gaelic, of which some were constructed by the author using multiple sources (see list at end of glossary), and to the best of her ability, as no authoritative pre-constructed versions of the word's pronunciation were found.

Á vegginum Ásgarðr \ ar-veG-in-uhm ars-gar-thr \: Lit: Upon the wall of Asgard. (This expletive was completely contrived by the author, and has no proof of historical merit, as far as she has been able to find.) Old Norse.

Aerariae secturae \ ahyuhr-ar-ee-eye sec-toor-ahy \: Latin "copper mines". [note: classical pronunciation]

Ankou \ ahn-koo \: Breton Mythology. A Celtic death god known as "Master of the World"; Grim Reaper.

Armoric \ ahr-mawr-i-k, -mor- \: A native of Armorica. (Brittany)

Bǫllr of Óðinn! \ Bah-klr ahv O-then \: Lit: Balls of Odin! (This expletive was completely contrived by the author, and has no proof of historical merit, as far as she has been able to find). Old Norse.

Bealltainn \ byăll-tènn \: The Celtic May Day Festival. (May 1 or 2). Scottish Gaelic.

Cailleach Bheur \ kaely-lyach vveer \: The old hag of the ridges in folklore. Scottish Gaelic.

Caislean Credi \ kahsh-lee-ahn kreh-dee \: "Hill of Credulity"; The place of coronation for Scotland's Kings at the Abbey at Scone. Survives as the present Moot Hill. Scottish Gaelic.

Castelaine \ kahst-l-eyn \: Note: Author-coined feminine form of *castelain*, which is a medieval term for the male governor of a keep.

Compline \ kom-plin, -plahyn \: "Night Prayer." The last of the seven canonical hours, or the service for it, originally occurring after sunset and before bed.

Corpsish \ kawrps-ish \: Note: Author-coined word (because corpse is an older word than cadaver) with the intended meaning: pale, haggard and thin. Of or like a corpse.

Cruach na Beinne \ kruăch nă baynn \: Ben Cruachan in Argyll. Scottish Gaelic.

Dæll \ dal-l \: Gentle, easy (to manage). Old Norse.

Garbh Uisge \ gărv ishka \: River Leny. Scottish Gaelic.

Greek fire \ Greek fire \: A Byzantine incendiary mixture, composition unknown that, when wetted, exploded into flame, and was then shot through syphons or catapults.

Haust \ howst \: Harvest. Old Norse.

Hymenaeal \ hahy-muh-nee-uhl \: Archaic. Marriage song.

Í móti vetri \ ee moti vetree \: Lit: "At the onset of winter". Old Norse. See: *Ynglinga saga* by Snorri Sturluson.

Ingeniator \ in-jen-ee-ah-tore \: Latin "to devise in the sense of construct, or craftsmanship". Root of *engineer*.

Inverleith \ eenn-vare-llhay \: Medieval name for Leith. Up until the 16th century, Leith had two settlements, one north, and one south of the Water of Leith river. The south settlement was a trade port; while the north settlement was more a fishing village, and under the jurisdiction of Holyrood Abbey.

Kœrr logi of mitt fýst \ korr loGi ahv miT fuhst \: Dear flame of my desire. Old Norse.

v

Leòdhas (Isle of) \ Lioh-yhas \: Isle of Lewis. The Largest Island of the Outer Hebrides, Scotland.

Lia Fáil \ lee-ah fowl \: Stone of Destiny. The coronation stone for the High Kings of Ireland up through Murtagh MacErc (6th century AD). Scottish chroniclers in the 13th century expanded the legend to say that the Stone of Destiny was the same as the Stone of Scone, that it was brought to Scotland by the brother of Murtagh MacErc, and never returned. This legend, then, I believe would have made for good theater in William the Lion's court.

Llyn Tegid \ khlin teh-gitt \: Bala Lake in Gwynedd, Wales.

Matins \ MATT'-inz \: "Sunrise Prayer". The second of the seven canonical prayers, fixed at sunrise.

Mildr \ Mill-der \: Generous. Old Norse.

Napron \ na-prau \: Apron. Middle English.

Nones \ nohnz \: The fifth of the seven canonical hours, or the service for it, originally fixed for the ninth hour of the day (or 3 p.m.).

Pasche \ păsk \: Medieval term for Easter or Passover.

Regnum Aragonum \ rai-nyum ah-reh-gon-uhm \: Latin "Kingdom of Arragon".

Samhainn \ sah-win \: All Hallows Day.

Scut \ skuht \: a short tail, especially that of a hare, rabbit, or deer, from old Norse *skutr*. A medieval slang term for female genitalia.

Seed wool \ seed wool \: Cotton wool not yet cleansed of its seeds.

Sext \ sekst \: The fourth of the seven canonical hours, or the service for it, originally fixed for the sixth hour of the day taken as noon.

Sìdh Chailleann \ shee haaly-unn \: Schiehallion is a prominent mountain in Perth and Kinross. The name Schiehallion is an anglicised form of the Gaelic name *Sìdh Chailleann*, which is usually translated as "Fairy Hill of the Caledonians".

Sruighlea \ Stree-lye \: ancient burgh of Stirling. Scottish Gaelic.

Svanfríðr \ svahn-fri-thra \: Beautiful swan. Old Norse.

Sverð of Óðinn \ Svairth ahv OhthiN \: Lit: Sword of Odin. (This expletive was completely contrived by the author, and has no proof of historical merit, as far as she has been able to find.) Old Norse.

<u>Tarse</u> \ tahrss \: Medieval term for penis.

<u>Terce</u> \ turs \: The third of the seven canonical hours of the divine office, originally fixed at the third hour of the day, about 9 a.m.

<u>Uachdar Àrdair</u> \ ooh-ahkgh-ar aar-dare \: The town of Auchterarder. Scottish Gaelic.

<u>Uisge Abha</u> \ ishka ahva \: River Awe. Scottish Gaelic.

<u>Uisge Beatha</u> \ ishka beyha \: Lit: "Water of Life", a.k.a. whisky.

<u>Uisge Theamhich</u> \ ishka haym-ekh \: River Teith. Scottish Gaelic.

<u>Whitsonen Day</u> \ hwit-sahn-en dey \: Whitsunday, Pentecost. A major holy day and festival celebrating the descent of the holy spirit to the apostles.

<u>Widow's Terce</u> \ wid-ohs turs \: Not to be confused with the religious term for the third canonical hour. In Scots Law, immovable property bequeathed by the husband to his widow upon his death.

<u>Sources</u>:
Covington, Michael A. "Latin Pronunciation

Demystified." University of Georgia, *Program in Linguistics*, last revised March 31, 2010

MacAlpine, Neil. *A Pronouncing Dictionary: To which is Prefixed a Concise but Most Comprehensive Gaelic Grammar,* Stirling & Kenney, 1833

Maceachen, Ewan. *Maceachen's Gaelic-English Dictionary.* Inverness, Northern Counties Newspaper, revised and enlarged 1922

Guðlaugsson, Óskar. "Pronunciation of Old Norse (standard)." Old Norse for Beginners Website: https://www.notendur.hi.is/haukurth/norse/, 2000

Slocum, Jonathan & Krause, Todd B. "Old Norse Online: Base Form Dictionary." University of Texas, *Linguistics Research Center* Website: http://www.utexas.edu/cola/centers/lrc/, last updated December 2013

Vikings of Bjornstad Group, The. "Old Norse Dictionary: English to Norse." The Vikings of Bjornstad Website: http://www.vikingsofbjornstad.com, last updated 2014

<u>Additionally, the following websites were immensely helpful:</u>

Forvo.com, Icelandic
Forvo.com, Swedish
Forvo.com, Scottish Gaelic
Forvo.com, Latin

Omniglot.com, Old Norse
Omniglot.com, Scottish Gaelic
Omniglot.com, Latin

Lexilogos.com, English to Scottish Gaelic Translation

Translate.google.com, Icelandic, Swedish (audio sample)
Translate.google.com, Latin (audio sample)

Wikipedia.com, Old Norse
Wikipedia.com, IPA for Icelandic
Wikipedia.com, IPA for Swedish
Wikipedia.com, IPA for Scottish Gaelic
Wikipedia.com, IPA for Latin

* * *

PART ONE

------ ❖ ------

A Knight's Quest

*"Time is now to arise, from tables costly to part us;
Now doth a virgin approach, now soundeth a glad Hymenaeal."*

From Hymn to Hymen by Catullus

*"That kiss again; she runs division of my lips.
What an eye she casts on me? It twinkles like a star."*

The Jew of Malta (Act VI, scene iv).

CHAPTER 1
Perth, The Highlands
Scone Abbey, March 1207

MORGANA CAMBEL SAT at one of the many trestle tables in the great hall of William, King of Scots' royal court and, as she'd done every night this past fortnight, surreptitiously gazed at the object of her deepest desire: Robert MacVie, Highland laird and knight magnificent. He'd won yet another tournament that day on the lists, and the coin and prestige that went with it as well. Just as he'd done the three times she'd watched him on the tourney field these past days.

She'd heard he'd entered the contests as more of a necessity for quick coin than a bid for acclaim. He did a quick scan of the chamber and she straightened. His gaze lighted e'er so briefly on her before settling warmly on her cousin, Vika, who sat speaking to one of the many other warriors present in the hall. Morgana sighed softly. *If only he could like one such as me.* But, 'twould ne'er be, she knew. For, she was quite certain that not he, nor any knight in fact, would e'er willingly take a lady like she with no power of speech, whom the priests were sure the devil himself had taken hold of, and who had little to offer for dowry, either—perhaps the biggest impediment of all.

Ah, but he was a handsome one, was he. Aye, handsome as the devil with whom she was accused of consorting. Sable hair and steel-gray eyes. Dark brows and a strong, square jaw. And bulk. Aye, what bulk the man had!

As she watched, he leaned to the side and said something to one of his comrades. Morgana's eyes dipped longingly to his wide, masculine lips. What would it be like to have her own seized by them? To taste him on her tongue?

"You want him, do you not?" Vika said next to her ear. "I can arrange it, if you'd like. Would you like that, my pet? I've grown bored, but you might enjoy a bit of his style of possession."

Possession. The word sent a thrill of excitement through her, making her womb throb, making the tips of her breasts harden. She didn't hesitate. She nodded.

Vika's laugh came from deep in her throat. "At the chimes of midnight, be settled on the third bench in the chapel. Wear the scarlet cloak I gave you, and keep that white hair of yours covered. We look enough alike otherwise, that he's sure to think you are me."

Morgana nodded again and gave her older cousin a grateful smile.

Song of the Highlands

"Now off with you. 'Tis nearing that time now. And wear a bit of my herbal tincture as well—you'll find it on top of the table, next to my comb, in my chamber. Place some on the curls of your sex—do not ask me why, for 'twill all become clear later."

Morgana felt a heated blush bloom on her cheeks, but she gave her cousin a jerky nod before rising from the bench she'd been seated upon. After signaling her farewell with a dip of her head to each of the others at the table, she hurried out of the hall, quelling the guilt that immediately rose up inside her. She was eighteen summers, she told her conscience, with her nineteenth fast approaching. Well past marriageable age and with no prospects for husband. Or lover, for that matter. And she'd remained chaste for as long as she was willing.

Aye, 'twas true that before, when she'd been in the nunnery, she'd had a different idea of what was proper. But since joining the court a moon past and seeing just how liberal the morality was here, her perspective had changed. Drastically. Now she saw the benefit in experimentation prior to wedding. Especially since it had become clear to her that her own chastity upon marriage would not be the sticking point she'd always believed 'twould be.

In short, she wanted to begin living her life, as it no doubt would continue to be: Sans husband, sans bairns. It made her sad to give up that dream, but to molder on the shelf the rest of her life seemed pointless. And her cousin had just given her the most perfect way for her to be initiated into her carnal education: With the first man she'd e'er desired to mate with, Robert MacVie.

* * *

Vika nodded and gave Robert a conspiratorial smile when he caught her eye again. *Aye*, she thought, *plan your little scheme, but you'll soon find you've tested a much worthier opponent—and lost!* She'd learned from one of her sources that day that her sometimes lover, Robert MacVie, with whom she'd made plans to play one of their little lovers' games—this time, one of her favorites, ravishment by a stranger—was in fact planning an abduction and forced pregnancy on her, an heiress to a vast holding, in order to obtain an open assent to his troth. Which, she knew, he desperately needed in order to pay his clan's debts.

This would get her cousin out of the way for a bit as well. Thus aiding her cause with the man she, herself, had set her eye upon, Guy de Burgh. Unfortunately, that man, thus far, could not be swayed. And had, these past days, been spending a bit too much time in Morgana's company for Vika's liking.

She watched Robert rise from his seat and stride out of the great hall. Ah, to be a fly on the wall and see his face when he at last discovered he'd taken the wrong lady! But would Morgana be *taken* before he discovered the switch? Vika chuckled. She truly did hope so, for 'twas clear the lass was deeply enamoured of the knight.

And, in truth, she wished her cousin a better first time than she, herself, had endured nearly half her own age ago when she'd been forced to wed the old man to whom her father had given her. Vika's brows drew together, her smile of a moment before disappearing, as she absently rubbed the pad of her thumb o'er the nail of her middle finger. Aye, 'twould be a shame if Morgana didn't at least get her first taste of the culmination of a woman's desire. And from the one she so clearly wanted.

Vika sighed. She'd simply have to wait until they returned on the morrow to find out, she supposed.

* * *

'Twas a long and bumpy ride to where e'er Robert was taking her. Morgana hadn't known exactly what to expect when she'd settled on the bench in the chapel a few hours past. But she certainly hadn't foreseen being gagged, blindfolded, and tied up. Nor, hefted like a sack of grain into the back of a wagon and taken to God knew where in the middle of the night. She would have been deeply afraid that she was the victim of some violent man's scheme, had she not continued to hear Robert's voice speaking in muted tones to what seemed to be at least three other men throughout the journey.

The cart began a long, rough ascent some three or more hours into their travel and she rolled and slid until she finally found purchase against one of its sides. The air was growing colder as they progressed, but she was well protected from the wind by the covering o'er the top of the cart.

'Twas not long before she heard Robert call a halt and the conveyance came to a creaking, shivering stop. In the next moment, she was hauled up and o'er someone's—Robert's?—shoulder and bounced roughly as he moved up some steps and through a narrow doorway.

He set her on her feet, but only long enough to fling wide her cloak and slit the front of her gown and chemise down the front. 'Twas done so quickly, she barely had time to realize what had happened before she was lifted in his arms and positioned on what she assumed was a narrow bed with tall posts at the end, because he spread her legs wide, wrapped her knees around the posts and then scooted her down to the edge. It made her thighs burn and quiver, to be spread in such a manner. Tears of strain leaked from her eyes, making the blind o'er them grow damp.

He still had said not a word to her and now she was beginning to be afraid. Was this how 'twas done then? Somehow, she'd gotten the impression that 'twas a gentler act than this. Her heart pounded so, that she could feel its pulse hammering in the side of her neck. She couldn't catch her breath.

The same two beefy, long-fingered, warm hands that had dealt with her legs, now took hold of her bound wrists and lifted them o'er her head, tying them to a post on that end as well.

Oh God, what was he going to do to her? Why had she agreed to this? *Would he kill her now?* She was completely helpless—totally at his mercy. A dank smell of must filled her nostrils, the sound of a man's rough grunts flashed in her memory. She began to quake.

But then something wonderful began to happen. Those same huge, strong hands commenced a slow, sensual glide o'er her bare breasts, down her rib cage, and o'er her abdomen, then up again to tease the peaks of her breasts. A warm, suctioning feeling came next, along with the sensation of puffs of hot breath against her sensitive skin. A hot thrill ran through her as first one crest and then the other was caressed in this manner, followed again by gentle fingers as that humid suction traveled down and o'er her abdomen and settled with blindingly pleasurable accuracy o'er the apex of her sex.

Morgana's back arched and every muscle in her frame went rigid with sheer delight. Her mouth opened wide under the gag and she felt a silent scream in her throat. His tongue began a magic dance and she started once again to quake and tremble—this time, with pleasure. He rolled her nipples between his thumb and forefinger and pinched them, causing a slight pain. She saw pinpricks of light behind her lids just before her womb convulsed, and then she splintered apart.

As she was floating back down to earth and hearing her breathing, still harsh, but slowing to a bit more of a normal meter, he shocked her by starting the process all o'er again. This time, when she felt that ultimate bliss, she began to cry. The pleasure was more acute this time, almost painful in its scope. She prayed he would stop now, for she knew she wouldn't be able to take another from him so soon.

Somehow, he must have known, because she felt him rise up between her thighs. Felt the wiry hair from his own muscular, hard thighs tickling and softly abrading the tender skin on the insides of her legs. She felt something warm, something long and thick, smooth, but with a blunt, rounded tip caressing the outer lips of her sex. Was this his manly yard? She'd ne'er seen one, but she'd heard the ladies speak of them. It certainly matched their descriptions.

She felt the blunt tip pressing into the center of her. She barely had time to get accustomed to the odd feeling before she was ripped asunder by his rough, rapid entry. She jerked and tried to pull herself back, but he had hold of her hips and rammed into her again. *This cannot be the right way.* Scalding tears burned her cheeks. *Surely, I will die from this.*

* * *

"God, Vika, you've been practicing," Robert growled. "Loose your grip on me, else I'll not last long enough to pleasure you." He knew he wasn't supposed to speak—this was one of the requisites she'd given him for this lovers' game—but he couldn't keep silent. Christ, she was squeezing him in a hot, moist vise along every inch of his cock. And it felt good. *Too* good.

But she didn't comply. Instead, she tightened around him even more. He jerked and shuddered, grinding into her e'er harder as he lost the battle and, with a vociferous shout, erupted inside of her. Just as he began to slow, as the last eddies of visceral satisfaction were rippling up from his tarse, into his loins, and out into his being, she lifted her hips and started moving against him. When he felt the strong muscles of her canal begin to milk him, he rose up on that crest again with a ragged moan and this time he thought he'd die from the eviscerating pleasure it gave him.

When 'twas over, when the only sound in the small chamber of the stone cot was the hiss of their breath as they struggled to fill their lungs, Robert slowly slid out of his lover and walked over to the wall sconce. Swiving Vika had ne'er been that bone-numbingly satiating before. Hell, his ears still rung from the explosive climaxes she'd given him. Which bode very well for their marriage, a thing he was determined to have with her.

And this night, and the nights following, with them having no means of preventing conception of a babe, would seal the bargain. For, he'd spend inside her how e'er many times it took to get her with child and force her to give him her hand. And the coin that came with it.

He'd not used the sheath on his cock, as she'd demanded he use in her note, but she'd told him before that she could ne'er tell when he used the thing in any case, and this game proved to be a perfect opportunity to begin as he meant to go on. 'Twas a desperate plan—and one that could easily go awry—but 'twas the only one he had at his disposal. In fact, he might just get hanged for such a reckless move, but he had no other choice open to him, not any longer, and he was determined to take complete advantage of it.

After lighting the end of the torch he strode over to gather up a taper from the trestle table by the hearth and lit it as well. He arched a brow, studying the hearth for a split second, but then decided he'd best light the thing after he'd made Vika more comfortable.

He turned back toward the bed, took a couple of steps, then stopped short. First shock, then unmitigated anger, filled him. "Was this your idea, or did Vika arrange it?" All at once he realized the lass—What was her name? Oh, yes, *Morgana*—still had the gag in her mouth.

With angry strides, he took the last few steps over to the bedside and loosed the ties that bound her. Tho' 'twould not give her a voice, he knew, for he'd heard the tale these past sennights that she'd not said a word since she was a wee bairn. And what e'er had caused her to lose her voice, had also turned her dark hair the color of the silver moon on the blackest, most starless night of the year.

His eye scanned down to her sex, to see how dark were the curls that covered her mound. 'Twas then that he noticed the blood. On her sex, and on her thighs.

He lifted the hem of his shirt and looked beneath. His cock was red from it as well. He had a bit of it streaked on his right thigh and his groin hair was damp with the stuff. *Blood of CHRIST! A virgin.* He'd forgotten she was an innocent not long from the nunnery.

He turned his attention back to his newly initiated lover, at a bit of a loss as to what to do, as this was the first one he'd e'er taken. He was going to strangle Vika for this, he truly was. For, now that he'd had time to think on it, he was convinced that this was one of Vika's *amusing* tricks she liked to play on her unsuspecting lovers. Or—had she learned of his own scheme and decided to confound the plot? Aye, knowing Vika and her court minions, 'twas no doubt the case.

* * *

Morgana blinked and looked around. She was inside a very masculine chamber. There were hunting knives, bows for hunting, and other weapons hanging from the far stone wall. Her eye settled on Robert's visage at last. She'd avoided it at first, feeling a bit too shy after what they'd just done, to look him fully in the face. Besides, he was angry now that he'd discovered the switch. She saw where his eye was settled and looked there herself. *God in Heaven!* Her pulse spiked. *Is this punishment for my fleshly lust?* She'd known there would be blood, but not this much. Had Robert torn her? Was her womb ruined? It had certainly hurt more than she'd been told it would.

In fact, she'd been sure she'd die from the searing pain of it. But then, when she'd heard his ground-out words, his moans of rapture, felt his body straining toward that ultimate joy as her own had done, she'd realized 'twas because of the satisfaction he was receiving by being inside of *her*, and the feeling had changed to one of pleasure.

Oh, there had still been a terrible burning sensation, but that had been overtaken by the growing delight until, finally, she'd been able to ignore the hurt, and begun to enjoy the feeling of him stroking in and out of her. Enjoyed it to such a degree that she'd found that ultimate bliss once more, but this time with him deep inside her and finding his own bliss as well. She'd thought it wonderful. And incredibly satisfying. Her breathing calmed. Aye, wonderful. So, surely not a punishment then? But the gore of it must be why virginal ladies are ne'er told in detail about the carnal act, for they'd ne'er agree to it then.

She tried to bring her legs up o'er the posts, but she

was too stiff, so she settled back. Mayhap 'twas best, for now, not to move very much until she was sure that she was all right. She turned her head and looked at him again, motioning as best she could that she needed something with which to cleanse herself.

Thanks be to heaven, he understood her and turned toward one of two buckets and a ladle that sat in the corner. There was a trunk next to them, from which he pulled a linen cloth. First, he washed himself. Then he brought one of the buckets of water and the cloth o'er to the end of the bed and settled on his knees between her thighs.

* * *

" 'Twill be cold. Ready yourself." Robert bent to the task, ignoring Morgana's sharp intake of breath at the first contact of frigid, damp cloth to hot, tender skin.

Black. The hair on her mons was as black as his own soul. And the flesh beneath, as red and succulent as the ripest winter berry. He felt his cock stir to life, but ignored that, too. He'd not chance another time with her. At least, not until they were back at the abbey and had access to the means to prevent conception.

He'd made sure there was naught like that here when he'd planned the adventure. He pressed his lips together in a thin line. Aye, he'd expected to stay here with Vika for at least a moon. Her father had left the King's court two days past and would not return for quite a time, mayhap even two moons. It had been the best and only opportunity Robert had had to try to get Vika to agree to wed him, for no one would look for her during those sennights, understanding that she was with her current lover.

* * *

Morgana flinched when Robert pressed a bit too hard as he wiped away further remnants of her first carnal experience. He lightened his touch, but remained as mute as she. What was he thinking? Was he still angered by her and Vika's duplicity? Had he enjoyed taking her? And, more importantly, *would he do so again, now that he knew her identity?*

That question plagued her more than she was willing to admit to herself. For, truth be told, his gentle cleansing of her was making her blood heat for him again. But, mayhap, 'twas too soon to do the deed again? She knew not for certain.

How often could a man perform the act? Was it once a night? Once a sennight? Or once a moon? Mayhap that was the reason her cousin had taken so many lovers. If ladies could take a man more often than a man was capable of performing, then that would certainly make sense.

* * *

" 'Tis unlikely you'll conceive this first time but, if you do, there is a woman I've heard spoken of that knows what can be done about it," Robert said into the silence, startling his mute companion enough to make her jolt. Ignoring the reaction, he dropped the cloth into the water and swirled it around, ridding it of the blood and making the water turn an even rosier hue in the process.

He shrugged. "Otherwise: Bastards are whelped everyday; one more will make no difference." He gave her a piercing look. "But you'll get no wedding vows from me, so do not think a babe in your belly will sway me to do so."

Morgana nodded slowly. She had no worries, for the court ladies had said 'twas not so easy to get a babe started if you'd just finished your flowering—which Morgana had only recently done. Two days ago, in fact.

Robert relaxed his shoulders. Good. The lass understood how things would be between them. He knew his words had been harsh, but he'd give her no quarter—he could not afford such a luxury. 'Twas best that the lass kenned from the beginning that theirs would not be a prelude to marriage; this was no carnal affair leading to a love match.

He took in a deep breath and released it, then turned back to the job at hand. After wringing out the excess moisture, he returned it to his silent companion's gorgeous, lush tail. Aye, but he'd fuck her often—and well—once he could get his hands on the means to prevent childing. That promise he could give to her—and to himself as well.

"All right. 'Tis done," Robert said as he plopped the rag back into the bucket and stood up. He walked over to the door and, after opening it, tossed the contents of the bucket out onto the snow-covered ground. He turned and placed the container back where he'd found it, and then started building a fire in the hearth.

He had to admit, he liked how silent the lass was. 'Twas rather pleasant for a change not to have a lady bleating in his ear after giving her a good fucking. Lord, how they could go on about this thing or that. Mostly to do with fashions, which he thoroughly abhorred. Or worse, some bit of chatter they'd been privy to that they simply could not wait to share with him. And if he e'er wanted to get between their thighs again, he had to pretend *interest* in those dull-as-dirt tidings.

He heard strange scraping and creaking noises coming from the direction of the bed and looked up. Morgana motioned that she needed a bit of help getting her legs back o'er the posts. He nodded and quickly accomplished what she'd evidently been struggling to do these past moments as he went about his business. He felt a small twinge of conscience that he hadn't thought of helping her before, but quickly let it go. 'Twas not his fault the lass was in this position. 'Twas her own—and Vika's.

And he was out an heiress now, which his clan desperately needed if they were to keep their land. He refused to feel sorry for her, or feel bad for what he'd done with her—*to* her—nor for how...how *rough*...he'd been with her.

Nay! He must stop that line of thought, else he *would* begin to feel compunction. And that was the last thing—the very last thing—he needed to be feeling at this moment.

* * *

Morgana straightened her torn gown and chemise as best she could before wrapping the cloak around her. The hood of the thing had fallen back during those first minutes in the lodge when Robert had settled her on the bed.

"Are you hungry? I've a bit of mutton and cheese in

yon satchel," he said, tipping his head and nodding in that direction as he spoke, tho' he didn't look up from his endeavor at the hearth. "There are a few bannocks there as well, I believe. Serve yourself, if you desire something."

Where have you brought me? she wanted to ask. She'd been thinking about the possibilities these past minutes and had decided that she was more than likely at a hunter's cot—she knew not whose—up in the hills.

She stood and walked with a bit of a slow gate over to the satchel. Her canal was desperately sore. Her thighs were aching and wobbly as well. But, she was more hungry than pained, so she crouched down and rummaged inside the satchel until she found the rough-woven bag with the food inside it.

She needed a knife. Lifting her gaze, she scanned the wall. *Ah-ha!* There, not too far up for her to reach, was a small dirk. She took it down and wiped it off on her ruined gown before placing the food on the table and cutting a portion of mutton and cheese for herself. She cut some for Robert as well, before taking a couple of bannocks from the sack.

She rapped her knuckles on the wooden surface to get his attention. He was finished with the fire and now stood staring at the flames. He looked up and, it seemed to her, it took him a moment to focus on her, so deep in thought had he been. She pointed to his portion of the food and picked up a bannock, holding it out to him, her brows arched in question.

"In a moment. No need to wait for me. Eat." He turned his gaze back on the flickering, crackling orange and yellow flames.

Morgana ate, but there was little joy in the endeavor. Robert was troubled, that much was clear. And it had something to do with her being here instead of her cousin, but no matter how hard she tried to puzzle it out, she could not ken the importance of such a thing. Oh, she heartily understood why any man would be vexed to find that his lover had sent another in her place, but this was not anger she saw; nay, this was worry, deep and anguish-filled.

Had her night of forbidden adventure cost the man for whom she'd been pining these past sennights some terrible price? Had it something to do with the reason he participated in so many tournaments?

* * *

Robert stared, unblinking, at the smoke rising up from the licking hearthfire he'd just kindled. What the hell was he going to do? King William had refused his petition for more time to repay his father's debts, so he now had only three moons more to earn the coin. And that sum was much too great to earn, even were he to win every tourney given in that time. He'd even offered his knight services to the Macleans for coin, but that, along with the tourney winnings, was not enough. Not by far.

He'd failed. Failed his clan, and failed himself.

Robert's eyes grew dry and started to sting. He clamped them shut and pressed his forefinger and thumb against their lids a moment. As he did so, and for what must have been the thousandth time since he'd first learned of the extent of his late father's debt, he wondered *why?* Why had his father been so set against the Norman earl, Roger de Burgh, whose land abutted the south portion of their holding, that he had spent all his coin, and borrowed against future earnings as well, to fight the man? Had it something to do with Isobail, Robert's sister, and the affair she had with the earl's son, Guy, so many years ago now? Or had it more to do with the humiliation Guy caused her afterward? He'd asked Isobail that very question as she lay dying o'er a year ago, but she'd had no more an answer than he.

The rapping noise began again and he turned toward it. It took him a moment to understand the lass's hand movements, but when he did, he answered, " 'Tis nearing dawn now. My clansmen will return for us later today." He shrugged. "Or the morrow, at the latest, I'm sure. For, once they realize we got the wrong lady, they'll not continue with the original plan." He noticed the weariness in her eyes then. "Go to bed and get some rest. I'll join you there later—worry not, I'll not fuck you again without some means of preventing a babe."

He turned back to the flame then, back to his gloomful thoughts of the previous moment, back to his ruminating. There *must* be some way to save his clan! He had three moons, *three* moons to find that means, and he'd not give up until the King came with his army—or sent his new tenant with his—to claim his property.

* * *

Morgana was a bit stunned by Robert's blunt declaration,

but she'd already realized he was a man of few words and, she supposed, if she were to continue an affair with him—and it certainly sounded as if he wasn't averse to that idea—she'd simply have to accustom herself to such.

Her eye wandered o'er to the narrow bed, tucked against the far wall in the corner. 'Twas barely wide enough—or long enough—for his tall, muscular frame. She'd no doubt need to lie on top of him for them both to fit upon it. That lewd thought gave her both a thrill of excitement and a twinge of guilt. She ignored the latter and basked in the former. After all—hadn't she only several hours past given herself permission to begin enjoying her life a bit? 'Twas not so evil, what she craved, was it? 'Twas not murder she committed, after all. She caused no harm to another, instead giving only pleasure. A tingle of remembered delight traveled down her center at the recollection of just how much pleasure was given and received. Aye, 'twas not evil, she'd not believe it.

She rose from her stool and walked with great purpose over to the bed and, now that the chamber was filled with warmth from the hearthfire, she did as she always did: Took every last stitch of clothing from her frame and got under the blankets. She rolled onto her side, facing the wall, ne'er looking back at Robert. But she felt the heat of his gaze upon her, even still.

With a contented smile and a weary sigh, she closed her eyes and fell into a deep sleep.

* * *

Robert was so painfully erect now, he knew he

couldn't last the night without relief. The image of her naked body was now burned into his mind for e'er more. God, but the lady was lush, more lush even than Vika—and that lady had one of the best figures he'd seen. Morgana's, however, was on a higher plane. Like some warrior goddess of old, her pale-pink nipples sat upon the peaks of her round, high breasts, begging to give succor to her man. Her silvery hair glistened against milky-smooth skin, and tickled the dimples at the base of her spine, just above her lovely, curved bottom. Rounded in a way that a man with big hands, like himself, could get a good grip on. Her waist was long and sweetly curved inward between her ribs and her narrow hips. And her limbs. Tho' she was only of medium height, her legs were long and straight, her arms the same.

He'd noticed her of course, in court these past sennights. For she had a beauty that few could ignore. She and her cousin shared similar features. But with Morgana, the contrast of her pale hair and cerulean blue eyes was much more striking. Add to that, her perfectly sculpted cheeks and chin, her feminine straight nose and a set of full lips that would give any man carnal thoughts, and 'twas no wonder that he'd felt stirred by her.

But he'd not dared to follow through on his lust. For she was a virgin just from the nunnery, a poor relation of Vika's that could not aid his cause. Because he needed a wife—an heiress—to save his clan. Besides which, until this eve, he'd been sure that Vika felt threatened by her cousin. Would have, in fact, discontinued her affair with him if he'd attempted a seduction of Morgana—even tho' Vika otherwise encouraged him to take other lovers, as she did herself.

His eyes traveled o'er the hills and dales of Morgana's curving form. 'Twould be the ultimate test of his will not to fuck her again until they were back at the abbey. Ah, but then, when he finally did have her again, he'd spend some time enjoying all those feminine treasures she'd been hiding beneath her modest lady's attire all this time.

He turned away from her and, after quickly giving himself manual relief and cleansing himself once more, he went over to the food Morgana had laid out for him on the table and choked it all down. He hadn't had an appetite since first hearing the sum his father owed. That was nearing three years ago now. But he'd begun forcing himself to eat more since speaking with his sister as she lay dying all those moons ago, after she had told him he looked as if he were the one nearing his last hour. It had made him finally admit to himself that if he wanted to continue winning tourneys he would need to not only keep up his strength, but build it. And that meant eating, whether there was an appetite to do so or not.

After washing the last bite down with a bit of the *uisge beatha* he dug out of his satchel, he stripped off his shirt, doused the flames on the torch and the taper, and got in bed. It took a minute, since Morgana was now well-cradled in the realm of Hypnos, but he finally got her positioned on top of him so that he could stretch out a bit more and rest. Surprisingly, he was asleep himself in a matter of minutes.

CHAPTER 2

"*PATER NOSTER, QUI es in caelis Sanctificetur nomen tuum—*"

Robert was jerked from one of the deepest, most untroubled sleeps he'd had in three years by the sound of an angel singing. He opened his eyes and realized that 'twas Morgana who sang so sweetly. She was sitting up, with her back against the wall. The light from the hearthfire allowed him to see that, tho' her eyes were open, she was not awake. There was something unearthly in the far-off look in her blue eyes, in the moon-glow silver of her hair streaming o'er her shoulders and down her torso, giving him only a teasing glimpse of the succulent fullness of the breasts beneath.

Stunned by the sight, stunned by the sound, he didn't try to awaken her, instead allowing the lovely image and ethereal lyric resonance to build a tide of exaltation inside him. For hers was the purest, most enchanting voice he'd e'er heard.

"Et ne nos inducas in tentationem;
Sed libera nos a malo."

And then, as he watched, Morgana heaved a contented sigh and, closing her eyes, settled back on top of him with her head on his chest and her left hand curved o'er his opposite shoulder. She was silent once more, and clearly sleeping soundly now. Almost as if it were habit, he wrapped his arms around her and brushed a light kiss on her brow.

So, her voice was not ruined, as the rumors attested. Did this happen often? And if so, did she know of it?

His body was stirring, his blood beginning to heat, as he held her to him. He wouldn't be able to remain much longer like this without exploring the curves she so freely offered up to him. Why *had* she offered herself up to him? Given him her maidenhead so willingly? 'Twas a puzzle he'd only just now begun to study.

He'd already worked out in his mind how he had continued to be duped, even after stripping her down and having a good taste of her. It had been pitch black in the chamber, and her figure was similar enough to Vika's to not cause him to question. They'd not kissed, as was Vika's requirement, so there had been no way of telling from that type of encounter. That left only the tasting. But the lass—or Vika, as he'd thought her to be—had put a good amount of herbal tincture on her curls there, masking the natural scent as well as the taste of her.

His fingers traveled down and o'er her rounded derriere cheek and lightly caressed the soft, silken, hair-covered lips of her scut. He'd taste her again later and learn just what flavor hers would be.

Morgana moaned in her sleep and lifted her bottom to his exploring fingers.

He snatched them back. None of that now. But later, after she'd rested a bit more. 'Twas the least he could do for her, to allow her some sleep, after the night he'd given her—she'd given him.

He turned his mind back to puzzling her out. Nay, she'd not resisted, not seemed afraid when he'd gone through the steps of the abduction and seduction that Vika had demanded. Well, there had been his moment of entry, when she'd tried to pull herself back with the ties around her wrists, but he'd thought 'twas part of Vika's performance, and had redoubled his part as the seducer, ramming himself even harder into her then.

'Twas truly a wonder to him that all that time it had been a novice, an innocent, taking what only a lady more proficient, more practiced, would have found pleasure in. 'Twas no wonder the virgin's blood had flowed and smeared to such a degree. But, in the end, she had found pleasure in it. And remembering his own second climax from it, made his blood fire, his tarse grow achingly hard.

He rolled her off of him and leapt to his feet. He looked down at her sleeping form, his lungs blowing, his fists clenched at his sides, and his brow and upper lip damp with sweat. Desperation driving him, he turned and strode toward the door, flinging it wide and walking out into the bitter cold late morn air.

As he stood on the porch, he crossed his arms over

his chest and tucked his hands under his arms. It didn't take long for the frigid air to soften the raging erection.

When Robert's eyes finally focused on the scene in front of him, he bit back a roar. Then, unable to keep completely silent, he ground out, "Blood of Christ!"

While they'd been inside, fucking, eating and sleeping, a storm of a great magnitude had blown in and covered everything, including the only path up to the cot, with several feet of snow.

And.... Was it growing colder, even as he stood there? He shivered and turned, walking back through the doorway of the dwelling and just barely managing to not slam the door behind him.

'Twould clearly be days, mayhap even a sennight, until his clansmen could get to them. And he needed those days to work on another plan for obtaining the monies needed to rescue his holding, save his clan. How many tourneys would he miss in that time? How much more coin? His eye was drawn to the lovely lady resting in the corner. And how e'er was he to keep his cock out of that delectable, tight tail in the meantime?

* * *

"Do you know that you sing in your sleep?" Robert asked a couple of hours later. They were seated at the trestle table, eating another portion of the mutton and cheese. He offered her a bit of bread and she took it. Thankfully, he'd planned for himself and Vika to be here for much longer a time, so there was food aplenty in the storeroom, and wine and ale as well.

Morgana's brows drew together in confusion. She placed the fingers of her hand against her throat and adamantly shook her head, as if saying, "tis impossible.'

Robert nodded. "Aye, you do. The *Pater Noster*, in fact." Her eyes grew round at his declaration.

Just the name of that prayer was enough to send a chill through Morgana. She'd had a dread of it since she was a bairn, but she had no idea why. And he said she *sang* it? In her sleep? Her heart began to thud. Her breath caught in her throat.

An image flashed e'er so briefly in her mind. Horrifying and awful. 'Twas *Ankou*, the death god of old. And he held a limp and lifeless lady in his arms. *"Say naught. Else you shall be next."* The image, the voice, faded just as quickly as it came, as it always did, before she could learn its meaning. Conjure whom he held.

She stood and walked a bit away, crossing her arms over her chest and staring, unseeing, at the wall above the bed.

Robert watched her. It clearly distressed her to learn of her slumber-song. "I thought you would be pleased to learn that your voice was not ruined, that you might someday be able to speak again."

Morgana ran her fingers along the length of her larynx. Was it possible? Could she speak? She'd not been able to utter a word for years now. She opened her mouth and tried to force a sound from her throat, but to no avail. 'Twas no use, no matter how hard she tried, she could not utter so much as a squeak.

"You're trying too hard. Relax your throat and then try again."

She did as he suggested, but still no sound. She shrugged and shook her head.

"Finish your meal." Robert took a long pull from his tankard. As he set it back down on the table, he smiled e'er so slightly. 'Twas a strange twist, was this, him trying to get a lady to *talk*! Mayhap, 'twas best to let her be silent, for who knew what silly, dull utterances would spew from those lips once she did gain her voice? Nay, he much preferred the silence. It allowed him to think, to plan, to try to figure out what the hell he was to do next to garner more wealth.

He studied her then. Besides, 'twas a boon, this, having at his disposal the best part of a lady, her voluptuous sex, sans the worst, her bleating tongue.

* * *

Just as the sun was going down, Morgana, feeling a bit chilled even with the heat from the hearthfire and the woolen gown and linen chemise Robert had brought from a trunk for her to wear after she'd at last risen that morn, walked to the peg on the wall and took down the scarlet cloak Vika had given her a few days past.

As she grabbed hold of it, she became aware of a strange lump under the material. She opened up the cloak and made a quick search. 'Twas sewn inside the hem. More curious than caring of ripping out threads, she opened the hem and took from it a small pouch. Once she'd loosened the string holding closed the top, she maneuvered her fingers inside and pulled out two items: A small square of seed wool and a vial. The pouch still seemed as if it had something in it. She felt inside, and discovered more seed cloth. Curious. She shrugged and opened the vial. There was a paste of some sort inside it. She sniffed. It had a definite scent of vinegar, along with ginger and possibly anise?

She sealed the vial and was just slipping it back into the pouch when Robert burst back through the door, his arms laden with more peat and kindling. His eyes dipped to her hands and widened.

"Where did you get that? Never mind, I care not."

He took another step inside and kicked the door shut with the heel of his boot. After dumping his burden next to the hearth, he strode up to her and took all of it from her.

He lifted his gaze to hers. "Know you what these are?"

She shook her head, her brow furrowed.

"These, used together, will prevent a lady from conceiving." Robert's heart raced. He'd denied himself all day, afraid that if he even touched her, tasted her, as he'd sworn he'd do this morn, that he'd not be able to stop himself from fucking her as well. And now he could. Fuck her, taste her, play with her, do every lewd, carnal thing he'd imagined doing to her these past sennights.

"Take off your clothes and lie on the bed."

Morgana's jaw dropped open. Her breath hitched. Her heart tripped. He was going to take her again! Finally! Joy and desire warmed her, melted her, readied her. She'd wondered if he would, after he'd told her that there was little chance they'd be leaving within the sennight. Even tho' he had sworn he wouldn't until they returned to the abbey.

With trembling hands she unlaced her gown and

walked over to stand by the bed.

* * *

Robert turned back to the hearth and placed some more peat on the flame. It took a moment for the peat to ignite, but when he was assured that 'twould not go out, he rose to his feet and turned toward the bed. He bit back a loud guffaw. "Morgana. Take your legs from 'round the posts and settle yourself further up on the bed." After a split second of thought, he added, "Keep your thighs spread."

They'd both bathed earlier in some snow water Morgana had heated and poured into the small tub he'd taken from the storeroom. There would be no herbal tinctures masking her natural scent and flavor from him this night.

He was rock hard, to the point it hurt, but he was damned if he would rush things the way he'd been obliged to do last night. He took up the seed wool and vial and strode over to her. Then he opened the vial and dipped the cloth in the paste. He placed it at her entrance and pushed it deep inside her. She flinched and bit her bottom lip. She was no doubt still sore from last night. He'd have to take it easy with her later. He pressed the seed wool up against the mouth of her womb.

Afterward, with his fingers still deep inside her, he leaned down and took one of her round pink nipples into his mouth and began a soft suckling as he gently stroked and manipulated her cushiony inner walls, teasing her clit with his thumb. 'Twas not long before his fingers were saturated with her love juices.

He lifted his mouth from her slightly and rolled his tongue around the hardened tip of her breast. Her tight cleft squeezed and released, squeezed and released when he did that, so he knew she liked what he was doing. Her breath blew harsh now, and her hands fisted in the blanket at either side of her hips.

He trailed his tongue down the milky blue-veined mound, across the pearlescent valley between, then up the other, taking that turgid peak between his teeth and tugging it lightly. She gasped and lifted her hips high off the bed. He clamped his mouth around it then and sucked hard, moving his fingers in and out of her in a rapid motion.

She arched her back and he turned his gaze to her face. Her eyes were clamped tightly shut, but her mouth was opened wide. She thrust her head backward, the tendons in her neck strained, a flush traveled up the milky, smooth skin of her chest and o'er her face. And then the soft, fleshy muscles of her canal convulsed, and convulsed, and convulsed around his fingers. He groaned. She was beautiful when she came.

He trailed open-mouthed kisses down her torso and o'er her flat belly. He nibbled the skin there. It tasted of sunshine, had the scent of clean, womanly flesh. An image flashed in his mind of her succoring their babe, but he pushed it away, refused to acknowledge such an image as something he wanted from her.

The muscles of her tummy trembled beneath his lips and tongue. He raised up and repositioned himself on his knees between her thighs. He kept his fingers deep inside her moist, hot sheath as he settled onto his stomach and lowered his head.

He began to feast upon her then. Her sex scent, her flavor, was the most intoxicating combination he'd e'er encountered. Sweet and fertile. 'Twas the scent of woman, and he couldn't get enough of it.

* * *

When Robert's tongue began the same erotic torment to that ultra-sensitive place where he'd concentrated his seduction the night before, but this time, with two long fingers inside her, stroking her, Morgana's entire being went rigid with delighted rapture. Her thighs began to quake. She shuddered. He'd send her reeling again in no time.

A stray thought flitted through her mind: How e'er could Vika have grown *bored* with his lovemaking? But in the next second, her canal did its mad dance around his magic fingers once more and she was again straining and panting as waves of pleasure coursed through her.

Tho' her canal was still sore, Robert's skillful ministrations had brought forth such profound delight that it quickly o'ertook the stinging ache his long, thick digits had initially caused her.

* * *

Robert made her come one more time before he lifted his mouth from her clitoris. He took a moment to revel in the highly sensual image before him: His fingers deep inside the lush, red-lipped cunt of his naturally black-haired lover. He dipped his head and took one last long suck of her clit, gratified when her muscles tightened around his fingers and she jerked a bit.

Then he slowly drew them out of her and raised up

onto his knees once more. He tossed his tunic and shirt up and off o'er his head and then untied his braies and pushed them down.

Morgana watched as Robert's linen undergarment snagged on his manhood and caused it to bob a bit, like a jack-in-the-box. Her eyes widened and her jaw dropped. No wonder it had hurt so bitterly! He was huge!

"We fit together fine, Morgana, calm yourself."

He repositioned his knees on either side of her hips and walked forward, grabbing another pillow and placing it under her head and shoulders at the same time. "Take hold of me in both your hands and put me in your mouth."

Morgana's heart skipped a beat. She ran her tongue o'er her suddenly parched lips, but did as he demanded. The flesh was a deeper tone than the rest of his skin, slightly ruddy, in fact. And 'twas warm—hot, really—to the touch. Hard. Like silk covered iron. No wonder it had felt as if she'd been torn asunder the night before.

She could hear the meter of his breathing begin to change, grow short and rapid. Did he enjoy feeling her hands on him then? She took a chance and looked up at his face. His cheeks were flushed, his head bent back, his mouth slightly open, and his eyes were closed. She smiled. A sense of womanly satisfaction filled her. Aye, he liked it well.

She lifted her head and took as much of him into her mouth as she could fit, continuing to hold him with both her hands fisted along the length. The blunt round head of the thing filled her mouth and she started exploring it with her tongue. She heard Robert gasp and he shuddered rather forcefully, so she continued along in that same vein. Some deep, primordial need rose up in her and she began to suckle. Lightly at first, but then with e'er more avid glee.

Robert's head was spinning. He leaned forward and took hold of the bed posts for support. "Christ, Morgana. You have the mouth of a proficient." Of their own volition, his hips began to rock, forcing a bit more of his cock into her mouth. Morgana took it, and then loosed her grip on him enough to allow his pulsing shaft to move through them and into the divine suction of her hot, wet, tongue-teasing mouth. His cods drew up higher still, his sack tensed and thickened.

Morgana felt Robert's manhood grow thicker, more turgid, the muscles beneath the satin-smooth skin contracting against her palms, felt with her tongue a tickling rush under the skin of it and inside a large vein. Then she tasted something a bit salty. Was this his seed then?

Robert yanked out of her mouth, out of her grasp. "Nay, we'll save that for another time." His face was as scarlet as her cloak and damp with sweat. He pushed himself back and lay on top of her, tossing the extra pillow to the side once more. When he was fully atop her, he took her face in his hands, bent his head, and gave her the most sensual, gentle, sublime kiss she'd e'er dreamed of receiving from him. She wrapped her arms around him and hugged him to her. He ran his tongue along the line of her bottom lip and nibbled at it with his teeth before softly sucking at it.

This, this was how she'd imagined the first time would be. She reveled in the tenderness of his assault.

When Morgana opened her mouth a bit wider, Robert took advantage, sending his tongue into its dark, sultry recesses. She tasted of heaven, of silvered moons and twinkling, starry nights. Of home.

He began to move his hips, pressing his erection against her mons and belly. "Open for me. Wrap your legs around my waist." After she'd done as he demanded, he trailed a hand down to her breast, stopping briefly to tease and tweak the nipple, and then went lower still, o'er the rest of her torso. He raised his head and looked into her eyes as he lifted his hips and positioned himself at her portal. And this time, with slow, gentle pushes, he entered her.

They were both gasping for breath by the time he was fully seated inside her.

Morgana ran her tongue o'er her parched lips as she studied her lover. The black centers of his pale gray eyes had grown large, his lips open, his cheeks flushed scarlet once again. There was a look of ecstasy on his face that gave Morgana a deep satisfaction. So much so, that she felt a thrill run through her, straight into her canal. It clenched around him.

Robert jerked. "Christ!" He tossed his head back and gritted his teeth, feeling his seed rise up again. He'd ne'er had a lover like her, who could make him spend so quickly, so violently.

He dipped his head and kissed her again, this time showing her the explosive passion he was feeling for her. He was out of his head now. He rocked and strained, pushed and pounded away at her. He wanted to devour her. He fisted his hand in her hair and yanked her head back, ignoring her gasp as he forced her to take all of his tongue, just as her tight cleft was taking the full length of his tarse.

All at once, her frame grew rigid beneath him and her thighs widened. In the next moment, the strong fist of her cunt began to milk him, begging him to give up his seed.

He jerked up, straightening his arms as he plowed e'er harder into her clenching womb. With a shout, he let loose his seed at last, shuddered with the intensity of the release it afforded. And then he collapsed on top of her, his breath rasping and loud. She wrapped her arms around him and kissed his shoulder. Joy tripped o'er the corners of his heart, but to the feeling, he shut tight his mind, shut tight his soul.

CHAPTER 3

ROBERT AWOKE LATE the next morn. He opened his eyes and realized Morgana wasn't in bed with him. For a moment, a dark panic assailed him, but then he heard a rustling noise to his right and looked to find her preparing their meal for the morn.

He smiled. His wee vixen lover had wrung him dry, it seemed, but he'd clearly given her more vigor. They'd spent the better part of the night discovering each other, finding new positions that they both enjoyed. Learning just how many climaxes they could have in a row before they swooned. His smile turned into a sheepish grin. That was the last part of the night he remembered. Evidently, it had been he who had swooned first.

"Is—" His voice was a croak. He cleared his throat and started again. "Have you taken the seed wool from you yet? I can aid in that, if you wish."

Morgana turned to him and nodded, indicating with

her hands that she'd done the deed and then washed up when she arose this morn.

He rolled to his side and sat up, placing his feet firmly on the floor and grasping the edge of the mattress in his hands. "What smells so good? I confess, I've a grave hunger this morn after the trial of strength and endurance you put me through this night past." And, surprisingly, he *was* hungry; he didn't lie.

Morgana lifted the lid to the pot she had hooked to the spit o'er the hearth and took out a spoonful. She walked over to him and pushed it under his nose. His eyes crossed trying to look at it, but she didn't give him time, instead simply shoveled it between his teeth.

"Mmm. 'Tis tasty," he said between chews. "Rabbit?"

Morgana nodded. She'd been assigned to the kitchens at the nunnery, a thing, it turned out, that pleased her well. For she loved to cook and she loved to feed those she cared for.

He took hold of her other hand and raised it to his lips, placing a kiss in its palm. "Lovely."

Morgana trembled. Was he talking about her? Or the rabbit stew?

After the previous night she'd shared with him, her heart had grown e'er fonder, and she craved to know that he might be feeling a bit of the same hopeful joy that she was feeling now.

She leaned down and kissed him on the lips. 'Twas a bold move, she knew, a romantic gesture. For, she knew, much deeper feelings could be relayed in a kiss than in the act of copulation of which so many at court partook.

Her heart warmed when he returned the kiss in like fashion. She smiled into it, then grinned when he did the same. He whacked her on the bottom, saying, "Finish cooking my meal, woman, else I'll not have the energy to finish where we left off this night past."

Morgana twirled away and happily continued her endeavor. She wanted to sing, so filled with elation was she. So she tried. But the effort was futile, as it always was. She shrugged and placed a bit more spice in the sauce.

Robert rose and quickly dressed. Then he grabbed the two iron pails from the corner with the intent of filling them with snow and then heating it on the hearth for a quick wash. When he opened the door, he nearly dropped the buckets. Morgana's uncle, Donnach Cambel, an earl in King William's court, and at least twenty of his soldiers were sitting astride their mounts just outside the cot. One of his clansmen was bound and sitting behind another of the men. 'Twas clear he'd been beaten nearly to death. The man gave him an apologetic look and Robert gave him a short nod of understanding.

He stepped outside and closed the door behind him, then took the steps down and walked to within ten paces of her uncle.

"Have you my niece inside that cot?"

"Aye."

"You'll wed her then." The earl lifted his arm in a signal to one of the horsemen in the back and that man made his way forward.

'Twas a priest, Robert quickly saw. A feeling of doom filled his breast. He was well and truly stuck. There would be no way for him to e'er pay his father's debts and he would lose it all. Everything he'd been fighting to keep these past three years was crumbling into dust right before his eyes. And all because of his desperate scheme to abduct and wed an heiress.

Vika. She was to blame for this as well. A ball of hatred formed in his gut. For if she had not arranged for the switch, had simply not arrived for their tryst, then he'd still have three moons in which to find another fortune. Or....

Robert ground his teeth, swallowing a roar of anger and betrayal. Mayhap, this had been the plan all along. Mayhap they'd thought to foist Morgana, the poor relation, the mute, hardly marriageable lady, off on him. And Morgana had willingly gone along with the plan, knowing 'twould be her best chance of getting a husband. Aye, the scope of their vile plot was growing e'er more clear to him.

"I'll go inside and get her," Robert said. He turned and went into the cabin once more, stormed over to Morgana, and yanked her up by her upper arm. Her head whipped around and her eyes went wide with dread. "So. You thought to trick me into marriage, did you? Well, you'll not be pleased for long, I trow, when you discover the depth to which my fortunes have sunk. You'll be lucky to have a roof o'er your head in three moons' time."

Morgana's brows drew together and she shook her head in confusion, in denial of his accusation.

Robert's laugh was derisive. "To think, 'twas I who was plotting to trick your cousin into a wedding, as I and my clan desperately need the coin she can provide. What a foul twist it has all taken."

Morgana tried to break free of his hold, but he tightened his grip, hauling her up against his chest. "Your uncle awaits us outside, my sweet, with a priest in the ready to bless our vows. 'Tis fitting, I think, that you'll be wed in these rags, as they're likely to be the best you'll see for many years to come." He swung around and dragged her by the arm out the door, down the steps, to stand in front of the priest.

The gaunt, black-haired man of the cloth stood silent, his craggy mien rigid with disapproval, his back stiff with it, and his hands tucked around the holy book, which he held with great piety against the front of his thighs.

* * *

Morgana was stunned, horrified, in fact, that her uncle had caught her thus—with her lover. And the look on the priest's face made her cringe inside. Aye, he, like the others like him she'd met at court, surely already believed her a consort of the devil, now he no doubt felt he had the final proof of it.

The priest looked directly at her then, his black eyes piercing her, sending a trickle of alarm, a strange feeling of awful recognition, through her before it vanished as quickly as it came. 'Twas no doubt dread of his power and position, she decided. And then, he began a slow incantation:

"Pater noster, qui es in caelis

Sanctificetur nomen tuum—"

Morgana's ears began to ring. Her heartbeat quickened and she swayed, nearly falling forward, but Robert caught her up against him. The priest did not falter; he continued on to the last of the prayer.

Afterward, he settled his gaze on Robert, saying, "Will you, Robert MacVie, willingly wed this lass?"

"Aye, I will," Robert said between clenched teeth.

"And Morgana Cambel, do you willingly wed this man?"

Morgana pushed away from her lover and shook her head.

"Aye, she does," the earl interjected.

She turned toward her uncle and motioned with her hands, with the shaking of her head, that she absolutely would not agree to such.

The earl stepped forward and slapped her across the face, so hard that she stumbled. "You will!"

Robert caught her before she fell. Now, he was confused. *Hadn't* Morgana been part of the plot? And then: Had it been a plot, or had it been a very unlucky happenstance that the uncle arrived back much, much sooner than was expected?

The earl grabbed her away from Robert and began to shake her. "You will wed this man now, else I'll lock you away until you agree to do so. Which will it be?"

"Release her," Robert said, his voice dark with anger.

The earl looked at the bloodlust shining in the mighty warrior's eye and thought better of arguing with him. He let go of his niece and stepped back. "We'll return to the abbey, but be prepared to wed my niece in three days' time. 'Tis clear, she needs a bit more *persuading* as to just what is her duty."

One of the earl's soldiers brought forth a white palfrey with a gray mane. From the look of joy that settled on Morgana's countenance, 'twas clear the horse was a favored mount. Robert watched her avid reaction to the beast. Had she not seen the horse in a while? The way she pressed her cheek to its neck, as if greeting a long-lost friend, made him wonder.

* * *

'Twas clear to Robert that the snow storm of two morns before had been mostly concentrated near the cot, for, as he and the band of soldiers continued to travel down the path, the snow became much less dense, the traveling much easier. It answered the lingering question of how the earl—anyone, for that matter—had traversed the hillside to get to them.

Morgana rode up nearer the front with her uncle and the priest. The fact that she still refused to wed him softened his feelings for her even further than they already had been by their torrid night of passion.

'Twas a boon for which he'd not deny gratitude that the law—both that of the church and that of the state—decried that both parties must openly attest to their willingness for a particular marriage match, else they could not be wed. Which would allow him the chance to find another heiress.

* * *

Vika followed the servant into Morgana's chamber. She waited for the youth to settle the tray of food onto the table and walk back out before she spoke. "So, was it all that you'd dreamed, my pet?"

Morgana felt her face flame, but she nodded.

"Good. He can be a bit...I know not...less than generous, shall we say? Sometimes?"

Morgana gave her a confused look.

Vika grinned. "But I see that was clearly not the case for you. 'Tis glad I am of that." She wandered over to the table and tore a piece of venison away from the shank and popped it in her mouth. After a moment, she said, " 'Tis a shame the King sent a messenger to turn my father back from his journey to our holding, else your adventure would have gone undiscovered."

She pivoted to face Morgana. "But my father is now quite set upon you wedding your seducer. And, after all, 'twas the King's greatest wish that you be brought from the nunnery and given the chance at a husband."

She walked over to where Morgana sat by the hearth and knelt down, taking both Morgana's hands in her own. "You must agree to wed him, my pet, else my father is quite set on punishment until you do." She paused briefly before continuing, "And he can be quite brutal, as I learned on more than one occasion when I was a young lass, and before I agreed to wed the old man he chose for me. Thanks be to heaven that I'm out from under both their controls these past three years since the old man's death." Vika squeezed Morgana's hands. " 'Tis no use fighting my father—he always gets what he wants in the end." She lifted her hand to Morgana's cheek. "Go to him now, before he can begin his punishment, and tell him you've reconsidered, that you will wed Robert MacVie."

Morgana shook her head, giving her cousin a pleading look for understanding.

"Why? Why will you not wed the man? I know you've been pining for him for quite a time now—all of the court knew, I think, except Robert."

Morgana felt the hot blush of mortification rise up her neck and face. She ignored her cousin's question and jerking her hands from her cousin's grasp, motioned for her to explain.

Vika chuckled. "*Morgana!* Your eye rarely moved from him when e'er he was in the same chamber. You went only to the jousts that he was competing in. 'Twas plain. As plain as...as...well, as the stone cross upon *Caislean Credi*, that you desired him."

Morgana covered her burning face with her hands and closed her eyes tight. What a fool she'd made of herself. All the court must have laughed heartily at the nearly beggared, white-haired mute, with little chance of drawing such a one's eye, following him around like some eager hound.

Vika patted Morgana's knee. "Do not fret so, for, 'tis plain now that Robert likes you as well, is it not? Or—he did take you again after he discovered the switch, did he not?"

Morgana's cheeks burned even hotter, but she slid her hands away from her face and, giving her cousin a joyful, wide-eyed look, nodded her head.

Vika grinned. *So.* The lass had been well-fledged, it seemed. Good. 'Twas good to learn of such things from a man you desired. An image flashed in her mind then of a Norse warrior—bright-haired, proud, and strong—but she scuttled it back into the dark recesses of her memory, turning her thoughts back to her cousin. "And you found the gift I left for you—sewn in the hem of the cloak—and used it?"

Morgana's nod was sheepish.

"Well, then. You see? All is well. You must wed your lover and appease my father's ire."

Morgana's mien turned sad again and her shoulders slumped. She shook her head.

Vika sighed loudly. "*Why?*"

Morgana began a mad explanation, her hands and lips moving rapidly.

Vika sat back a bit and nodded her head. "Aye," she said with a sigh, "I know of his troubles." She got to her feet and began to pace, chewing thoughtfully on her thumbnail. "I do not know the sum that he's seeking, but surely my father will settle a sizeable dowry on you and that will help his cause—if not relieve it completely."

Morgana knew differently. She'd already been told, in angry detail, of what she could expect from her uncle in the way of dowry now that she had humiliated the family with her wanton behavior: Naught.

Vika stayed another hour continuing to try to convince Morgana to change her mind, but Morgana refused to budge in her conviction that she must not stand in Robert's way of finding and wedding the heiress he clearly so desperately needed.

She settled at the table then and ate as much of the meal as she could stomach. 'Twould no doubt be the last for quite a time.

Afterward, she rinsed her mouth, bathed her face and slid, naked, under the blankets and linens atop her bed. It took her quite a while, but sometime in the wee hours of the morn, she at last drifted into a troubled sleep.

* * *

Morgana was wrenched from her bed not long after by her uncle, the priest standing not four paces away, and told to dress quickly.

Scarlet flags of humiliation colored her cheeks as she hastily threw on the chemise and gown her uncle tossed in her face.

" 'Tis the dungeon for you until you agree to wed that cocky knight who ruined you. And after you've given the priest your confession, he'll mete out your penance."

Dread filled Morgana's breast. The dungeon? Were there not criminals there, chained and diseased, awaiting their final plea to the King, or their final end? Her resolve wavered, but then her heart overrode it. Nay, she'd not be the cause of Robert's downfall. And surely her uncle would relent after a time, when he saw that she would not give in to him.

With her head dipped in deference and her hands clasped in front of her, she followed behind her uncle, the priest directly at her heels.

She lifted her eyes, but not her head, to her uncle as they walked down steps and through the halls and chambers of the abbey toward the tower dungeon. His gate was purposeful, his back rigid, his arms swinging at his sides. He was not a tall man, only an inch or two taller than herself. But he was wide. Not completely gone to fat, but not as lean and muscular as she'd been told he had been in his youth. His torso was long, but his legs were short and stubby.

They were going deeper and deeper down a winding stone staircase, getting e'er closer to that dark pit she'd heard tales of from some of the soldiers. Her heart, already pounding hard in her chest, began to race e'er faster, tripping and skipping the further below they went.

Her uncle paused and Morgana barely missed running into him. He took a lit torch from its sconce before continuing on his trek, ne'er saying another word to her.

She could hear the harsh breathing of the priest at her back. 'Twas clear the man was growing winded from their long march to her doom.

At last, her uncle came to a standstill directly outside a door with a bar across it and a lock the size of the man's head in its iron latch.

* * *

"Where has your father taken Morgana?" Guy de Burgh asked, sitting down next to Vika at table as she broke her fast in the great hall a bit later.

Vika swallowed back the waspish, jealous reply before it tripped off her tongue, instead giving him a sad look and shaking her head. With a slight shrug, she said, "I know not."

" 'Tis rumored that he's put her in the dungeon, with the felons. If that be the case, we must get her from there forthwith."

Vika looked at her hand and rubbed the nail of her middle finger with the pad of her thumb. "I think, if 'tis true that she's in the dungeon, that my father would keep her locked in a chamber by herself, not in with the others there." She lifted her gaze to Guy's. "Besides, 'twould only cause my father to be more angered—at me, and my cousin—were we to attempt such a feat."

"Help me find her, at least. I must see how she fares. We can either bribe the guard, or you can distract him with your beauty and wiles. Either way, I care not."

"Why care you so much about my cousin? Surely you've heard, as have I these past hours, that my father has denied her a dowry because of her conduct with Robert MacVie." She lifted her brow in speculation. "Unless...do you want her as lover, mayhap? After Robert?"

Guy's teeth ground together. Vika was the exact opposite, it seemed, of her cousin. The lady was selfish to a fault, ne'er doing anything unless it might serve her own interests. Even with regard to her cousin, for whom, 'twas clear to all, she deeply cared.

The truth was, he liked Morgana. In fact, these past sennights, as he'd gotten to know her, he had come to the decision to give her his troth. He had no need for a wealthy alliance; he had plenty of his own. But he did need an heir. And, since he had destroyed his chance to wed the one woman to whom he could have—*had*, in fact—given his heart; a lady such as Morgana, whom he liked well, seemed the perfect solution.

"I intend to give her my troth."

Song of the Highlands

Vika turned a bit more toward him, her eyes narrowing as she rested her forearm on the table. There was an edge to her voice when she said, "You do know, my father intends her to wed Robert, her seducer, to take the taint off the family name."

She leaned forward and said softly, "If 'tis a wife you seek, I've a need for a husband now that my own dear departed's nephew has taken possession of the family's holding. And, unlike my cousin, I can bring a great fortune with me." She ran her finger down the front of his tunic in direct line to his groin. "We could meet after supper and practice a bit of amorous sparring, if you wish to..." Her tongue darted out the corner of her mouth in reaction to what her finger found, then she said with a purr, "...*discover* how we get on...?"

Guy grabbed hold of her hand and, not gently, placed it back on the table. "I think not."

Vika felt angry heat rise to her cheeks, but she sat back and gave Guy a bored smile. With a shrug, she said, "As you wish." 'Twas not as if she'd been in the least serious about wedding him, in any case, but a mutual seduction? Well, that was another matter, entirely. She took a breath and added, "As far as my aiding you with my cousin, *I* think not." She rose to her feet and, with a demure courtesy, turned and walked from the great hall.

Guy narrowed his eyes as he watched Vika move smoothly toward the exit. He hardened his jaw. He would need to find another way in which to see Morgana. But how? After another moment, he, too, rose and departed the great hall, another plan forming in his mind.

* * *

Robert had heard the rumors as well, of course, but there was little he could do for Morgana without destroying his clan. Aye, his conscience was sore. Aye, he worried for her welfare. Aye, his dreams had been filled with her the night before. And, aye, if things were different, he'd wed her with little remorse.

But. He was his clan's only hope, and he would not forsake them o'er a woman. No matter how gentle, how giving, how lovely, how restorative, how overpoweringly desirable, she was.

He rammed the bottle of *uisge beatha* back in his satchel and mounted his steed. He was off to a nearby holding to woo another heiress he'd learned of this morn. Mayhap, if all went well, he'd return here in a few days' time with a new bride. And then, surely, the earl would release Morgana from her prison.

* * *

Morgana sat crouched in the corner of the dank, dark cell. Her breathing, harsh, and her skin, clammy. She'd not stopped quaking since first smelling the odor of fetid meat and spew, the damp must that pervaded the chamber. And her uncle had not left even one taper for her.

Her head flashed first one way and then the other. All about her were the sounds of scurrying vermin feet. They'd bite her, she knew, if they were allowed near her. And such a wound could send her into a mad, foaming-mouthed fit until death at last took her. She shivered.

Song of the Highlands

When the sound came closer, she *swish*ed her cloak across the floor, as she had been doing all day, to try to keep the rats at bay. Thankfully, as it had the many times she'd done so before, it worked again.

Morgana ran her dry tongue o'er her parched lips. Before the door had been slammed shut, and all light had been extinguished, her gaoler had shown her where to find the bucket that held water and a ladle from which to drink. But knowing that the rats were no doubt taking full advantage of its bounty, she'd relinquished the full of it to them.

However, her thirst was now great and, if the gaoler did not return before dawn to refill the bucket, she'd be forced to take up a bit from the tainted container.

She heard a low moan and the sound of rattling chains coming from another chamber. Panic filled her breast. "Mama!" she mouthed the word without realizing she'd done so. There was something about this place, these sounds, that niggled at her memory, that brought forth some hidden fear in her.

The violence of the sudden quakes and shudders that took hold of her frame sent her reeling. She fell hard against the two cold stone walls that met behind her, making her bite down on the inside of her cheek and delivering a new wave of searing pain through her system. The hurt sent the phantom fear flying, but brought the misery of her circumstances back to her threefold. Tears formed in her eyes as she gingerly returned to her former position.

Both the earl and the priest had taken turns with the crop. Her back felt afire and she wondered if they'd broken the skin; if blood had been let as well.

'Twas her penance, this mortification of the flesh, to cleanse her of her impurity. To teach her to honor the Lord's will and follow the righteous path. To wed the man whom she had allowed to desecrate her.

All at once, she heard a mighty scuffle just outside her door. There was a brief, loud, startled-sounding yell from her gaoler, a muffled *thud*, but then all was silent once more.

She heard the scrape of a key turning in the lock before the door was flung wide. She squinted and blinked as harsh light came through the opening.

A tall, broad man stood in the entrance. The glow of the torch was behind him, so she could not see his face. *Robert!* Joy filled her as she struggled to rise, but her heart sank when 'twas Guy de Burgh's voice she heard saying, "Please, allow me to aid you," as he took three long strides toward her and extended a hand. She let her friend help her to her feet.

"The guard has been taken care of, but we must make haste if I am to get you free of here before he wakes."

Morgana's brows slammed together in confusion, but she allowed Guy to lead her out of her gaol and into the brighter corridor.

"I've a plan, Morgana. We'll hie ourselves to my holding and wed on the way. I know Bishop Richard de Prebenda in Dunkeld quite well, and I've no doubt he'll bless the vows."

Morgana shook her head and stepped away from Guy.

Song of the Highlands

Guy took both her hands in his and said, "But do you not see? This is the best solution for all. I will give your uncle a very generous bride price for you and you will then be well-wed, as your uncle wants."

Morgana's head had not stopped shaking throughout Guy's speech. She yanked her hands from his grasp and pointed toward the entry to the stair. When he didn't budge, when he continued to give her a pleading look, she jabbed her finger three times in the same direction she pointed, then stomped her foot for emphasis.

"What if.... I know of the debt your lover has, and is trying to pay to King William. I also know that he's been given only three moons in which to pay the balance of it. He'll not be able to do that with only his winnings from the tourneys he's been in, so he's scouting for an heiress. I'll pay his debt—all of it—if you'll agree to wed me." 'Twas the least he could do in any case, since 'twas his vile behavior when he was still a squire, a lad of seventeen summers, toward Robert's sister, Isobail, that had been the cause of old Laird MacVie's unrelenting war against the de Burgh's, even after Guy's father had abandoned his own desire for the fight.

Morgana's jaw dropped. She stared at her friend, trying to gauge if he truly had meant what he'd said.

Guy smiled and nodded.

Thoughts flew 'round in Morgana's head, so quickly, she became dizzy from them. Even were Robert's woes not a problem, she'd still not let her uncle force a wedding on him; one he clearly had no desire for, as he'd so bluntly told her at the cot.

But she might be able to help him—help his clan—and then, mayhap, he would find contentment, stop worrying so, enjoy his life a bit.

As she continued to think it through, she nibbled on her lower lip and gazed, unseeing, at the floor. She liked Guy. He'd been kind to her when so many of the other knights had ignored her. She lifted her gaze to him. He was a good choice for husband. Better than she had e'er dreamed of having, in fact. A slow smile spread o'er her countenance and she began to nod, unhurried at first, but then e'er faster.

Guy grinned and took hold of her hand. "Let us make haste, then. Worry not, I shall send a missive to your uncle informing him of our marriage as quickly as 'tis done." He looked down at her bedraggled clothing. "I wish we had time for you to retrieve another gown, but we do not." He shrugged. "We shall simply make haste to obtain one for you upon arriving at the village outside of Dunkeld."

Morgana nodded.

Guy turned then and, with her trembling hand still clasped in his, he led her down the stairs. It seemed only minutes later that they were settled on their mounts and Guy was speaking to the guard at the gate. The guard, unaware of which lady Guy was traveling with, allowed them to exit with no question.

CHAPTER 4

ROBERT SETTLED ON the ground next to the fire he'd built a while past. His journey to the nearby holding had been unsuccessful. Not because the lady had little desire to wed him, but because the father had no desire to give his daughter up to him. He was full aware, it seemed, of all of Robert's debts and troubles.

And he would have been back at the abbey by now, if his horse had not gone lame from a stone caught in his shoe. He'd gotten the stone out, but the horse's hoof was still a bit hot, so Robert thought better of continuing the journey without first allowing the animal a long rest.

Robert sighed and scrubbed his hands o'er the tired muscles in his face. 'Twas going to be harder than he'd first thought to find another heiress within the allotted time. But find one, he must. It mattered little at this point the lady's age, looks, or character. As long as there was a fortune attached, he'd take her. He'd worry about his lack of heir later. 'Twas too much for him to ponder now.

But his return to the abbey sooner than he'd hoped would allow him to do the thing he'd been fighting his conscience not to do since watching the earl haul Morgana off her palfrey this day past: Go to her and see how she fared. If he could conceive of a way to steal her from that dungeon and speed her off to safety, he'd do that as well. But, at least at present, he'd not been able to think of one that would not end in his losing all hope of saving his clan when he was hung from a gibbet for his crime.

* * *

A shuffle of feet sounded close to the tent Robert had erected with the heavy wool plaid he carried tied behind his saddle. On instant alert, Robert drew his dirk, scrambled to one knee, ready to strike. So caught up in dire thoughts had he been that the trespasser was full upon him before Robert had marked his presence. Giving a silent growl deep in his throat at his own stupidity, Robert gripped the hilt of his blade with more force.

"Whoa, friend," The man said, skidding to a halt with his palms out in front of him, showing Robert that he carried no weapon, when he saw Robert's intent to strike. "I but saw the glow of your fire, and hoped only to share the heat of it this frore night in exchange for a bit of ardent spirits I've brung from my homeland."

Robert eyed the man from top to bottom, noting first the tangled skeins of silver-yellow hair, coming from beneath the hood of his finely-made fur-lined cloak, that hung down against the sand-and-wheat colored bristles on his chin; the crystal-blue eyes that held a hint of humor, and no rancor; the sword sheathed at his side, its hilt jutting from one side of the cloak. At last, his sharpened sights settled on the man's boots—clearly North-man made. His gaze returned to the intruder's as Robert slowly sheathed his weapon and settled back to sit again. "What are you called?" he asked as he indicated with a nod that the man should join him. He was not fully convinced of the man's benign intent, but he would share the fire and test his purpose.

The man grinned, and Robert could not help but notice the whiteness, the straightness of the man's teeth. "My thanks, and I am called Grímr, Grímr Thorfinnsson," he said, and quickly—and much too carelessly for Robert to become alarmed—unsheathed his sword and lay it on the ground, then settled at Robert's left, facing him.

"Where is your horse?"

The man jerked his head toward the darkness beyond the fire and said, "I've tied it to the same tree as yours now is."

"What brings you to the King of Scots court?" Robert was only guessing at this by a very slight degree, as 'twas plain the man was of some wealth, and there was no doubt at all, by the fineness of his weapon, that he was a warrior as well, which meant to Robert that he no doubt intended to enter a tourney or two. Although, 'twas a bit odd that he traveled alone, hence a bit of uncertainty, and suspicion, remained in Robert regarding that conclusion.

In answer, the man took out the skin of drink and two silver bowls from the pouch strapped around his shoulder, poured out some sweet-smelling brew into each, handed him one, drank fully of the other, then, as Robert did the same, said, "I come to retrieve my woman."

The back of Robert's throat closed up and he held his breath to keep from humiliating himself by coughing. *Blood of Christ. What is in this brew, goat piss and rotted pippins?* Instead of making an answer, he simply nodded and wiped his mouth with the back of his hand. Finally, the burn receded and he was able to speak. "I was sure you were going there to compete in the tourneys."

"Nay, I've a fight enough on my hands, once I find my woman, to bring her to heel."

This made Robert grin in spite of his dour mood. "They can be a handful."

The man's easy grin flashed again as he gave a nod of his head, and said, "Aye, that be truth. Both in the good, and the bad way, I trow," and Robert was reminded of his longtime friend, Callum MacGregor. That memory, along with the pleasant vapors the man's brew produced in him, brought about a sudden sense of kinship with him that would usually take years to engender in Robert otherwise, and he grinned himself, saying, "What do you call this spirit you have shared this night?"

The man shrugged, grinned even broader, and

poured them both some more. "We call it *björr*."

"*Björr*," Robert repeated, then drank his second bowlful down and wiped his mouth again on the back of his hand. The burn wasn't so great this time, nor the taste either. " 'Tis good."

"Aye."

'Twas not long after the third bowlful that the both of them were nodding off into slumber where they sat, but before they did, Robert said, "I am called Robert MacVie, Laird and Chieftain to the clan MacVie. My lands are west of here near *Cruach na Beinne* and the *Uisge Abha*. You will always be welcome there."

"I doubt I shall e'er find myself in those parts, but I thank you for your generosity, friend MacVie, and I shall return that invitation to you as well. My lands are on the northwestern isle of *Leòdhas*. You will always be welcomed there."

Something niggled at Robert's memory regarding that place, but so full of drink and so weary of spirit was he that the thought drifted away before he could capture it. *I will think more on it on the morrow.* But, when the morrow came, when the morn dawned, his friend of the north was gone, and all that remained in his mind of their conversation was the man's name, that of the thick-head producing brew, and a vague recollection of inviting him to be his guest at a holding he had every belief he'd not be in possession of for more than a few more sennights' time.

Robert moaned low in his throat and dropped his sore pate into his hands. He was even more of a fool than he'd been trying to talk himself out of believing himself to be these past moons.

He made quick work of pulling down the tent and tying the blanket back in its place on his horse.

Aye, fool he may be, but he'd not quit his efforts. He owed his clan his loyalty and, aye, even his life.

* * *

Guy and Morgana were almost to Dunkeld nearing dawn, when they were overtaken by her uncle and twelve of his soldiers. If 'twere not for Guy's immediate offer of a bride price for her, Morgana was sure her uncle would have had him hanged, drawn and quartered where they now stood.

But, much to Morgana's relief, the bloodlust left her uncle's eye when the offer was made.

Donnach Cambel turned his gaze to his niece. "Come here, Morgana. Stand beside me." When she and her palfrey were safely settled next to his own, he returned his gaze to her Norman companion. "She's to wed Robert MacVie in two days' time in the chapel of the abbey at Scone."

Morgana's head jerked around, her eyes wide as she stared at her uncle. He had already contracted the chapel? He must be as certain that she would agree to wed Robert as she was that she would not.

"But what does Robert MacVie have to offer her?" Guy shrugged, shaking his head. "Naught—less than—as I've heard tell of it."

" 'Tis of no consequence. The lass must wed her seducer. 'Tis as the Lord wills it." The Norman and his family had the ear of both King William, and through the Earl of Pembroke, King John of England as well—

a much too dangerous alliance for Donnach's ends. Nay, 'twas the better, safer way for him to hie his niece off to the almost destitute MacVie holding. For, if the lass e'er did regain her memory, she could cause him a great deal of trouble. Trouble Donnach had only barely been able to avoid with the King thirteen years past when all eyes turned on him after the attack on his brother and his family. An attack that ended in bloodshed and death.

Guy started to move up beside her, but Morgana adamantly shook her head. The fear in her look and the way her eyes shifted rapidly from her uncle, back to Guy, told Guy all he needed to know. He halted and waited until the mounted party were well up ahead before continuing on his journey.

He had not gone more than a mile forward before he reined his horse in and turned back. There was naught left for him at King William's court. He'd done well in the jousts he'd competed in, as was his liege lord, Guillaume le Maréchal, the Earl of Pembroke's desire, but his own endeavor, his search for a wife, had not been so successful. Mayhap he'd have more luck in Cambria this next time.

With that thought in mind, he kneed his mount into a full gallop. If the weather held, he'd be at Cilgerran Castle by the time of *Pasche*.

* * *

Morgana was dragged from her mount by her uncle and shoved ahead of him. "Get you back to the dungeon. 'Tis clear the flogging you received this morn past did little to cleanse your soul."

Morgana stumbled and nearly fell forward when he shoved her again, this time with even greater strength behind it. Her back was on fire from his rough handling and tears of fear and shame formed in her eyes. Her limbs, her frame, were quaking so badly, she could barely keep herself upright.

'Twas in this manner that they continued on until they were inside the dank, odorous cell once more. Her uncle had said naught else during the forced march to her prison, but once the door was slammed shut behind him, he settled the torch in its hoop on the wall, picked up the crop, and said, "Bend over and grasp your ankles."

Morgana shook her head, pleading with him the best she could, with her expression, with her hands, not to beat her again.

"Do as I say, or 'twill be twice the punishment for you. I'll not have a willful whore for family."

Tears of utter dread streaked down her face but she turned and did as he'd bade.

In the next second, her skirts were flung o'er her head and the crop came down on the tender flesh of her buttocks and thighs in swift, repetitive, searing, strokes.

* * *

Robert had just come out of the stables when he'd seen Morgana's uncle pushing his niece through the doorway of the dungeon tower.

He'd raced to catch up to them, but by the time he'd made it into the tower, they were already nearing their destination. He could hear the sound of their footsteps coming from somewhere below him in the stairwell. While he was still descending the stairs, he heard the echo of a door slamming. He continued on, listening at first one door and then another, until he came to one in which he heard the distinct *thwack*ing sound of something—a crop, mayhap?—meeting flesh. He pushed on the door and it opened.

"Leave her be!" he roared. In the next instant he was between the earl and Morgana. He took two of the strokes to his shins before he was able to wrest the crop from the earl's hand.

The earl, sweating and red-faced, his shoulders heaving with each new breath, looked up at him. There was a gleam in his eyes that caused the hairs on the back of Robert's neck to rise. 'Twas clear, the man did not even see who was standing before him, so thralled was he by his means of punishment.

Robert heard shuffling behind him but dared not turn his back on the man. "Morgana, go back to your chamber."

"You have no right to give her a decree such as that! I am her guardian and she must do as I dictate!"

"She is my betrothed. From this day forward, you have no right to her." Robert's heart pounded in his chest. *What am I saying?* He wasn't going to *wed* the lass—he had to find an *heiress* for his clan! On the cusp of that thought, he saw a blur of white hair pass next to him. When he looked, he saw the daubs of blood that stained the back of Morgana's pale gray gown, and was livid. After that, no matter how he tried, the words would not rise up in him to negate his previous statement. He was in deep, deep, *deep*, trouble.

* * *

Guy shoved the velvet purse filled with most of the coin he'd gained from the tournaments these past sennights, along with a rolled scroll, into the young novice's hand. "Take these directly to the King. He'll have audience with you immediately if you say you've a missive from me."

The youth nodded and tucked both in the billowing sleeves of his habit before turning and making his way on foot down the path leading to the abbey at Scone, where the King held court.

'Twould be well past nones by the time the novice arrived at his destination, but Guy's conscience and pride were soothed by the knowledge that by nightfall, not only would Morgana be well out from under her uncle's iron-fisted sway and under the protection of both her betrothed and the King, but that Guy would have at last paid the debt he owed to the MacVie clan for his part in their financial ruin due to his youthful dalliance with the lovely Isobail.

* * *

"So, you wish to wed the lady Morgana Cambel?" King William asked Robert late that evening. Robert was on one knee at the base of the King's throne in the royal court chamber. His liege had sent forth a decree to Robert that he wished to meet with him after dinner.

Robert had a yawning dread that the King may have reconsidered even the three moons he'd given him to repay his debt and would now tell him that he wanted the payment in full forthwith.

But this question he'd asked gave him pause.

"Aye, my lord King, I do." Tho' he still had no idea how he could do it and still pay his debts. His clan was going to kill him. Beat him, flay him, roast him o'er a spit, fire flaming arrows into him, then kill him.

And he'd help them.

King William nodded his head. His red hair had long turned to gray, but there was still a youthful, yet speculative, twinkle in the old man's sharp gaze. "Because the lady's uncle demands it?"

Robert swallowed hard. "Nay, sire."

King William's eyes narrowed. "Because you *love* the lady?"

Robert's heart began to thud. What was King William's purpose? Would he scorn the match? A thrill of relief coursed through him. But then, immediately on its heels, came remorse and an even stronger sense of purpose. He would not leave Morgana in the violent hands of her nearly mad uncle. "Nay, sire," he answered honestly. He dared not lie to his liege. "But I like her well. As she does me, I trow."

King William settled back in his chair. "Donnach told me he found the two of you hidden away in a hunter's cot up in the hills. Is this true?"

"Aye, sire."

King William studied the nails on his beringed right hand. "And did you force the lady?"

"Nay, sire."

The king looked at him. "But you did tup her?"

Robert cleared his throat. "Aye, sire."

King William smiled. "Well then. I see no reason for

the wedding not to take place as Donnach has arranged. We'll leave for the chapel at the morrow's dawn." He rubbed his hands together. "Now, I do believe I've a wedding gift for you that you'll not forswear." He paused, a jolly grin splitting his countenance. "I've decided to forgive a portion of your debt, Robert MacVie. Exactly half, in fact."

Robert's heart began to race so rapidly, he grew dizzy.

"And the remainder you may pay me o'er the next five years."

"My...my thanks, sire."

" 'Twas a boon that you chose my darling Morgana to seduce. For I've had a soft spot in my heart for her since she was no more than a babe. 'Twas my fondest wish, after the horror of her youth, that she would have the chance to be a wife, have bairns." He sighed. "Aye, 'twas a boon for you, and a good decision on my part to demand that Donnach take her from that nunnery and bring her here to me."

Robert cleared his throat again and nodded. "Aye, sire."

"Off with you then. You've a wedding to prepare for, and I've six more subjects with whom I must meet before supper."

Robert rose to his feet and bowed before walking with a lighter step than he'd had in many, many moons out the door.

There was silence in the chamber a moment as the King watched the young knight's departure, and then he said to the high steward, " 'Tis a fine thing, and only fitting I trow, that Guy de Burgh sent such a heavy purse to pay MacVie's debts—and the extra half I shall receive o'er the next years will aid in my campaigns against the upstarts, eh?"

"Aye, that it be, sire," the man replied.

* * *

"So, it all turned out well for you after all," Vika said later that night as she sat in Morgana's chamber watching the lady's maid put salve on her cousin's welts and sores. "Tho' if you'd only agreed to the match when I told you to do so, you'd not have near the number of marks on your flesh that you bear now." Vika let out a loud sigh of frustration. "Did I not tell you? My father can be quite cruel in his punishments."

Morgana kept her gaze on the older woman's ministering hands, but she nodded.

"Ack! But enough of that. It turned out well in the end."

Morgana swiveled her head and looked at her cousin, one brow lifted.

Vika chuckled. "Do not give me that look, my pet. It *did* turn out well. You shall be wed to the man you've pined away for these past sennights, and he's had half his debt forgiven by the King—and the other half he has *five years* to repay!"

Aye, Morgana thought, but for how long will Robert remain hers alone? She'd seen too much of the ways of the flesh here at court these past sennights to believe he'd stay true for e'er more.

She returned her gaze to as much of her sorely-abused backside as she could see. Nay, she'd not ruminate on such dreary thoughts. No matter what the outcome with Robert, she was determined to remain cheerful, to enjoy her new life, and to be thankful that she'd now be able to have the bairns she'd dreamed of, but had given up hope of having.

And who better to sire strong sons than her mighty, virile, handsome lover—soon to be husband—Robert MacVie?

In some future time, when he left her bed for good, she'd not break her heart o'er it. Nay, she'd busy herself with other things that she enjoyed, like cooking and raising her bairns, and she'd ne'er bat an eye at his wandering. Not one eye.

* * *

'Twas as Vika was making her way across the courtyard to meet her lover of the evening that a strong arm swept around her waist and a large, gloved hand clamped o'er her mouth and nose, nearly suffocating her. As the man hauled her into a dark alley between the stone walls of two of the abbey's inner structures, she struggled to free herself from his grasp.

This abduction felt too real to be a lover's game and her heart raced with fear. Would he slit her throat? Strangle her? She redoubled her efforts to get free, but she was fast losing consciousness. She hadn't taken a full breath since her captor got hold of her and her mind was swirling, her ears ringing.

But just when the soft ebon mist began to surround her vision and she was near to swooning, he dropped her to her feet, pressed her up against the wall—she started to scream, but he stuffed a gag in her mouth—

then jerked her hands behind her back, bound them, and yanked up her skirts. When he had both her legs bent o'er his arms, he leaned down and nuzzled her ear.

Oh, God. Let me live through this. Her blood turned to ice and she began to shake. She screamed behind the cloth, twisted and bucked.

But then, an all-too familiar voice said, "This is how you like it, is it not, Vika, *my love?*" In the next second, he was pushing inside her.

"Ohhh, *God!*" she ground out in a wash of relief and instant desire, tho' 'twas muffled by the gag. The sound of his voice alone had sent a flood of juices into her canal. He had always had that effect on her. Always. Since their first meeting when she was but a young bride of twelve summers. He stroked into her again and she tightened around him. Would he like her new trick?

He jerked. "Aargh!" And then: "*Vika.*" There was heartbreak in his voice, as if he knew well of all the lovers she'd lain with since him.

But then he began to take her in earnest. He kissed her neck, with a rough, biting suction, pounding into her so deep, so voraciously, she could feel him battering the mouth of her womb. "Come for me, Vika," he said as he strummed the pleasure point at the apex of her sex with the pad of his thumb.

Her womb quivered but she shook her head. She didn't want to come for him. She fought hard not to do so. 'Twas not fair. He had much too much power o'er her for her liking. 'Twas another reason, mayhap the *true* reason, she'd left the isle of *Leòdhas* after her husband's death. To get out from under this Nordic warrior's control.

But 'twas no use. "Nay! Nay! Nay!" she moaned through the cloth. Her limbs quaked, her tummy trembled, her sheath violently convulsed around his erection.

He ripped at the neckline of her gown and chemise. "I want to hear you come apart," he said, pulling the gag from her mouth at last as well. But she was in the throes of such an intense release, she was barely aware of what he was doing. As she was over the edge of the crest, however, she felt the same hot, humid suction on the tip of her breast as she had a moment before on her neck. It sent her careening once more.

"Aaahhhh! Aaahhhh! Aaahhh! God!" She heard her keening cries, felt the hot tears streaming down her cheeks, touched the stars he handed her once more.

No one else had e'er been able to do this to her, tho' Lord knew, she'd tried to find another who could. That stray thought flitted out of her mind just as he hauled his head back and, with a harsh, gravelly yell, spent inside her.

They were silent for a time, both recovering, catching their breath, awaiting lucid thought to return.

"What do you here, Grímr?" Vika asked finally. Her voice was hoarse from the strain she'd put it through. He'd unleashed her hands and she'd wrapped her arms around his neck. Her legs were secured around his waist as well and he pressed his torso into hers, nuzzling her ear with his lips.

"I've come to take you home, Vika. You've our daughter to raise, remember?"

She closed her eyes and willed the mist that formed there at the mention of her bairn to vanish, still, her heart broke a little. Ignoring the pain, she said, "My life is here now."

"Your life is with me, with our daughter."

She slowly shook her head. "I've been beaten, I've been prisoned, I've been starved, all to be forced into submission to a man's will. First by my father as I grew, then, after he bartered me to Hákon, by him as well."

"So you told me, so I saw," Grímr murmured.

"I'll give you yet another reminder, then: I'll not be another man's chattel e'er again. I have no use for bairns, I have no use for marriage. And the only use I have for men is what dangles 'tween their thighs."

"Aye, you said that as well. Still, I believe you not."

She pushed against his chest, but 'twas as immovable as a mountain. "Aah!" she screamed in frustration. "Then you are guiled at your own peril, for this I swear: 'Tis true." A shadow of heartbreak darkened his countenance, and she fought her conscience, determined to be cruel to assure he would ne'er return to her again. "I only lay with you—bore Halla—to gain my freedom from Hákon."

"Now, I *know* that's not true," he said, his voice soft, gentle.

She turned her face away and let out a weary sigh. "You should find a good woman to wed and be mother to the lass," she murmured.

He touched the rough pads of his fingers to her chin and forced her to look at him again. "*You* are Halla's mother. She needs you, Vika. She asks for you almost every day." He leaned back and took her cheeks in his gloved palms. "She has no understanding of why you left her, left *us* so soon after birthing her."

Vika was silent for a time. She studied the ties at the neck of Grímr's shirt. "And what of her aspect? Has she the look of me?"

Grímr smiled. "Aye. Very much, in fact. Except for her pale blonde hair. That, she gets from me. But she has your amber eyes."

Vika started to weep in earnest. She could not hold back the tears any longer. "I cannot return with you, Grímr. I beg you to understand! Do you *want* me to perish there? Shrivel, like a piece of dried fruit? For, 'tis truth, that is surely what I would do—and quickly—were you to force me to return with you."

"Do not cry, little one." Grímr leaned down and kissed her. 'Twas a gentle kiss, soft, sweet. *Loving*.

Panic filled Vika's breast and she shoved him away. "Nay! You must leave here, Grímr. Forthwith. And do not return. E'er again." Vika dropped her legs back down to the ground and Grímr took a step back.

"Vika—"

"Nay, Grímr. I am dead to you—and to Halla as well. 'Tis time and past for you to begin anew." Vika let her gaze fall to his chest. "Find a wife from your own homeland and bring her back to the manor you inherited from my husband. Build a life with her and Halla. And forget me." Meeting his eyes with a steadfast gaze, she said, "All right?"

Grímr took another step back, did a sweep of the abbey's walls with his gaze, as if he had thoughts of forcing her to go with him. But thankfully, 'twas well fortified with armed men, now that the King had taken up court there, and clearly he decided against it, for in the next moment, he spat out, "All *right*." He turned then and stormed off, quickly disappearing into the inky blackness of the courtyard.

Ne'er to be seen again. The words tripped across her mind and pierced, like the points of sharp daggers, into her heart.

After a moment, Vika lifted the torn edge of her gown and chemise o'er her bared breast and trudged into the courtyard as well. But instead of heading in the direction she'd been going prior to her surprise meeting with the avid lover of her first blossom, the man whose memory still haunted her restless dreams, she turned back toward the abbey, back toward her chamber, back toward the comfort of her own feminine power.

CHAPTER 5

*R*OBERT TOOK HOLD of Morgana's hand. "'Tis done."

She looked at him and nodded.

"I'll meet you in the great hall of the abbey in a half-hour's time."

Morgana blinked. She motioned toward the wagon her uncle had arranged for them and cocked her head in question.

"Nay. I detest the things." He did a quick scan of her attire. "But 'tis clear that you've a need for such, as that gown must weigh a ton."

Morgana clamped her palm o'er her mouth to hide her grin. The gown *was* a bit excessive for her liking, but she'd not had the heart—nor the courage—to say *nay* to such an expensive loan from the Queen. 'Twas made of an unusual royal blue woven-silk cloth—velvet, 'twas named—got as a royal gift from a legate of *Regnum Aragonum*, and lined in ermine. There were rubies sewn around the neckline in a repeating arabesque design that had also been used on the lower half of the wide sleeves.

And, aye, 'twas heavy.

Robert led her over to the conveyance and lifted her onto the seat.

She winced. The abrasions on her backside were still quite tender, even tho' the lady's maid had put more salve on them prior to helping her dress this morn. Thankfully, Robert didn't notice her discomfort.

He surprised her then. He leaned in and gave her a quick kiss on her mouth, and a treacherous warmth spread through her. Afterward, he looked at the driver and nodded before turning and walking away.

Morgana shrugged, but a thrill of joy bounded about in her rapidly beating heart. Would they be able to enjoy each other this eve, in spite of her sore backside? She prayed they would, for she truly did not believe she could wait another day—or, the good Lord forbid, a sennight?—to have him inside her again.

* * *

Robert took a longer route back to the main building of the abbey. He needed a bit of time to grow accustomed to his new status as husband before greeting his comrades and fellow clansmen in the great hall.

The vows had been exchanged and blessed with only Morgana's uncle and the King and Queen as witness, which pleased Robert greatly. He'd had horrors of having the entire court bear witness to his wedding. Aye, a privy ceremony was much more to his liking.

But now 'twas time for the true test of his mettle. For he had no doubt that he'd be at the center of all his comrades jests this day, with no relief until many hours from now, when he and Morgana were at last allowed to go to their marriage bed.

Tho'—*Christ's Bones!*—was there not some humiliating tradition involving that as well?

If 'twere not for the fact that this match was being celebrated by the King himself, Robert would find some way to abduct his bride and spirit her off to his holding without delay.

* * *

" 'Tis sorry I am that I was not able to see you wed this morn," Vika whispered in Morgana's ear an hour later, resting her hand atop her shoulder, "but my father strictly forbade it." She'd just arrived and was about to move past her to settle at her place further down the table. "Do you forgive me, my pet?"

Morgana looked up at her cousin and placed her hand o'er Vika's. She gave it a slight squeeze and followed that with a smile.

"Good." Vika sighed and straightened. "Well, I'm off to the nether ends of this King's table. Lord, but I hope I haven't been seated next to a driveling old fool!" She swayed away then and Morgana grinned, shaking her head at her beautiful, black-haired cousin's dry wit.

She scanned the chamber once again. *Where is Robert?* 'Twas well past the time he'd said he'd meet her here and, by the dark spots of color on her uncle's cheeks and his strained expression, 'twas evident that he was growing quite vexed with her new husband.

Song of the Highlands

At last, her eyes lit upon him.

Thanks be to heaven! He was not more than five paces inside the chamber, but he'd clearly been waylaid by a few of the younger warriors. All at once, great roars of laughter erupted from the lot, with each in his turn slamming his palm down upon Robert's back. And the answering sheepish expression on her husband's mien told her exactly what they were jesting about.

She sighed. Poor Robert. This could not be an easy day for him. For, she'd learned quickly that he was more a man of action than of words. And not only that, he'd always seemed more interested in being victorious in the contests of skill, and in the winnings he received from them, than in any of the glory that was lavished upon him afterward.

Nay, he would not be liking the amount of notice he was receiving, she decided.

She fluttered her fingers to gain her uncle's eye, then she motioned toward Robert. Her ploy worked, for in the next second, her uncle was off the dais and storming toward her new husband.

It didn't take him long to extricate Robert from his comrades and soon the two of them were settled on either side of her. She heard her husband say under his breath, "Christ's Bones! Will this day ne'er be done?"

He'd splayed his hand on the table next to their wine goblet. She took hold of it and gave it a light squeeze. When he turned his gaze to her, she smiled. She was pleased when her tactic succeeded and his shoulders visibly relaxed as one side of his mouth tipped up in a begrudging smile.

Trumps sounded and they both turned their gazes toward the entrance leading from the King's privy chambers into the great hall. A hush fell o'er the assembly as the tall arched doors were flung wide and the King's attendants stepped o'er the threshold. King William came into the hall next with his Queen Consort, Ermengarde, on his arm. His aged stride was still purposeful, his bearing still straight, as he strode to the dais and, after seating his Queen, settled into his wide, oaken chair to the left of the earl. He nodded to the pages lined up near the door leading to the kitchen's corridor and the young lads filed out to retrieve the first course of the feast.

The feast progressed for twenty courses, during which pipers and harpists played. Afterward, a troupe of players acted out the ancient tale of how the blessed *Lia Fáil*, the Stone of Destiny, on which Scottish Kings accept their crowns was first carried from *Hispania* by the tribes of old and brought to the Hill of Tara on the Isle of *Éire*, then to Dunstaffnage Castle in Oban where 'twas built into the wall, before finding its sacred place at Scone for *Cináed mac Ailpín* to be crowned.

When the play was done, the King signaled to Robert that 'twas at last time for the couple to retire to their marriage bed. Robert let out a sigh of relief, but 'twas short-lived. For, he had no sooner taken hold of Morgana's hand and stepped off the dais with her, than they were both lifted from their feet and hoisted onto the shoulders of four of his clansmen. They were led away amongst a clamor of hearty well-wishes.

Robert gritted his teeth, but did his best to force a

smile to his lips. *Would this day ne'er be done?* 'Twas surely nearing the hundredth time he'd thought those words since first seeing Morgana this morn. All he wanted, all he had been able to think clearly on these past hours, was stripping her of that ridiculously ornate dress, as well as every other scrap of cloth between him and her naked flesh, and partaking once more of the lush bounty of her frame.

When they, and the boisterous ruck that carried them, were up the stairs and nearing his bedchamber door, Robert did a quick twist and jumped down from his clansmen's shoulders. He rushed to stand in front of the portal with his arms crossed over his chest and his legs spread. "That's as far as you'll be going with my bride. Put her down. Gently."

"But—"

"Nay." Robert stepped forward and lifted his arms to Morgana. "Come, Morgana."

Morgana didn't hesitate. She reached her arms out and fell into his embrace. The clansmen were forced to let go of their hold on her.

Robert pressed his nose into Morgana's soft moon-spun hair and took a deep breath of the fresh, clean scent of it. "Goodnight," he said to his comrades and swung around, barreling them both inside the chamber, then slamming and barring the door behind them.

* * *

Robert scanned the chamber, thrilled to find it empty of maids. 'Twas not until he'd barred the door that the thought had dawned that he may still have others to oust from their presence. Now, well pleased with their solitude, he folded his arms over his chest and leaned against the heavy oaken wood. The side of his mouth quirked with amusement—at her, at himself—as he watched Morgana begin to strip off her dress. All these hours he'd believed he'd be somehow dealing with a shy bride, that he'd need to maneuver a bit to get her naked again.

Thanks be to heaven, 'twould clearly not be the case. Did she want him as badly as he wanted her? 'Twas a thought to which he'd ne'er truly given time before, if a lady might actually feel real desire for *him*. Not just for the fucking, but for the man doing the fucking. 'Twas rather a novel concept, but now the thought had taken hold, and 'twould not let him go. He had to know if what she was feeling now was the common desire to mate that most had after getting a taste of the mad, orgasmic rhythm, or if 'twas specifically *him* that she wanted inside her.

After all, she had run off with *Guy de Burgh*, he'd found out from one of his comrades. Which had sent a hot, violent jealous rage coursing through him. Another thing that he'd ne'er experienced before. There were many firsts for him where Morgana was concerned. Some pleasant, and some—like the jealousy—not so pleasant. "Did you fuck de Burgh?"

Morgana stood naked now and shivering a bit, as the fire needed tending. Her brow furrowed and she shook her head.

"So I'm still the only man you've allowed between those creamy thighs?" Robert's eyes dipped to the apex of the appendages in question and then back up to his

Song of the Highlands

bride's visage. Her eyes were wide now as she nodded her head. A lovely blush pinkened her cheeks.

Robert grinned. He'd gotten the truth from her, 'twas evident in her aspect, as well as her bearing, and he liked the answer well. He kicked off his shoes.

With a short nod, he strode toward her, hauling off his tunic and shirt as he went. When he was no more than two feet away from her, he unlaced his braes and shoved them down, stepping out of them and kicking them aside in the next second. "Turn around and draw your hair o'er your shoulder."

Morgana did as she was bade. What was his game? Her heart pounded in her chest. Not with fear, but with anticipation. She'd been aware of him for hours, his heat, the abrasive touch of his large and calloused hand o'er hers, the muscular arm that brushed against her breast as he reached for this tidbit or that. Aye, she had spent long minutes imagining those same hands on her body, those same arms wrapped around her, as they had been those nights they'd been together at the hunter's cot.

"Bend over and grasp your ankles."

Morgana's heart leapt into her throat. A convulsive swallow worked in her throat as she whipped her head around. Those were the same words her uncle had given her before he'd begun to *mortify her flesh*. And all knew, a husband had the right to beat his wife. Had she wed a brute, then, without knowing it?

"I want to see what damage your uncle caused you."

Relief flooded her as her heart settled back into a less rapid meter. She nodded and bent low at the waist, taking hold of her ankles.

She jerked when the rough pad of a thick finger trailed o'er the outer flesh of her sex.

Robert bit back a growl. She was bruised and abraded there as well. Her back, buttocks and thighs had raised welts on them; some, where the skin had been broken and the healing had begun.

Morgana felt her canal grow heavy and damp with each stroke of her husband's finger. The flesh ached a bit when he pressed on it, but she truly cared not. The pleasure he would give her, she had learned well, would soon override any discomfort she now felt.

" 'Twill be a chaste marriage bed this night," Robert said under his breath.

Morgana straightened and turned. She took hold of his forearms and, shaking her head, wrapped them around her. Then, rising up on her toes, she kissed him full on the mouth as she settled her own arms around his neck at the same time.

Robert's manhood jerked against her belly and her mons. She felt it grow larger still. His arms remained lightly around her, barely touching her skin. She crowded closer against him and rubbed her nipples into the wiry hair on his chest, her pelvis against his erection.

Robert's will snapped. "Bend o'er the bed. Put a pillow under your belly."

It took a moment or two, but after she was finally positioned the way he wanted her—he'd spread her legs a bit wider and lifted her arms o'er her head—Morgana at last began to be taken by her husband.

The first thing she felt was that same rough pad of his finger trailing lightly o'er the outer flesh of her sex before making a shallow dip inside her canal. He traced the dew he brought forth down to the sensitive peak and began a slow manipulation of it, sending hot and cold thrills coursing through her.

He continued in this vein for quite a while, but each time her limbs would begin to quiver, each time the muscles of her back and thighs tightened, he would withdraw a bit.

Morgana could feel her heartbeat pounding inside her sheath. She craved the release he was holding just out of reach. She was hot. Burning up. Moisture gathered on her face and neck.

Robert gently took hold of the outer lips of Morgana's lovely red scut and pulled them open. Then he bent his head and ran his tongue along the scarlet inner lips, taking a slight detour to send his tongue inside her several times. She was saturated and the flavor was so sweet, so womanly, it made him drunk with the need to find completion inside it.

But not yet. He didn't want to hurt her. Not after the beating she'd received. So he sent his tongue further south, to the hard nubbin he'd been teasing these past minutes, and flicked and softly sucked on it until he once again felt her muscles gather for release. He sent two fingers inside her and massaged the inner walls. In the next second, they were tightening and convulsing around his digits.

Morgana caught her breath, her body strained and worked as she spread her legs wider still and began to move forward and back, clenching and releasing the blanket in the same rhythm as her sex.

He sent her over the edge twice more before he stood up and slid to the hilt into her.

On his third stroke, she was cresting again. She arched her back and rose up on her elbows.

Robert leaned forward and kissed her fevered, humid cheek and then took advantage of the position she was in by molding her breasts in his hands. As he rocked into the trembling, writhing fire of her, he tasted her, nibbling and suckling her earlobe before moving on to the soft flesh of her neck. He rolled her tight nipples between his thumbs and forefingers. "Aaahhh!" he cried out as her snug passage clamped around him even tighter. He tweaked and pulled at the taut peaks, sliding almost completely out before ramming himself high into her. He did this several times and, with each new thrust, he felt her tense before a shudder ran through her.

She began to move against him wildly, slamming her abraded, beautiful buttocks against his abdomen.

His own thighs and stomach began to quake in reaction. "Morgana!" he yelled, and then, in more strangled tones, "Blood of Christ!" as the first surge of ecstasy, the first, second, third bursts of seed went deep into her undulating womb. Finally, as the bliss he'd found inside her was ebbing, and just as had happened the first night—and the next night as well—a second, violent wave of rapture crashed through him. He jerked uncontrollably, yelling so long and so loudly that his throat burned from the strain.

A black mist invaded the edges of his vision. Before he swooned, he managed to move aside and crash face-first onto the bed beside her.

* * *

Morgana twisted her head and rested on her other cheek. Robert was asleep. Again. Was this common? For, tho' she felt rather drowsy, she in no way wanted to sleep right now. Nay, she'd far prefer to spend a bit of time with her husband, now that no others were about. Make that her *awake* husband.

After another moment, she lifted herself up off the bed and went to the washstand in pursuit of a damp cloth with which to cleanse herself.

After bathing, she opened her clothing chest, which a servant had brought to Robert's chamber sometime during the day, and dressed in one of her linen chemises. Afterward, she spent a bit of time folding and hanging up their hastily discarded wedding attire before building the fire higher and settling next to it with one of Robert's shirts she'd found on a peg. It had a small tear in the sleeve and the hem was coming out. She'd mend it for him.

As she sewed, her thoughts remained on her husband. She was still in a state of shock, really. All these sennights, she'd pined for the man now sleeping peacefully on their marriage bed, but with no hope of having him.

Yet, within a matter of days, she'd not only become his lover, but become his *wife* as well! Morgana felt a song rise up in her, so strong, that she thought she'd expire from the need to release it into the air. She opened her lips and mouthed the words, straining and struggling to emit even the softest of sounds. But 'twas no use. She rubbed the pads of her fingers o'er her throat to ease the strained vocal chords as she turned her eye to the man to whom she'd given her vows with only the nod of her head earlier that day. 'Twould not be long, she knew, before he'd grow weary and angry with her for her lack of speech. What man wouldn't?

And then he would find another lover.

All at once a new horrifying thought flashed through her mind: What if he sent her away? Sent her back to the nunnery to molder before she e'er had the chance to make a babe with him?

Or worse: What if he sent her back *after* she gave him an heir? Her heart wrenched at that thought.

"Morgana, come to bed."

She jumped.

Robert's voice was craggy with sleep and he hadn't even opened an eye as he'd made the demand, but the fact that he wanted her near him forced her fears at bay and within seconds she was beside their bed, discarding her chemise. She shoved at him in a bid to get him positioned with his head and feet facing the right direction.

Tho' he ne'er opened an eye, ne'er said another word to her, he must have understood what she wanted from him, for he crawled and rolled until he was settled with his head on the pillow at the other side of the bed. She gave a silent giggle and got in beside him. It surprised her when he immediately tucked her up against himself, his arm under her bosom and his lips against her temple.

Within moments, she was fast asleep.

* * *

Morgana awoke to the scraping sound of the hearthfire being tended. She opened her eyes and turned her head in that direction. 'Twas her husband doing the deed. Blinking and rubbing the sleep from her eyes, she wondered, was it dawn already? Her gaze tracked to the window. There was still no light coming through the shutters' slats.

Robert lifted his gaze to her. "Get up and dress. We're for my holding in a half-hour's time." He rose and went to the washstand. After rinsing the remnants of their lovemaking from his groin, he quickly dressed and walked toward the door. When he was nearly through the opening, he turned and said, "I'll return in a bit. Be ready." And then he was off, with not even a smile to soften his words.

Morgana leapt to her feet and scurried to the washstand herself. She was just finishing her ablutions when the same lady's maid, Modron, who'd aided her with her injuries before, scratched on the door before entering. "Your husband sent me up to put more of this salve on your flesh," Modron said. She moved with a rather agile gate for one so aged to stand at Morgana's back. Then, with efficiency, she proceeded to do just that.

Morgana shrugged. 'Twas clear the servant was bound to do Robert's bidding, whether 'twas to Morgana's liking or nay. Fortunately, Morgana was rather pleased to have a bit more salve on the tender marks the priest and her uncle had administered.

"Your husband has arranged for me to travel with you back to his holding, to continue as your lady's maid," the older woman said. There was a pause before she continued, "Does that please you, m'lady?"

Morgana looked back at the servant and nodded, giving her a warm smile as well. 'Twould be a comfort to have another woman with whom she was familiar to travel with, to aid her as she got settled in as mistress of the keep. *Mistress of the keep!* Oh, dear Lord. How was she e'er to dispense such duties when she had no voice with which to command? Morgana bit down so hard on her lip, she tasted blood.

The maid's gaze dropped to Morgana's abused mouth and she cleared her throat. "When I was young and before my husband's death, before I lost all to that greedy Norman King Richard's proxy, Guillaume le Maréchal, I was mistress of my own holding in Cambria. If...if it please you, m'lady, I could dispense your bidding to your staff each day?"

Morgana felt a wave of relief crash o'er her. She gratefully nodded her head. Something about the older woman's voice brought a long-forgot warmth, a sense of safety and comfort to her, calmed her.

Modron smiled. "Well then, 'tis settled."

Morgana had only just completed dressing a few minutes later when the door to the chamber was flung wide and her husband strode in. "Good. You're ready." He stepped aside and allowed several male servants to enter who quickly heaved the chests filled with clothing and other personal belongings onto their shoulders and walked back out.

"Your things have already been loaded on the cart," Robert said to Modron. "My lady and I will meet you down in the courtyard in a short time." With that, he swung the door open a bit wider and watched as Modron dipped a courtesy and scurried out of the chamber.

* * *

The alewife's cot in the stews of Perth was already teaming with men and women that morn. In a shadowed corner, through the haze of hearthfire smoke, two men sat across from each other at the end of a trestle table, both disguised in the rougher apparel of the lower classes.

"Did you get a good spy of her?" the man said.

The other man shrugged, nodded. "Aye. Good enough."

"We're to follow her to her new husband's holding; somehow, get behind the gates. 'Twill take a bit of time to arrange it so that there is no suspicion of our purpose."

"Aye," the other man said with a nod.

"And then we will devise another test, to see if her memory of us, of what we did, is truly lost."

The other man scrubbed his fingers across his well-trimmed red beard as he thought o'er the man's words. He nodded at last, saying, "Aye, 'tis a good plan."

The man did a quick scan of the smoky, raucous chamber, dipped a glance to his half-empty cup, took a long pull, almost in afterthought, then leaned across the table closer to his partner and said just above a whisper,

"She has a dread of the song, this I know for sure, but no recollection of why 'tis so...*and* no recollection of me, either, 'tis clear, and no doubt because the disease I took from the whore two years past has left me with little meat on my bones and pocks on my face. But the earl is right to worry that a scheme is in place to rout us as the culprits of the ambush, so we will watch and wait, and scheme ourselves, and above all else: Not get caught!"

* * *

Robert shut the door and walked over to stand in front of Morgana. Before he'd completed his last step, he hauled her into his arms and kissed her. He tried to keep his embrace light, but when she slid up his body, pressing those lush breasts of hers against him as she went and opened her lips to him, he tightened his hold. He drilled his tongue into the soft, succulent orifice she'd proffered so sweetly and mimicked, in crude detail, exactly how fast, how deep, and how hard he wanted to plunge into her other delectable cavern. With first his tongue and then his cock.

He was still a bit stunned by how quickly and easily she was able to give him a second release each time they swived. And this past night's had surprised him, for he'd nearly fell upon her in a dead swoon immediately afterward. A thing which had now happened twice to him with her, but had ne'er before happened with any other. And 'twas not something for which he was proud. That rather embarrassing reaction this night past, he hoped, had only occurred because he'd had little to no sleep in the three nights since they'd returned from the hunter's cot. And the other time—well, it had been after fucking her several times, and they'd been *trying* to make the other swoon.

Aye, 'twas no doubt that he had been wearier than he'd realized which had given him such a reaction. For he'd stayed awake the first night after their return, worrying, planning and scheming o'er his new conquest. The second night, he'd spent out in the cold on the heath with his temporarily lame horse, and the third had been filled with anxious anticipation of the next morn's exchange of vows and the horrid feast that would follow.

God, but she was sweet. He loosed the ties that closed the side of her gown and ran his fingers and palm down into the bodice before capturing one of her breasts. He lifted it up and out. "I'm not going to fuck you," he said against her mouth, "but I want a bit of what this abundant tit of yours offers."

He moved his mouth further south, avidly tasting and nibbling the soft skin of her face and neck. She tasted so good, he couldn't keep himself from biting and sucking the tender place where her neck met her shoulder. When she jerked and stiffened, he soothed the spot with the tip of his tongue before continuing his mouth's journey down her chest and o'er the rise of her breast.

He wasn't so gentle when he opened his lips wide o'er her nipple and drew hard on its peak, teasing the hard nubbin that grew tauter still with each new flick of his tongue.

When he had her trembling and straining against

him, when he knew she would now be as avid to fuck as he would be all day, he released her.

They both stood staring at each other, the black centers of their eyes magnified and their bodies rigid. The sound of each grating breath they took echoed in the chamber like the wind o'er *Sìdh Chailleann*.

Robert dipped his gaze first to the place on his wife's neck and then to the swollen, hard tip of her breast. There were white indentations in both places where his teeth had been. And within each, the skin was swollen and red. A bit abraded, even.

There was something about her that made him want to leave his mark on her.

"Straighten your gown. 'Tis time we left." He turned and strode to the door. After swinging it wide, he turned back. "Come."

Almost as an afterthought, or so it seemed to Morgana's dazed mind, Robert held out his hand to her.

She hurriedly tightened the laces on her gown and realigned the neck of the shift beneath so that it covered her well. Then, with a bit of a skip in her step, she walked toward her husband and placed her hand inside his calloused palm. When a very slight, but warm smile curved his lips and a twinkle lit his eye, she grinned and happily allowed him to lead her out of the chamber.

* * *

A while later, as their wagon shuddered and jerked, and began to move out the gate, Donnach Cambel seethed and worried. *'Tis the basest of fortune that the meddling Norman paid so much of the MacVie's debts.* Instead of having his mute niece well out of the way again, and too poor to be of any danger to him, he'd now have to spend good time and coin to have her watched—and if need be, killed. But, what tormented his mind even more, was *why* the King had suddenly insisted the lass be brought from the nunnery and presented at Court. *How had he learned she still lived?*

PART TWO

A Lady's Journey

*"But, soft: behold! lo where it comes again!
I'll cross it, though it blast me. - Stay, illusion!
If thou hast any sound, or use a voice.
Speak to me."*

Hamlet (Act I, scene i)

*"Mad call I it, for to define true madness,
What is't but to be nothing else but mad?"*

Hamlet (Act II, scene ii)

*"O, that way madness lies; let me shun that;
No more of that."*

King Lear (Act III, scene iv)

CHAPTER 6
The Highlands, Scotland
The MacVie Holding, May 1207

MORGANA SWUNG HER arms in a lively arc as she walked around the corner of the keep. 'Twas nearing two moons since she and Robert had returned to his holding and all around her was activity. Some were hard at work repairing portions of the fortress's structure and others, like herself, were preparing for the *Beálltainn* festival that eve. The warm yellow beam of the sun's rays had melted the last of the snow a fortnight past and now kissed her cheeks, giving them a slight rose tint.

She'd received a missive from her cousin that morn. Vika was still bold as ever, it seemed, openly giving forth every shameful detail of who was with whom at the King's court. But there was a rather worrying, and telling, omission: With whom was Vika spending time now that Robert was gone?

Morgana shrugged and shook her head. Her cousin was a bit of a puzzle, brazenly giving her body up to men, yet ne'er giving any of them the slightest hope of winning her hand, or her heart. A thing that was so far removed from Morgana's own desires as to be nearly unimaginable.

She allowed her palm to rest lightly o'er her lower abdomen. Had Robert's seed at last taken root the eve before? She prayed so. She'd had her flowering twice since their first time together, and Modron had explained that her monthly courses would stop when a babe began to grow there.

The sound of metal striking metal jerked her from her thoughts and she turned toward it. A contented smile formed on her lips for, there, not more than thirty paces from where she stood, was her dark-haired, handsome husband. Bare to the waist, he hefted the long handle of an iron hammer into the air again and blasted it down on top of a long, heavy spike.

'Twould not be many more moons before their keep was back to the condition Robert had told her it had been in when he was a young lad—before his father's compulsive need to make war on the de Burgh's had o'ertaken his duties to his clan and fortress.

Aye, the *de Burgh's!* She'd had no idea that Robert's family was so closely linked to Guy's. Not, at least, until she'd arrived here and heard the tales from a few of the more vocal clanswomen who spun for the keep. And then Robert had utterly shocked her last eve, after their first loving of the night, when he'd lain on his back, tucked her up against his side, and *talked to her!* Not in short, blunt commands, as was his usual way, but in expressive words. About his days as a young squire, about his hopes for the future, and about how consumed his father had been in trying to destroy the de Burgh's—so much so, that his sire had put their clan and holding at risk.

And 'twas upon hearing him speak to her thus that her heart had truly tumbled. She sighed. Aye, 'twas going to be much more painful than she'd e'er imagined when he left her bed for another's.

But, she was sensible. Especially so after seeing at court just how faithless most marriages were. For now, however? Aye, for now, she'd enjoy every last moment of this mad, surprising, *fortunate* twist in her fate.

Modron walked up and stood next to her. "Think you the rowan arch will be completed in time for the festival?"

Morgana smiled, but didn't turn her eye from the flexing, sweaty bands of muscle across her husband's abdomen and chest. She nodded and motioned with a wave of her finger toward the center of the courtyard.

"Ah, I see now. But...what e'er is your husband working on then?"

Morgana shrugged one shoulder and shook her head. She knew she no doubt had a worshipful look upon her countenance, but she couldn't tear her eyes from the sight of him. And she truly cared not what he was making. She just hoped it took a long while to complete, so she could savor the view for a bit longer.

Aye, she had enjoyed watching Robert at the tourneys; watching him meet each new challenge, each new test of strength and prowess. And not only win, but far surpass his opponents.

And to think, 'twas all to save his holding, to rescue his clan from total ruin. Not for the renown had he competed, as so many of the young knights she'd met at court had done. Nay, 'twas for a much nobler cause than that.

All at once, Robert's eyes locked on hers. He gave her the most heated, conspiratorial smile she'd e'er seen—or that he'd e'er bestowed upon her. Her nipples tightened under the light wool of her gown. When his eyes dipped to them and an avaricious spark lit their pale gray depths, her canal grew heavy and damp, pulsing in readiness for his next invasion.

"Breathe, or you shall be in a swoon in another moment," Modron said in a low voice.

Morgana gave her an absent nod, but forced air into her lungs as her maid—who had also become a dear friend these past sennights—had advised her to do.

"My, but your husband is a virile one. 'Twill not be much longer, I trow, before he's bred a strong son 'neath your heart."

Morgana lifted her hand to that rapidly beating organ and lightly rubbed it with the tip of her fingers.

Her husband clearly misunderstood her action for, in the next second, he was striding toward her. And in not more than five after that, he had her lifted into his arms and was marching them in the direction of the keep's front entrance.

Aye, Morgana thought happily, 'twould not be many more days, she was sure, until she'd have his babe growing inside her.

* * *

God! The way she'd looked at him—as if he were invincible, mighty, as if she thought he was a god. It both frighted and thrilled him. And now, Robert was so ready for her, he nearly dropped her twice before he made it into their chamber and tossed her crosswise on the bed. He flipped up her skirts, shoved down his braies, clamped his hands under her knees, spread them wide, and entered her. When she came immediately, it almost caused him to shoot his seed, but he gritted his teeth and growled, somehow managing to keep the unbearably pleasurable impulse at bay so he could enjoy gliding in and out of her a while longer.

He'd ne'er desired any woman to this degree, and 'twas beginning to bring on an uncontrollable panic. And not only that, but there was, expanding inside him, some other emotion. Foreign in scope and foreign in experience. Even when she was nowhere in sight, his thoughts were on her. And not just thoughts of fucking her, which he could almost understand. Nay, they were other thoughts, other images that at first were nebulous, but with each passing day, were becoming so strong, that one in particular had burned into his consciousness and would not let him go: Her, round with his child and holding another.

He'd ne'er, *e'er* cared for the young ones. Had only e'er thought of them in terms of his responsibility to his clan and his family. But there was something about Morgana that made him think of babes in a different light. Made him want to be a *father* for Christ's sake!

Made him want to be the father of *her* bairns—*their* bairns. Together.

On the cusp of that last realization, he shot his load. High and straight, deep and purposefully, pushing the seed against the mouth of her trembling womb.

And afterward, they both came again. First her, then him when he felt the strong muscles of her canal tugging and sucking hard on him. "God, Morgana, I lo—*argh!*—what are you doing to me?"

Later, as he held her dozing form close against his side, softly rubbing his lips against the silken strands of moonlit hair at her temple, he recalled what he'd been envisioning just before he'd climaxed, what he'd nearly said—what he *had* said—and his lungs stopped working. The walls of the bedchamber suddenly seemed to close in on him.

But then, in the next second, he realized that he had no doubt been speaking of the way she was fucking him, and his world righted a bit. He was at last able to take air into his lungs once more.

* * *

Atop the gorse-covered mound about a mile from the fortress, the two *Bealltainn* fires were lit on either side of the path, one on a carn and the other in the ground. The rowan-wood arch decked with bright yellow flowers was placed o'er the pathway leading to the fires so that couples might pass through two-by-two.

Robert had said little since Morgana had awakened after his spontaneous dash with her to their bedchamber earlier that day. His silent reserve, a thing she had grown accustomed to these past sennights, worried her now, for he'd been more solemn than usual as well. But then he took hold of her hand to walk the last distance up to the *Bealltainn* fires and her anxious thoughts settled a bit.

In the dark purple and deep blues of near-night, she heard the rumbling, chattering sound of far-off joyful voices behind and in front of her. And over to her right, she saw the darkening shadows of clan herdsmen with their cattle preparing for the rite of running the animals between the two fires to cleanse and bless them against illness and injury for the next twelvemonth.

A cool breeze buffeted her gown, causing the skirts to cling to her legs. She halted, shivering a little as she tugged at the material. Her husband must have noticed, for in the next second, he hauled her up against his side and lightly rubbed his palm up and down her arm.

She looked up at him, hoping to see that shadow of a smile he sometimes bestowed upon her, but she found only the same shuttered look she'd been receiving from him for hours now.

She didn't hold his gaze for long, however, for he looked away almost immediately, turning his attention back to the fires that crackled and spat a bit further ahead from where they stood. They resumed walking then, but after only a few paces he dropped his arm from around her. Her heart did a little dip in her chest at the loss, but soared once more when he twined his fingers through hers again.

When they were close to the fires, Robert waved to one of his clansmen and dropped her hand. "I need to speak to Dugan. Go stand with Modron," he said, and walked away. He'd not even looked at her while he'd spoken to her. *What is he thinking?* If only he would tell her what he was displeased about—*with her?*—she might be able to lessen his displeasure.

She did, however, go stand with Modron.

The older woman turned a surprised eye upon her, but smiled, saying, "I thought not to see you again 'til well past morn after the way your lusty husband behaved this afternoon. I thought he'd not let you out of the chamber again, even for the fire rites!" and handed her a flagon of ale.

Morgana blushed, but returned the smile, and accepted the proffered spirits. She shrugged, took a long swallow, and looked toward the dancers that waved flame-tipped torches as they moved around the smoking, crackling blaze.

After a few more minutes, she and Modron strolled closer to them, and clear of the path that the herdsmen and cattle would take in just a while.

They were not in their new position long before an older, unwed clansman took Modron by both her hands and hurried her into the throng of revelers.

Morgana chuckled silently into the palm of her hand and shook her head when Modron looked back at her with a pleading look in her eye.

Just then, the muffled male shouts, the frenzied rush of hoofed feet and the *swish!* of rowan branches against rough-trod path and fleeced hide came from behind her and she turned toward the sound. The herding had begun.

All about her was madness and mayhem. At first, Morgana was amused by the sights and sounds around her, but then an unaccountable dread began to grow inside her. Images, colors, blurred and her mind spun, *she* spun, looking in all directions for her husband. *Where is he?* Her skin went clammy, causing her chemise to cling to her breasts and tummy. A gust of wind blew across her, making her shiver, and sent sparks and ash into the air.

And then she saw him—nay, not Robert—but Him. *Ankou.* Standing on the other side of the *Bealltainn* fires, the hood of his long, black cloak pulled forward so that only an ebon void could be seen where a visage should be.

The tankard slid from her nerveless hand. She doubled over, her arms about her middle, unable to breathe. *"Say naught. Else you shall be next."* The disembodied, rasping voice floated up from somewhere deep in her memory, and again, the fleeting image of *Ankou* carrying the limp form of a dead woman in his arms taunted her understanding.

"Morgana! What ails you, child?" 'Twas Modron. "Laird MacVie! Make haste, your wife!" the older woman called out.

In a flash, Morgana was enveloped and lifted into a strong pair of arms. He held tight to her as he took the path back to the keep in great strides. "We'll be back home soon. Do you need a physic?" His voice sounded strange, a bit strained, as if fright had hold of him.

Morgana lifted her head and shook it. She was feeling much better now. Calm, in fact, since her husband was holding her. She placed a soothing kiss on Robert's tensed jaw.

She felt his shoulders relax beneath her hands. "When I get you settled, you are going to tell me what happened."

Morgana smiled at his choice of words but nodded.

* * *

The man in the cloak looked in all directions, ensuring he wasn't seen by any others, before he slipped silently back into the rising mist and trudged down the opposite side of the mound toward his waiting stallion.

* * *

It took a while, but between Morgana's large hand gestures, her mouthing of words, and her miming of incidents, Robert finally felt he kenned the whole of what had happened to her up on the fire mound.

On the morrow, he'd obtain ink, parchment, and quill, as she'd assured him she knew how to read and write. And then, he'd told her, he wanted her entire life's story writ out. For, 'twas clear to him now, that there was much in her past which he needed to know if he was e'er to understand what was causing her sometimes strange behavior and fright.

* * *

"Did she see you?" the first man asked.

"Aye," the other answered, then took a long pull on his tankard of ale.

"Think you that she remembers then?"

The other man shrugged and shook his head. " 'Tis hard to know, but by her reaction, I'd say she recalls at least a bit of it."

Song of the Highlands

"If it comes to it, we shall kill her. If Morgunn hasn't come back from the dead and aided his wife in her escape from me, as Donnach and I suspicioned, this daughter is still a threat, as is Gwynlyan. I kept Gwynlyan too long as it is, I confess. I should have killed her years ago once her usefulness in my bed was at an end."

The other man nodded. "I've kept a close vigil of the comings and goings, and have seen no one that matches the description you gave of the mother. Where e'er she is, she is not on this holding."

"Where else would she go?" The first man rubbed the pad of his thumb o'er the round ruby set in the silver ring on his middle finger. "Nay, do not relax your guard, she will come. I am sure of it."

* * *

"You sang in your sleep again this night past. You've not done so since we wed, mayhap since that first night at the hunter's cot."

Morgana's hand froze halfway to her mouth. She looked at her husband, wide-eyed, and slowly placed the crust of bread back on the trencher, swallowing convulsively. She'd sung? Had she sung the *Pater Noster*? Again? She opened her mouth and tried to speak the question; tried to at least mouth it, but the words wouldn't form.

Robert reached over and placed his hand o'er hers. "You truly cannot make a sound now?"

She shook her head.

" 'Twas again the *Pater Noster* you sang. And 'twas lovely, Morgana. I've ne'er before heard a voice as melodious as yours."

Morgana blushed. He'd not said anything as sweet before. His usual manner of speaking to her was blunt or involved the more vulgar love words.

"Why the *Pater Noster*?"

Morgana's brows slammed together in confusion. She shrugged and shook her head.

"Scribe your thoughts to me and I'll read them after dinner this afternoon." Robert cringed inside. What was happening to him? He actually *wanted* to know a lady's thoughts? Nay, had actually *demanded* as much? He leapt to his feet. "I've a new tower wall being constructed that I need to o'ersee." He turned and stormed toward the entrance of the great hall. *Christ's Bones!* What mad sickness had taken hold of him? And he'd still not worked out in his mind why he'd been impelled two nights past to impart so much of his own thoughts to *her*.

He truly did not recognize himself any longer. Mayhap, he'd caught a fever. He lifted his hand to his forehead. Aye, a fever. A fever which had caused him to lose his mind.

But an afternoon with his soldiers, doing man's work, might be the remedy. He hoped.

Morgana could only stare at her husband's receding back. What e'er had come o'er the man? He'd acted as if stinging bees had gotten inside his braies, he'd leapt up and darted away so quickly.

With a shake of her head, she resumed breaking her fast. Afterward, she'd do as Robert wanted and scribe as much as she knew of her life's story. Her stomach did a little flip. Including her feelings regarding the *Pater Noster*.

* * *

Morgana watched with envy her maid, Modron, organize the weavers for their day's labors. 'Twas the task she herself was bound to do as castelaine of the keep, and tho' she held great gratitude to Robert for securing such a warm, generous, and competent companion for her to aid her in these tasks, it also brought to bear, each time she beheld it, and with e'er more clarity, the absurd and ill-conceived desire she'd borne all those sennights at court that she could e'er be a true help-meet, a true wife, to any man of rank and land. *Why had the King believed it possible? Why had I?* 'Twould have been better had she stayed at the nunnery, where her duties were simple, and guided by others, and there was little need for the spoken word.

"What ails you, m'lady?" Modron said, jolting Morgana from her brood. "You've lost all countenance! Here,"—she hurried her over to a bench and sat down beside her—"settle here for a moment. Eithne, bring our lady a cup of water from the cask! Quickly!"

Morgana bolstered her courage, forcing the uncertainty back from where it had sprung, took a long, soothing drink of the cool water, then, after handing the ladle back to Eithne, turned to Modron with a gentle smile and placed her hand in hers. "I am well now," she mouthed.

Modron patted their joined hands with her other, then started to rise, but Morgana waylaid her, tugging her back to settle beside her once more. As the weavers were well-set upon their duties, and well-away from the corner nook in which the two of them rested, Morgana, feeling again the close bond they'd formed since her wedding, took that moment to ask the question that had been burning within her these past moons, that she had yet to draw the courage to query, lest she be perceived as too prying. Sliding her hand from Modron's, she mouthed as she folded her arms and rocked them as if rocking a babe, "What became of your bairns?"

A jubilant bubble of relief and joy rose in her chest when Modron did not turn from her, but instead studied Morgana's face with eyes full of wonder and affection, then said, "Tho' I bore several, I only went to childbed with one. My first—a daughter. Lovely, she was. She sang like an angel on high, all noon and night, and the sound of her laughter was as high and bright as a harmony of faery bells." Modron sighed, blinked several times, as if sweeping away tears, and looked away, saying, "But. After my husband's death, she went to live with others who were better able to care, protect, feed, and clothe her." After taking in a deep breath, which straightened her spine, and brought her shoulders back, she said with finality, "And, alas, I've learned she has no memory of me, and it has been decided that, for now at least, I must keep it such. Let us go to the larder now to take our stock of the stores there, shall we?" And with that, she rose with her hands clasped loosely in front of her, and waited with patience for Morgana to rise as well and begin the trek to the larder, so that she might follow behind.

Song of the Highlands

* * *

'Twas a few hours later, after quite a bit of laborious, physical work, that Robert finally felt calm again. He stood back and examined all that had been accomplished since his return to his holding.

Scanning the outer wall and gatehouse, he noted that the repairs were going well—better, even, than he'd first expected.

He had only been back here a handful of times these past years as he'd done all he could to raise the coin needed to keep the land in their family. And in those years, and clearly for many years prior, very little monies had been allotted to the maintenance of the fortress and keep. A thing that, now that he'd been given a reprieve from paying the remainder of the debt so quickly, he intended to change.

His earlier unease regarding his reactions to his bride had, thankfully, and at last, receded back from whence it had sprung. And now that it had, he was determined that 'twould remain there. For, he was now convinced, those reactions were merely some strange and temporary madness brought on by his elation and profound relief regarding his not losing his clan's holding. Aye, he was back to his old self, he was sure.

He could not, however, ignore the fright she'd taken the night before—nor her ethereal song as she slumbered. For, as her husband, 'twas his duty, his avowed duty, to keep and protect her. And for her own safety, he must not only learn why she'd been so afraid, but if, as well, it had aught to do with her loss of speech.

The bells began to toll and all work came to an end for the time being as everyone turned toward their own hearths to partake of their dinners. Robert did the same.

* * *

An hour later, after their meal, Robert placed the sheet of parchment down on the table and lifted his eye to his bride. "So. You remember naught of your youth prior to your life at the nunnery." He turned his sights back on the curving lines of writing. All at once, he recalled his liege's words to him the eve before their wedding.

He sat forward a bit, drilling Morgana with a steady gaze. "King William said there was some horror in your youth. What could he have meant?"

Morgana's heart began to thud and her palms grew moist. She shrugged and shook her head.

"No one has told you?" Robert's brows drew together even more when Morgana shook her head again. As he scrubbed his fingers across his chin, he stared at the hearthfire. " 'Tis strange, I trow."

Morgana could do naught but shrug again and nod.

After another moment, Robert whipped his head around and said, "Think you that *Vika* knows the tale?"

Morgana had avoided learning of her past since first arriving at the King's court. But somehow, now that she had Robert's strength behind her, she felt better able to delve into that time. She shrugged, motioning that she could send her a missive to query her.

"Aye, do that." He picked up the second sheet and quickly read it. His eyes grew round, then narrowed when he read the part where she'd seen *Ankou* at the *Bealltainn* fires the night before and that it caused her to see a recurring image of him carrying a dead woman in his arms. This was something she had not been able to explain well the night before with her usual means of communication. He'd only understood that she'd been frighted by the rough and noisy fire rituals, that it had reminded her of something she didn't like.

He looked up and studied her troubled visage for a moment. "*Ankou?*" He shook his head in confusion.

Morgana lifted the quill and dipped it in the vial of ink. Taking the sheet of parchment from his hand, she then wrote out who the creature was. With a bit of a shaking hand, she gave it back to him.

Robert read the newly-writ words. "A death god?" He shook his head again. "I've ne'er heard of this creature."

'Twas Morgana's turn to be confused.

She took the parchment again and wrote a bit more detail.

After Robert had scanned her newest addition, he said, "I'll ask Dugan and some of the others if they saw anyone about the fires last eve that fits this description." If a stranger had been amongst them, he needed to know. Not only for Morgana, but for the safety of his clan and his fortress.

He shuffled the pages together and rolled them up as he stood. "Go about your chores. I'll see you at supper." He strode out, his mind already on his coming conversation with Dugan, his lieutenant.

Morgana sighed as she watched her husband's

determined departure. She supposed 'twas wishing for the moon to think he'd e'er give her a kiss—even a pat on her hand—before he left her side. With a small shake of her head, she rose to her feet as well and walked toward the door leading to the spinning and weavers' chambers. Time to find Modron and learn what progress she and the others had made this day.

* * *

Morgana awoke that night to the feel of the blunt pad of her husband's long finger wedged between her closed thighs, strumming the sensitive bud of her sex. "Open, I'm going to fuck you now," he murmured against her ear. She felt the weight of his engorged manhood rubbing against the crease between her buttocks. She curved her back, pressing her swollen labia against it and lifted one leg, draping it back and o'er his own.

His breath was harsh, bathing and buffeting her ear canal as he positioned himself at her entrance and pushed high and deep. There was some resistance, but by the third thrust he was all the way in. "God, I love fucking you. Your cunt is so tight. Hot. Slick."

The words sent her into a spiral of ecstasy. He didn't always speak to her while they made love and it thrilled her to hear his voice, no matter how ribald the speech, while he was mating with her. For, somehow, she understood, that when he spoke, if he spoke, it meant that he was in the throes of such pleasure, he could no longer keep silent.

She moved against him, pressing herself down on him, forcing him within her so high it hurt. She wanted to please him, to give him all of herself. And she'd learned these past moons what did please him: He liked burying himself inside her as far as he could go; he liked even more when she helped him do so. What e'er he wanted from her, she would give him. She wanted to bring him delight, bring him contentment, bring him joy. She wanted...she wanted to make him love her.

As she loved him.

CHAPTER 7

ROBERT STRODE TOWARD his bedchamber the next day in search of Morgana. He'd spoken to most of the revelers of two nights past and had not found one who'd seen the stranger described by his wife in her writing.

He wondered if the man, this *Ankou* creature, had been some phantasm of the mind brought about by the mixture of liquor, smoky air, and revelry.

He flung the door wide and took two long strides inside before he realized his wife was on their bed with her back to him.

Not at all where he'd expected to find her.

"What ails you?"

She shook her head and waved her hand in a shooing motion.

He ignored her decree and marched over to the bedside. 'Twas then that he heard the unmistakable sound of *weeping*. His skin crawled. Blood of *Christ*!

Song of the Highlands

What the hell was he supposed to do now?

He looked first here, then there, desperately searching for something to offer her.

Why him? He had no idea how to deal with a wet-eyed female. His sights finally lighted on the ewer of water on the washstand. He took the several steps over to it and quickly poured some out into the pewter cup that rested next to it. When he was once more standing at her back, he thrust the vessel under her nose. "Drink."

She shook her head and sniffled. When her shoulders began to quake with great sobs, he felt a panic rise up inside him the likes of which he'd ne'er known. Not even the time he'd ridden out alone on the border and been ambushed by a band of freebooters when he was a lad of only eleven summers had he experienced such a dread as this, so profound in its compass as to render him utterly frozen with it.

Another long moment passed as his mind spun with disjointed thoughts about how he should handle this. Finally, he set the cup on the table next to the bed and, after taking more than one very deep breath, he sat down next to his distraught bride. Having absolutely no idea how to calm her, he did the first thing that came to him. He patted her head. "You're all right. You can stop weeping now."

Morgana turned and looked at the big hulking man that was her husband through the tears pooled in her eyes. The expression on his face would have made her laugh if the pain of her heartbreak wasn't so acute. He looked lost and highly uneasy. A first for her—and no doubt for him as well.

Then he did something that startled her, broke her heart a bit more and, miraculously, began to mend it as well: He leaned down and kissed her on her mouth. The kiss was so gentle, so dulcet. There was more behind that kiss than comfort and she exulted in it.

She lifted her hand to the short stubbled beard that covered his jaw and stroked her fingers through its somewhat coarse, dark mass.

When he broke away at last, he did not move his face far from her own. His eyes showed less alarm now, showed that familiar spark that she'd come to know so well these past moons. "What ails you?" he asked again, softer this time, but with just as much steel behind it. She would not—could not—refuse to answer this time.

She lifted her skirts and showed him what she wore beneath. Her face crumpled once more as a new flood of tears gushed from her eyes and down her hot cheeks. She flung the skirts back o'er her legs and flipped over on her side, hiding her face in her hands as she silently bawled her heartache away.

Robert cleared his throat and darted a look at the exit. *Where the hell is Modron?* She was much better equipped to handle these female doings than he. "Do you need an herbal for the pain?"

Morgana stopped crying. She did laugh then, snorted actually, so he had to know she was laughing at him, which made her feel contrite. She turned her head and, looking at him, shook a negative.

Then, seeing how distressed, how awkward, he truly was, she crossed her arms and mimed cradling a babe in them. Then opened them and shrugged, shaking her head.

His eyes widened with understanding—and not just a bit of relief.

Robert's hand trembled as he lifted it to his wife's hip and softly stroked the rounded curve of it. His mind churned. "So—you are sad because you aren't childing yet?"

She nodded.

Again, the image flashed in his mind of her in that very state, with his babe in her arms. But this time, there was also an ache attached that squeezed his heart like a vise.

Mayhap next time.

He cleared his throat again. "My sister, Isobail—she died near the time of *Samhainn* two years past—it took near a half a year after she was wed before she...umm...did."

That made Morgana's heart sing. Not just the tidings that it could take a bit longer than she'd hoped to conceive a babe—for Modron had told her the same thing this morn—but that Robert had again revealed something about his family which had naught to do with his father's ill-desired legacy. She smiled and asked him, as best she was able, to tell her more about his sister.

To her great surprise and e'erlasting delight, he did just that. He scooted her over and settled on the bed beside her, wrapping her in his arms. He spent the next hour telling her about the elder sister he'd loved so dearly, but whose life had ended much too soon. He also told her about David, Isobail's son. That he was being cared for by, and fostered as page to, his best childhood friend, Callum MacGregor and his wife, Branwenn. That the lad's father had died not long before Isobail and that Robert had been in no position to care for his nephew at that time. It had been a necessary arrangement, Robert said, for which he would forever be grateful to his friend.

Morgana wanted to meet David, now that she knew of him. The cogs in her mind began to turn, but every thought scattered when she felt her husband's warm lips and teeth nip and suck the tender skin just under her ear.

"I've questioned my clansmen," he said against her earlobe, then took it between his teeth and tugged. A tremor of pure desire traveled through her. Its destination: Her eager portal. "None saw this creature you described." He ran the tips of his fingers along the bare skin just beneath the neckline of her chemise. Her nipples puckered and she tried to turn onto her back. He wouldn't allow it.

"God, I wish I could fuck you right now."

Her heart tripped. Eyes wide, and brows lifted in question, she turned her head and looked into his heated gaze. Would he think her base? Vile? She had to know, had to take that chance, for she wanted him inside her just as badly as he claimed a desire to be there.

With a pounding pulse that worked in both anticipation and fear, she loosened and lowered the neckline of her chemise and gown, pushing it down until she was giving him a full view of her breasts. When his eyes heated and his breath came more rapidly, and he said naught to stop her, she lifted her skirts, unlaced the undergarment beneath and draped her leg back o'er his own, opening her thighs to him.

Her husband's nostrils flared, the steel-gray of his eyes disappeared as the black centers opened wide. She didn't even blink as she reached around and lifted his tunic, then ripped at the linen that covered his loins. When his erection sprang free, she stroked it, bringing up a bit of seed as she did so.

Would he say her nay? Would he leave her wanting? She would pleasure him thus, or with her mouth, if he so desired. But she craved the release he could give her as well, with only a few deep strokes into her with this, his lovely, long, hard-muscled appendage.

If only he would.

He swooped and she gasped in surprise before he took her mouth in a hot, carnal, devouring kiss. In the next instant, she was on her back and her calves were o'er his shoulders. He pressed forward then, his arms straight as he balanced on his palms and pushed into her. He'd ne'er taken her like this before, and the point of entry stung a bit, but the feeling of being filled by him was instantly gratifying.

* * *

"Another first," Robert mumbled. He didn't realize he'd said the words aloud until Morgana nodded. Then her eyelids fluttered shut and she arched her back. When he saw the rose blush begin to move o'er her chest and neck, to flush her cheeks, he changed the meter of his plunging; began to move with shallow strokes instead. He didn't want her to come yet; he enjoyed keeping her right there with him, on the edge. Enjoyed watching those lush breasts bounce in time to his rhythm.

His eyes scanned down to her pale pink, tightly wound nipples and his mouth watered. God, he'd love to suck on them awhile, but he knew she'd climax then, so he waited. Later. He'd savor them later, mayhap after they'd enjoyed each other.

Enjoy each other. Was that not what the ladies called it? Mayhap, he should use that phrase with Morgana.

Did his coarse speech offend her? He'd ne'er really thought about it until now.

He did a slow glide almost completely out of her and then sank inside her again, up to the hilt. It caused her breasts to grow rosier still, the nipples taunting him further to take a taste. He dipped his head to do just that, but halted at the last moment, his lips hovering o'er that tantalizing crest. Nay, he'd wait. He forced his head up. 'Twould be a first, as well—enjoying a lady's breasts *after* the climax. He'd ne'er tried that. But the thought excited him.

Could he make her come again that way?

God, but her scut was slippery. He raised up a bit further and beheld the place where they were joined. *Beautiful.* It reminded him of their first time together, of the virgin's blood. He'd ne'er thought anything of fucking a lady, even during this—what did they call it? Ah, yes—*flowering* time. But he'd ne'er before met any— even Vika—who'd allowed him to try it with them.

Until Morgana. 'Twas what he'd meant before by 'another first', tho' she'd no doubt believed him to mean their current position.

She was so free with her gifts to him, with her body. What e'er he wanted, she enthusiastically gave.

And she wanted his babes! He still felt stunned, and *honored* that she'd wanted his bairn so badly she'd wept when his seed hadn't taken root. No one—*no one*—e'er had liked him so well.

A wave of absolute joy—different than the ecstasy of release—filled his being, warmed his chest. What the hell was this feeling he kept experiencing when he was with her—or just thought about her? The question evaporated when she grasped hold of his buttocks and undulated her hips, forcing him to move faster and deeper into her. He threw his head back. "Aaaahhhhh!"

And lost control.

No more thought, only the ardent, strident, assiduous pursuit of visceral delight.

* * *

Morgana's whole frame began to quake. He'd kept her on the precipice for so long! And now she was near to touching heaven. It felt so good, so *goooood*. Please, *please*—oh, God! He pounded into her even faster and she tossed her head from side to side. Finally, finally, her canal began to convulse. She saw the sparks and colored lights behind her eyes, felt her body grow rigid with the unmitigated pleasure of being taken so fully, so voraciously, by the man she adored. Her eyes flew open for a split second. "*Robert!*" she cried. And then darkness.

* * *

Robert folded Morgana's limp legs o'er the backs of his own as he collapsed on top of her. Sweat dripped from his brow onto her chest before he could wipe it away and his breathing was so ragged it echoed in the chamber. Still locked snugly inside her warm womb, he rested his forehead on the pillow to the right of her ear, just managing somehow to remain up on his elbows, so as not to completely crush her. His mind spun like a top, his ears rang, but still he managed a grin.

He'd finally made her swoon first.

His eyes went wide. *She'd called out his name!* He lifted his head. 'Twas an effort, but he managed to raise up a bit more and study her slumbering visage. She'd spoken her first word in God knew how long, and it had been *his name*. Something important, something profound, settled into place inside him, somewhere in the vicinity of his heart. He trembled as he gazed at her, studied her, memorized every lovely curve, every gentle line of her countenance.

Then he kissed her lips. Softly and reverently. *I love you, Morgana.* The words, which expressed that unknown feeling, took him by surprise as they flitted across his consciousness and took up permanent residence in the center of his chest.

* * *

When Morgana woke, the sun had already begun to lower in the sky, as evidenced by the receding line of sunlight across the dim bedchamber's wooden floor. She looked around, for Robert, but he was not about. The chamber was silent, except for the slight hiss and crackle of the hearthfire.

She yawned and her body moved into a long, satisfying stretch. The edge of the blanket dipped below her nipples and she realized she was no longer in her gown and chemise. Curious.

With a flip of her hand, she tossed the blanket aside and sat up. Her eyes scanned her body and the bed covering for vestiges of the mess the two of them had made earlier. Naught. She was bathed clean and—dear Lord!—she had a new wrapping on her lower half as well. 'Twas not possible, surely! Aye, she did sleep soundly, she knew, for the nuns had chided her often enough as she grew, when they could not wake her for matins, but this? Nay, surely not. 'Twas too mad. She giggled. Aye, but he *had* made her swoon first, and that no doubt sent her into an even deeper slumber than was her habit.

She nibbled on her bottom lip. Robert? Had Robert, *her* Robert, ministered to her as she slept? She shook her head. Nay, 'twas more likely he'd asked one of the young chamber maids to do the deed. Her cheeks grew hot at the thought. But then, after another moment of horror, she sighed and shrugged. 'Twas much too late now to waste time cringing about.

She got to her feet and dressed in one of her prettier gowns. 'Twas the pale blue one with the snug-fitting bodice and waist; the one that had caused a warm light to shine in her husband's eyes, a small smile to curve his lips, the last time she'd worn it.

* * *

"She's written the tale out. Her husband's been bandying the pages about in his effort to find me."

A gust of wind blew at the hem of the other man's long, dark tunic. The material made a *whip*ping sound as it tossed to and fro. "Have *you* read it? Does she mention the ambush?"

"Nay, I've not read it." The man turned the woolen cap in his beefy, calloused hand. "But naught has been said about the ambush, nor all that happened afterward, either, so 'twas likely not revealed in her script."

"Good, good." After a pause, the other man said, "And no one suspects you of the deed the other night? Even tho' you've only been amongst the apprenticed masons for less than a sennight?"

The man shrugged and shook his head again. "It seems so. Not a query have I gotten in regard to it, at least not as yet."

The other man nodded, his shoulders visibly relaxing. "I'll meet you here again in two days' time. I'll give you further instruction then. For now, keep on as you have been; gathering as much information as you are able about the lady and her memory of that time."

The two men parted then: One moving back in the direction of the fortress, the other turning toward the hermit's cot he'd discovered upon his arrival.

* * *

Modron took one more quick look o'er her shoulder before slipping out the door of the keep.

'Twas past the chimes of midnight, and all but the night guards on the curtain wall were well abed. The air was crisp and calm, filled with the dust of ground stone, dank with the scent of still-wet mortar. Her son-in-law had done well in his bid to repair and furbish his much-ignored fortress these past moons.

It had taken Vika near to two moons to reply to Morgana's query regarding her past, but the letter had arrived this morn, and since that time, all had been in flux. For Vika, it seemed, had decided upon a visit.

Since their arrival at this holding, Modron had allowed some of her disguise to fall away. She'd slowly stopped applying as much of the pale gray ash to her face and golden brown hair, discontinued the slower, slightly stooped gate she'd employed during her few sennights at William's court.

But now, she feared, she'd be forced to resume the guise. And that worried her. For Morgana had noticed and commented upon her changed demeanor, but had accepted Modron's explanation that the rustic air away from the bustling court had been the reason; it had been a balm to her aching bones and vitalized her weary flesh.

As she'd done each eve since arriving o'er three moons past, Modron nodded to the guard and escaped the walled fortress through the postern gate.

The nights had become warm enough to enjoy the cool bath by moonlight in the clear water of the burn she'd discovered that first day. 'Twas hidden in a dense crop of pine, oak and spruce not far inside the wood. The place she liked to bathe had been dammed by the trunks and branches of fallen trees, so there was a deep pool in which she could immerse her tired and sore body, cleanse it for a few hours of the smothering ash.

At its edge, she quickly doffed her gown and chemise and then inserted the torch into the natural nook she'd made between three large stones. Afterward, as she always did, she walked directly into the depths until she was chin-deep in the still-frigid water. And, just as always, within a few minutes, her body stopped quaking and she began to glide and swim.

'Twas not long before her mind turned to her daughter once more. Only three days past, she'd discovered that Morgana was with child. The news had both pleased and stunned her. Even now, she was having a bit of trouble imagining herself as a grandmother.

Yes, she was of an age to be one, as she was just past her thirty-second summer, but still it seemed too soon, somehow. For, so much of the life she'd been promised—had expected to have—had been stripped from her while she was prisoned away in Brittany these past thirteen years. And now, she wanted to live again; enjoy life, enjoy her newly gained freedom.

Modron twisted and dove under the water. After several strokes, she reemerged, sweeping her hair back off her forehead with the palms of her hands as she lifted her face to the silvery moonbeams that gleamed above her.

Still, her mind would not settle, and her thoughts crowded in once more. But, she must make sure she, and most importantly, her daughter, were free from harm first. Recalling the bloodied, striped flesh of her daughter's back Modron had tended in those days after Morgana's prisonment by Donnach and the vicious priest—another of Donnach's minions, she had little doubt, tho' she'd not gotten a view of the man—and recalling as well her own anguished impotence at not being able to contravene, Modron was e'er more certain that Donnach would not rest until he'd destroyed Morgana as well. With a shiver, she sent a small prayer heavenward for both guidance and assistance in gaining the protection and the justice she craved for them both. And, aye, she knew that her being here in Alba, and this close to Morgana, would instantly bring danger, if 'twere discovered. Yet neither of their lives were safe as long as the savage devils remained untried and free. She was not meant to survive the attack, this she'd come to ken not long into her captivity.

She dove again, and paddled hard, yet the anger and unease remained.

Nay, her captor had gone against orders, had wanted her too feverishly, to destroy her that day.

But after her escape…. Aye, 'twas why she'd disguised herself, created a new identity, gotten herself inside William's court. It had not been easy, but her experiences there when she was a young wife and mother had aided her in her device; had allowed her to remain unnoticed as she sneaked about and maneuvered her way into her daughter's chamber and life.

And then, when she'd learned that her husband's brother, Donnach, the unsuspected man behind her husband's murder, behind her and her daughter's abductions, was successful in forcing a marriage on her little lass, Modron had made sure that Robert allowed her to travel here with them. If Donnach had further villainous intentions toward her family, as she suspected he did, then she was determined to stop it this time.

Rolling to her back, she glided through the moon-kissed ripples, allowing the silken-soft, cool bath to soothe her abused skin, her tightly drawn muscles.

After a long moment, a sigh escaped. Aye, she'd wavered many times o'er the past moons between revealing her ruse (or at least warning Robert about her worry) and keeping silent, especially after Morgana's strange vision the night of the *Bealltainn* fire and feast. But, when no real danger was found, she decided it best to keep silent. 'Twas clear from Morgana's inability to speak, and from that vision as well, that she was in no state for another blow. Besides, Robert, being a man, was better made for hand-to-hand battle with a known enemy, and this required a woman's facility for cunning and stealth, if the traitors were e'er to be rooted out.

"You're still as lovely as ever, my dear Gwynlyan."

Modron gasped and took in a mouthful of water. Swiftly, she whipped into an upright position and crouched up to her chin in the burn. Coughing as she crossed her arms o'er her chest, she turned in the direction of the voice, and froze, her eyes wide with shock and disbelief, her jaw slack.

He smiled, but it didn't reach his eyes. "Aye, 'tis I, your husband."

She opened her mouth to speak, but no sound came forth. *Morgunn.* He'd survived somehow. *Praise be.* "How?" she managed to ask at last.

Morgunn glanced down at the folded garments near his foot. After lifting them in his hand and thrusting them out toward her, he said, "Clothe yourself first, then I shall tell you."

She nodded and waded a step toward the bank, but then halted. "Place the garments on yon bolder and turn your back to me while I dress."

The smile did reach his eyes then. "Surely 'tis not shyness you are feeling—not with all that we were, all that we shared."

Modron bit her lip. Aye, 'twas shyness. After all, it had been nearly fourteen years since he'd last seen her in the bare; much had changed—settled—since that time. And...there were the scars now, as well. "Please. Turn around."

The smile left Morgunn's face, but he did as she'd asked.

She darted out of the water and, as quickly as she was able with wet skin, tossed first her chemise and then her gown o'er her head and tugged the resistant hems down o'er her dripping, chilled frame. While she tied her knotted, damp hair with a leather thong, she turned back to the man she'd wed with so much hope in her heart twenty years prior. "All right. I'm ready to hear your tale."

He swiveled to face her then. Crossing his arms over his chest, he said, "After my brother's accomplices left with you and our daughter—"

"So you do know of Donnach's treachery."

His jaw clenched. "Aye," he ground out, "and he'll pay. This I vow."

She gave a quick, decisive nod of agreement, then prompted him on with his tale, saying, "After...?"

"Aye, after the fiends left with you, your cousins,

Giric and Alaxandar, the men I'd sent to arrange the next delivery of copper and who were to join us on our journey that day, fished me out of the water and brought me to a nearby kinswoman's cot. They'd come upon the grisly results of the ambush just as the convoy was leaving—and just as the conspirators tossed my limp, bloody carcass in the loch. The dear woman worked a miracle somehow, for I survived the bastards' swords—and the near-drowning as well."

Modron could not take her gaze from the man before her. In so many ways, 'twas as if no time had passed. And yet. He was older, as was she. Where before, his hair had been long and straight, black—so black, the sun's rays could make it seem streaked with deep blue—and he'd always had it tied with a thong, now 'twas cut short, in the way of the Normans, and there was just a touch of gray at the temples.

But, Lord, he still had the powerful build of a Highland warrior, still had the rugged handsome appeal that had drawn her to him when she was but a lass of twelve summers and he, a young squire of fifteen.

"Do you still love me, Gwynlyan?"

Modron's pulse pounded. *Did* she still love him? Her heart could not answer. Too many years had passed, and her time of grieving her loss, his death, had long receded into history. All that had been left, until just moments ago, had been warm memories of her youth and resentment at the loss of her love, her life.

Morgunn snorted. "Nay, do not answer." He turned and walked a few paces away. His arms akimbo, he stared out into the darkness of the forest. Neither of them spoke for long minutes afterward. The only sound between them was the quiet hiss and crackle of the torch's flame or the occasional scurrying of some woodland creature.

"How long have you known we were here?" Modron asked at last.

Morgunn swiveled to look at her a moment before turning back to his perusal of the black shades in front of him. "Nigh on a moon."

Her brows shot higher. "Have you been here that long then?"

He shook his head. "Nay, I only arrived this day past."

"Where were you?" Her throat ached from the effort not to scream the words, for she'd meant more by them than what he'd no doubt kenned. And 'twas growing more plain to her with each passing moment that he'd left her to rot in her prison, left their daughter to nearly do the same in that nunnery she had been shoved into...afterward.

Morgunn turned. He took two steps toward her, then halted, as if he knew she'd not allow him closer, as if he *did* know what she'd meant. And when he spoke, he proved it. "For almost nine years afterward, I was lame from the sword wounds. Giric and Alaxandar sheltered me until I was well enough to be moved, then they found a place for me to live and a nurse to take care of me." He took another tentative step toward her. She stepped back, crossing her arms over her chest. "I was not in my right mind, Gwynlyan. The near-drowning had affected my reason, somehow. But, finally, with the aid of that good nurse, with her healing skills and my own determination to o'ercome my weakness, finally, about four years past, I at last regained my strength, my full mobility, and my reason. I've been looking for you and our daughter e'er since." He turned his head and gazed toward the pile of wood and debris that made the dam. "Tho', 'tis truth, for most of that time, I believed I was searching for your graves."

"I was in the land of the *Armorics*, locked away in Alaric's seaside fortress," she said, tho' there was little emotion in the sound.

"Aye, I know."

"You *know*?" she accused with a start.

Morgunn sighed. His hands clenched, then opened, then clenched again at his side. "Did it ne'er occur to you to wonder why you were finally allowed to leave? Given berth on a barge from there to the port near the King's court?"

'Twas Gwynlyan's turn to take a step forward. Her heart began to thud in her chest. "You? How?"

"How did I find you, or how did I gain your release?"

"Both."

* * *

Morgunn would have given his hard-won right leg's agility at that moment to fold her in his arms, to feel the comfort of her lovely frame—the other half of his own—securely in its natural place once more, but he knew she was not yet ready to allow such from him. He could see, in the rigid way she held herself, hear in her voice, how deep the hurt had gone. Aye, 'twould be a long, difficult struggle to regain her love, regain his place in her life. But, he was bound to do it, as, for him, there was simply no other choice. He was hers, had been since the first time he'd seen her, met her, on the rolling moors of Carn Dochan and Bala, near the old Roman fort of *Caer Gai* in Cambria.

"I found Angharat, your lady's maid, back with her family near *Llyn Tegid*," Morgunn said at last. "She told me of a rumor she'd heard not long after my brother's deceit. A rumor that you and our daughter were not dead—that you had been hied off to some fortress in the duchy of Brittany, and my daughter was ensconced in a nunnery there as well, but that she, being a woman of little power or means, feared making accusations that she had little way of proving, knowing that her own family would be in his sights next, were she to do so." He scrubbed his hand across the back of his neck a few times. "I had no other choice then. I risked all and went to Bishop Richard in Dunkeld, undisguised, allowing him to recognize me, and told to him the entire tale."

He heard her gasp. Morgunn looked up once more, and seeing his wife's surprised, beautiful mien, he wondered again if he could e'er win back her love. "He arranged a private meeting with King William. Once I revealed the betrayal to him as well, he agreed to press Donnach to bring Morgana to court, to try to stir Donnach's fear that his crime would be discovered so that he might again begin to plot."

Morgunn took in a deep breath and turned his gaze upward, focusing for a moment on the twinkling stars above as he continued, "In truth, our King had not been as startled by the revelation as I'd believed he would be," he settled his gaze on his wife once more, "and when I inquired, he yielded that he'd suspected my brother's hand in the deed all these years past, but could ne'er gather enough evidence to charge him, so had finally left the matter in God's good hands to punish."

Restless, Morgunn turned and walked a few paces away. Turning back, he said, "After my meeting with King William, I went to Brittany, to Alaric's fortress—for who else among my brother's comrades would have done the deed for him?—and bargained for your escape with the night guard." He took in a deep breath and slowly released it. "I ransomed you with my father's sword."

Gwynlyan gasped. "*Morgunn!* 'Twas your most prized possession, the key to your birthright, your final proof of his will that you hold *Aerariae secturae* upon his death!"

Morgunn shrugged. "I had no choice; I could not leave you to rot in that place. By some act of God's good will, or their own blundering dull-wittedness, our attackers did not take it with them when they fled. For that, I am eternally grateful. For, I wanted my family returned more than I e'er wanted that land or the wealth that came with it." He snorted. "All that land e'er brought me was grief, from the moment my father forced it upon me."

Gwynlyan walked over to stand in front of him, so close, he could reach out his hands and pull her into his arms.

If only she'd allow it.

He gritted his teeth and clenched his hands at his sides to keep from doing as he craved.

"But, 'twas our only home," she said at last. "And he bequeathed it to you—and the sword as well—to show all that you were the son of his heart, bastard-born or nay."

"Aye, and the bequeathing of it only made my brother covet it more. I have little doubt now that Donnach's plot against us was set in motion on the very day our father was interred in his tomb."

"Truly? As long ago as that?" she asked, turning and, crossing her arms over her chest, she scanned her eye o'er the light dancing on the water. The next she murmured, as if to herself: " 'I'd ne'er conceived...."

Morgunn swallowed the bile that rose up at the memory. He'd lost all because he'd wanted so desperately to believe his brother's missive, to believe that, at last, the man had come to terms with their father's betrayal of Donnach's mother, of their father's devotion, not only to his new wife, Morgunn's mother, the woman he'd wed within days of Donnach's mother's death, but also to the son they'd conceived out of wedlock. Instead, Donnach had used Morgunn's desire to mend their torn clan by hiring men to lay in wait for him and, worst of all, his wife and child. "I'd suspected, but didn't want to believe...," he replied softly.

Gwynlyan stormed away several paces. "Why did you not tell me?"

He felt a new crack in his heart at the loss of her nearness, the renewed stiffness in her frame. "I was trying to protect you; I knew how distressed you were already. Why give you more worry if I could come to some agreement with Donnach?" He sighed and shook his head. As if drawn by unseen silver chains, he stepped toward her, stood next to her once more, gazing at her fragile-boned profile. "You were so young, Gwynlyan. *We* were so young. Mistakes were made, I admit that, and I ache inside knowing that you have suffered so long at the hands of my brother's cohorts."

Her head whipped around, and a shadow of an unknown emotion passed across her countenance, lit her eyes, at his words. But just for a fleet moment, and then 'twas gone. Gone before he could capture its meaning. Gone before he could form a question. But in its wake, an unease twisted in his gut that he would not acknowledge. Instead, he turned away. Turned away from the feeling and turned away from her. Turned away from the lovely eyes that held so much pain, so much accusation in their moon-gilded reflection.

He faced the darkness of the wood once more. "You made a mistake, when you agreed to wed me, 'tis plain, but—"

He heard her gasp, heard the crunch of twigs beneath her feet as she moved in some way behind him. "Nay!" she said. He felt her rush toward him, then halt, just inches away from him.

He continued as if she'd said naught, "—if you will give me a chance, I'll do all I can to make amends for the harm I've caused you."

Gwynlyan stunned him in the next moment when she took that last step and flung herself into his embrace, gave herself, her trust, into his keeping once more.

CHAPTER 8

MORGANA OPENED HER eyes and blinked rapidly against the bright sunshine coming through the window. As she stretched, she turned her head to look behind her. The dip in the pillow where her husband's head had been was all that was left as proof of his earlier habitance.

This day was the anniversary of her nineteenth year of birth, or so she'd been told by Vika in one of their many dark-of-night, hushed confidences during her stay at King William's court. All her life—at least the life she could remember—she'd not known, and so the nuns had simply marked the beginning of the next year of her life on the day of Christ the Lord's birth as well.

This day, however, was to be special. For, once Robert had learned of it—Modron, bless her, had pressed Morgana to tell her if she knew the date, then scurried off in secret to inform him—he'd insisted that they have a feast to mark the day. She sighed. She smiled. She settled her hand o'er the babe Robert had given her, tucked snug in her womb.

As had become her habit these past days since discovering her childing state, she rose from the bed and quickly dressed before hastening out the door to meet Robert by the latest portion of the fortress to be repaired.

He'd changed since that day two moons prior when she'd revealed her deepest desire to him, and even more so, since discovering he'd successfully bestowed it to her.

Morgana's hand flew up to cover the big grin that spread across her countenance. This past night, he'd even used the words *enjoy you* when he'd tossed her gown and chemise o'er her head and onto the floor; tho' the words had seemed to stumble out, as if they were much too large for his mouth. She stopped short, staring across the bailey, her eyes wide with wonder, for she'd only just realized that she'd not heard him say the other, lewder, term in at least a *fortnight!*

She shook her head and resumed her buoyant stride. He'd been so gentle with her, too. As if he'd break her, or hurt their babe, if he moved too quickly, went too deep. And he was always resting his palm o'er her belly now. Measuring each day the growth of his son—aye, he was sure 'twas a son he'd started inside her!

One time, a few days past, she'd awakened to hear him whispering, his lips nearly touching the small mound. It had taken her a moment to realize he was talking to their babe. Promising their wee one that he'd ne'er do what his own father had done. That he'd leave this world knowing that the legacy he left to him was intact.

That had broken her heart. When she'd stroked her hand through his mussed hair, he'd jerked, but then he'd lifted up, taken her into his arms, and kissed her. The kiss had been almost desperate, as if what he needed, only she could provide. And when she'd wrapped her legs high around his waist, urging him to enter her, it had quietened his demons, allowing him to find his rest afterward.

As she turned the corner, she saw him standing with the master mason. His brows were like angry thunderclouds shadowing gray-lightning eyes. Mayhap 'twas not the best time to interrupt him. She'd just taken a step back, was about to turn around, when he looked up, directly into her vision. The storm clouds vanished and in their place a small smile and a definite twinkle took their place. He lifted his arm and waved her over to him, but then, as if he couldn't wait for her to reach him, he began to move in her direction as well.

He'd left the master mason in the middle of his speech. The man flapped his arms like a goose throwing off water and stalked away, shaking his head and muttering under his breath. Morgana grinned.

The closer they came to each other, the longer Robert's strides grew, until he was directly in front of her. Then, he did the most wonderful thing! He hugged her and gave her a quick kiss on the lips. Just as she'd hoped he'd do, but had begun to doubt he e'er would.

"How is my son?" he asked, drawing back slightly. Not waiting for her answer, he splayed his hand o'er her belly. "Same size as earlier this morn." There was actually *disappointment* in his voice!

She rolled her eyes at him, but she nodded and smiled to take the sting out of the gesture.

He looked behind him and studied the progress of the work being done a silent moment, before turning back to her and saying, "The master mason wants to tear down that portion of the wall"—he pointed toward the northeast side—" and extend the bailey by a hundred feet. 'Twill mean extending the mound, building it up as well. I will need to use some of the monies intended for the additions to our living quarters. Dugan says that we've needed that extra training area for a few years now." He lifted his hand and stroked it up and down her arm. "But...if you say me nay, I shall tell him we will keep the bailey as it is."

Morgana was stunned. So stunned, in fact, all she could do for several heartbeats was stare, her mouth agape, into her husband's steel gray eyes.

That familiar shadow-smile touched his lips and he brought his hand up to her chin, gently pressing it up so that her mouth shut as he stroked his thumb at its corner. "What say you?" he prompted.

Morgana took in a deep breath to still her pounding heart before shaking her head. Then, motioning and mouthing the words, she told him that the fortifications must take priority o'er the dwelling.

Robert gave her a brief nod, then turned and strode over to the master mason. They spoke for a few minutes before her husband returned to her side. "There is a place I liked as a lad—a place in the wood where a burn flows. We dammed the water and made a pool to swim in. Would you like to go there with me now? Have a privy"—he leaned forward, rumbling the next two words low in her ear—"more carnal feast to honor your day of birth?" he finished as he straightened again. "Mayhap, take a bit of food to enjoy afterward, as well?"

Morgana felt the heat rise in her cheeks, but nodded in sheer delight, taking hold of his hand.

He looked back at the master mason and raised his arm in farewell, then turned with her and strode with her toward the keep to get the supplies they'd need.

* * *

Hours later, the two of them were settled by the side of the burn. She, enjoying a bit of the wine Robert had brought along, and he, still dozing in the dappled, fluttering light of the sun trickling through the heavily-leaved tree branches above their heads after the torrid loving they'd shared. Morgana scanned her eye about the secluded area and her sight was dazzled by some sparkling, waving thing attached to a fallen tree branch a few paces away.

She rose to her feet and walked closer to the object. 'Twas a silver chain. When she unsnagged it from the piece of dried wood and held it up high, she realized 'twas a necklace. And suspended from it was a cross of the ancients. In the center, where the two stems of the cross joined was a strange stone, green in color—as green and vibrant as the high grass of the glen this time of year. There were emblems carved into the circle surrounding the junction, emblems that caused her skin to crawl, made her sweat, brought on a vision of fire and clashing swords, a woman's hysterical screams. *"Morgunn! No!"*

There was only a vague realization that she'd actually cried out the words herself, that she was crumpling to the ground, before all went black.

* * *

Robert was jarred to full wakefulness by the sound of his wife's voice. A bit dazed with sleep, it took him a moment to find her as he jolted into a sitting position and looked around. When he saw her recumbent form splayed on the ground a bit away, he bellowed, "Morgana!" then leapt to his feet and jogged over to her.

As he knelt down next to her, he turned her over onto her back so he could see her face, feel her cheeks and brow. Her skin was cool, cooler than it should have been, and clammy. White. White as hoarfrost on the heath in winter. "Morgana," he said near her ear. It took two more attempts, but finally her eyelids fluttered and opened. Her brows came together as she gazed up at him in confusion.

"You swooned. Is it the babe?" he said anxiously, running his hand and eye down to her belly. "Are you in pain?"

His wife shook her head and tried to sit up, but Robert pressed his hand to her shoulder and forced her back down. "Rest a moment longer."

After retrieving the cup of wine she'd left near the blanket they had been sitting on, he lifted her up only far enough to drink some of it down. "Are you sure the babe is well? That you are well?"

Morgana swallowed down the remainder of the red liquid in the cup before answering him. As she pressed the vessel back into his hand, she nodded her reassurance.

Robert helped her to her feet. "We should return to the keep. I want you to lie down and rest for the remainder of the afternoon. Just in case."

She nodded and walked over to their pallet, the necklace, which now lay half-hidden in the bracken, entirely forgotten. She tried to fold the blanket, put away the remains of their meal, but Robert would not allow it, instead simply scrambling it all together in a ball and tying it to her mare's saddle. "You'll ride back with me on my steed. My thighs can cushion the ride a bit more for you."

* * *

Gwynlyan waited until her daughter and son-in-law were well away before scurrying from behind the oak. When she'd learned the two were off together, that she would also have some time to herself, she'd rushed here to retrieve her cross. But, when she'd discovered the lovers here already, she'd turned back with the intention of returning later that night. She hadn't gone far, however, before Robert's cry had come to her, holding such fear, that she'd hurried back. 'Twas with no little amount of relief that she'd found 'twas naught dire, that her daughter had only succumbed to a swoon quite common to those who were breeding.

It took a bit of searching, but she at last found what she'd come for. Somehow, this night past, the necklace that she'd worn since she was a lass of twelve summers had slipped from around her neck.

Somehow. Nay, not *somehow*. She knew exactly *how.* She bit down so hard on her lip that she tasted the iron-ore flavor of blood on her tongue.

Morgunn. She'd nearly allowed him to enjoy her the night before. When she'd felt the long-remembered, long-missed comfort of his embrace, realized her love had not died, but had grown stronger, she'd been in such a daze of wonder that she'd not recalled the scars. Not, at least, until he'd nearly had her completely unclothed again. Not until she'd seen his own reminders of their shattered dream, broken trust, slashed across his chest in a raised white stripe.

Then she'd remembered her own, and could not let him see her thus. He'd always thought her beautiful, perfect. As so many young swains had when she was a lass. Why, even tho' she had been happily wed, during those years at William's court, she'd had troubadours sing of her beauty. And it had been a heady thing, to know that she was so alluring to so many.

But, no longer. And, 'twas her intent, that Morgunn, tho' she loved him, would ne'er see, ne'er know, of the scars that marred her back, nor the years she'd spent as her twisted captor's concubine.

She was a grotesque and defiled version of her former self, and no man, most of all her husband, should e'er be expected to want her again.

* * *

'Twas just past the chimes of midnight, when Robert was once again brought from a deep slumber by Morgana's beautiful song, that he recalled her words before her swoon. When she lay back down and rolled onto her side, he wrapped himself around her and began to try to slowly awaken her by brushing her hair away from her face and kissing first her brow, then her cheek, and then her neck. The ploy worked and she stirred.

"Who is Morgunn?"

Her eyes flew open and she tried to disengage, tried to rise from the bed. But he wouldn't let her go. Held tight to her, not ungently, but in a manner from which she could not get loose.

"Who is Morgunn?" he asked again.

This time, she answered him. She rolled her head on the pillow and met his gaze. *Father.* She mouthed the word. She didn't know *how* she knew it, but she did. The Morgunn the woman had plead for had been Morgana's father. And the voice Morgana had heard crying out his name must have been that of her mother. A tear trickled out of the corner of her eye, tickling her temple.

Robert brushed it away with his thumb, doing the same to the next, and the next. He pushed the fear—the restless, need to run, fear—that her tears caused him down deep and leaned forward. He kissed her then. As gently as he was able.

This was new to him, this *lovelonging* thing. But he was determined to do it right. Treat her the way he thought he was supposed to treat her. Blood of Christ! *Talk* more.

"Did you recall something of what happened that day? To your father?"

Morgana's tears went dry. Her muscles tensed. Her heartbeat doubled. Her skin grew clammy.

She knew not. She knew *not!* All she could do was shake her head and hide her face in the pillow.

Robert's own heartbeat increased. "Be you at peace, Morgana," he said, then leaned down and pressed his lips to her pate. "All is well. I'll not press you any further." But 'twas clear he'd need to redouble his efforts to find the key to her past, for her hauntings were coming more often and with more force, and that could not be good for their unborn son.

He caressed her arm, then turned her onto her back and was relieved to feel her become pliant under his touch. "All is well," he repeated.

As he stroked her hair and nibbled at her lower lip, he recalled again the magical sound of his lovely wife's voice. Mayhap, if fortune shined upon him, she would regain her voice one day, and for e'er more; she'd say his name—tell him she loved him—before they were aged and gray.

At that last thought, his heart began to thud with a warm joy inside his chest. Without realizing it, his hand splayed o'er the mound of her belly where his son grew. When he felt the soft comfort of her own settle o'er his, he was shocked to feel a bit of moisture gather behind his lids.

In answer to that perturbing experience, he opened his lips wide and plundered her mouth with his tongue, changing the tender kiss into a torrid one in seconds. What he needed was a good fu—damn!—*coupling* to exorcize his unease.

***

"The cousin comes," the man said. "She shall arrive here shortly from Perth. Do you think she knows who devised the destruction of Morgunn and his family?"

The other man shook his head. "Nay. She knows little of that time, of all that happened." He turned and strode toward his mount. "But she might, if pressed by the husband, tell him of the lady's mother and father." As he dug inside the satchel attached to his saddle, he turned his head and looked back at his fellow conspirator. "And that might bode very ill for us. For, with enough of a nudge, the other one might begin to recollect all. And, once she does, our fortunes—our very lives—will be at risk." Tucking a carrot under his steed's nose and watching him eat, he continued, "If only we could end this now, cleanly. But Donnach is right: If the King suspects him, then he's no doubt watching that naught amiss befalls the mute."

"Aye, but 'tis taking longer than was originally planned."

The other man nodded. "Still, we must continue to look for a means to kill her that will raise no questions." He turned to face his companion once more, his hands clenched at his sides, his jaw tight. "For, we will not be safe until *all* of that line are ended. This time *for e'er more.*"

***

'Twas not long past the nooning meal the day after their lovers' idyll at the burn, and directly upon being distracted in her mending of yet another of Robert's frayed shirts by a strong beam of sunlight coming through the window of her bedchamber and refracting off her fine silver needle, that Morgana at last recalled the cross necklace.

The image appeared, seemed to float, warped and stretched, before her eyes, then tunneled, receded, sped and swirled, into a black void. As terror spread, like cumbrous molten lead through her veins, her heart pounded, her body separated from her will, from her mind, as all sensation departed.

Mama!

Mama!

Mama!

The word clanged through her brain like the tolling of a bell, while she watched, as if from a distance or dream, the needle drop from her trembling fingers, followed by the shirt, as her legs brought the rest of her frame up. One of her feet stepped forward, but found no purchase. In the next second, the floor hurtled toward her forehead. In the far distance, a *thud* sounded before all went dark.

* * *

Robert took the steps two at a time that led up to his bedchamber. So greatly pleased was he by the progress thus far on the furbishing being done to the northeast wall that he'd decided to take a small moment away from the activities, to yield to his yearning to see his wife so soon again after the nooning meal, to rest his hand on the warm mound of her belly, 'neath which his heir nested snugly, and, aye, to give Morgana his thanks once more—nay, for the first time—for her calm understanding of the practical use of what funds they had. He felt the not-oft used muscles in his cheeks stretch as his mouth formed a grin. 'Twas dawning on him more each day what an excellent wife he'd stumbled into wedding, and he knew he didn't deserve her, knew he'd somehow been blessed, and was thankful all the more for it.

With added vigor, and an unaccountable lightness in his breast, he said, "Awake, wife!" as he swung the door wide and strode forward. " 'Tis too pleasing a da— Morgana!" He rushed to the nook near the window where she liked to sew and knelt down by her prone form. Rolling her over onto her back, he saw at once that a thin sheen of sweat dampened her flushed brow and cheeks, yet she was so still, with not even a flutter of a lid to let him know that she still lived, breathed, that he frantically pressed his ear to her chest to listen for a pulse. *Praise be to Heaven.* 'Twas there, and steady. He yanked off the filet and wimple she wore and tossed them aside, hoping the added coolness would help to revive her. Afterward, in one fluid motion, he lifted her in his arms and took her to their bed.

Settling her gently upon it, he kissed her brow before his eye anxiously swept the room and landed on the ewer and bowl on the washstand. In only a matter of a brief few moments, he'd jogged the distance there and back and had the moist cloth against her flushed skin, soothing it.

Her eyes fluttered and his lungs expanded, allowing, at last, a full intake of breath.

"Morgana." He touched his lips to each lid, then pressed a much more furtive one against her mouth.

Song of the Highlands

"Awake, my love."

Her lids lifted, and in the depths of her lovely blue eyes, he saw warm recognition, immediately followed by confusion as her dark brows furrowed.

She pushed against his shoulders and tried to rise, but his strength was greater, and he pressed her back down to the pillow. She looked around, mouthing, "What befell me?" with a flutter of her hand.

* * *

As Morgana shifted her gaze back to her husband's worried countenance, as she felt his hand settle o'er her belly, as she heard him say, "You swooned again, Morgana," she recalled with clarity the necklace she'd seen at the burn, and, immediately on its heels, the fear it evoked. *Had it truly been there, or had it been some new madness of mind?* 'Twas what she now believed her vision of *Ankou* had been all those moons prior (and what she secretly worried was what Robert now believed as well). *If I reveal that I've had another vision, will he regret the bad bargain he made in me?*

"Is it the babe again? Should I call for Modron?" He half-rose to do just that, but she yanked at his arm, and he settled again next to her, except this time his expression showed perplexity.

"Nay!" she mouthed, shaking her head vigorously. Going purely on emotion and against her conscience, she put her hands together as if in prayer, tucked them against one side of her cheek, and half-closed her eyes, showing him she simply needed to rest. She soothed her hand o'er his arm. "Fret not," she mouthed, then curled up on her side. "Supper," she mouthed.

Robert nodded, leaned down and brushed a kiss on her brow, then rose, saying, "Rest you well, then, and as you say, I shall see you at supper." He turned and departed the chamber.

Morgana lay there, still and tense, for quite some time afterward, fearing that he'd send for Modron despite her wish otherwise, but once she was sure that she would be left alone until the evening meal, she turned her mind once more to the necklace. Why would the sight of a simple piece of jewelry, real or imagined, send such terror through her veins? Without realizing she was doing so, she fisted her sleeve in her sweaty palm. *'Tis madness! It must be!*

Closing her eyes, she took in a calming breath. Nay, she must not panic. Before she mentioned the necklace to her husband, before she gave him the real truth about her swoon today—only one day after she'd frightened him with a like experience at the burn— she'd journey back there and look for the necklace. If she found it, then she'd know 'twas not some trick her mind had played, some madness that might have her in its grip.

Biting down hard on the side of her finger until the pain o'ercame the dread expanding in her breast, she allowed the other unsettling thought to seep through: If she found the necklace, found it to be real, then *who did it belong to?* Friend or foe?

* * *

Late that night, not long past the chimes of midnight, yet well after Morgana and Robert had retired for the night, Morgana remained awake, unable to find her rest.

Her mind would not settle, no matter how she tried. She lay there, still, measuring her breathing, measuring her husband's. His hand rested, warm and protective, o'er her hip, their curved frames nearly touching.

She closed her eyes and tried yet again to clear her thoughts, to drift into slumber.

A noise, sounding suspiciously like a dropped shoe, came from beyond the door that led into the small antechamber of their own that her maid, Modron, occupied. Her ears pricked and she lifted her head from the pillow. She had to strain, but, aye, she could hear other shuffling about going on. If shoes were involved, it meant a late-night assignation. Was Modron meeting a lover? A thrill of both joy and adventure coursed through her, for she loved her maid, and wanted her to find another mate, a mate as perfectly right for her as Robert was for Morgana.

A wedding feast! Aye! 'Twould be wonderful to host a wedding for Modron here among their new clan.

After a quick glance to confirm that her husband still slept soundly, she rolled out from under his hand and off the bed. She'd follow. She couldn't sleep anyway, and she simply *must* know if the lover was that handsome clansman who'd danced 'round the Bealltainn fire with her maid that night. If 'twas, how long had they been lovers? Since the feast day? If so, how had Morgana not been aware before?

Morgana made swift, silent work of dressing, all the time listening to the sounds coming from Modron's chamber. Modron had a door that exited into the corridor, so she'd not be coming through their own chamber, and Morgana did not want to be too late to follow. In another moment, she was ready to go. She waited until she heard the muffled *creak* of Modron's door opening, then waited again to hear her pass outside her own, then waited yet again, to allow Modron a good ten paces lead, before Morgana at last departed her chamber.

She merely wanted to know the identity of Modron's lover, she told her chiding conscience. Aye, she knew 'twas a deceitful thing to do to her maid. If Modron had wanted to share the tidings with her, she would have told her already. But, Morgana simply had to know. And she simply could not bring herself to query the maid on such privy matters. Which told Morgana, she truly was doing a very bad thing. Still, she continued on.

Modron carried no taper. She went with the assured steps of a woman who'd made this journey many times, Morgana thought.

Her maid did not depart the keep through the front entrance. Instead, she took a more indirect route, going first through the great hall, then out the side door that led into a short exterior covered walk, walled on one side, which connected the keep to the chapel. She did not go into the chapel, however, she veered to her right and traversed the narrow, cobbled expanse between the two buildings that led directly into the courtyard. She was headed for the postern gate! Where was she meeting this lover, anyway? The glen? The burn? His own cot? Morgana's imagination spun with all the exciting possibilities. If 'twas his cot, unfortunately, 'twas possible Morgana would not actually see him, she thought, as she began the lightless stealthy hike between the buildings.

Her breathing increased. This much shadow and gloom made her uneasy. It always had, she knew not why.

Sometimes, when she was but a young lass at the nunnery, she'd grow dizzy and swoon, if she was alone too long in the dark, much like the whirling feeling she'd experienced earlier today when she'd recalled the necklace.

She'd not taken more than three steps when she felt a presence behind her. The hairs on the back of her neck stood on end. Her heart began to thrum. Fear made her quicken her step, made her swing her gaze around as she moved. All was black as pitch. Her breathing quickened, grew harsh. Sweat beaded her upper lip. *Light! Get into the light of the courtyard where the guard can see you!*

She began to run, caring not if Modron found her out. She was near the edge between night and moonlight when two arms swept around her, one o'er her mouth and nose, cutting off her air, and the other o'er her shoulder blades. The hooded black cloak he wore was all too familiar.

"You're mine now," he rasped close to her ear. He began dragging her back into the darkness, and she fought him. Writhing, scratching, kicking, elbowing. His hold remained strong. He would kill her. Take her into the underworld now. Just like the legend told.

Her clawing hands brushed the brooch attached to her cloak. She ripped it from the wool and jabbed the sharp end deep into his arm. He grunted and his grip loosed long enough for her to stomp down hard on his instep and yank out of his hold.

She ran. As hard as she could, she ran. Toward the light. Toward safety. Tho' she did not hear him behind her, still she turned her head, she could not keep from doing so, and saw only a yawning void. She kept running, kept moving. And barreled into a hard wall of sinew and bone. *'Tis him!* Arms enfolded her, and from somewhere far off, a familiar voice soothed, " 'Tis all right, Morgana, 'tis only me," but still she struggled, panting, frantic to be set free.

Again, the voice came to her. " 'Tis Robert, Morgana! What is amiss?"

All she could do was point, point in the direction from which she'd come, and mouth, "*Ankou!*"

"*Ankou!*" her husband repeated. Then, in one movement, he looked down that gloomy, dark expanse, released her from his embrace, and took off between the buildings, the lightless chasm soon swallowing him up.

She stumbled further into the courtyard, into the moonlight, for the moment, all thoughts of Modron forgotten.

* * *

The mute's husband, looking right and left, darted past where the apprentice hid, huddled under his cloak in the corner and holding his breath, and on down the aisle between the two rows of long benches in the chapel. As the husband reached the alter, he slowed then stopped, arms akimbo, his lungs blowing hard in the exalted silence of the church. He looked all around, to each side, then forward and back.

After another moment, the husband jogged back up the aisle and returned through the door leading to the outside passageway. The apprentice sucked in several deep breaths. He waited there for another quarter-hour, afraid to leave lest the husband sent guards out in search of him.

* * *

'Twas many long, terror-filled moments later before Robert jogged back to Morgana. Placing his hands on her shoulders, he studied her visage and murmured, "There was naught there, no one there."

She stared up at him. *There was! There was!* If only she could shout the words.

Her frame aquiver with uncontrollable quakes, she collapsed into his arms, gripping tight to his back, fisting her hands in his linen shirt.

"Fear not, you are safe. I'll ne'er let anyone harm you, Morgana. I swear this on my very soul. Do you believe me?"

She didn't answer, too shaken was she, and needing first only the comfort and security of his strong embrace. Somehow, he sensed her need, and stood there with her, holding her tight for a sustained moment while her trembling waned.

After another short time, he touched his fingertips to her cheek, touched his lips to hers, before slowly drawing away. "What was it brought you out here in the middle of the night?"

Her heart tripped. She opened her mouth to explain,

but then clamped it shut. Nay, she'd not betray Modron in that way, nor her own shamefully inquisitive doings either. After all, hadn't Robert once told her he found such actions loathsome in her cousin, Vika? Nay, she'd reveal naught of her reasons for being here. So, she gave him a limp shrug.

"You told me you saw *Ankou* earlier."

A shiver ran through her. She nodded.

His brows slammed together. "*Ankou*. Aye, *Ankou*," he said, and she heard a small thread of disbelief in his tone. " 'Twas but another of your dreams, Morgana."

A dream! She'd not dreamed him…surely? She glanced back into the black void again. Or…had she? She'd been frighted, she'd tingled with dread, had even recalled her reactions as a bairn to the dark. And then he'd appeared. Seemingly, out of nowhere. Added to that, were the events of the past days; the visions with regard to the necklace she'd found at the burn. She could no longer be sure. Mayhap, yet another of her illusions had forced itself into her waking life. And this time, she'd dreamt the creature had tried to carry her off, just as he did the dead woman in her recurring vision. *This is some kind of madness. It must be….*

Her husband pressed his lips to her forehead. " 'Tis all right, Morgana. You are safe." He turned them both in the direction of the front entry of the keep. After they'd taken several paces, arm in arm, he leaned down and whispered in her ear, "I have just the remedy for such night terrors. By the time I'm done with you, you shall be too weary to wander about in your sleep, or to dream either, for that matter.

Song of the Highlands

In spite of her remaining nervousness, in spite of her worry regarding her soundness of mind, in spite her growing fear that Robert's patience with her would soon begin to thin, her pulse increased and anticipation took the place of all her dread thoughts and feelings. She smiled up at him and gave him an eager nod.

* * *

When all was quiet as a tomb for an extended time, the apprentice risked rising and going to crack the door open and peek out. The area was completely deserted. Awash with relief, he let himself heave an audible sigh, then slipped from the chapel, down the cobblestones, and, keeping to the shadows next to the wall, headed for the courtyard and postern gate.

His partner would not be pleased at his lateness. No doubt, he'd been waiting on the mound for more than an hour by now. The apprentice had been hiding in the darkness, away from the night guards' eyes, when first the old maid of the mute's, and then the mute herself, had walked past him where he stood leaning against the stone wall of the keep. The maid's wanderings he found curious, and may have followed her, had the mute not been the better prize. In truth, he'd not had a plan. He'd acted in the moment, wanting to frighten her, see if, with the addition of force, her memory, her voice would return. But, clearly, it had not.

Would he have killed her? Aye. No doubt. And 'twas possible Donnach Cambel would not have been pleased. He rubbed the puncture wound she'd left in his skin and recalled that she'd dropped the brooch where they'd struggled. It took him only a moment or two to retrieve it, wipe it clean of his blood, and drop it nearer the end of the cobblestones just where the courtyard began.

She'd gotten away from him, and he'd only followed a step or two, before deciding his best course would be to flee instead. But, he'd not, not right away. He'd lurked in the blackness, watching her exchange with her husband first. Tho' 'twas dangerous for him to do so, he wanted to know. Know for sure that she did not, would not, could not identify him as anything other than an unknown attacker. And his gamble had paid. For, she'd not recognized him from his work here on the fortress. She'd again thought he was phantasm—a harbinger of death. And mayhap he was.

The wind was high this night, the moon full, as he trudged across the glen toward the mound. To keep the hood o'er his head, he held it on with his hand, and the hood flapped against his cheek.

But there was still the question of the mute's mother. Where had she gone after her escape from Alaric? If only she would show herself here! They could kill them both, and then this plan they'd hatched would be finished. And he'd be a wealthy man at last.

That missive they'd received from Donnach several days past warned them of his worry that he is now under the King's suspicion once again. A merchant that Donnach had dealings with told him that a proxy of the King's had visited him, and had queried him about his connection to the earl. Donnach wrote again that he dared not be seen near this place, for fear, if death be the mute's fate, that 'twould cast an even greater shadow of doubt upon him with his liege once done. Tho' truth told, the apprentice thought 'twas more the earl's religious fervor, and his belief that as long as blood was not directly upon his hands, that his sin was venial, not mortal, and he'd not be eternally damned.

As he arrived at the base of the mound, a figure separated itself from the dark night and moved toward him.

"You are late," his partner said.

"Aye."

"Why?"

"I dozed, did not awaken until not long ago. My pardon," he lied. The deed was done, and all was well. Why give his partner reason for fury toward him?

* * *

Robert shut the door behind him with a *click* and followed his wife, both with his eyes and with his feet, as she moved with grace further into the chamber. His heart was still beating faster than its normal meter, his worry for her not near to lessened. Even tho' he'd found no evidence of there having been someone in the lee between the buildings, and even tho' he was almost sure that what e'er had happened in the lee had been part of the night wandering dream she'd been having, still he'd have that area watched from this point forth. For this night, he'd sent one of the guards below stairs to stand watch there the rest of the night. He'd meant every word of what he'd vowed to her earlier. He'd not allow anyone to ever harm her. Not *ever*.

His wife began to loose the ties on her gown, and the sight of Morgana's bare flesh jerked him from his dour thoughts. He hurried to aid her, brushing her hands away. In the blink of an eye, he had her exactly as he liked her best: Bare from head to foot.

Resting his hands lightly on her hips, he leaned down and opened his mouth o'er her nipple, suckling softly. Immediately, she began to tremble, grew e'er more pliant in his embrace. He used the tip of his tongue to torture the peak until it puckered to the exact degree he wanted, then he began to do the same to the other.

The flesh above her breasts was a fiery flame. Her breath caught, then turned to pants as she dug her nails in his shoulders. When her fingers began ripping at his own clothes, he lifted his head and said, "Nay, not yet. Let me enjoy you first with my mouth. Then, aye.... Aye, then."

Her agreement was given with a jerky nod of her head and he swept her up into his arms and placed her on the stool she used when mending his clothes. His tarse grew another painful inch remembering how oft he'd watched her doing so, and how oft it led to him spending his passion 'tween her thighs. But this night, he wanted to make her burn for him as well, as she balanced upon that stool, and again, and again, each time she sat upon it thereafter.

On his way, he lifted a pale silver veil from off the top of her clothing chest and tossed it o'er his shoulder, then settled her upon the stool. She gave him a look of such confusion, he had to bite back a grin. Coming down onto his knees, he spread her thighs wide and gazed at the glistening dark curls, at the lush red inner lips only slightly hidden now by the hair. Sweeping a hand around her head, he held it in his palm, leaned forward and kissed her hard on her mouth. She responded in like fervor, gripping the back of his head in both her hands as well. When he sent his tongue between her teeth, he sent two fingers inside her as well and she broke the kiss, arched back, opened wider for him, and began to undulate against him.

"Hold on to me, Morgana," he said, and slid his fingers from her. He made quick work of securing the long veil around his back and under his arms, then released first one and then the other of her hands from him and tied an end onto each wrist, showing her how he wanted her to also hold tight to the silk. The center of her eyes, black with desire, gazed at him with confusion, but trust shown there as well, and as he knew she would, she nodded her agreement.

He brought her into his embrace for a quick hug, kissed her cheek, then pressed on her shoulders, making her tip back, as he said, "Now, you'll ride my tongue until you shatter. Lean back further. Yes that's right." He began first with her breasts again, because their taut peaks beckoned him, taunted him. And as he did so, she dropped her head back and arched in to him.

As he began to trail his lips and his tongue down her torso, spending an added moment kissing her belly, as it held his son as well, she gratified him by slowly leaning e'er further backwards. By the time his mouth and tongue found her scut, she was near to horizontal, and he used that advantage to press her thighs open wider still. Her arms trembled with the strain, but she took all that he offered, when first, he spread her lips and sent his tongue deep inside for a long drink of her, before sliding it out and using it to softly tickle the red scalloped folds.

Her breathing grew ragged, her skin, the color of red berries, and it sparkled like the first dew of the morn upon them. Her visage was contorted with the pleasure he gave her—and the pleasure he withheld. She began to tug violently on the ends of the veil, and he knew if she had a voice, she'd be screaming for him to make her come.

Finally, he gave her what she begged for. But not quickly. Not at first. Slowly, leisurely, until her head began to toss back and forth, until she began to yank e'er harder on the silk, until he at last gave her *exactly* what she craved.

While his tongue danced and fluttered, he sent two fingers deep inside her, pumping them in and out, reveling in the cushiony, wet feel of her, the strong grip of her. The stool had grown slippery with the mist on her skin, with the flood of juices from her womb. He wrapped an arm around her back, just above her bottom, to keep her atop her seat.

When she began to work and gyrate her hips, when the muscles in her thighs, in her belly, in her shoulders began to quake, he caressed just the right place inside her, allowing her to go o'er the edge at last.

After the storm was over, he loosed her silken bonds, drew her to him, wrapped her limp, lung-heaving form in his embrace, then settled a soft kiss on the nape of her neck, tasting the clean flavor of salt and Morgana. In the same movement, he lifted her into his arms and rose to his feet, allowing the silver veil to drop to the floor, then strode to the bed, made quick work of undressing, then settled upon her, between her thighs, and deep inside her.

A shudder of delight ran the length of him, and he let out a loud groan.

He started to move, sliding, sliding, sliding in and out of her slick heat. Beginning to tremble himself, so ripe was he to spend, he pressed his fingers to her cheek, turned her head so that she faced him now, and said, "Open your eyes, Morgana. Take me to heaven."

Languid with spent passion, her lids fluttered open and she smiled. Tho' her skin was flushed from their ardent exertion, still he knew that she blushed as well, and it made his heart expand in his chest. "Beautiful," he said, and then she began to strain beneath him, to caress his back from hip to shoulder, to arch and open her thighs wider for him, and he knew she was as close as he to gaining rapture.

Her canal convulsed around him and her head went back. "Robert!" she cried out, and he bucked and strained, ground out her name, then came along with her on a long shout.

* * *

Later, after they'd both cleansed themselves and stood next to the bed, Morgana yawned so long and so hard, that her whole frame quivered.

"You'll sleep well now, I'll wager," Robert said, and there was no mistaking the self-satisfied pride in his tone.

Tho' she felt her face grow warm, Morgana could do naught but nod sleepily and tumble onto the bed. This time, she was asleep before her head hit the pillow.

* * *

Morgana washed and dressed quickly the next morn, with the pressing intent of going back to the lee between the keep and the chapel. She wanted to see for herself, in the light of day, where her real life and her dream life converged. She'd clearly used the brooch on something, whether imagined or real, she knew not, for 'twas no longer attached to her cloak. And there was still some glimmer, some meager fraction of a glimmer of hope that she'd find definitive proof that she was not going mad, was not conjuring in her mind the events in the lee this night past.

It took mere moments to retrace her steps of the night before and soon she was standing in the walk between the two buildings, gazing out at the cobblestoned area in front of her. A clansman stood guard halfway between the doors and the opening into the courtyard, she was surprised to note. The fact that Robert had clearly ordered him there meant he, too, had doubts that what she'd experienced had been merely a dream, and it went a long way toward easing some of the dread she was yet feeling that now Robert, as well, believed her going mad and truly would begin to regret his marriage to her.

Tho', truth be told, tho' some still remained, the passion she and her husband had shared this night past went far in diminishing that dread, as well as diminishing the contempt she'd felt for herself and for the mad visions she'd had of *Ankou*. Just as he'd known it would. A flutter of love brushed o'er her heart, and in spite of all that had happened in the past days, she smiled.

The lee was a peaceful, common-looking space, and at this early hour of the morn, still mostly shaded. Tho' the west wall was receiving some light from the sun, the east wall was in shadow. She'd seen this area, of course, many times these past moons; she'd just ne'er taken much note of it until now.

When the guard greeted her with a nod of his head, she replied in kind and took a step off the walk onto the cobblestones. Keeping her movements casual, she began to closely study every inch of the area, with particular regard to the section where she believed she was at the time she first saw the creature. All looked in the common, expected way. There was no blood on the stones, and as yet, no sign of her brooch. Which was odd. Mayhap, she did not lose it here? Mayhap, she'd only dreamt she'd fought her attacker with the brooch. If he was naught more than illusion, why not the stabbing of him as well? *Hmm*. Mayhap, instead, it came away from her cloak in her mad dash toward the light this night past?

She headed with more purpose toward the courtyard, intent on searching the ground where she'd stood waiting for Robert's return, but continuing to scan the ground in between there and here as well. 'Twas just past the corner of the keep that she found the brooch, tilted on its edge and cradled against a tuft of weeds that were growing against the front wall.

Her pulse raced. With a shaking hand, she retrieved the jewelry, all the time praying that she'd find proof—*Ankou*'s blood—on the sharp pin of it. She looked closely, turning it o'er in her hand, first this way, then that, but 'twas as clean as when she'd put it on this night past. The crushing weight of her disappointment made her collapse against the wall of the keep for a time. She'd lost it in her flight from a creature that was not there. A creature formed only in her mind. *Why?* Why would her mind play such horrid tricks on her? And when she was in such high spirits, planning a wedding, believing she was about to discover her maid's true love? It made no sense. *Why Lord? Why do you punish me so?*

She stood quiet and still, waiting, waiting, waiting, yet no answer came. Or…mayhap it did, for a thought struck: Could it be that 'twas not a punishment but a trial He gave her? If so, then she must be up to the challenge. For Robert and her babe—and the promise of more to come—were worth all the fight she had in her to o'ercome these mad visions. And she would. She must.

Even with her new resolve, it took some time more for Morgana to gather the strength to stand tall again, but at last she did, and, her movements purposeful, she drew the brooch through the cloth of her woolen cloak. There was still the matter of the necklace with which to deal. Would that prove fruitless as well? She prayed not. If fortune was with her, then she would find it in the exact place she'd seen it last, and know that 'twas not yet another illusion come to haunt her waking hours, come to prove her frailty of mind. As well, 'twas possible, if she did find the thing, the having of it would make known to her why it brought on such dreadful feelings, dreadful visions. Wouldn't that aid her in her struggle to win against it?

And, if she did not find the necklace? Well...the truth was, she knew not what she'd do then.

* * *

Even with all Morgana's worry, 'twas not until after she'd broken her fast that she was able to take the trip back to the burn, but 'twas with Modron and a guard along as well. She knew without attempting such, that the gatekeeper would give argument and no doubt inform her husband of her plans, were she to endeavor the journey outside the fortress walls without an escort, for all had heard of her childing state and of her recent swoon at the burn. No one knew (or at least she prayed 'twas so) of her terrible waking dream of this night past, nor of her nocturnal wanderings.

As they journeyed, she made no mention to Modron of her knowledge that, deep in the night, her maid had gone to meet her lover, believing it best to leave it in the past, and, if 'twas not for the dire reason for the expedition they were now set upon, Morgana would have found some joy in the warm, sunny day, in the vivid pinks and yellows and purples and greens on the glen, and in the butterflies that danced upon air there.

After securing their mounts to trees, they went down near the water's edge. As Robert had done the day prior, the guard descended the incline in the terrain ahead of the women and then gave purchase with his arm and shoulder as they took the few awkward steps down themselves. 'Twould be difficult to search for the necklace without the other two seeing her doing so, but Morgana felt confident that she was capable of the small deceit.

While the guard unfolded the blanket and laid it out for them to sit upon, and while Modron walked closer to the water's edge to watch the antics of the bright blue dragonflies that hovered and sped about above the moss-covered bolder a bit further upstream, Morgana strolled over to the place she'd spied the necklace two days past.

The fallen branch was still there.

Her heart raced with joy. *I am not utterly mad!* Sending a furtive glance in the direction of her two companions and finding them still occupied with their own endeavors, she scanned the ground around the fallen branch with added fervor. In only moments, however, her initial eagerness stumbled, then fell like stone, leaving a weighted, twisting fear in the pit of her stomach.

Still, she was not ready to admit defeat. With another brief look to the other two beforehand, she crouched down and began to run her hand through the debris and vegetation on the ground.

With a start, she heard the guard boom, "Did you drop something, m'lady?"

Morgana's heart leapt into her throat as she jerked her head up to look in his direction. She gave him a vigorous nod as she rose to her feet, pretending to place one of her rings back on her finger and lifting it up for him to see at the same time she did so.

I am. *I am going mad.*

CHAPTER 9

VIKA PUSHED THE stableman's hands away when he tried to help her from her cart, then she promptly mounted the wooden steps he'd placed next to it, taking them down to the ground. Her cousin and Robert would learn soon enough about the babe in her belly without her sending the entire court into a dither of excited chatter beforehand. The guards who'd traveled with her would be returning after a bit of rest and refreshment, so she had little worry that they would stay long enough to learn of her childing state before their departure and carry the tale back with them.

She'd not received her cousin's missive until a few sennights past when it had finally made it to the small manor house to which she'd fled once she'd discovered that she was breeding. The dwelling and its bit of land and rents had been part of her dowry upon her marriage to the wretched man her father had forced her to wed, and bequeathed back to her as part of her widow's terce upon his death. It had been the only place she could think of where she could abide for a time while she made her plans for the babe. The letter had come at a very opportune time for her, however, for she was growing too thick in the middle now to continue hiding her condition from her servants for very much longer—and 'twould not be long then until one of them revealed it to her father. A thing Vika was determined to keep from him as long as possible—mayhap forever, if she could somehow contrive to do so. Her father had renounced all further dealings with Morgana and Robert after the embarrassment they'd caused him, so there was little worry that he would e'er hear news of her from this clan.

And, as soon as this one was whelped, 'twould be sent to Grímr, where the other one he'd planted in her was biding as well. The babe would be better off without her, just as was Halla, the young one she'd borne nearly three summers past.

She hadn't taken more than three steps toward the entrance to the keep when she saw Robert emerge and trot down the stone steps. Clearly, he was deep in thought about something, for his eyes scanned the courtyard, glancing off of her, as they moved past her toward the north side of the fortress. In the next second, however, his head whipped around and his eyes lit upon her with a friendly warmth in their depths. He jogged over to her.

"Vika!" he said, taking both her hands in his in greeting. "Morgana will be pleased to learn that you've arrived." He turned his head and dropped one of her hands in order to motion to one of his men to announce her arrival to Morgana. "Come. There's fresh-made ale in the great hall." He took hold of her elbow and pulled her in that direction.

Vika shook her head and smiled. Still the same old Robert. Always ordering, ne'er asking. It had been rather vexing to her while they were lovers, but now that they were cousins—and friends, she supposed— 'twas only a mild irritant. She'd only e'er been able to command him when they played their erotic games. But, how e'er did poor Morgana stand it, otherwise? Truly, she must be a saint.

When they walked through the doorway to the hall, a servant tried to take her cloak from her shoulders, but she resisted, saying, "Nay, I'm just a bit chilled. I'll keep this on a while longer."

Robert looked at her as if she'd gone mad, but, thankfully, did not comment. Instead, he made arrangements for the ale and a bit of a light repast to be placed before her at table.

Vika was just raising the cup to her lips when Morgana swept through the entrance and hurried over to where they were seated. She didn't give Vika a chance to rise before she placed a kiss on her cheek and settled down beside her.

Robert reached over and took hold of Morgana's hand. This gesture, alone, was enough to shock Vika, but when she also saw his expression soften and a tender light spark his eyes as he regarded his wife, the greeting to her cousin clogged in her throat and all she could do was blink at him.

She recognized that look all too well. 'Twas the exact look she'd received from Grímr much too oft during their time together on *Leòdhas*. 'Twas *lovelonging*! A remembered feeling of smothering dread hit her like a hot gust of wind, nearly knocking her from her seat, and she leaned against the table for support.

'Twas only when she felt Morgana's hand on her arm that she realized her cousin had been trying to give her some news. Vika turned her stunned gaze to Morgana and almost lost the battle to stay upright all over again when she at last understood the tidings. *Morgana was breeding as well!*

Except this child, 'twas quite clear from the effusive hand movements and joyous grins on both her companions visages, was very much wanted. As was the common way. Aye, 'twas only she, herself, that was the bad one for not feeling elation o'er this same fruitfulness within herself.

Vika forced a smile to her lips and gave Morgana another hug. Their bellies came close to touching, but Vika managed to back away just in time. She would not reveal the fact of her own childing now that she knew her cousin was so pleased to be in the same condition. She'd hoped for a bit of solace, mayhap, even understanding, but knew now she'd not find it here. 'Twas clear 'twould be best to depart in no more than a day or two hence—to where, she would simply have to use this time here to consider—and not return until well after the birth of this babe she carried.

* * *

'Twas as Robert was taking the last swallow of his ale a few minutes later, having dispatched Vika to her newly-prepared bedchamber where she would rest until the next morn, as she'd declined taking supper with them due to fatigue from her journey, that his eyes once again settled on his wife.

'Tho she sat quietly beside him, with a smile still upon her lips, he could also see that she'd grown pale, and her countenance was drawn.

"The babe is making your stomach roil again. Go up to our chamber and rest."

She shook her head and indicated that she had duties to attend.

He stood up, lifted her in his arms, touched his lips to hers—because he could not fight the urge to do so—and strode out of the great hall, not stopping until he had her out of her gown and lying on her back on the bed in only her chemise.

"Rest. My son needs it, and so do you."

The fact that she gave no protest, only nodded her head, told him he was right in giving her this command.

Again, he bent down and touched his lips to hers, this time cupping her soft cheek in his palm as well. She lifted her hands and pressed them to the back of his head, deepening the kiss, and he almost relented, almost accepted what she offered, but worry for her and his son gave him the strength to pull away.

"Rest," he said again. "I know you did not sleep well this night past, and so you must sleep now. Do not leave this chamber until I come for you this eve for supper. Aye?" He waited for her nod of agreement then turned and departed the chamber before the fire in his loins made him change his mind about bedding her, made him slake his need deep inside her.

* * *

Late in the afternoon, and after a much-needed, tho' guilt ridden, rest, Morgana pulled the needle strung with dark blue thread through the cloth that would, when the scene was completed, be her son's tapestry showing his father on his steed, with the MacVie forest and burn in the background. She was also working on another, larger one, which was to be hung in the great hall. It depicted Robert, in all his knight's armor, on the tourney field with lance in hand, charging toward his opponent. The recollection of his bravery and expertise, of his handsome, active body, brought a sigh to her lips. Even with the queasy stomach, and the weariness she'd felt earlier, she still wished he would have lain with her, taken her, as she'd hoped, as she'd asked, as she'd wanted.

Feeling restless, she stood up, dropping the square of cloth, and walked to the window. She could see that work was ending for the day for most of those down in the courtyard and realized with a start that she'd idled near to all the day away already and the sun would be setting in but a few more hours. If she wanted to complete the stitching on the burn this afternoon, she must get back to it without delay.

As she was about to turn back to her chair to take up her sewing again, a clamor began at the gates, portending a visitor's arrival. Soon, a man on horseback, and of some prominence, as evidenced by his dress, entered the courtyard with but a few men riding in his wake. Tho' she could not discern his features from this distance, nor his heraldic badge, still Morgana felt a twinge of recognition. 'Twas not until Robert strode out to meet him, and after the man had dismounted and they both began walking toward the entrance to the keep, that she at last knew his identity. *Guy de Burgh!* A thrill of pleasure at seeing her old friend was instantly replaced by worry that he was here on some dire duty that would not bode well for Robert. *Is this to do with the war between the MacVie's and the de Burghs?*

* * *

It had shaken Robert more than he wanted to admit when he'd been advised that a small band of de Burghs were at his gate, saying they came with no quarrel, and requesting entry. Of course, he granted his permission. He could do naught otherwise, as they were his closest neighbors, and he, at least, wanted a final end to the ill-will between the two families. And, this was as good a time as any to try to get some clearer answers about why the feud between his father and Roger de Burgh lasted so long, and was so virulent that it nearly brought Robert's clan to ruin.

He'd heard not one word from, nor had his scouts at the border the two families shared seen one sign of, Roger de Burgh, or his men, since Robert's father's death—and Robert had certainly had no reason or desire to continue the war, so had kept the peace with silence and distance, and hard work on the furbishing instead.

Now, he could not help but wonder if the old man

was ready to take up the fight again. Well, if 'twere the case, then Robert would do all that he must to squelch the man's bloodlust first, and keep the calm.

But, if the man would not....

Well, at least Robert's outer wall was near to complete now, and he, and his clan, would stand and fight, and this time, win not just the battle, but the war!

As he approached the guests, he cleared his thoughts and focused on the man at the lead, and was shaken again when he realized 'twas not the father, but the son—the man who'd taken his sister's virtue, then broken her heart, sending her into a season of immoderate sensuality—who'd requested entrance. And, Robert recalled with a hot shaft of jealousy through his middle, Guy de Burgh was also the man who'd fled with Morgana and attempted a clandestine marriage to her.

A low growl erupted from him and Robert gritted his teeth. His fists clenched reflexively as he continued toward him, but he willed them open. For the sake of what was best for his clan, he must not grind the devil to a pulp without more current provocation. And, the man did tell them that he came bearing no quarrel.

* * *

The flash of violent hatred that passed o'er Robert's countenance before he quashed it with a renewed look of wary welcome and keen interest sent a jolt of alarm through Guy. Tho' he knew he still had much to make amends for where his vile treatment of Isobail was concerned, still he believed most of that enmity toward him would have been put to rest now that he'd paid

Robert's full debt to the King.

Well, mayhap 'twas best to behave as if he believed naught amiss.

When Robert was but a few feet from him and said, "I welcome you to my holding, Guy de Burgh," Guy slid from his horse and dipped a nod to Robert saying, "My thanks, Laird MacVie. I come bearing tidings that affect both our families."

"Take these men to the alewife's cot," his host said o'er his shoulder to the man that Guy assumed to be Robert's lieutenant.

On a turn toward the entrance to the keep, Robert replied to Guy, "Come inside and we'll share some ale as well while we speak."

Guy was only able to gain a small, surreptitious impression of the furbishing thus far completed inside the walls of the fortress as the two of them walked together in silence. He'd seen the expansion that was being done to the northeast wall, of course, as they came up the road that led to the gates of the MacVie fortress, but was quite curious to see the changes within the walls, also. Ah, well, mayhap another time, if all went as he hoped.

"How is your lady, Morgana?" Guy said into the silence that remained between them after Robert had ordered some ale be brought to them and they'd both settled on chairs by the hearth.

* * *

The fireball of malignant jealousy spread once again through Robert's center, but was quickly replaced by seething determination. "She is well. She bears my son in her belly." Robert would be damned to the fiery pits of hell before he'd tell this man, this competitor in all things, anything further regarding his wife. "What are these tidings you bring?"

By the rapid lift and drop of one side of Guy's countenance, as well as the spark of humor that flared e'er so briefly in his eye, Robert knew he'd somehow revealed his weakness—his jealousy—to the man, but Guy answered his question without comment on the other, and his countenance grew grim as he said, "My father is dead."

* * *

Tho' she was expected to await Robert's arrival to escort her down to the evening meal, and 'twas at least an hour until that time, Morgana, with a burst of rebellion she rarely acted upon, due to her strict upbringing with the nuns, and her natural ill-ease at being unable to speak, flew to the chamber door, flung it wide and swept out the door, down the corridor, and on down the stairs. 'Twas truly exhilarating! A bubble of mirth floated up and she felt her throat work in silent giggles.

By the time she'd made it to the bottom, she could hear the deep sounds of two men's voices coming from behind the closed doors of the great hall, and she did not hesitate, but simply heaved them open and stepped inside. The noise from her entry turned the heads of the two men toward her and, catching Guy's eye, she sent him a wide smile and dipped a courtesy.

* * *

Robert's eyes narrowed as he watched with interest

his wife's renewed vigor: Her cheeks, pinkened with health; the sparkle of her lovely smile; the limpid glimmer of merriment and wonder—and attraction?—in her blue eyes; all of which combined, seemed a near to palpable bright beam of light aimed entirely at, and for, *Guy de Burgh*.

For the second time that day, Robert's fists clenched at his sides, and this time, he did not relax them. He wanted desperately to tell her to go about her business, to leave them to their dealings, yet he knew if he did so, especially knowing his wife and Guy's past bond, he'd only prove to his guest his shaken faith in Morgana's loyalty that much more by doing so. "Morgana, I believe you are acquainted with our neighbor, Guy de Burgh from your time at King William's court?" Lifting his arm, he summoned Morgana with a gesture of his hand. "Come, give him your welcome."

* * *

An hour-and-a-half later, Robert nearly choked on his half-swallowed bite of meat, when first Vika, who sat on one side of the man, and then his wife, who sat on the other, both hurried to give Guy a drink from their cups after he'd burned his tongue on some portion or other of his meal. Vika had had a seemingly miraculous return of vigor at learning of Guy de Burgh's arrival earlier; in fact, had all but prostrated herself and spread her legs for him right there in front of all, from the moment she'd entered the great hall for the evening meal, which—Robert gritted his teeth—Robert had been obliged to allow Guy to partake of when his clearly-smitten wife had proffered the invitation along with her welcome earlier.

After clearing his throat of the blockage with a long pull on his ale, and then clearing his throat loudly enough to gain the others' brief glances, he dipped determinedly back into his trencher and turned his mind to the other matter: Roger de Burgh's death.

His wife's interruption earlier had curtailed all discussion in regard to the tidings and how 'twould affect the bitter connection between the two families, and now Robert wondered if Guy de Burgh intended more than only a discontinuance of violence, if he intended, instead, an actual alliance between them.

Again, Robert lifted his gaze briefly to the ridiculous tableau playing out before him, but this time quelled the ire that immediately rose within him so that he might study the man and his behavior with more acuity, and without prejudice. His eyes narrowed. Aye, 'twas clear by the easy smile, the relaxed posture, the amused look in Guy de Burgh's eye, the complete lack of tension in any portion of his visage or frame, that the man was quite content—nay willing—nay, *determined* to thrust himself into the good graces of the lot of them. *Especially the ladies.*

* * *

Guy had had enough experience with jealous husbands, suitors, and competitors to know Robert was near at his limit, and 'twas no doubt past time that he disengage from the attentions of the women and turn his own attention back to his host, especially as he'd not as yet accomplished what he'd come here to do. Which was to end the feud between the two families for good.

"I would beg to continue our earlier conversation in privy with you, Laird MacVie, after our meal, if you will?" he said, and was relieved when Robert gave him a silent nod, tho' the man's eyes watched him with much distrust in their depths as Robert lifted his ale to his lips.

Thankfully, the ladies took their leave not many moments later, and, after the remains of the meal were cleared, with the great hall once again void of all prying ears, Robert returned to the hearth area with Guy following.

Guy had, of course, been privy to chatter regarding Robert's brusque constraint in words and in manner while they both were at court, and, as well, Isobail herself had told him very much the same of her young brother during their long-ago amour. Therefore, it did not come as too great a surprise to Guy when Robert did little more than rest his hands on the arms of his chair and give him a dark look without a word spoken to prompt Guy further to begin what e'er he was fixed to speak upon.

"My father took a bad fall from his steed two moons past, and tho' it seemed in the beginning that he would recover his wits and his health, alas, he did not. Upon the dire mischance, I was, of course, sent for, but only arrived a fortnight ago from Pembroke, and found that I was too late to say my farewells. As I am his only heir, I have been released from my duties to Guillaume le Maréchal so that I may take up my duties as lord and baron of our lands here." He paused, waited for Robert's nod, then continued, "I will begin my journey

Song of the Highlands

to King William's court on the morrow, where I will give him the tidings of my father's death, and swear my allegiance to him as well, but before I do so, I want to end the war our fathers waged between our two families."

* * *

Robert had every intention of ending the war waged between his father and Guy de Burgh's, but first, he wanted answers. Narrowing his gaze, he leaned toward the man who'd so vilely used Robert's gentle, beautiful sister. "I know—at least, I believe I know—why my father despised yours, but why, pray, did yours despise mine? There was naught my father did that any man would have done were his own daughter so viciously and openly spurned by her seducer."

Guy gave him a surprised look. "You know not?"

Robert ground his teeth. *If I knew, why would I ask, you pretty-faced pustule!* "Nay," he growled.

The chamber went very still, the only sound, a nervous clearing of the throat from his guest. Finally, when Robert was near to yanking the man up by the neck of his indigo tunic, he responded at last: "Your father.... My mother.... God's teeth!" he exclaimed, scrubbing the back of his neck, then doing the same to his cheek. "I did not foresee the need to reveal to you this wretched tale."

A sickening knot of dread formed in Robert's gut. He needed naught further to be said—in fact, he desired that it not be with a savage vengeance. "Aye, we shall call an end to the strife, then." He stood. "Come, I am sure you have much to do in preparation for your departure on the morrow. I will walk with you to the courtyard."

Guy blinked in surprise, but remained firmly seated. An overwhelming need filled him to purge his conscience, to do what was right, to even things between them, especially now that he knew that Robert had not been privy to all that had led up to the hostilities. So, instead of responding to Robert's words, he continued on with the tale, saying, "Your father and my mother met many times in secret."

Robert turned his back to him. "I care not to hear more. I know what my father was, what he was apt to do when any lady caught his eye, be she wed or nay, and I need not hear the particulars." And there was a time when Robert admired his amorous adventures, when he merrily followed in the man's footsteps. *Until he left me in debt and despair. Until....*Morgana. He swung back to face him. "I ken in full now, the reasons for your father's hatred of mine. Let us speak of it no more."

"Ah, but I find I must. And you must hear it all, else naught will truly be well and right between us. For, I need you as my ally—and, I wager, you, I, as well—as we are each other's closest neighbor. Surely, you ken that?"

Robert narrowed his eyes at him, but finally he gave him a nod to indicate he should continue his tale. Guy de Burgh cleared his throat and Robert, feeling the need to quench the dryness in his mouth—and to give himself a small reprieve to recover from the angry shock he was feeling—walked to the buttery and brought forth two tankards more of the ale the butler had left for them earlier. Once Guy de Burgh had swallowed down a long draught of it, wiped his mouth on the back of his hand, and filled his lungs with a new breath of air, he continued, "We—my father and I—did not learn of this until after…." A shadow of what Robert recognized as grief passed o'er the man's countenance as he sat forward, resting his elbows on his thighs, then dipped his head. "We did not learn of their affair until after I found my mother had hung herself from a tree in our wood by a plowman's rope, with letters to me, to my father…and…to *yours* pinned to her cloak."

Robert's knees went weak. He sat down with a *thump*. "Y—Your mother committed self-murder?" He feared he knew the answer, but still he asked it: "Why?" It must have taken place years earlier, while he was being fostered at the Macleans, during his squire training.

Guy de Burgh lifted his head and met his gaze. Robert could see the tortured pain reflected in the man's eyes, and sympathy stirred within him. It deepened further, and was compounded with an even greater anger at his deceased father, when his guest verified his suspicions, saying, "Because your father spurned her when she would have left us for good to be with him as his wife, or concubine, she cared not which."

Robert leapt to his feet and strode several paces away. Without turning to face his guest, he said at last, "I…see."

"There is more I would tell you—more that regards your sister and my...connection."

Robert did turn then. "Aye?" he said with much more fire behind it.

He watched Guy de Burgh resettle in his chair before saying, "After...after the inquest by the coroner and jury, with my father unable to bear the shame of being known by his neighbors and peers to be a cuckold, a mere challenge to the death seemed not enough to my father to balance the scales between him and his rival, *Kenneth MacVie*." His guest cleared his throat. "You must understand that I, as well, held much rancor for your father—your family—as I'd not only lost my mother, not only learned of her desire to betray us, *but* had also been the one to find her swinging by a rope in the wood." He took in a deep breath and released it before continuing: "So, 'twas with a large measure of ease that my father was able to induce me to gain retribution—an eye-for-an-eye, if you will—by seducing, then spurning the cherished daughter of his enemy: Your sister, Isobail."

The ball of fiery anger in Robert's gut sent the blood rushing to his head, and he was at Guy de Burgh's throat in two strides. "I should enjoy wringing this pretty neck of yours with naught but my bare hands!" But when the man did not attempt to escape, only gasped for air as sweat drops formed on his face, grew red as a woman's cunt, Robert regained control of his rage and thrust him from his grasp, then stumbled back, filling his lungs with deep intakes of air.

Guy de Burgh straightened, resettled on his chair—

with no little amount of strain, 'twas clear to Robert—as he coughed, gasped, and rubbed his gullet. When he spoke again, 'twas with a wheeze. "It should give you a good amount of comfort, and a satisfying feeling of retribution, as well, that I have been tormented by a ne'er-ceasing lovelonging for your sister all these years, and have ne'er found another that could claim my heart again. It went to the grave with her and I shall ne'er retrieve it. Tho', in a small way, it gives me comfort that 'twill always reside with her." Using the arms of the chair to lever himself up further, he continued, "So, you see, the punishment I wished to levy on your father, came back to me a hundred-fold." He turned his head, his gaze drifting to Robert-knew-not-where before he murmured, as if only for his own ears, "And I've much longer in years to bear it than your father e'er did, I fear."

There was a time, not very many moons ago, that Robert would not have recognized, would not have believed, Guy de Burgh's heartache to be free of deceit, but now he did recognize—oh, aye—and he did believe, for his own heart was owned by, and fully in the hands of, his woman, his wife, his Morgana. "I...I see." He cleared his throat. "Although I cannot offer my forgiveness for what you did—I know not whether I e'er will be able to do so—I will not bankrupt my clan again by continuing the strife between our two families." He took in a breath. "And, as you say—and as I know well myself—'tis better for all that we two form an alliance."

Guy de Burgh drank down the last of his ale with an

audible swallow and, as he settled the tankard on his knee, met Robert's eye once more. There was a look of surprised regret reflected in their pale green depths before he said, "I had believ—Nay, I had *hoped* I would find at least *some* bit of forgiveness had already risen within you when I arrived earlier, but I see that is not, and will not be so, no matter how much silver I yielded in your name."

"Wha—"

"And, alas, I suppose if 'twere my sister whose honor and virtue had been defiled, I'd not be so easily softened in my hatred with coin alone, no matter how dire the need for it, nor how timely the gaining of it might be."

Robert's pulse pounded in his ears. Numbly, he staggered and fell back into his chair, his gaze frozen on Guy de Burgh's countenance. With effort he said, "Am I kenning aright? 'Twas your coin—not the King's good favor—that washed away half my clan's—my father's—debt?"

Guy straightened. "Half? 'Twas *all*. And, aye. I sent it with a messenger—a young novice—to King William the same day your wife's uncle brought to an end our planned escape to be wed."

" 'Twas not the King then…."

"Nay, and 'twas for the full amount owed by you."

"The King has played me false."

"Aye, as is his right—tho' not, I agree, a most honorable dealing."

Robert's gaze sharpened. "And I'm still to pay him *more*—the other half, so is his decree—o'er the next five years." He pounded his fist on the arm of the chair. "I thought him generous!"

"I've fiefs under both King John and King William, and must support them both with subtlety and cunning. However, when I see King William next, I will mention the funds I gave on your behalf, and see if I might wheedle him into forgiving the other half as well—tho' I doubt not that he will continue to give the belief that he was behind the coin given you."

With a hand rubbing the back of his neck, Robert rose and strode a pace or two away then turned back to Guy de Burgh, saying, "This does change things between us." And, in a quieter tone, more to himself, "Aye, it does." His gaze sharpened on his guest. "I shall find some way to repay the debt, tho' at present, I know not how."

Guy de Burgh bolted from his seat. "Nay, I'll not take a penny from you. 'Twas repayment for the harm I did your family—did Isobail—but also, 'twas a keeping of a promise given to your wife, Morgana, before you were wed, when I inveigled her to escape with me. I gave her my oath I would pay your debts if she would consent to be my wife."

Robert's gut tightened yet again into a raging ball of jealousy, making his face hot, but he swallowed the bellow that rose in its wake and allowed the man to continue.

"Tho' we were thwarted in our plan, she would have kept her side of the bargain, so I kept mine. And there is also the fact that, tho' I do not love her with the passion I still hold for your sister, I do care for her and

I'll not see her living in penury because of my foolish, callow, faithless deeds."

Robert took a step forward. "She'll not live in penury, no matter what happens regarding this holding. I can support my wife. She'll not want for food or shelter—or clothing, either."

"I see I have offended you, and that was not my intent, but I ask that you do not trouble yourself further regarding the coin I gave the King on your behalf. Even—"

"I will, I mus—"

"—if you cannot see it as remuneration for the wrong I've done your family, then simply know that for me, it is, and is also not less than I would do for a friend." As if he'd only just heard Robert's words, Guy de Burgh sighed and said, "But, if you must repay it in order to be at ease, then take what e'er time you need to do so. For now, I have done what I came to do, and I must return to my own holding and prepare for my journey to King William's court." With a dip of his head to Robert, he strode out of the great hall.

Robert was too stunned to stop him—and, in any case, had naught else to say to the man. That same dread that had roiled in his innards for all those moons after learning how deeply his father had gotten them into debt, roiled within him now, mixed with the jealousy and knowledge that his wife would have had better fortune had she wed the Norman. Robert sunk down into his chair once more and dropped his face into his hands.

* * *

" 'Twas not the King who forgave my debt, but Guy de Burgh who paid it—did you know this?" Robert said to Morgana an hour later as he stood over her with his arms crossed and watched her take another stitch in the small tapestry she was making for their babe.

Her head shot up and she stared at him, wide-eyed, a moment before shaking her head and dropping her hands, filled with needle and cloth, into her lap. Relief crashed through his veins, for, aye, he believed her.

It had not been until a mere quarter-hour past that the thought had taken root in him that she'd known of Guy's beneficence all along, yet had kept the truth from Robert, out of fear of his response—or more worrisome—loyalty to Guy, deliberately allowing Robert to continue in his belief that 'twas the King's beneficence instead. And with only half the debt paid!

Coming down on his knees, he reached for her cheeks and brought her face toward him so that he could quench the thirst for comfort he could only receive by a deep draught from her supple lips. Afterward, he settled his head in her lap, his cheek cushioned by the cloth she'd been plying her artistry upon. With soothing, soft fingers she combed his hair off his forehead, when he placed his hand on her belly. "Modron said that we should feel him move sometime nearing the feast of Saint Michael," he murmured, "but I hope 'tis sooner."

She leaned down and touched her mouth to his temple, and he felt more of the tautness in his shoulders wane.

"Morgana, what am I to do about this debt I owe to

the man who spurned my sister?" He lifted his gaze to hers and, brows furrowed, lips pursed, she shook her head.

Robert settled his head back in her lap. "He told me why his father hated mine so, why he was determined to ruin our clan. His wife, Guy's mother..." Again, he lifted his head, resting his gaze on Morgana's gentle countenance, and again the tension that had returned with the recollection of Guy's words eased in him enough so that he could continue, "...She committed the gravest sin, Morgana, and all because of my father's perfidy, his faithlessness." Robert gripped his wife's hands. "She committed self-murder." Robert's voice cracked on the last. He was still finding the guilt o'er all that his father had caused hard to bear. As well as the guilt of knowing that, if not for the horrors he'd suffered in trying to save his clan o'er the past three years, he'd with certainty have continued down that same path, wedding and siring children with what e'er woman suited his purposes for power or position, while he bedded as many others that struck his fancy as he could who might fulfill his baser needs, be they wed or unwed. And, even with that, and actually *because* of that, he'd still almost wed a woman for nearly that very same purpose. And, he had little doubt, knowing himself and Vika as he did, they'd both have conducted their marriage with little or no fidelity. But, by some fortunate twist of fate, or mayhap—though, knowing the blackness of his soul, he did question this—the benevolent grace of God in Heaven, he'd been given the precious gift of Morgana. And he would ne'er take the gift of such for granted.

* * *

Morgana worried her lower lip between her finger and thumb as she paced her bedchamber a bit later, after Robert's departure. Had Guy paid the monies Robert owed because of his oath to her, or mayhap, because of the bond he had formed with her while they were at court? She was beginning to believe 'twas the case. She'd queried Robert about Guy's reasons, but by that time, he'd returned to his usual brooding, quiet self, and had wanted only the comfort of her body, which, of course, she'd more than willingly given.

If only there were something she could do for her husband, to ease his burden, as any good wife would and should do. But how? She had no fortune to cull from—and in any case, that fortune no doubt would have already gone into Robert's hands at their marriage, if she'd had one. But still.

She swung around and began the trek across the floor once more.

Was there some way, some means she'd not already pondered, of bringing more coin into Robert's coffers with the methods that were already available to them?

She halted and lifted her gaze. *Or....*

Should she send a missive to Guy—request that he forgive the debt, as he'd sworn he'd do when she'd agreed to run away with him?

But, if Robert discovered she'd done so....

Morgana shook her head. Nay. She would not betray her husband's trust by doing such without his knowledge and agreement.

Should she ask Robert if he would allow her to do so?

Nay. On this she was certain he would ne'er agree. There were too many years of enmity between the two, and her husband's sense of honor was strong. Nay, he was bound to pay the debt and he'd not allow Guy to forgive even a fraction of it, even if Guy could be persuaded to do so.

But how, then, might she aid her husband's cause? Nibbling her thumbnail, and taking another turn across the small expanse of floor, her eye scanned then caught on a newly-dyed length of crimson wool one of the weavers had brought to her a few days past for her approval. An idea struck and Morgana rushed over and lifted the cloth, noting again its fine weave, its lush texture.

A grin bloomed on her countenance and she pressed her cheek into the softness as she whirled 'round and 'round. This was the answer! She'd expand their cloth trade! Hadn't they sold all their goods on the first day of the fair during this past Whitsonen day? Those fairs went on for days. If she could manage to gather more clanswomen to weave, spin, and dye, why, she just *knew* they could triple their profit at next year's fair!

And wouldn't her husband be relieved? Mayhap, even proud of her? Or, at least, he might find the strain of her spells and lack of speech easier to bear.

On that last thought, Morgana's determination grew six-fold. If this might not only increase Robert's purse, but lessen the burdens forced upon him, then she would do what e'er she must to succeed.

Song of the Highlands

* * *

Tho' the knowledge and worry o'er the coin he owed Guy de Burgh was well-entrenched in Robert's mind, he had not forgotten the reason for Vika's visit. Unfortunately, she did not come down to break her fast until the nooning meal of the following day, having sent word early that morn to them through a servant that she was still tired, and would rest in her chamber a bit longer. This, of course, reminded Robert of her sudden burst of energy the day before when Guy de Burgh arrived, and brought forth the irritation at both Vika's *and* his breeding wife's reaction to the man.

But, now that the afternoon was well upon them, and he and Morgana had spent the nooning meal with Vika, learning what she knew of Morgana's past, his ire had eased.

"Your revelations earlier aided me in understanding some of Morgana's fear, but there is much more to be learned I trow," he said to Vika as they strolled in the herb garden.

" 'Tis sorry I am, but there truly is naught else I can tell you," Vika replied. Morgana had grown weary and had retired to her chamber for a nap after their meal. Vika wished that she could do the same, but she feared giving any indication of her condition, so, instead, requested a turn about the garden, in hopes the fresh air would revive her. "The brigands have ne'er been captured, and 'twas clear their purpose was robbery of weapons and goods, as all the guards were stripped down to their braies. Even the wagon that had carried my cousin and her mother and father was ne'er discovered afterward." She'd said all this before, but she could see that Robert needed to hear it again, was still attempting to piece it together in his mind.

"Aye, and 'twas only when Morgana came to court that you discovered she'd survived the attack, that she'd been living in the land of the *Armorics* in a nunnery all these years."

"Aye, 'tis truth."

"What confounds me is this: Why had your father not told you that Morgana survived the attack, that she was alive and well in Brittany?"

"This confounds me not." Vika shrugged. "I was young as well when it happened—a mere lass of eight summers—and now my father and I see each other little. For much of the years of Morgana's exile, I was wed and away on my husband's island demesne, and since his death, and my freedom, I have removed myself as much as possible from his sight, even at court."

"And since King William told me himself that he'd demanded Morgana be taken from the nunnery and brought to his court, signifies that he, as well, knew of her exile all these years."

"Aye, 'tis no doubt truth."

"And you have heard *naught* of the details surrounding Morgana's rescue? You have no names of anyone whom you may have heard discuss her circumstance when she first arrived at court?"

"Nay. All in my acquaintance knew naught of her history. If there were any at court who remembered that time, they were not among my friends." She paused, furrowed her brow. "But, I am disposed to believe that the matter was not well known, for you ken how rampant the chatter is at court, and 'tho I may not have associated with those who were privy to information about that time, if there had been stirrings among them, I would have heard it—and so would have you, I trow." Spying a planting of flowering lavender, she bent to take in a long whiff of its sweet scent.

"Aye, you are no doubt right. Which leaves only the King for me to go to for information. I would beg an audience with him, if I did not have so much to o'ersee here. I confess, her history would be of little matter to me, if 'twere not for Morgana's sudden hauntings. They put her in a terror so strong that she swoons most times."

Vika straightened and faced Robert. "She has hauntings? I had no notion...I thought 'twas only the one time, with this strange *Ankou* creature."

Robert's lips pressed together in a thin line as he shook his head. "Nay, there have been more than one. One night she even rose from our bed and, dreaming, wandered off outside. When I found her, she was awake, but in a terror, believing yet again that she'd seen *Ankou*." He paused long enough to take a breath, then continued, "Did you not see how pale she became as you spoke of the ambush?

Vika nodded, but said naught, allowing him to continue.

"I thought mayhap she was remembering—feared she would swoon—but knew also that I could not deprive her of the knowledge she's been craving these past moons." His look sharpened. "And she sings in her sleep. She's the voice of an angel. Know you of this?"

"Nay! Truly?" Vika nibbled the side of her lip. "Tho' I do recall that, as a wee lass, she did sing as a songbird, but now...how is she able? I thought her throat had been harmed—mayhap even crushed, and that she had lost the ability to make any sound." Vika turned and gazed blindly at the color spectrum of herbs and flowers before her. " 'Tis strange...." She swept around and grabbed Robert's hands, squeezing them. "Yet miraculous! Robert! She may speak again, does this not please you?"

He started walking again, and she fell in line. "Aye," he said, "at first it did, but now.... Now I wonder if 'tis not more another incident linked to the violence and fright she suffered as a bairn than a healing begun." He inhaled deeply, clearly in an effort to soothe some panic in himself. "I know not how to ease her."

Once again, Vika was stunned by the changes she saw in Robert. 'Twas clear to her that he was suffering from some very deep emotions. A thing, until just now, she'd not fully believed him capable of. "Fear not, she is stronger than she may seem to you."

He was silent a moment before saying, "Aye, she is strong in many ways. But this...this...I know not."

Vika gave him an awkward pat on the shoulder. "She will be fine, you shall see."

Coming to an abrupt halt, he turned and faced her once more. "Aye, but what of our babe?" Robert startled her by gripping her shoulders in his large, warrior hands, but before she could protest the sting he caused, he said, "Vika, you are a woman."

The way he said it as if he'd just now been seized with the truth of it vexed her, but seeing the wild frenzy in his eyes helped her to ken the vulnerability in him, and therefore the humor in his declaration, thus blunting the ire (at least, a bit). She smiled. "Aye. I *am* a woman."

He pressed his fingers into her flesh with more force and she twisted, squealed.

"Tell me what to do," he said, but lessened his hold, then dropped his hands to his sides, releasing her altogether.

Vika had no notion how to aid her poor cousin, tho' she wished fervently she did. However, still stung by Robert's words, the imp inside Vika rose to the surface, spoke for her. "Why, Robert, 'tis clear! For, as you say, your babe is in jeopardy. You must sing to her—"

"Sing! Nnn—"

"Aye! Sing! Every morn before rising and every eve before sleeping." The round-eyed fright in Robert's eyes and the rise and fall of his Adam's apple told her he was extremely close to believing her. "If you truly care for your wife and your babe's welfare," she went on, "you will do this thing I say! For I've heard this o'er and o'er from the older matrons at court who had weaknesses during their babe's ripening. They say their midwives told them that a soothing song sung by the babe's sire was the only, and best, thing for a childbed to go smoothly and with little duress."

Aye, revenge was sweet. *You are a woman!* As if he didn't have familiar and personal knowledge of such! She tipped her head to the side and did a slow shake of her head, inhaling on a shrug. "Of course, if your pride is stronger than your care for your wife and unborn son, I understand." *Last nail.* "And, worry not," she said, with a pat on his shoulder, "I'll not tell Morgana that you were too weak of character to perform such a minor task for her and the babe."

She heard a grumble erupt from him, but then he said, "All right. I'll—I do not believe this!—I'll try it." He narrowed his eyes at her. "This had better not be one of your tricks."

She gave him her best look of innocent surprise. "Robert! I would ne'er trick you about something as important as this!" Who knew? Mayhap Robert's singing *would* soothe Morgana and the babe. Or, if not soothe, then surely give them great mirth. For was it not true that 'twas healthier to laugh than to cry? And, how could demon memories break through when such jollity and glee were being had? Nay, she was not doing a harm to her cousin, she was sure.

* * *

Chewing on her thumbnail, Morgana absently closed the bedchamber door behind her and stumbled over to the stool in the nook by the window. In one movement, she collapsed upon it and brought the hose she'd been mending for Robert into her lap with trembling hands.

While her mind churned with dread thoughts, her fingers worked, first fumblingly pulling the threaded needle from the soft wool, then beginning the looped stitching by rote.

The only knowledge Vika had had of the *Ankou* creature had been tales she'd been told as a child by Alaric Albinus, a friend of her father's. The name sent a tingle of dread down Morgana's spine, but 'twas no doubt due to her melding of the name with her vision of *Ankou*, now that Vika had told her of his connection to the tale, so she did not allow it to take root. Pausing in her stitching, she closed her eyes and took in two deep breaths.

There. 'Twas gone.

With newfound vigor, she set her fingers back to work, willing her hands to still their shaking. But, after only a stitch or two, her mind, of its own volition, swerved back to her cousin, and what little she'd been able to glean from her.

Vika had been able to impart little about Morgana's mother and father, other than there had been an attack on their caravan as they were returning home from the King's court. Yet, what she had learned was enough to send rivulets of fear through Morgana's veins. An image—a memory? Or simply more proof of her growing madness?—kept forming in Morgana's mind, and try as she might to force it back to where e'er it had come, 'twould not be beaten back this time. 'Twas a lurid and vile tableau of a man grunting and moving fiercely atop a woman, with his hand clamped o'er her mouth as he bit her breast. That same dank smell that would always bring about such a terror in her pervaded the place in her vision. The image, the scent, the sounds he made, brought with it a stray, confused thought and feeling that he was suffocating the woman, tho' Morgana, as she gripped the hose in her fist and tried to shut her mind to the vision, understood that he was actually forcing himself upon the woman. When his hand at last released his victim's mouth, Morgana saw that the woman's lips, her teeth, were red with blood. A chill tripped o'er Morgana's skin, making icicles of her fingers, when the woman said, "I'll never be yours. Never," and the man replied, "You already are."

A high-pitched ringing began inside her head, her perception tunneled, making her mending seem far away before she blinked and looked up. The room spun and a dark fog crowded the sides of her vision. *Nay! I will not swoon!*

With an effort that seemed more than she could bear, she closed her eyes and managed to force a slow, calming breath into her lungs. Then, leaning forward on her stool, resting her head between her knees, she relaxed her shoulders, hoping that by doing so, she would keep herself from tumbling to the floor, tumbling into darkness.

After several silent moments, Morgana at last felt well enough to sit up again.

Still, her ribs, her lungs, felt too tight to breathe properly. Rising, she dropped the mending back into the basket and went to her bed to lie down. When she'd settled there curled in a ball on her side, in the dark cocoon that the closed drapes surrounding the bedframe afforded, the furs pulled snugly o'er her, and her hand placed protectively o'er her growing babe in her womb, she allowed her thoughts to stray back to the vision she'd just had.

If what she'd seen had been a memory, then she did not want to know more. Her brow furrowed. Tho', she did wonder (and wondered also, if Robert believed the same), if the remembering of all that had happened would somehow bring back her voice.

She pressed her lips together and nibbled on the bottom one.

But if she allowed the memories free rein, would they grow stronger? So strong that she could no longer have any control o'er them? So strong that they sent her even further into madness? Aye, 'twas that fear that convinced her 'twas better for her and her babe, and even for Robert, if she endeavored to learn or recall no more of that time. Even if it meant ne'er regaining her voice. Aye, even then.

And, what if 'twas not a memory?

Her heart raced and she gripped the side of her finger between her teeth.

If 'tis madness, then she would fight it with all that was inside her. She would not give in to it. She would make note of what things brought on the spells, and she would simply keep well clear of them.

For, even tho' it had not been easy these past days to keep the secret of her visions regarding the necklace from her husband, to maintain the pleasant and peaceful guise as she went about her daily tasks, she'd still managed to do it.

But, what if they grew stronger still? Plagued her more often? Were even more vile than the one she'd had moments before? What then? Nay, she'd not give them purchase. For, hadn't she only moments before vanquished them? She could do so again. And again. And again. She must. For Robert and her babe, she must. Nay—she *would*.

Feeling steadier now that she'd made that decision, she rose from the bed and went back to her mending by the window. She'd dropped the needle in her haste earlier and, after a few sweeps of her eye o'er the floor, she at last retrieved it from under the stool.

Settling back once more into the soothing task of her wifely duties to tend her husband's needs, her mind wandered to Robert, and his relationship with Vika.

It had been a shock she'd not been expecting, to watch her husband and his ex-lover together. A shock that, she had little doubt, had more to do with her current worry that her husband may have made a bad bargain in her—more so, even, than she'd fretted about on the day of their wedding—than any true belief that his desire for Vika lingered still.

She shook her head and forced her thoughts back on her task. The hole mended, she lifted up the leg covering for full inspection. Aye, that would do nicely. She smiled with tenderness. *Poor Robert.* He was so oblivious to such things as this. A man of action, was he, with little care for the torn seam here, or the hole in the toe there.

Dropping her hands that held the hose back into her lap, she lifted her gaze and peered out the window. From this vantage point she could see past the barbican to the verdant sun-soaked glen beyond, and further still, to the full and lush stand of trees that was the MacVie forest. Several miles past that, she knew, but had yet to see it, was the loch that their little burn fed into. Her gaze lifted. Onward still, like earthen sculptures of a recumbent female form, the peaks and slopes of *Cruachan Beann* buoyed the clouds above them and split the horizon.

Recalling the oft-retold legend of *Cailleach Bheur*, the old hag of the ridges, she'd heard from the spinners not long after her arrival here, she smiled. If only she could stave her unease in the same way the old hag staved the font on the mountain's peak each eve to keep it from o'erflowing and flooding the land.

Resting her palm o'er the small mound of her belly, she sighed. *No more fretting.*

* * *

That night, well after the compline bell, Gwynlyan trod the path to her, and now Morgunn's, secret haven. She was close enough to the burn to hear the rush of water as it slammed against rock, the splash of nighttime creatures as they searched for food or mates in their aquatic home, smell the wet ground, the must of the damp green moss, that during the day would nearly blind the eye with its bright green color, but now, in the dark and dim of the nighttime forest, would appear as shades of gray, black, and deep, deep green upon the rocks and stones along the burn's edge. As she continued to walk, she enjoyed, as well, the sharp tang that wafted up to her of young fern leaves and other new-grown plant life crushed beneath her feet.

Morgunn would not be pleased with what she would tell him, but there was naught else she could do. Until that afternoon, when she'd hidden behind the trunk of the large oak near the northwest corner of the garden, and listened to her son-in-law speak so frankly about Morgana's plight, she'd had no notion of the extent of her daughter's distress, nor Robert's increasing worry for her and their babe because of it. 'Twas time to reveal themselves to her, to help her mend with the knowledge that her family had not been slain, but had survived the attack, to enfold her in the warm refuge of their love once more.

Coming to the area near the burn where the land sharply sloped, she grabbed hold of the low-lying branch she used for leverage each eve, and carefully began her descent. She'd managed to get a foothold with her first initial step down, but when she placed her other foot, the right one, down ahead of the first and attempted to lift her left, 'twould not give way, as a bundle of unearthed roots had somehow snarled around her ankle. In seconds, she'd lost her balance and begun to fall, her mind already whirling with images of the torch fire taking flame to her and the forest around her. A scream formed in her throat, but was muffled before she had time to think how, by a scarred and calloused hand across her mouth, as, at the same time, a long, muscular, familiar arm enveloped her from behind and pulled her up against a chest as hard, but with much more heat, as the symbol stone of the ancients that stood proud on the heath near *Aerariae secturae*.

"To lose you now," warm and charged with desire, a smoky whisper puffed against her ear, "when I've only just found you again...nay, lass that will ne'er do." He stepped back and brought her with him, not releasing his hold on her until he was sure she had her footing once more.

After a silent moment, in which they both stood drinking the other in, Morgunn wrapped his long fingers around her fist, then slowly slid the torch from her hand, in a bold, sensual reminder of more intimate past caresses. Her fingers trembled. Still, she managed to say with some modicum of poise, "Hardly a lass."

The soft kiss he bestowed upon her ash-toned lips stunned her more than his words that followed.

"To me, in my heart, you will always be a lass, *my* lass."

And you will always be my brave warrior husband. "I have tidings," she said briskly to cover her desire for him.

With a nod, he took her by the hand and led her to higher, yet still secluded, ground, edged as it was by the dense crop of heavily-leaved trees. Once he had the torch secured by soil and rock in the ground, had her settled upon his mantle beneath the canopy and resting against the trunk of a birch, he said, "Tell me of what you have learned."

"Our daughter suffers, is preyed upon by images from the ambush, tho' I know not what images they might be." *Of the hours Alaric rutted 'tween my ungiving thighs?* She prayed not.

Morgunn swung around, pummeled his fist into the trunk of a tree, bowed his head. "He shall pay for all he has done to us. He *shall!*

"Vika, as we believed, knows little of the details surrounding the assault on us, so in the end, did little to aid our daughter's memory of her past." *Or, mayhap, 'twas of shivering in a dark corner of that devil's cot singing with her ears covered to the violent sounds?* "She was able to give Morgana some information about her life prior to the ambush, and I saw later that Morgana was soothed by this knowledge."

"Then how is it now that you believe she is tormented by memories of the assault?"

"I followed Robert and Vika into the herb garden after the nooning meal, hid from sight, and watched for others who might have followed as well—there was no one."

"Good."

"Aye, of that I am thankful. But as I watched, I listened," Gwynlyan continued. "Robert revealed to Vika that Morgana has been haunted by sudden flashes of memory that make her panic and swoon. She sings in her sleep, which pleased him at first, as he believed she was recovering her voice, but now he worries 'tis somehow connected to the violence and fright she suffered. He fears for his unborn babe."

Morgunn growled, scrubbed his hands o'er his face, then strode over to her and collapsed down next to her with his back to the forest and his legs drawn up. Resting his arms on his knees, he said, "And what of you? You have stayed close to our daughter. Surely, if 'twas so bad, you would have seen signs of it as well?"

Looking off in the distance, she said, "Aye, I have." As she spoke, she absently touched her fingertips to the place above her breasts where the cross hung, beneath the coarse brown wool of her gown, and felt its imprint push into her flesh. "Near to a sennight past—'twas the day after we first met here, in fact—she and Robert came to this very spot. I happened upon them when I returned to retrieve something I'd left the night before. When I discovered them, I turned, and started back toward the holding. I'd only taken a few steps when I heard Robert cry out her name. I rushed back, but discovered that she'd merely swooned." Gwynlyan clasped her hands in her lap and brought her gaze back to Morgunn, saying, "I thought then 'twas only due to her childing state. But now.... Now I believe 'twas more than that." Again, she lifted her fingertips to the cross hidden beneath her clothes, wondering how much she'd need to reveal in order to convince him to do this thing.

"Aye? What makes you believe such?"

Taking in a deep breath for courage, she tugged the chain and brought it out, exposing the ancient amulet.

Morgunn's eyes widened. His gaze riveted upon the piece, he reached out and lifted the cross from its perch between her breasts. "I remember this.... 'Twas my mother's...and 'twas my gift to you...." Bringing his gaze back to hers, he said, "How do you have this still? I cannot believe Alaric, or one of the others did not steal it."

Nay. She could not tell him the whole of it. Not yet. So, she lied. "I hid it in the hem of my gown, and later, I found other places to hide it, so 'twould not be taken." The last part, at least was truth.

Smoothing the pad of his thumb o'er the emblems, he murmured, "This is the thing you came back to the burn for that day?"

"Aye. But...now, and especially after what I o'erheard this day, I believe that the viewing of it is what sent Morgana into a swoon. That she recalled holding tight to it, holding tight to me, while the sounds of the men attacking came from outside our covered cart." Unable to bear the twin needs inside her to both crumple into his strong embrace and to cringe away at the same time, and knowing that he'd cringe away, as well, were he to fully learn the extent of her fall from honor, she slipped the amulet from his grasp and tucked it and the chain back behind the cloth of her white chemise and brown woolen gown. Feeling him settle back into his previous position as she did so, and keeping her eyes down, in a pretense of concentration on the task, she continued, "The day after, Morgana came here again, this time with me and a guard—," she did look at him now, "—and I found this odd at the time, but dismissed it as mere chance—she dropped a ring at the exact place where I'd retrieved my necklace the day before, following her swoon. After she placed the ring back on her finger, and for the remainder of the day, she was somber, seeming thoughtful, even." Gwynlyan clasped her hands together in her lap. "I am convinced now that her reserve was due to the fact that she did not find what she came back here to find: my amulet necklace. A link to her past, and possibly something that made her recall us, the ambush, and the violence of that day." Her earlier unease forgotten with her newly revived sense of purpose, she grasped hold of his hand, squeezing tight. "She suffers, and 'tis time for us to reveal ourselves to her, so that she may be calmed by the knowledge that all the terror that befell us did not result in our deaths, as she has been told...as all still believe."

In the long, tense silence that followed, Morgunn dipped his head and studied the edge of the makeshift pallet they sat upon. Finally, he said, "Do *you* believe her babe is in danger from these flashes of memory?"

Gwynlyan could be naught less than honest, tho' she knew that her answer would no doubt decide it. She dropped her gaze from him, looked first at her twined hands, then lifted it up toward the break in the canopy, which allowed a moonlit view of the rushing burn, of the moss-covered stones and plant growth on the far bank. "I confess, I have not thought of much else since hearing our son-in-law's words, but...," she shook her head, brought her gaze back to Morgunn, "nay. I believe the babe is well-nested 'neath Morgana's heart, and will not loose itself so easily."

His spine straightened. "Then—"

She gripped his forearm. "Yet, there is also the babe's mood to be pondered. A mother's mood affects the mood, the mind, of the babe she carries. 'Tis well known."

* * *

Morgunn leapt to his feet and thundered over to the slope in the terrain that led down to the burn. The same place, not an hour past, where he'd snared his long-lost bride and saved her from a terrible tumble down to the river rock that edged the burn below. His arms akimbo, he glared at naught, at the silver-shine on the water, at the moon-glisten on the back of a lone frog squatting on the bank, watching with bulging, round-eyed intent the flies buzzing o'er and 'round the rotting center of a fallen tree.

He squeezed his eyes shut against the ache in his heart, forced the words past his lips that he knew could harm his grandbabe, would, no doubt, harm his wife's new-kindled trust in him. "We cannot."

Immediately from behind came the angry rustle of skirts, followed by the snap and crunch of twigs and forest floor debris as Gwynlyan rushed up to stand at his side. "Aye, we *can*, we must!" She yanked at his sleeve and he turned to face her, letting his arms fall to his sides. "Morgunn, did you not ken me before? Our daughter needs us! Her unborn bairn needs us!"

Looking into Gwynlyan's large, lovely, dark eyes—eyes that now held panic—he lifted his hand toward her cheek, but halted the motion halfway, fearing, nay, *knowing*, that she'd not allow the touch now. "Aye, they do, but they need us not in the flesh. 'Tis too soon to show ourselves—"

"But, Morg—"

"Nay, Gwynlyan. Forget not our purpose, for more lives are at stake than just the babe's. We must strike first if we are to regain all we have lost, if we are to be safe from my brother's deadly duplicity. Stealth is our best, mayhap, only weapon against our foes."

Without thought, he took hold of her hand, then was pleased when she did not immediately pull it back. " 'Tis my final word. I beg you, argue with me no more on this, for we have other pressing concerns to discuss before this night begins to wane into morn."

At first, he thought she'd ignore his request, as she slipped her hand from his and turned away. But when she only walked back to sit under the tree again, then patted the place beside her and smiled, he took in a long breath of relief and returned the gesture before joyfully doing as she'd bade.

PART THREE

A Bond Broken

*"My son — and what's a son? A thing begot
Within a pair of minutes, thereabout: A lump bred up in
darkness."*

The Spanish Tragedie (Act III, scene xi)

*"What outcries pluck me from my naked bed
And chill my throbbing heart with trembling fear."*

The Spanish Tragedie (Act II, scene ii)

*"He was my comfort and his mother's joy,
the very arm that did hold up our house—
our hopes were stored up in him."*

The Spanish Tragedie (Act III, scene xi)

CHAPTER 10

'TWAS WITH SOME consternation the next morn that Vika found herself alone in the great hall. All had already broken their fast, and were about their daily duties, leaving Vika to cast about in her own company. She tried for a time to search out her cousin, but at every end, she discovered she'd just missed meeting her, and Morgana had flitted off to her next destination.

It became apparent that Vika would do best to simply enjoy the quiet time, and content herself with seeing her cousin again at the nooning meal.

With that thought in mind, she decided to explore her surroundings a bit more. After a quick return to her chamber to replace the pale rose-colored silk veil and silver filet she wore o'er her hair with a plain white wimple, and the matching gown with a plain brown woolen one for her excursion, she made her way to the courtyard. 'Twas a bright day, with ne'er a cloud in the sky, she was pleased to find, and feeling a new surge of excitement as she gazed about her, she smiled. Robert's fortress was not a large one, not the size by half of her father's demesne. But this one was rife with possibilities, and she could see immediately the improvements upon the old structure, even envision how the final outcome would look. 'Twas clear that Robert was replacing much of the original earthwork, timber, and thatched roof portions with stone, as well as expanding the walls and furbishing the barbican. The keep, that held the great hall and the living quarters, was a stone tower with the chapel attached on one side and the kitchens on the other. If any furbishing had been done to it, 'twas not visible to Vika's eye.

Not far from the kitchens, and through a tall wooden gate, lay the herb garden that she and Robert had meandered about in this day past. For a brief moment, she contemplated taking another stroll around it, but the exercise held little interest, so she abandoned the notion in favor of a newer adventure, in pursuit of which, she sauntered out of the courtyard, through the arched opening in the stone wall, and into the outer bailey.

As she eagerly took in her surroundings, she first heard the sound of iron against stone and the muffled, low tones of men's voices, then saw the collection of master carpenters and masons, along with their journeymen and apprentices, against the north wall. Several of the men looked up and saw her, then bent their heads back to their tasks. *Naught for me here.* With a sigh, she turned back and entered the courtyard once again.

Wandering around the side of the kitchens, she was surprised to spy a battered, somewhat tumbledown section. 'Twas attached to the back side of the keep, but clearly part of a much older section. Curious, and with naught else to occupy her time as she burned away the last hour until the nooning meal, she shrugged, smiled, and sallied forth, intent on a bit of exploration before dinner.

* * *

The apprentice looked o'er his shoulder a third time and, seeing the master mason still occupied with the ingeniator, moved through the gate leading into the courtyard. He'd managed to make his way over here in time to learn the direction in which the lady had gone, and was determined now to see an end to this.

He'd ne'er been one to miss an easy opportunity, especially one that seemed to have been handed to him from the Fates themselves. Nay, he'd not spit in those ladies' faces, he'd not. He'd long grown weary of this watching and waiting. He wanted action, swift and sure. And if Morgunn and Gwynlyan were alive and e'er drifted out of their hiding holes, then he'd hasten to do the same to them. Donnach had grown soft in his old age, but he'd not. Nay, he'd not.

The ancient wood plank door with black iron braces had been left ajar and the apprentice silently stepped across the portal of the timeworn timber, wattle and daub structure into the dim, cool entry. Across a ten-foot expanse, a stone hearth, long dead and cold, gaped like an open maw in the wall. Cobwebs hung down, sheer as moth wings, in every corner and crevice, and the smell of dirt and rotted wood came to his nostrils, nearly bringing on a sneeze before he clamped his fingers to his nose, holding his breath a beat until the urge to do so passed. Midway, and to his right lay a staircase made of heavy splintered wood and iron. From above, he heard the shuffle of footsteps, the creak of old boards, and, with what little light the open doorway afforded, caught sight of a fall of dust and earth floating down from above with the movement. The sound spurred him into action. At the base of the stair, he looked up and found that it made its first turn some fourteen steps up. He'd hide in the black cove of that landing above and when she descended, he'd have her.

With his plan set, he softly placed his foot on the first step.

* * *

Vika clapped the dust from her hands and perched them on her hips. The light from the three paneless windows brightened the chamber and streamed across the wood plank floor. It illuminated the dust floating in the air about her as well and a sneeze caught her by surprise. 'Twas time to depart this hovel, for she'd found naught but an empty broken chest, cobwebs and forsaken vermin nests on this ill-conceived adventure. Clearly, all items of interest had long since been hauled from here into the newer portions of the keep. She wondered why Robert hadn't torn this section down, since 'twas clearly long left vacant, and at this point, more of a hazard for fire than aught else.

With a sigh of disappointment, she stepped over to the windows, closed and locked their shutters again, then ambled back to the doorway leading to the stairs.

* * *

Hearing the lady's foot treads coming e'er closer, the apprentice hunched further into the dark corner of the landing and, with hands up and ready, he held his breath.

* * *

Absently humming a bawdy tune Grímr had taught her years before, Vika thought, *At least, at the nooning meal, I shall have a bit of respite from my boredom,* as she lifted both her skirts and her foot to descend the first step.

Something—someone?—yanked on the back of her skirts. *"A-a-a-a-a...!"* she screamed. Her other foot left the ground and her body projected forward, anchorless for mere seconds before she dropped, crashed, hurtled, rolled, and bumped against wood plank and iron railing, each board crunching and bruising another portion of her frame. This time, her shoulder, the next, her hip, the next her shin, the next her spine, and finally her head against cold, ungiving iron. *The babe!*

The world spun. Black mist crept along the edges of her vision. Her hands went to her womb. Morpheus brought oblivion.

* * *

Horror filled the apprentice's breast, cutting off his wind, as he gazed down at his victim and saw hair as black as a raven's wing poking from the wimple on her head.

He'd murdered the wrong lady! 'Twas Donnach's daughter he'd sent to her grave. And now, he'd be a dead man for sure. The thought put wing to his feet and he leapt down the stairs, across the prone form, and o'er the threshold of the door. A trickle of sweat fell into his eye and he rubbed the sting viciously with the soiled and calloused palm of his hand as he looked first right, then left, scouting the area. His breath blew harsh and loud in his ears as, finding that all was quiet and still, he headed back to the site under construction. With luck, he'd be back among the others with ne'er a one having noticed his absence.

Aye, that be the best way to go about this. For, 'twould be as good as a confession were he to scurry off now, and a roasting for sure when he was caught. Aye, 'twas a good plan. For, with no witnesses, neither his partners in this scheme they brewed, nor Robert MacVie, would suspect 'twas more than an accidental misstep on the lady's part as she came down the stairs of that abandoned and broken relic.

Approaching the bailey a bit to the side of the entry allowed him visual access to the company of men working on the repairs and renovations to the fortress. None faced his direction, and all seemed concentrated on their own task. He could not see the ingeniator, nor the master mason, however. So, skirting even further to the side of the entryway, he pressed himself against the stone wall and, with heart pounding and palms sweating, he took in a deep breath and peeked around the edge of the opening.

A sigh of unutterable relief gushed from his lungs

when he saw that the two had moved even further afield than they'd been when he'd left here not more than a quarter-hour past. Their heads were still bent together, discussing some aspect or other of the drawing the ingeniator held of the planned changes to be instituted to the stronghold.

Not daring to hover there another moment gawping at the assembly, he walked through the entry with a purposefulness to his mien and step, glanced to his side, found a barrow of crushed stone, grabbed it up by its handles and pushed it o'er to the area that needed it. When one of the men only barely lifted his gaze to him and said, "Aye, 'tis good. Bring us another, will ye? I think 'twill take two loads for this portion," he knew for a fact that no one had realized his absence.

But the question still remained: *How to end the other's life so he could return to his own?*

* * *

His wife pressed her palms to the back of Robert's tunic and pushed him forward. She'd been near to frantic by the time he'd arrived in the great hall for their repast a quarter-hour ago and, after quite a flurry of hand and mouth movements, he'd at last discovered that she'd been in search of her cousin for the past half-hour, after discovering that Vika had, in fact, been in search of her that morn as well, and now Morgana could not find her.

He had little doubt that Vika had simply strayed off to meddle and pry into things that were of no business of her own, as was her way and, 'twas almost certain, out of her own boredom. He'd wager she was even now not far from where they stood. However, Morgana would not be eased, as she evidently believed it a much too rare occurrence for Vika to not at least return from her wanderings to join them for the meal.

And now, he'd been sent on the mission of finding her. He ground his teeth, but did as his wife bade, for he was more concerned for her and their babe's health than he was worried for Vika and what e'er mischief she might brew by poking her nose where it didn't belong. Let the meddling creature miss a meal for her misbehavior. 'Twould serve her right. Especially after the mortifying lyrical affair she'd teased him into performing for his wife last eve. He felt a flame of humiliation spread from his gut to his cheeks. Aye, it had not been long into his awkward song and his wife's dancing eyes and pursed, amused lips, that he'd known for sure he'd been deviled and tricked by his trouble-making ex-lover for her own wicked amusement.

Although.... Now that he thought more on the matter, his wife *had* slept much more peacefully, with barely a stir against his side the remainder of the night, so 'twas *possible*, he grudgingly supposed, that Vika had, in fact, given him good advice, even if 'twas not her original intent.

Robert blew out a gruff sigh and shook his head as his feet moved down the steps of the keep and into the courtyard. He scanned the perimeter, but all was quiet. Everyone *else* was having their meal.

But not him.

Nay. Not him.

His stomach growled.

Then *he* growled.

Vexing woman!

But. He loved his wife, and she was awaiting her meal as well. Which both spurred him onward, and angered him even more at Vika's antics.

Dark clouds had rolled in o'er the last minutes, hiding the sun, and turning the daylight to dusk, but again, he looked all about him, this time making a slow turn as well. The wind whipped at his face, and he felt the first drop of rain splash upon his cheek. He gave it a rough swipe and growled low in his throat. *Where in the name of Christ the Lord and all his disciples would she have wandered away to?* That was when his gaze snagged on the original keep his great-grandfather had built in, so the legend told, only a day, to stake his claim and fortify his position as King David's proxy in this region.

* * *

Somewhere between dream and waking, Vika struggled to free herself from the torpor in her limbs and eyelids that held her, like leaden weight, unmoving and unseeing. She floated, yet she knew she touched the cool ground, for it pressed into her cheek, her hip, her thigh and knee. Trying to think around the ache in her head, and knowing in her very center that she must not stay much longer as she was if her babe had any hope of surviving—if *she* had any hope of surviving—she at last captured and clung to a word, a phrase: *Help me!*

It took all the strength, the will, she had to form the words on her tongue, to force the sound from her throat, and after several tries, she was at last successful.

Unfortunately, what erupted was no more than a

mere whisper and moan.

After lying silent, after forcing her muscles to relax, chiding her throat to do so as well, in another moment, she rallied her vigor once again and this time, her voice was much stronger. Now understanding what she must do, she relaxed again, built her strength again, and waited, again, to send up another cry for aid. *Surely, 'twould not be long now. Surely.*

* * *

Robert almost didn't find her. In fact, he'd made the decision as he trudged toward the scarred and crumbled opening to the old keep that this would be his last stop on this bootless errand his wife had sent him on. For Vika was a woman full grown and, if she wanted to skip a meal, so be it, but he would not. Nay, he would not. And neither would his breeding wife. So, after an irritated and perfunctory scan of the unlit, dusty interior in which only dank and dark met nose and eye, he'd swung back around and taken no more than a step when his keen warrior's hearing registered a distinctly distressed, yet nearly silent, moan.

He skidded to a halt and listened. In the next moment, a strained, but recognizable cry for help emerged from the doorway behind him. A rush of alarm surged in his chest, tripped, like ice-cold fingers, up his spine and neck. He wheeled around, jogged through the door and, this time, looked more closely. "Vika! What hap—"

"Ro—a-ow!"

"Be still," he said in a rush, hurrying to her and coming down on his haunches. "You fell down the stairs?"

"Mmm? I-I know not...I-I remember not..." she said with little breath and winced with the effort.

"Where are you hurt?" he asked, at the same time, running his hand o'er her limbs, her frame, looking for breaks. "Tell me if I hurt you."

" 'I—I'm so glad—" She sucked in a sharp breath, then, in a pained voice said, "My head. 'Tis my head. It pounds so, and I feel wobbly, and quite sick."

Robert's lips pressed together in worry. She'd clearly swooned from the injury, and with as many years of warrioring and tournaments as he'd had, Robert was quite versed in the dangers that might come from a sound strike to the noggin. "You've hit your head, and 'tis no doubt jumbled your brain a bit. I'll carry you to your chamber, then I'll fetch the clan's healer."

Vika nodded, then rested back, closing her eyes.

"Nay!" He tapped her cheek several times with the pads of his fingers. "You mustn't sleep, else you may not waken again."

She took in a deep breath and gave him a slow nod. When her eyelids lifted more slowly than they had before, he knew she was struggling to comply, struggling to do what she must to survive.

* * *

"Nay, Wife Deirdre, there is no need, I tell you, to burden my hosts with this worry o'er my childing," Vika pressed again, this time, grasping the old woman's arm, keeping her beside the bed, where Vika reclined. 'Twas nearing sext, almost a full day since the fall, and tho' her head still pained her, she'd at last been allowed an uninterrupted night's sleep, and was now only mildly sore, with no churning stomach to contend with any longer. "My babe is well! Even now, it moves within me." She splayed the healing woman's gnarled hand o'er her belly. "Do you not feel him kick?"

"But m'lady, ye 'ave 'ad a very bad tumble, a hit ta th' pate, an' there's still a danger ta yer babe. I mest tell me laird o' yer condition, as was 'is behest, and as is me duty ta 'im." She pulled free of Vika's death grip on her hand and marched toward the door.

"Bu—"

"Rest, m'lady," Wife Deirdre said o'er her shoulder as she pulled the door wide, "an' I sh'll return wi' yer broth in no' more'n a 'alf-'our's time."

"B-Bu—" The door closed with a decided snap, and Vika fell back more fully against the pillows. *Bedevil the woman!* After seeing Robert's tender care for Morgana, the way he doted on her, the way he puffed up like a cock in the roost at his coming fatherhood, Vika was sure now that once he learned of her condition, he would storm 'round like an angry bull, and no doubt grind into a fine dust her will to keep the identity of the babe's father to herself. And Morgana. Vika's heart sank. Morgana, who would be the perfect mother—already was, as far as Vika could see—would ne'er understand Vika's need to be free of any bond that would keep her under a man's control, to give her babe away, into the gentle care of its fierce and loyal father.

She rolled her head to the side and a sharp pain pierced her skull. Wincing and squeezing her eyes shut, she rubbed her forehead with her fingertips. She simply would not tell them that bit. Opening her eyes, she curled on her side and stared at the hearthfire. Aye, that would do. And all that would be left would be for her to dodge Robert's (and no doubt Morgana's) questions. For she knew, she *knew* that if Robert discovered her plan, he'd conspire with Grímr to hie her back to that damnable island inhabited by the bold, the possessive, the sometimes raging, the ofttimes brave and true, summer wanderers of the far north.

* * *

Smoothing her palm o'er Robert's rigid, broad back as she climbed the stairs behind him in an effort to calm his temper, Morgana worried and wondered again what the healer had said to him regarding Vika that could have put him in such a fury.

He'd slammed the door to the keep, stormed toward the stairs, and begun the climb, leaving the poor healer gawping on the front steps, and putting Morgana in such a shock as she'd watched his progress across the antechamber to the stairs, that it had taken her a moment to rush to follow him.

The healer had inquired after Robert's whereabouts near a quarter-hour past, and Modron had advised that he would be found on the training field this morn. Clearly, what e'er tidings she bore him were not good. *Had Vika not been following the healer's advice?* If so, Morgana would stand firm with her husband, even in his anger.

She had no time to wonder further, for in that instant, Robert came to Vika's chamber door and nearly knocked it off its hinges flinging it open.

Morgana scurried around him and positioned herself a bit to the side, and several paces from both Robert's scowling countenance and Vika's stunned, yet mutinous, one.

"Is it mine?" he barked, arms akimbo and feet spread.

Huh? Morgana's brows drew together and she shifted her gaze to her cousin.

Vika's eyes widened, then narrowed on Robert before she relaxed back with a slight smile curving her lips, crossed her arms over her chest, lifted a brow, and returned Morgana's gaze with a speculative one of her own. "Why my dear cousin-in-law, do you not think this a subject we two should discuss in privy first? I'm sure this is not the way you would have your breeding wife learn of your bastard bairn."

Morgana's breath caught and would not release, her heart raced, her knees buckled, her head spun. As the wood-slatted floor sped toward her, darkness enveloped her.

* * *

Vika pulled the comb through her long, black tresses and gave a small defeated sigh. She felt very bad for Morgana. Truly, she did. 'Twas rotten fortune all around that her childing state had been discovered, and rottener fortune still that she had been enticed to use Robert's masculine conceit in his own virility against him.

In spite of her sore conscience, she smiled.

Aye, she should have known the man would immediately jump to that conclusion upon hearing she was breeding. In truth, the thought that he would do so had ne'er crossed her mind. Nay, she'd been much more fearful of either her father, or worse, Grímr, learning of this babe he put inside her before she could have it and ship it off to him, while keeping herself clear from both their clutches.

But, now that the idea had been formed, it seemed the best and surest way of keeping Robert's infernal, arrogant meddling at bay long enough for her to heal from her fall and *get as far away from them* all *as possible*.

Recalling the crushed look on Morgana's countenance in the brief moment before she fell into a swoon, the bellowing of Morgana's name that burst from Robert's lips as he rushed to catch her before she hit the unyielding surface, the soft thud that followed when he was not successful, the evil look he sent her as he lifted his wife in his arms, and the parting retort he made upon his swift departure, *"This is not the end of it,"* sent a spike of guilt into her belly and tingle of cold dread down her spine. *No matter what he says, what he does, no matter the misery I've caused Morgana, I must not relent.*

* * *

Robert leaned forward on his stool when Morgana's lids fluttered and her lips parted e'er so slightly in her sleep. Her cheeks had more color now, which sent a sweep of relief through his veins and allowed the muscles in his aching shoulders to relax at last. Clearly, she was dreaming. He only hoped 'twas a pleasant repose, and not filled with what e'er images, whether of the current circumstances they'd found themselves in, or her violent past, that would distress her and, therefore, their babe, even further. When she'd roused from her swoon not long after he'd arrived with her in his arms and settled her on their marriage bed, and been anxious and upset to the point that Robert worried for her and his babe's health, even after he'd assured her that all would be well, he'd bade the healer give her a sleeping draught.

Now, he brushed a soft kiss o'er her warm brow, then, because he felt his own need for comfort as well, he settled a brief kiss on her parted lips also. After a prolonged moment, he rested his palm o'er her silken pate, moved his lips just above her ear, and began to gruffly sing again one of only two songs he'd e'er learned, and those o'er multitudinous cups of ale:

> *"Nay, young rascal, fondle me not!*
> *Fer I'll not share yer lowly cot*
> *Ye—"*

The sweet caress of Morgana's breath blew against his neck and his heart melted. Without realizing he was going to do it, his voice, his words changed to a song he'd heard at court, but had no notion he'd learned, tho' he altered them a bit to fit his lady:

> *"O! Lovely wench,*
> *Methinks I am lightheaded from love;*
> *Thine locks, the color*
> *Of the silvered moon that shines*
> *O'er the glen,*
> *Doth beckon now my heart from*
> *Its dark, dire grave..."*

A small hand landed on his shoulder. He started.

His heart plummeted into his stomach as mortification washed through him. Cheeks burning, he lurched upright and whipped his head around to stare, frozen, at Modron, Morgana's gray-haired lady's maid.

"Aye?" he said gruffly.

* * *

"Be easy, Laird. Your lady and the babe she carries are well, you shall see," Gwynlyan soothed. Even tho' she seethed at his stupidity in allowing Vika to deliver such a blow to her daughter, she also saw well that her son-in-law was smitten to his core with Morgana, and would ne'er knowingly do anything that would cause harm to her feelings or her health. And that, she was determined, was what her mission this day would be: To give this fierce warrior, this brave knight, this noble leader of his clan, a bit of well-needed tutoring in proper behavior with regard to the gentler sex.

After taking a last quick glance at her slumbering daughter, her son-in-law bolted to his feet and strode to the washstand, there splashing his ruddy cheeks with the water in the bowl and saying, "Aye, 'tis as you say." While patting his face dry with a cloth, he turned back to her and said brusquely, "Is there aught else you wanted?" clearly intent on her swift departure.

But, Gwynlyan was not near finished with this quest, and tho' 'twas a very fine line of proper deportment she trod, as slender as a blade's edge, in fact, still she ventured forth boldly, saying, "Aye, Laird, there is. I've heard a tale from Wife Deirdre that the lady Vika admitted she is carrying your bastard bairn after you challenged her with the query in front of m'lady, and that is the reason m'lady swooned." *Are you the biggest oaf in all of Caledonia?* "I thought surely the healer had wrongly kenned you, and so I came directly to ask what truly passed, so that I may end this false tale before it spreads further, Laird."

'Twas with no little satisfaction that Gwynlyan saw a renewed flush invade his cheeks before he said, " 'Tis no chatter you heard, but truth."

"I...see. I *would* wonder at the reason for allowing your wife such a shock, Laird." *You dolt.* "Although," she rushed to say, "I am sure 'tis merely my feeble, female mind that stumbles o'er the complex strategies of a great male mind such as yours, Laird."

A metallic thud sounded near the bed and they both swung their gazes in that direction. Morgana had risen, but was swaying on her feet rather precariously. The pewter cup that had held her sleeping draught rolled on the floor and stopped a foot away from where she stood.

Gwynlyan and Robert moved simultaneously.

"—Here, let me pour you—" she said.

"—Morgana! Get back in—" he said.

...And collided mid-stride, with Gwynlyan unable to keep her balance and flying back. She would have toppled onto her bottom, had Robert not made a grab for her and saved her from that ignominious end.

* * *

Robert spent only the briefest second assuring himself that Modron was well-planted back on her feet before striding to his wife's side and sweeping her up, then back on the bed.

She shook her head and tried to rise again, but he pressed her shoulders back down until her head touched the pillow once more.

When she shook her head again, caressed away the tightness and worry on his brow, around his mouth, with her delicate, sweet touch, then sat up once more, he relented and stepped back a bit, but kept his palm on her shoulder, tracing her slow pulse with the pad of his thumb on her warm, silken neck.

She swiveled her gaze to Modron and reached her hand out to the woman. After the too-perceptive-for-her-own-good servant had sidled up to the bed next to him with her hands primly clasped in front of her, his wife surprised him by taking Modron's hand and squeezing it.

It didn't take long for either him or the older woman to gather from Morgana's mouth movements and gesturing at him with her free hand that she had heard the woman's last statement to him. She was now intent on reassuring her that he'd acted rightly, as he believed also—even tho' the woman had pricked the sore of his own self-doubt, making it chafe and bleed to the point where he, once again, and possibly for the hundredth time since his wife's upset and swoon, questioned his decision to do so.

In truth, it had not been a thought-out decision, for he'd not even known she had followed him until he'd felt the quiet strength of her hand on his hot back as he strode up the stairs and, 'twas truth also, that he'd been more focused on his anger and—aye—fear that his suspicions regarding the paternity of Vika's unborn bairn would prove true. His wife's presence had seemed a calming ray of sunshine in the center of the turbulent storm brewing in his insides, and knowing he'd be telling her of it despite her wish otherwise, he'd not thought....

Aye, he'd not thought, not until Vika had shot her barb, not until he'd seen it strike true by the look on Morgana's face in the moment before she'd crumpled to the floor, and moments later, when she'd awakened and been so distraught o'er all that the news entailed.

A tug on his tunic brought him out of his troubled musings and he centered his mind and sights firmly back on his wife and her maid once more. Except, the maid was nowhere about. The blasted woman was as light-footed as a cat, much more nimble than he'd e'er conceived possible for one so late in years.

His wife's hand movements caught and kept his attention when he realized she was telling him that Vika must stay with them at least until her babe was born and, 'twas vexingly clear as well, that Morgana intended to raise the bairn herself—with, or without his consent!

"Christ's Bones, you'll not!" He needed *uisge beatha*. *Now.* "Nay!" His heart raced, his palms sweated, and the heavy burden of guilt—and the inevitable—weighed upon his conscience, but still he whipped around and stormed toward the door as if he could outrun the hounds of his own personal hell that growled and nipped at his heels. After swinging the portal wide, he halted midstride, turned, and warned:

"We'll not—argh! *I'll* not!" With more than a little satisfaction, he yanked on the door and slammed it behind him, creating a quake that could be felt in the wood planks under his feet, and a bang so loud, King William himself no doubt heard it all the way in Perth.

CHAPTER 11

MORGANA RELAXED BACK against her pillow with a furrowed brow and nibbled her lip. Her husband, tho' blustering about, would do what was right in the end, she was sure. And her cousin, whom, 'twas now clear to Morgana, had had more as purpose for her visit than a simple desire to aid Morgana in learning the events surrounding the attack on her family, would no doubt be relieved by, as well as amenable to, her babe being left with them to raise.

Feeling restless and needing to set things in motion, she swung her legs off the bed and stood up. Light-headed and swaying, she grasped hold of the edge of the bedside table for support. The effects of the sleeping draught, which Wife Deirdre had promised would not harm her babe, had still not fully abated she realized. But, determined to see the task done, she remained where she stood. After a time, at last feeling more steady on her feet, she stepped over to where the deep-blue gown she'd been wearing earlier was hung on its hook and began dressing, pulling it o'er her head, wiggling and twisting until she had it well-settled o'er her frame and had the chemise she wore beneath adjusted and aligned properly as well.

After closing the clasp on the silver girdle around her hips, combing, and re-braiding her hair and placing a silk veil of the same silver hue as her girdle o'er her locks, then holding it in place with the silver filet made of the same delicate and finely linked chains as those of the girdle, she took a moment to caress the cool, smooth sapphire encased in silver filigree which hung as a pendant on one end of the girdle. The filet and girdle had been gifted to her by Robert not long after she'd given him the news that his seed had taken root in her, and because of that, they were now two of her most highly treasured possessions.

Gazing at the results in the silvered glass Robert had taken from his sister's childhood bedchamber and brought in here for her use, she gave a small mew of satisfaction that all was neatly in place before turning to leave on her mission.

With luck, all would be settled by nightfall.

* * *

An hour later, Vika watched with more than a little ire Morgana depart her chamber. Her accursed head still pounded with as much pointed precision as it had all the day long, and she was now despairing that she'd be in any state to away from this holding, these irksome cousins of hers, in stealth in the next day or two as she'd originally hoped.

Taking another long swallow of the bitter draught Wife Deirdre had given her to dull the pain enough to fall asleep again, she closed her eyes and allowed her head to slowly fall back as she drank it down. Afterward, she settled back and rubbed her temples with the pads of her fingers, trying to clear the haze from her brain enough to think how to deal with this new dilemma Morgana had foisted upon her in the past moments.

She was glad, she did admit, that Morgana and her babe had not suffered any lasting effects from her crash to the floor—nor from the distress Vika had caused her with the blunt lie she'd spoken. Nay, it seemed, her cousin was more than recovered, and ready now to remedy Vika's problem with a solution of her own: She expected Vika to stay until the babe was born, then leave the bairn in Morgana and Robert's care.

This, however, was *not* going to happen. She may not be the most honest, selfless person in the world, but she was not so deceitful she'd allow Robert to raise another man's bairn, thinking 'twas his own.

A growl of frustration erupted from her throat and sent answering spikes of pain pulsing into her brain. *I must leave. And soon.*

* * *

Late in the night, and several hours now since he'd stumbled back to his chamber, calmer with the liberal quaffing of ardent spirits, and fallen into bed beside his slumbering wife, Robert awoke with a jolt and sat up. His heart hammered against his rib cage as he blinked the sleep from his eye and looked around the chamber.

What had awakened him? And then he heard it. The sound. Not just any sound, but one that was so rare and precious, one that, even tho' he'd grown to know the hearing of it could only be more proof of some inner turmoil within his wife's mind, still, he had begun to crave its beauty more with each passing day. 'Twas his wife's voice. She lay curled on her side away from him, only the light from the hearthfire illuminating her, silhouetting the curve of her hip and limbs.

'Twas the softest of sounds, almost too slight to hear.

He leaned o'er her a bit to see her profile. Aye, her eyes were closed. Just as he'd expected. Once again, 'twas only in her sleep that she gained her voice. But, 'twas not a song this time. Nay, this time, she spoke; almost as if she were speaking to someone. Answering them. And her eyes came open, looked right at him.

"But King William said I could have the mare!"

At those last, much louder, words, Robert sat back a bit. Despite the seriousness of the moment, he chuckled. After all these moons of waiting to hear more from her, she spoke of a *horse!* Recalling the strange affinity she'd shown for the palfrey her uncle had brought for her to ride from the stables at the abbey that day he'd discovered them at the hunter's cot, Robert wondered now, if 'twas that same horse she spoke of now. Tho' that made little sense, as she'd not have remembered the beast—or, mayhap, 'twas only that she remembered the feeling and not the event? He shook his head. Yet another riddle in his wife's past.

He waited for more from her, but naught emerged.

She'd had a shock earlier that day—due to him—and he had little doubt that 'twas for that reason her sleep was restless. Was his babe affected as well? He placed his palm o'er the slight mound of her warm belly, willing his babe's continued health with the strong protection of his large hand.

Her generosity of spirit still had the power to humble him, and she forced him to be a better man because of it. How she knew, even before he did, that he would ne'er be able to forswear any offspring of his making, whether bastard-born or of legitimate stock, astounded and warmed him to his very soul. 'Twas a boon—a boon disguised as a blight—that Vika had tricked him into bedding her impoverished, mute, but oh-so-lovely cousin and that the unctuous, angered uncle had done as he'd done to force a wedding on him.

Brushing a kiss on her brow, he thought again of the irony of all that had come to pass. He'd planned to get Vika with his babe in order to gain her hand and with it, her inheritance, and now that he was well wed to the cousin she'd believed she'd been foisting on him, and that lady bore his babe 'neath her heart, Vika, too, now bore a babe of his as well. And, there was little doubt in his mind, or his heart, that were the tables reversed, if 'twas Morgana who carried his bastard, and Vika the legitimate heir, Vika would have expected he forsake his bastard child, and may have even banished Morgana from her home.

As he gazed down at his slumbering wife, her eyes came open again. Thinking 'twas yet another dream she was having, he remained still, watching her, and allowing her to lead the way through her dream.

She surprised him by raising her head up off the pillow and touching her lips to his. His tarse grew heavy, lengthened. This, he would ne'er try to halt. When she drew him down to her, he opened her mouth with his tongue and tasted the sweet nectar within. After a moment, she pressed him to his back and crawled on top of him.

As he cupped her full breasts in his hands, he asked low, "Do you sleep? Do you dream?"

She raised up and looked at him with mirth dancing in her eyes and shook her head, then leaned down again and began kissing him in earnest. As he rolled her nipples between each of his forefingers and thumbs, making them pucker, he felt her hand trail down his torso until it found his eager cock. His hips lifted and immediately he wanted to fuck, but this was so new. A side of Morgana he'd not seen, yet was thoroughly enchanted by. If he could be patient, if he could wait, then there might be more surprises from her to come.

The thought had barely made it across the transom before she rose up on her knees, then came down again, drawing his tarse all the way inside her in one long, swift glide. He arched, cried out.

And there it was, the next surprise. She was as ready to fuck him as he was her. So he settled his hands on her hips with the intent of helping her find the rhythm, but she gripped his wrists, shaking her head, and lifted them o'er his head.

" 'Tis like that is it?" he ground out in some amusement

between panting breaths.

She nodded and began to move, and a shudder ran through him.

"All right," he croaked. "Do to me what you will, my wanton wife."

All Robert's attention, all his strength, was centered on the delightful tug and slide of her tight, warm canal o'er his cock. His ballocks drew up so tight they ached. "Please. Faster, love. Deeper," he begged. The urge to find fulfillment clawed at his groin, and he gritted his teeth against it. Not until she'd found hers first.

Her breasts bounced to the same tempo as her fucking, and he took a chance and brought his arms down from above his head and molded the ripe mounds in his palms. She leaned forward, settling her hands on his chest and leveraged her weight on her palms. He pinched her nipples and she threw her head back, squeezing her eyes shut, and started to move in earnest.

"Ah, God! Aye, like that," he growled, and this time, when he put his hands on her hips to help her retain the rhythm, she allowed it.

Her breath came in small puffs, and when he lifted his hips high at the same time he brought her down on to him, her mouth came open on a silent scream. In the next moment, the walls of her canal gripped him tight and didn't release him for a sustained moment. It made it difficult to thrust into her, but it also made the pleasure so pure, 'twas near to unbearable.

As she continued to come, a rare, prolonged moan fell from her lips. He rammed her down hard on him and, on a prolonged moan of his own, shot his load deep inside her.

Morgana bent forward and dropped one final sweaty, carnal kiss on his mouth, then collapsed onto her back, lungs blowing.

"That was magnificent. *You* were magnificent," he said.

When she only lay there, still as a stone, he realized she'd fallen back to sleep, and he chuckled. He could use some more sleep as well. Yet he lay there awake for a while. Enjoying the pleasant glow of utter fulfillment—and contentment.

A time later, tho' his head still spun, he managed to rise and bathe himself, then bring the cloth to his wife, and bathe her as well. Afterward, he settled again beside her and wrapped himself around her before falling back into the blissful sleep he'd come to enjoy since their first night together.

* * *

The next morn at the table, as Morgana and her husband were quietly, and companionably, breaking their fast, Robert, with some concern in his tone, abruptly said, "Do you remember tossing me to my back last night, and riding me like I was prime horse flesh?"

Morgana's cheeks flamed. She dipped her head and gave him a shy nod.

"Good. I'd wondered…." He leaned close, caressing the shell of her ear with is lips, with his warm breath, and rumbled low, "Do it again later."

She shuddered, felt her nipples pucker, but forced

herself to glance up and give him another nod.

He planted a quick kiss on her lips, and said brusquely, "Good. Finish eating," and he crammed another bite of bread into his mouth and began to chew. It didn't pass Morgana's notice that she'd managed to gain a shadow of a smile from him, and had also sparked a twinkle in his grey eyes.

She swallowed a sigh, then bit into her own crust of bread as well.

* * *

Later that same morn, Robert went to Vika's chamber with the decided purpose of learning her original plan regarding their babe she carried, as well as learning a bit more of the events that led up to her fall down the stairs two days past.

He was more than a little worried, however, when he arrived and found that Vika was still suffering from an ache in her head. 'Twas clearer and clearer that the fall she had taken, and the injuries she had suffered were even more serious than he'd originally believed. Even if Morgana had demanded her banishment, he would not have been able to fulfill her wishes in that regard, for Vika was not, nor would she be for some time to come, in any condition to travel.

Because of the distress he found her in, he took a much more gentle tack with her than he'd originally planned, taking up a stool and bringing it to her bedside, then resting his hand o'er the one she had limply lying at her side. "Were you able to rest at all during the night?"

She lifted a lid and one amber eye peeked out at him.

"Nay, not a whit."

" 'Tis not good for the babe."

Vika rolled her head away from him and focused on some distant object, he knew not what. "Aye, and we mustn't have that," she said with the familiar sarcasm he was used to hearing from her, "but if 'twere only me, then you'd not care a tittle." It made him hopeful that she was not as ill as he'd feared.

"I'd care."

She shifted her gaze to his and lifted an eyebrow, along with one side of her mouth. "Truly?" she said in a low, disbelieving tone, and again the sarcasm dripped in it as well.

He sat back on the stool and crossed his arms over his chest. "I'd care because Morgana cares." He sat forward and rested his elbows on his knees. "Now, since you are clearly well enough to jab and poke at me this morn, I've a few questions for you. The first of which is this: What exactly was your plan regarding this babe you carry before Wife Deirdre discovered your secret?"

* * *

Vika's heart leapt in her chest. *Oh, Lord. What to say? What to say?* She cleared her throat. Then she made a long production of sitting up and fluffing the pillow behind her *just right*. After that, she straightened and untwisted her gown before tugging the sleeves down further o'er her arms until they covered the upper portion of her hands.

"Viii-Kaa..." Robert growled at her.

She refused to be intimidated (even tho' she was,

just a little). She fluttered her lashes at him. "Aye?"

His eyes narrowed and once again he sat back with his arms crossed over his chest in that imposing posture he had an affinity for taking much too often in her presence.

It didn't take as long as Vika had striven for under his silent, hard glare, for her will to crumble, and her tongue to begin forming words. "All right. I'll tell you." *When I figure out what to say.*

She dropped her gaze and fingered the hem on her sleeve, the cogs in her battered, aching brain turning, as first one idea then another struck then was swiftly discarded. And her tormentor, bless his domineering soul, just sat there, like a king on his throne waiting for the trumps to finish sounding, in order to give some final decree. Mayhap a *bit* of the truth would not hurt?

"I *had* planned to tell you of the babe when I first arrived."

He dipped his head in an imperious nod, as if to say, 'As is right,' then said, "But you did not."

Vexing, vexing man! She lifted her gaze to his. "Nay, I did not." See? She could give short responses, too!

Except, that glare bore holes in her will again.

" 'Twas only after learning that Morgana carried your bairn, and seeing how joyous the two of you were, that I decided against telling you of my own childing state." There! She'd managed to give him the truth, yet not lie again about his fathering the babe.

Yet again, she was met with only silence, and the crushing pressure of those unrelenting steel-grey eyes upon her.

Then, her long lost friend, inspiration, struck. " 'Tis truth, I had not had time before the fall I took to conceive a new plan, once my original had been discarded."

She knew by the way her interrogator's shoulders relaxed and he dropped his hands to his knees, that he believed her. *Thanks be to heaven.*

"Well, 'tis all settled now. Tell me how you managed to take that tumble down the stairs."

At the word *tumble*, a brief, and confusing, spike of terror arced through her, but was swiftly followed by a renewed wash of relief when she realized Robert would not be forcing her to speak of his and Morgana's plan for her and her babe, and she answered gladly, "I remember not. I—" A vague, uneasy feeling settled in her stomach, as if there were something quite important, something bad, that happened just before her fall, but try as she might, she could not recall it.

"Aye?" Robert sat forward and placed his hand on hers. "You've grown pale. Do you need a tisane for your head?"

The throbbing *had* grown more acute in these past minutes, and she closed her eyes, saying weakly, "Aye, my thanks."

* * *

Robert silently shut the door to Vika's chamber not long later and made his way down to the great hall. He'd sworn to her that they would keep the fact of her childing hidden until 'twas necessary to reveal it, as only they, the healer, and Modrun knew of it, and he'd already gained the oath of the last two that they would keep their silence, and curb any chatter that might arise, by giving forth a different tale of events. That would afford Vika a bit more time to heal without worry of the tidings reaching her father. His brows drew together. As to the other, tho' he was much relieved at learning that Vika had not always intended to keep his babe with her a secret, her strange reaction to what e'er recollection she'd had regarding her fall now made him question further and, aye, worry as well. *Had* it been an accident she'd suffered? Or, as he was beginning to suspect, had there been a fouler reason for her fall? He'd ne'er completely put aside the notion that the dark figure his wife had seen upon the *Bealltainn* mound was not phantasm but, in fact, corporeal.

But who? Who among them would commit such an act? And for what purpose?

It bore investigating. And if he wanted to find the culprit, 'twas plain that the suspicion should be kept to himself, so that the ferreting out of the coward would be much easier. And, in the meantime, he'd keep a closer watch on both Vika, and his wife.

* * *

Over the next three days, Robert surreptitiously looked for clues, made casual inquiries, and questioned Vika further about all that she recalled of her fall, and the events that led up to it. Thus far, he had found little proof of evil-doing or foul intent. The only piece of information he'd managed to glean that struck him as odd, and therefore, put his suspicions on alert, was the tale he'd got from his master mason only moments past that one of the man's apprentices had slacked in his duty, had wandered away for a time on the same day as

Song of the Highlands

Vika's fall. Of course, the mason only told him of this as part of his report on the work they were now doing, and as an assurance that he'd taken the man in hand and dealt with his behavior, so that Robert should feel confident that the mason had things well under control.

But, the question remained, if this man did push Vika down those stairs and leave her for dead, why? There seemed no credible reason, other than pure madness, for a man of such low means, and whose livelihood depended so much on Robert's good will, to attack a guest at this holding.

Unless.

Unless he was not what he seemed?

But why Vika?

* * *

The apprentice narrowed his eyes as he watched the husband walk through the entry to the bailey where they were nearing completion of the furbishing there. He'd seen the master mason deep in conversation with the man only moments prior, and knew he'd relayed to him the fact that one of his men had been reproved due to slacking in his work.

He'd truly thought he'd not been missed. *What faulty fortune!* 'Twas not clear as yet whether the husband suspected any crooked deed behind the lady's fall, but he knew now he must confess his radical and unsanctioned actions to his partner in their scheme, for he had from him, at least, some chance of aid, whereas, if he scurried off now, there was every reason to believe he'd hurry his own end even further.

One of the other apprentices called him, jerking him

from his dark thoughts, and beckoned him over to help him move some debris. With a mental sigh, and a last calculation of how many hours more 'twould be until he could meet his partner on the heath, he tugged on his glove and strode over to the man.

* * *

Robert was still pondering the puzzle of Vika's fall as he walked across the courtyard when he heard his gatekeeper call to him, "Laird, there's a knight by the name of Grímr Thorfinnsson begging entrance."

Robert grinned. "Let him in."

* * *

Grímr spurred his stallion into a walk. When he was through the gate, his host called out, "Welcome!" and strode toward him as he dismounted and handed the reins to the stableman who'd jogged over to him.

"I hope you do not mind a guest for some bit of time, as I've dealings in the next shire, and thought of your generous offer as we shared a bowl of *bjórr* together on the road last winter."

"Aye, aye, as before: Welcome!" On a turn, his host continued, "Come. We shall share a tankard of ale together while I have a chamber prepared for you."

Grímr glanced around as he walked. "I see you are expanding the fortress. The work looks to be going well."

"Aye. I shall show it to you in a while, if you wish."

"I do. My thanks." He'd taken it as a benevolent sign when he'd discovered, after first traveling back to court, then on to her manor, that Vika had journeyed to the selfsame holding that he, himself, had been invited to as guest.

With a quick glance up, Grímr scanned the windows on the upper levels of the keep, wondering which one opened into her chamber. Tho' he'd left court last winter after his ill-begotten attempt to seduce her into returning to *Leòdhas*, and traveled back home to his daughter and his responsibilities, 'twas not long again before his daughter's pain, her discontent and inability to be comforted by any other but himself, made him once again vow that he'd not rest until he'd given her the thing she craved the most. For, she would not listen, would not believe, that 'twas her mother who refused to come home, but he who was somehow keeping her from it.

But, this time, he'd hardened his heart against Vika's wiles. Last time, when he'd seen her walking in the moonlight, all the tenderness, the desire, the gut-wrenching *need* for her had near to poleaxed him, had o'ercome all reason, and he'd acted on those emotions. He'd taken her, claimed her as his once more—or attempted to, at least. And, good God in heaven, how sublime it had been! Just as before, mayhap, better. And, once again, he'd let her see his weakness where she was concerned. And, once again, she'd taken his love for her and thrown it back, as if 'twere the vilest, the most putrid, of gifts. Because, as was nearly always true with Vika, the more a man pushed to bind her to him, the quicker she panicked and scurried away.

So, he'd show no mercy, he'd give no quarter, he'd offer no soft words, and he'd bring her back to their daughter, force her to take up her duty, even if he had to toss her in a chest and take her there by force.

* * *

Morgana peeked around the corner of the keep and saw Robert and his guest walk through its portal. *Praise be!* Her husband hadn't seen her, and tho' she was eager to learn who the blond warrior knight was, she'd not forfeit this chance at freedom. Her husband had been acting so strangely these past days since Vika's accident, always no more than a step or two away, where e'er she turned. And tho' his concern warmed her, it also thwarted her from being able to make a short survey of the place where Vika had taken her fall. She, herself, had ne'er entered there, believing it so tumbledown that it surely would be destroyed and rebuilt as a more permanent extension of their living quarters. And now, Robert didn't want her going there. He'd told her so. When he'd startled her out of her skin not three days past just as she was nearing its entrance. But, in this, she would not obey him.

For now, she simply could not keep her curiosity at bay another moment. Vika had told her that there was a rather lovely view from the windows on the second floor, and since Robert would be using the funds to extend the wall of the bailey instead of for the keep itself, she thought, mayhap, the old keep might still be used as a second area for the making of cloth, from raw wool to final fabric, with a bit of restoration, which she thought, surely, would not be too costly.

She'd already found several broken looms in a storage chamber, which she'd tasked one of the carpenters to fix, but she'd worried how she'd fit them into the already crowded space of the existing weavers' chamber.

Then, upon hearing Vika's words, it seemed a boon sent straight from heaven. Mayhap, if she were frugal with coin, but lavish with ingenuity, she might even be able to use some of the discarded materials from the fortress furbishing.

With a skip in her step; a smile on her face; bright images of the coming fair, with bags of coin and bolts of cloth changing hands; and a jaunty tune trilling in her throat (that she was thoroughly unaware of), she hurried toward her destination.

* * *

"Donnach will not be pleased by this," Alaric told the apprentice late that eve.

"Aye. This I *do* know," he answered. "But will you help me?"

His partner gave a loud sigh and said, "I will, but 'twill not be easy." Clearly agitated, he began to pace. Alaric's stallion snorted and stomped in reaction, and Alaric went to it and soothed it with a stroke of his hand on its corded neck.

"I've heard whispers that the mute one's voice is returning, that she sings, that she has visions. 'Tis time to act, and 'tis what I did—though, I admit, I should not have acted in such haste, nor should I have acted without speaking to you first. But, I believed the opportunity presented itself, and I could not let it pass...."

Alaric's brow furrowed. As he pondered what had been revealed, he tapped the pads of his fingers on his lips. After a moment, he said, "Aye, that does bring some urgency to this."

Hopeful now, the apprentice said, "I have another who has agreed to aid us—the same lass, in fact, who gave me those tidings regarding our quarry. She is a servant inside the keep. I've given her a tincture to mix in the mute one's wine. Soon, all of this will be done and we can return to our own holdings."

A growl burst from Alaric's throat, taking the apprentice by surprise, just as his partner's beefy fist connected with the apprentice's face. He stumbled and was on his arse before the sharp pain knifed into his skull and the blood from his lacerated lip drained onto his tunic. He ignored all and flung himself to his feet again rushing Alaric in the same motion. Now they twisted on the ground, pounding their fists where e'er they could find purchase.

After a moment, his partner called out, "Enough, Symon!" and the apprentice rolled away. The harsh sound of their ragged breaths filled the silence for a long moment until, finally, Alaric spoke again, saying, "This solved naught." Tipping his head back and pressing his palm to his nose in an attempt to check its bleeding, he continued, "And I fear you have taken a gravely rash step in using the servant to gain any end."

Symon sat up and tried to stanch the flow of blood from his lip using a portion of his torn sleeve. "Nay, there is no danger in that, at least. The lass will do aught I ask of her. She believes herself enamoured of me, and I've promised a wedding, in the bargain."

Alaric sat up as well and draped his arms on top of his knees. " 'Tis a folly I am angered by, but I see no way out of it now that you've revealed your intent to someone outside our circle."

"This *will* work, and then we can hie ourselves away before the husband has had time to learn any of our plan."

His partner did not answer; in fact, he remained deathly silent for quite a time. Finally, he said, "There is still Gwynlyan with which to deal."

"Nay, I do not believe so. I am beginning to wonder if she even survived the escape, for if she had—where is she then? Why would she have not shown herself at court, given the King her tale? 'Tis been too many moons since her flight. Nay, she does not live. She no doubt drowned in the sea, or was murdered by freebooters before she e'er made it to King William's court."

* * *

Grímr trod, with some stealth, down the stairs to the level below his own tower chamber, to the one where Vika had been housed. It had been a horrible shock to learn of the tumble she'd taken. Robert had told him, after some talk of his plans for his keep, and Grímr's false reason for being in the area, *and* after several tankards of ale, that his wife's cousin was on a visit here as well, and was recovering from injuries caused by a fall a few days past.

His innards had not stopped roiling since. And it had taken all his will not to blurt out his true purpose and storm the inside of the tower keep looking for her. But, if he was to be successful in his plan, he could not reveal it too soon. For now, however, he must find his daughter's mother and see how she fared.

He knew which door was hers, for he'd asked the young servant who'd brought him up to his own chamber earlier, and the lad had been more than willing to inform him of all he knew of the lady, the mishap, and the injuries she'd suffered. Grímr gave no indication of his presence beforehand, instead, simply opening the door and entering. 'Twas best, he'd learned long ago, when dealing with Vika, to give no warning of one's intent with regard to her, else she'd find a way to thwart it.

An old woman, no doubt the healer, was curled up on a pallet by the fire, and seemed to be full asleep, so he went to the bed on silent feet to pull back the drapes that covered the canopy, then settled next to her, pulling the drapes closed again, enveloping them in near complete darkness. She'd not awakened, which told him she'd no doubt been given a draught to aid in her sleep, and now he listened a moment to her soft breaths as she slumbered. It caused such a pang of longing, such a strong wish for what they'd had, that his breath caught in his chest. *Why could you not have been the woman I believed you to be?* On the cusp of the thought came renewed anger at himself, renewed resolve that she would not now, not *ever*, work her wiles upon him again, get beneath, over, or around the fortress he'd built to protect his heart from her. He was here for his daughter's sake, he reminded himself. Naught more. After a time, his eyes adjusted to the low light, and he could see the outline of her visage, the curve of her shoulders and hip as she lay on her side facing him. As he gazed down at the woman who'd sworn so long ago now to be his wife, he studied the wrist that was still bound in linen, the bruise that still marred her cheek and forehead, and clenched his fist, gritted his teeth against the impulse to feel them with the pads of his fingers, soothe them with the touch of his lips.

'Twas clear, as the lad had told him, that Vika's outer injuries were mending well. And, he could only hope, and pray, that the lad was also right about the injury to her brain: That she had not lost her wits with the pounding her head had taken in the fall.

Having found some solace from his worry for her now that he'd seen her for himself, and heaving a mental sigh, he slid from the bed and slipped out of the chamber without waking either the healer or Vika. 'Twas clear she could not travel as yet, and he would not leave without her, so 'twas a boon that he'd told Robert that he was not sure how long 'twould take him to conclude his dealings in the area, and Robert had extended his hospitality to him for as long as was needed.

Back in his own chamber, he doffed his clothing and swung himself onto his back on the bed, with his arms under his head. Staring up into the dark nothingness above him, his thoughts continued to churn and turn on Vika. He was as determined that she would be the mother to their daughter that Halla needed and craved, as Vika was that she could ne'er fulfill that duty. *But what if her wits* had *been damaged?* Nay, he would not think such. Not, at least, until he'd seen it for himself. So, he'd somehow contrive to visit her in privy on the morrow to find out for sure. *And, if her wits* are *gone?*

Well, he'd deal with that as it came. *And, what if she is cold as stone to our daughter after being forced home?* Rolling onto his side, he closed his eyes, turning his back on that dread thought, which slipped between the cracks of his resolve sometimes, unbidden.

* * *

Vika, feeling full of vigor the next morn, and refusing to owe it to the stirring dream she'd had the night before of a familiar pale-haired warrior she refused to give name to, hummed as she took the steps down to the great hall to break her fast. As she swept through the entry, a word of greeting trembling on her tongue, her gaze landed on the back of a blond head, skidded with heart-palpitating panic down the well-formed shoulders and back, then swung to Robert as he came toward her, hand extended, saying, "Vika. Come. Meet our guest."

She only had time to see a glimpse of the all-too-well-known visage of her former lover before she whirled and fled, without a word, out of the hall, up the stairs, and into her chamber, swinging the bar down to lock out any who would follow.

A scream burgeoned in her throat, so full that it caused a piercing ache to keep it down. Pressing both hands o'er her mouth, she paced in a frantic pattern about the chamber. *What to do...what to do...what to do...what to do.... Oh Lord, Dear Lord, what am I to do?*

A knock came on the door, and Vika stumbled as she swung around, her eyes wide with dread as she stared, unblinking, at the slatted wood.

"Are ye ill, m'lady? Th' laird sen' me oop to 'ave a

look a' ye."

With some relief that she had not made the true purpose of her flight known, she called out, "Aye, Wife Deirdre," and stepped to the door, lifting the bar, and opening it for the old woman. "My head began to pain me and it caused a sudden churning in my stomach. I feared I might purge, so I fled. 'Twould do me a great service if you would tell my cousins that I will rest in my chamber this morn, and should be well again by the nooning meal."

"Aye, m'lady. An' there's still some draught there on th' table nex' ta th' bed, if ye need it." With that, she departed, closing the door behind her, and leaving Vika once more to moil in her worry, wondering again how she might deal with Grímr's unexpected arrival, with keeping the fact of her unborn babe—his unborn babe—unknown to him until she was ready to reveal it, and also wondering how she was e'er to keep him from revealing the fact of their daughter, and Vika's abandonment of her, from her cousins, and even more fearfully, from her *father*.

On the cusp of that thought, the door swung open, and in stepped the exact last man she e'er wanted to see. "Grímr!" Her gaze swept o'er his shoulder to the passage behind him, but thankfully, he was alone.

He shut the door and leaned against it with his arms crossed over his chest. "Vika."

She took a step forward, then stopped short. "How—" Forcing a breath into her lungs, she started again with more bite: "Why are you here?"

"Do your cousins know you are childing?"

She blinked. "Wh—I-I'm not!" She turned and walked several paces away, wringing her hands. She *would not* swoon. "Why would you think it?" *Good God in heaven! He knows! He knows!* She closed her eyes and took in a deep breath, then swung around to face him once more, saying, "Clearly, that insult was a ploy to set me off the true subject. You have not answered my question: Why are you here, Grímr?"

His brow lifted, but, thankfully, he pursued his query to her no further, instead dropping his arms to his side and coming away from the door, he strode with ease, as if he were master of the keep, as if he were master of *her*, to the chair by the hearth and settled in it before saying, "I think you are full aware of my intentions with regard to you, Vika, so why do you waste precious breath asking me such?"

CHAPTER 12

GRÍMR WATCHED, WITH both ire and amusement, Vika glare at him in silence as she struggled to remain in control of her natural inclinations, which, he had little doubt, included at least a slap to his cheek, and at most an attempt to throttle him. Such fire. He'd been drawn to it from the moment they'd met—what seemed years and years ago now—and he was pleased beyond words to see it in her now, the healthy glow to her cheek, the near-ease she had in her movements, the quick-witted sparring they had shared thus far, all signified to him that she truly was fully on the mend.

And the babe.... Aye, he'd seen her in this state before, and no matter that the evidence of it barely showed beneath the layers of clothing she wore, nor the lie that fell so easily from her lovely lips, she most assuredly was childing. He knew from the glow to her skin, from the slight rounding to her face, from the evident blossom in her breasts. The jealousy, the fiery ball of anger at the thought of another man touching what was his, he ignored—or, was determined to do so. *And, if 'tis my babe she carries 'neath her heart?* He fought the joy that came with that thought just as vehemently. Still, he would allow the admission to himself that he was glad to know that the fall she'd taken had not flushed it from her womb. For, who knew? It might have been the final blow that would have caused her death, and then he'd not be able to fulfill his vow to his daughter.

Rising from the chair, he said, "I'll leave you to your rest now, *svanfriðr*."

"Bu—"

He shut the door against further speech. There was time and plenty for that in the days ahead. For now, all that mattered was that she had not sustained any lasting injuries. The matter of the babe, and whether he'd sired it, would have to wait. And, in any case, 'twas clear she had no intention of wedding another, whether he be father of her babe or nay, so even if 'twas proved to be another man's when 'twas brought forth at last? Again he fought back the instant burn of jealous rage that seethed in his gut, flexing his hand, then curling it into a tight fist at his side. Nay, even then, he'd not deny the babe a place in his home.

* * *

"I think it not at all so difficult a thing," Vika said, a brow arched as she rubbed the pad of her thumb o'er the nail of her middle finger.

Morgana's lips twitched with mirth in response to

her cousin's clearly nettled barb at Grímr's answer to Robert's query regarding the last joust Grímr had entered. For some unknown reason, Vika had been behaving with much hostility to their male guest, and had countered near to every comment the man put forth, as if he'd offended her in some way. Truly, Morgana had ne'er seen her cousin behave in such a manner to any man, especially one as handsome and virile as this one. Nay, 'twas more her way to use her tongue to seduce and charm than to taunt and vex.

"And, how many times, pray, have you fought in a tourney, so that you might be so knowing and assured of this opinion?"

With a turn of her head, Morgana's gaze rested again on Grímr. Aye, Vika had finally made him show a bit of ire. She shifted her attention to her husband. And, 'twas evident, Robert was so flummoxed by the situation, that he would only clear his throat and shovel another turnip into his mouth.

"There is no need for me to fight to know that what I say is truth," Morgana's cousin said, gazing down at the nail on her middle finger as she stroked it with the thumb of her other hand, "for even Robert uses that very ploy at least once in every joust he's been in." She stroked her palm up and down Robert's upper arm. "Is that not so, Robert?"

She'd purred his name, in a voice more suited to the bedchamber, and Morgana's earlier good cheer was replaced by worry, and anger. Morgana moved her hand toward the chalice of wine as if to pick it up, but knocked it over instead, directly into the pale-blue silk-covered lap of her cousin.

'Twas with no little satisfaction that Vika's antagonist for the meal burst into laughter, that Morgana's husband leapt off their bench to keep from getting drenched himself, and Vika screeched that her best gown had been ruined.

You must curb your willful anger and pride, Morgana, for they are sins, she heard the chiding voice in her head of Ma dame Aliénor, the abbess of the nunnery Morgana had been raised in, and Morgana's elation was instantly tainted with guilt. In repentance, she silently vowed to the rarified image of Ma dame to give her own favorite gown to Vika as recompense.

The page rushed over with a cloth and Morgana reached for it, then wrapped one arm about the waist of her cousin and used the other to daub at the stain, as they both exited the great hall together.

* * *

After the ladies had departed, Robert sat back, crossing his arms over his chest and studied Grímr with a raised brow. 'Twas all Grímr could do not to show his discomfiture in manner or word, instead composing his visage into an indifferent mein as he took a long pull on his ale and waited, this time, for Robert to speak his mind first.

It took much longer than Grímr e'er believed it would, but after what seemed to be several quiet, ponderous, moments, as the only sounds about them were of the pages clearing the remains of the meal from the table, Robert said at last, "I ken now why that island of yours struck a familiar chord within me when we met: 'Twas Vika's home as well, before her husband's death."

Grímr watched the door shut behind the last page carrying a loaded tray before saying, "You've caught me out. Vika was wed to my uncle—and, aye, we two are well acquainted." How well, he'd not reveal unless absolutely necessary to his own ends.

Robert's eyes narrowed on him. "The two of you seem at sixes and sevens."

Grímr shrugged. "Aye," he said, and took another pull on his ale, but did not allow his gaze to waver from his host's.

"All right," Robert finally said. "I see that you'll share naught more. But, I'll tell you this: If it comes to choosing between you and Vika as guest, I must, and will, choose my wife's cousin."

"As it should be. But, worry not, for 'twill not come to that, I give you my vow."

* * *

Vika paced her bedchamber, nibbling on her thumbnail. *Had her ploy worked?* Would Robert demand that Grímr leave, find another place to stay while he carried out the alleged *duty* that he'd come to do? She prayed he would, yet she feared 'twould take much more to push Robert to do so.

'Twas a shame she'd had to sacrifice her lovely gown for the attempt, but, she had to admit, 'twas worth losing it to see the e'er agreeable Morgana so vigorously protect what was rightly hers. Mirth rose up from Vika's belly and exploded forth in a snort. She wondered if Robert realized his wife had purposely spilled the wine, out of jealousy and umbrage.

Nay, no doubt not. For Robert had his eye to his meal and would not have seen the spark of satisfaction that glimmered e'er so briefly in Morgana's eyes before, sadly, her conscience o'ercame her bout of fiery will, and once more the illusion of docile kindness prevailed.

Even so, when Morgana had insisted Vika take the very lovely lavender silk gown, Vika did not refuse it. She ran her hand o'er the shiny white-and-purple violets embroidered around the low neckline with fine silk thread. 'Twas truly beautiful. Much more so than the gown Morgana had ruined.

With a sigh, she hung it on a peg, then settled on the bed for a short nap.

As she drifted to sleep, images of Grímr's reaction to her in the gown, of his handsome face and desire-filled eyes, of her cool reception of such open admiration, floated behind her lids, and she smiled.

* * *

Robert shut the door behind him as he came into the bedchamber behind his wife that eve after supper, and after the second round of sparring between his guests he'd been subjected to. "Those two are making my meals not settle well."

Morgana turned her gaze to him and gave him a small smile that included a shrug and a shake of her head.

"He is the nephew of Vika's husband, did she tell you?"

Morgana's eyes went round. She shook her head and lifted the filet and veil from her head, then put them away.

"I've told him that Vika will be the one to stay, should their animosity become a burden."

On a sigh, his wife nodded.

"Why did you give Vika your gown?" he said, walking up behind her and aiding her in disrobing for the night.

Her answer was a flurry of hand movements reminding him of the spill of wine at the nooning meal. He gave a gruff grunt in answer and opened his mouth o'er the pulse at her neck, more interested now in the soft, pale, succulent flesh feast laid before him.

The heartbeat under his tongue fluttered and sped, and a rush of breath beat, warm and moist against his cheek, as she lifted her arms up and around his head. In answer, he cupped her breasts, fuller now because she carried their babe in her womb, and tweaked their dark tips into tantalizing points.

When she tried to turn in his arms, he stayed her movement by dropping an arm across her belly, bringing her lush bottom up against his cock, and pressed his palm against her mons, prying her humid lips apart with his fingers and sliding them into her liquid heat as he teased her clit with the rough pad of his thumb.

In moments, she'd drenched his hand and her thighs trembled and opened. When she arched, went rigid against him, when he felt the first ripplings of her womb begin to contract, he pinched her nipple and sucked hard on that pulse point at the base of her neck.

She came so hard, he almost lost hold of her, almost

stumbled. And, as was becoming e'er more common, she vocalized her pleasure with a long moan.

Which only made his own need for completion more acute.

Lifting her up into his arms, he cradled her head in his palm and pressed a lip-splitting, passion and need-filled kiss on her mouth as he brought them to their bed.

"I would have had you where we stood, but I don't want to hurt the babe," he told her, as he quickly doffed his own clothing. Then, climbing atop her, he kissed her brow, lifted her limbs about his waist and drove home. "Blood of Christ, 'tis Heaven here, I swear."

In answer, she ran her tongue up his neck and bit down hard on his earlobe, which made him arch, which sent him deeper, which made him touch the mouth of her womb, which nearly made him spew his seed before he'd had time to enjoy the ride.

"Nay, none of that," he told her, then imprisoned her wrists above her head, gave her a small nip on her lower lip with his teeth, pressed his cheek to hers, and lifted and lowered his hips in slow, seductive movements, keeping them both riding the sharp edge between delight and torment, between the need to remain bonded, and the desire for release, for long, long minutes, until Morgana's face and chest were so flushed, and Robert's pulse was so rapid, that he feared they'd both burst into flame if they did not fall o'er that searing, pleasurable precipice soon.

With the very last bit of strength he had left, he

raised up on his knees and took her with the force he'd been depriving himself—depriving her—for much too long and, as his cock slid in and out of the tight, slick, engorged center of her, as her hips came up again and again to meet his, the world around them exploded into millions of flashes of starlight. Somewhere on the edge of his consciousness, Robert heard Morgana cry out her pleasure, and his deeper answering cry as well.

Sometime later, Robert awakened from his passion-induced sleep to find Morgana had bathed him, and was now settled by the fire, as so oft she was, mending yet another piece of clothing of his. Warmth filled his heart as he watched her.

Rising up, he walked over and settled on his knees in front of her, reached out his palm, and placed it on the small mound of her belly. "How is my son?"

She smiled and smoothed his cheek with her hand, mouthing, "He is well, worry not."

"But he needs his rest and, so wife, do you." Rising to his feet, he lifted her to hers at the same time, making her drop what e'er she had been working on. Tho' she tried to bend down to retrieve it, he would not allow it, and tugged her toward their bed instead.

He rolled her to her side and curled around her, stroking her hair from her forehead and cheek before dropping several soft kisses from her temple to her chin, then pulled her more snugly into him, with his hand resting lightly o'er their babe.

'Twas not long before Morgana heard the deep, slow breathing that indicated Robert had fallen back to sleep. She tried to sleep as well, she truly did, and she did know that Robert was right: She and their babe needed rest. So, on the advice that Modron had given that the sleeping draught she had begun to need so oft in the past sennight, for precisely such times, would not harm the babe, Morgana took just a drop or two in a cup of water, weakening the dose—just to be safe.

In moments, and tho' the babe was making her stomach churn a bit, she was sound asleep.

* * *

The next morn, Morgana's queasiness had not lessened, so she only nibbled on a bit of stale bread to break her fast before beginning her duties for the day, with Modron beside her.

As they walked together across the courtyard toward the weavers' chamber with Modron chatting pleasantly about tidings that the blacksmith's son was to wed the alewife's daughter, a sudden sharp pain in Morgana's head together with her already churning stomach made her halt her steps.

Modron made a fuss, trying to turn her about and walk them back to Morgana's bedchamber, saying she should rest a while longer.

But the initial flash of pain in her head had already settled into a bearable, dull ache, so she shook her head, and continued toward the weavers' chamber.

After only a small hesitation, Morgana was pleased to find Modron once more at her side, tho' the woman insisted that Morgana at least try to eat a bit of something more than the stale bread she'd had earlier, as the babe was no doubt telling her 'twas time to feed him something more substantial.

Song of the Highlands

* * *

Robert, drenched with sweat from the morn's training session, took several long swallows from the ladle of well water before picking up the bucket and pouring the remainder o'er his bare head and shoulders. Tho he'd still not found any evidence of malignant intent in regard to Vika's tumble, he'd come to the decision that 'twould be best to inform Grímr of his suspicions. For, tho' the two had little liking for the other, Grímr was still her husband's kin, and would be bound by honor to aid in her protection. In addition, and after much thought, he'd also decided 'twas best for Grímr to know of Vika's childing state, and that Robert was the sire. But, before he did so, he must verify all was well with his wife. Morgana would be about her duties now, so Robert headed toward the weavers' chamber, did a search and scan of the exterior, peeked in on the women, saw that his wife and Modron had their heads together working on something or other, then turned back toward the keep, feeling much more settled now that he'd confirmed his wife's safety.

* * *

A knock sounded on the door to Grímr's bedchamber, and he hurriedly pulled his shirt the rest of the way down as he strode over and opened it. "Robert," he said with some surprise, "is aught amiss?"

"Aye, mayhap. But I see that you are readying to leave on your journey to the next shire, so I will ask that you and I have a bit of time to speak later this eve, after you've returned."

Surprise turned to alarm, and Grímr pulled the door

open further as he took a step back, saying, "Nay, my business there is not pressing. Come inside, we shall speak now, if you will."

With a nod, his host strode through the doorway and, after a quick glance around, found a stool by the window and brought it over to place it next to the other by the hearth. After they were both seated, Robert said, "I have a suspicion that someone—I've yet to find out who—pushed Vika down those stairs."

Grímr's stomach lurched. "How know you this?"

" 'I've no proof as yet, only a suspicion stemming from the look in Vika's eye, the loss of color in her countenance, the first time I asked her to tell me how she fell. 'Twas as if a glimmer of memory passed within her, but 'twas gone again before she could hold it."

"Could it not be merely a reaction to recalling the terror she must have felt as she tumbled?"

"Aye, I have thought of that, but…. Nay, 'tis something else, I've a feeling in my gut, tho' she assures me 'twas merely a badly placed foot on her part."

Grímr rose from his stool and walked several paces away. "I think…." He swung back to face his host. "I believe you. I confess, I've been wondering at the oddity of Vika's fall since I've learned of it. She has always been so sure-footed. I've ne'er known her to trip, to take any misstep. She is pure grace when she moves."

Robert's eyes narrowed on him, and he knew he'd said too much, revealed too much, with that last observation.

"Aye." Robert's gaze continued to penetrate, and

'twas all Grímr could do to remain stoic in the dark quiet that followed until his host at last broke his silence, saying, "There is something more. Vika bears my babe in her belly."

A shock of rage, of virulent jealousy seared Grímr's gut. "You!" he bellowed, thundering toward Robert with hands outstretched, ready to throttle.

Robert leapt up, but stood his ground, prepared to fight, but clearer thinking prevailed, and Grímr halted his motion, his lungs blowing. He would not care. He would *not*. She would not have that power o'er him e'er again. And besides, he'd not be thrown out before he could take her with him—back to their daughter.

"Forgive my ill reaction, 'twill not happen again, I assure you."

His host gave him a short nod. After a brief, but weighted pause, he said, "So, 'tis as I thought. You were lovers."

He hesitated, not sure if he should respond with truth or falsehood. "Aye," he said finally. Turning, he moved several paces away and crossed his arms over his chest. "But, that was long ago, before she left *Leòdhas*." *And we've a bairn together as well.* Nay, he'd not reveal it. Not yet. Mayhap, not ever. And certainly not until after he'd had another talk with Vika about the one she carried now.

Robert sat down again. "Vika's father must not learn that she is breeding."

Alarm ran down Grímr's spine, his pulse increased. He walked over and settled on his stool once again as well. "Nay, he must not. 'Twould not be good for Vika if he did."

"We've kept it a secret thus far, and believe we can continue to keep it from reaching her father's ear, even after the fact of it can no longer be hidden."

"Fear not, I shall keep the secret as well."

Robert rose to his feet. "Good. And you will aid me in watching o'er Vika while I continue my search for the culprit behind her fall?"

"Aye." And 'twould give him the excuse he needed to be seen studying the design and daily workings of the keep to find the best time and means of whisking her back to their daughter, when she was well enough to travel again...if, as he suspected, she would not go willingly.

* * *

'Twas not until Robert was back in the courtyard that he was struck with a sudden realization: 'Twas *Vika* that Grímr had gone to court to retrieve all those moons ago. And, clearly, he'd not been successful, else she'd not be here with them now. Nay, she'd be off on that island, but still with Robert's babe in her belly. A babe, he wondered now, if he'd e'er have learned of.

He wondered as well, if Grímr's reason for being here had more to do with Vika and less with any real duty he was bound to in the next shire. 'Twas more than likely the case, and Robert would do well to watch closely the man's actions in the coming days, for he'd not allow him to away with her before the babe was born. Tho' by the waspish words she stung the man with when e'er they were within a foot of each other, he also believed he had very little to worry about on that score. For, Vika, 'twas plain, would ne'er agree to return to that isle with Grímr, nor, either, e'er give him purchase 'tween her thighs.

* * *

Grímr only waited long enough for Robert to get to the bottom of the stairs before taking them himself to Vika's bedchamber below. He swung the door wide and strode in, but a shriek of indignation, and a flying pewter cup that grazed his temple and brow before landing with a crash against the doorframe, halted his forward motion. And, the sight of familiar passion-hued bare flesh spun the hot ire in his gut into a blaze of unwanted lust before he controlled the impulse, turned his back to her, and shut the door, giving both of them time to recover.

"Leave!"

"Where is your maid?"

He heard a feminine growl, then the stomp of a foot. "LEAVE!"

He turned to face her and was both relieved and dismayed to find she'd covered her nakedness in a crimson robe. "Where is your maid?"

He could see her jaw working as she gritted her teeth before she gave her back to him and walked over to the table that held her comb. She pulled the tines through the dark locks several times before finally answering, "I left her at my manor."

"And the healer?"

She sighed and rolled her eyes, facing him once more. "She was needed in the village. What do you here, Grímr?"

"Is the babe truly Robert MacVie's?"

* * *

Vika's breath caught, formed a mass of dread that constricted her throat. Robert, the vexing villain, had told him her secret (her lie)! She swung around and walked to the window, folding her arms over her chest as she gazed, unseeing, at the courtyard below. *Aye! Aye! Aye! 'Tis Robert's!* She opened her mouth, the words forming on her tongue, and said instead, "Nay, 'tis yours. You are my babe's father, Grímr." She released a loud sigh and pressed her fingers to her lids to stem the tears that threatened to pour forth. *"Again."*

"He is certain 'tis his, so I must ask: How do you know for certain that I am the sire?"

"Because, with..." ...*with the others.* Nay, she'd not test his anger with that confession. "...with Robert, there was something used to hinder childing. And...I had..." She sucked in a breath to bolster her courage. "I had not been with Robert—or anyone—for near to a fortnight, as I had my flowering. With you...with you there was no time," she said the last with some bit of renewed fire. "There was no barrier. And after...." She swallowed and took in another deep breath to gain control of her trembling voice. "Well, after *you*, I did not again flower." Her voice cracked on the last.

"And you took no other to your bed?"

Oh, how she craved to lie—to tell him there had been many others after that night—but 'twould only make it impossible for her to give their babe o'er to him later, when 'twas time, after its birth, for he'd ne'er believe her then. So, in answer, and because she found her throat too tight to make sound, she simply gave a shake of her head.

"Vika…." There was such pain, such longing in his voice, and she tensed, shut her eyes against it. Then because he'd surely realized his folly, a low, angry growl erupted from him.

After a moment, he said, "Why have you allowed him to believe the lie?"

She heard the disgust in his voice, which always managed to work on her desire to please him—as well as her conscience—and whirled around, allowing him to see the tears she could no longer keep in check, and wailed, "B-Because I'm a vile, wicked woman! 'Tis what you believe, is it not?!" She swung back around and dropped her face in her hands. "And I am! I *am* all the things you said I was before I left *Leòdhas*."

She heard him take a step toward her, then halt just as quickly.

"What I said that day…I said in anger and frustration that I could not change your mind."

"Well, they are true."

"Nay, I think they are not. And, now you must tell Robert the truth about the babe."

She couldn't form sound, her throat was too clogged with tears, so she simply nodded as she swiped them from her cheek with the back of her hand.

He strode up to her and placed his large, protective hand on her arm, saying firmly, but gently, too, "And there will be no further resistance. You *will* return with me, once you are healed enough to make the journey."

She would not, but, 'twould only taunt him into

taking her away by force, if she did not give her assent, so she said in a grudging voice (tho' she did not lift her gaze to him), "Aye. I will."

* * *

Morgana was still suffering with a dull ache in her head, and her stomach had still not settled, by the time she came down for supper later that day, even after the rest she'd had at Modron's insistence after the nooning meal. But, she was determined to be a good hostess to her guests (and, besides, she had come to enjoy the sharp, and witty, exchange of words between Vika and the handsome warrior), so she took in several deep breaths, positioned a smile upon her lips, and took Robert's outstretched hand, so that he might lead her to her place at the table.

Unfortunately, her evening's entertainment was not to be. Vika had sent word down that her head was aching again, and she would take her meals in her chamber for a day or two. Morgana had little doubt that the true reason for her cousin's sudden aching head had more to do with the blond warrior knight, and less to do with the fall she'd taken. But, Morgana was still worried about her, so determined that she would visit her on the morrow, and see if there was aught she might do to ease her suffering.

As Robert and Grímr spoke of manly things of mutual interest, Morgana fought her own need to rest. She only managed to nibble at her meal, and, later as they ascended the stairs to their chamber, Robert asked her whether she was well, whether he should call for the healer, but she felt sure all she truly needed was a good night's rest, so she shook her head and pressed her lips to his cheek until she felt him relax. He nodded his head and smiled down at her, settling his hand o'er her belly, as he so oft wanted to do.

With a sigh of contentment that almost cured her aches, she closed her eyes with a smile and settled her head on his arm, climbing the stair from memory as she allowed him to blindly lead her where e'er he would go.

* * *

"Oh, God, oh, God!"

"Wha—?" Robert jerked upright late that night, jarred from sleep by his wife's cry. His heart leapt into his throat when he realized she was tossing from side to side with both hands on her belly. "What is wrong? Is it the babe?"

She didn't respond, but guttural moans burst from her throat. Then he noticed a clammy dampness seeping o'er the mattress under his thigh. *Christ's Bones!* He leapt from the bed and hurriedly lit a taper.

For several stunned moments, all he could do was stand there, frozen with dread and disbelief, blinking rapidly at the sight before him. There was a red stain, growing e'er larger, under his wife, as more of the blood flowed from between her thighs. With effort, he tore his eyes from the spot and settled them on Morgana's face. Tears ran in rivulets o'er her flushed cheeks. "I must call for Wife Deirdre," he told her numbly. Before he turned, he bent down and placed a kiss on her heated brow. "I'm sorry."

Please, he prayed, *do not take her from me.*

CHAPTER 13

$\mathcal{M}$AYHAP, THE BABE was still in her belly. Robert prayed that 'twas the case as he paced by the hearthfire a while later. After learning that he would not lose Morgana, he had turned his thoughts fully to his unborn son. Modron and Wife Deirdre were bathing Morgana now and speaking to her in hushed tones. Too hushed for him to understand. But what e'er they said soothed her, for her whimpers lessened by a small degree.

In the first minutes, as the healer examined his wife, Modron had explained to him what she believed was happening, assuring him that Morgana's life was not likely in danger. The older woman had even revealed to him then that she, herself, had lost a few wee ones as a young wife; that, although it wrenched at the heart, losing a babe this early in childing rarely threatened the mother's life. But, she also gave him a bit of hope, saying that sometimes there could be bleeding, where the babe was not lost.

There was a helplessness in him, a restless need to take action, *do* something, but what he could possibly do for his wife, he had no clear notion of. He crossed his arms over his chest and paced toward the window. After staring blankly out into the darkened courtyard a moment, he swerved around and headed back to his place by the hearth. When his foot caught on the leg of a stool, he flung it away with an angry kick. It skidded across the wood planked floor and made a rather satisfying *crash!* against the stone wall, splintering the wood and knocking off a leg.

* * *

Jarred by a clamorous clatter behind her, Gwynlyan whipped her head around and saw Robert's pained visage, his tensed stance, his chest rise and fall with each harsh new breath. Patting and soothing her distressed daughter's hand, she realized she'd best get her son-in-law out of here before she gave him the news. He was already behaving like a caged animal, and there was no telling what he would do once she told him the babe had flushed from Morgana's womb.

But when she tried to disengage from her daughter's grasp, Morgana tugged her back, refusing to release her. Gwynlyan turned and looked at her then. Morgana was adamant. She wanted to give her husband the sad tidings herself. She wanted the two women to leave her and Robert alone for a time so that she could do just that.

Gwynlyan looked to the healer to gauge her stance on this notion. The aged woman nodded her head.

Before Gwynlyan realized what she was doing, she bent down and kissed Morgana's damp brow. The look of surprise on her daughter's face brought her up short. She must take more care in future, if she was to continue on with the guise she'd been living under these past moons. But then Morgana took her hand and gave it an affectionate squeeze and Gwynlyan relaxed. Thankfully, she'd not been offended by such an undue familiarity from one of her staff.

* * *

A time later, Robert sat on the edge of the bed beside Morgana. When his wife's grief had turned into silent sobs, she'd rolled on her side, no longer facing him. And because Robert didn't know what else to do, he stroked the back of her head, then patted her quaking shoulder and said, "Do not fret. 'Tis a common enough occurrence, I'm told, and there will be other babes. I can give you another in not too many days' time, so Wife Deirdre said."

Her frame quaked even harder as she grabbed a fistful of her hair and covered her face with it, then rotated even further away from him, causing his palm to fall to the mattress behind her, and buried her nose against the pillow. The dread and anguish that had been gripping his innards these past hours, shot up through his center and lodged in his throat. His vision blurred, and he blinked it away, then took a deep swallow before saying, "Aye, rest. I'll find a bed in the great hall."

With that, he rose to his feet and strode to the door. He knew—he could *feel*—that Morgana still wept, and he would see that Modron and Wife Deirdre stayed with her the remainder of the night to keep her from becoming ill and to give his wife what e'er comfort she needed that he was clearly not providing.

* * *

With yet another swing of the heavy, long-handled axe, blade met surface, along with the gratifying sound of splintering wood, followed closely by the creaking and quivering of the old structure. Robert jogged back a few paces and watched as the entire left side of the old fortress finally came tumbling to the ground with an even more satisfying crash.

I should have called for Wife Deirdre sooner. Morgana had said she wasn't feeling quite right after their evening meal, but she had insisted there was naught amiss, and that she would feel better after a night's rest.

And he'd believed her.

He shouldn't have.

Striding over to the now half-torn-down keep, he lifted the axe again and slammed it down on the portion that still stood. Several times more, he repeated the action, and with each new cleave, another section fell.

With effort, he forced his mind on thoughts less heartrending.

He'd questioned the apprentice who'd slipped away from his duties the same day as Vika's fall, but the man admitted he'd been with his lover—a lass who served inside the kitchen—and she'd affirmed his tale as truth. As the lass was admitting to being lax in her own duties, which the cook, who was working at the table while they spoke, quickly punished her for, he felt sure she told the truth, and that the apprentice was not the culprit.

Robert was beginning to wonder if there *had* been someone on the stair with Vika. Mayhap, he'd been wrong. Mayhap, she *had* had an unusual moment of awkwardness, and simply tripped and fallen. Mayhap, Vika's pallid countenance, the strange look that had flashed in her eyes, had only been a reaction to the pain, or to the memory of the fall. He'd tried to question her again about the incident, more than once now, and each time, she'd been calm, had simply shrugged with indifference, and told him she remembered not. And Grímr had found naught thus far in his search either, so he'd told Robert last eve while they shared a tankard of ale before supper and awaited Morgana's arrival.

Well, no matter. He'd not have anything inside this fortress that was a danger to the women under his protection. And even tho' Morgana had thought it well enough to furbish and use, his master mason said not. So, 'twas past time to destroy it. And 'twas an added boon that with each swing of the axe, with each crack of the wood, with each boom and crash that followed, the ache of grief in his chest, the twisting, acrid guilt in his stomach, lessened.

Do I still name myself a father, if my babe no longer lives?

Robert's roar rent the air, the axe came down, the wood splintered.

* * *

Morgana scrubbed at her puffy, tear-streaked eyes and cheeks, and slid her feet o'er the edge of the bed until they were flat on the floor. From the vociferous snore that met her ear again, she knew Wife Deirdre's daughter dozed by the hearth, even tho' she sat upright in the chair, and still held the needle in one hand and her sampler in the other.

She would not lie abed another moment longer, wallowing in her grief, and being reminded with every turn of her head, with every slide of the blanket o'er thigh or breast, that 'twas on this very mattress, her son's life had begun...and ended.

She needed to move, to leave this chamber of death, and to set her mind, at least for a small while, on something other than her heartache and her chiding conscience that, with every new breath, wondered again what she'd done that had caused her to lose her babe. Or, if she'd done naught wrong, was she flawed as a woman in some way? Or, mayhap, even cursed by the devil, as the devout priest who'd flogged her when she'd refused to wed Robert all those moons ago now, had oft repeated to her with such surety.

Tho' she doubted the woman would waken, even were a band of ravening warriors to burst through the door, Morgana still slipped out of the chamber with barely a sound made. She'd thought she might visit the weavers' chamber, to check on the progress there, and to give her thanks to Modron once again for all the kindness and support she'd provided these past moons, and especially during the sennights she'd carried her son 'neath her heart, but now the thought of seeing all those women—all those *mothers*—sent a sharp spear of anger and, aye, *jealousy* straight through her center. *Why Lord? Why?* She felt a new wave of anguish, a new flood of tears gush forth, and she pressed her palms to her face, crumpled against the cold, stone wall of the stairwell. *What did I do? What did I do? What more should I have done? Oh, God, oh, God...NO! Cease this now.* Morgana slid her hands from her damp cheeks, gulped in several deep, calming breaths, straightened her spine, and stood tall on wobbly knees a moment before, with renewed purpose, she made her way back up the stairs, and higher still, to the small solar tucked away in the westside tower. There, she would sit and sew on the large tapestry meant to be hung on the wall behind their long table in the great hall. The smaller one, the one meant for her son's chamber, she would not think or look upon for many moons to come...if ever.

***

As the gates shut behind Grímr, he heard yet another crash of timber, and knew Robert was not yet done purging his anger, his sorrow, and no doubt his unease of mind o'er the blow of defeat he'd taken at the loss of his and Morgana's babe.

And now, Grímr could not give him another by revealing that the babe Vika carried was not his own, but Grímr's. At least, not yet.

Vika! Damn her! If she'd only honored their bargain three years past, they'd not be here now, she'd not be in some still unknown danger, their daughter would not cry herself to sleep so oft asking for her mother, *and* he'd not have to deliver a second blow to a man that he'd developed a bond of friendship with from near to the moment of first meeting him. *Damn!* He kicked his steed into a faster pace, ran him o'er the heath for long minutes until Grímr's ire was spent, and his horse was lathered.

Turning in the direction of a shaded copse of trees where, he could see, the burn wandered through, he moved toward it. After dismounting and stripping his steed's back of its burdens, he led it to the burn so that it might drink. As he did so, he turned his mind again to Vika, and her fondness for taking what e'er course was easiest at the moment, with little regard for the lasting effect such action might have on her. Grímr grumbled. Aye, on *her*. But, and more importantly, the effect it might, and too often *did*, have on those around her.

Once she'd agreed to return with him to *Leòdhas*, she'd revealed to Grímr the depth of her deceit. Not only had she allowed both Robert and her *mildr*, *dœll* cousin, Morgana, to believe Robert had sired a babe with her, she'd also allowed them to believe she'd leave the babe to be raised by them. Upon learning the last, he'd insisted they not wait a moment longer, insisted they must go to Robert and Morgana immediately and tell them the truth. But, she'd worked her wiles on him, with her tears and pretense of a need to rest, for the babe's sake, so he'd agreed to let the revelation wait until that eve, after supper. What a fool he'd been! *Again!*

For, nay. She'd not come down, she'd not honored even that bargain. Grinding his teeth, he yanked on a cluster of bracken, slicing it through at its base, then using it to groom the lather from his horse. For at least the hundredth time since she'd insisted on abandoning them, he asked himself: *Why? Why do I burn for her? What is it in me that craves such a selfish, deceitful, faithless lady?*

"Just as my heart no longer is yours, neither, now, *logi af mitt fÿst*, is the little trust I offered up this day past," he vowed.

He positioned the saddle on the back of the horse with a growl. 'Twas near more than he could stomach to know that this conniver was the mother of his bairns.

Finally, he mounted his steed once more and continued on his journey. Knowing Vika would be safe, hiding away in her chamber while he was gone, as she'd no doubt dread facing Robert and Morgana with her lie to them even more, now that she would be met with their grief o'er the loss of their babe as well, he forced the worry from his mind.

The trip to and from the west coast to meet with his men, to find out the progress of the repairs to his ship from the damage done it by the sea storm they encountered on their way here, and to give them notice that they should be prepared to leave within not more than a moon's time, should take him no more than five days, and he should be back six days hence. Hopefully, that would give his hosts time to o'ercome the shock. The last thing they needed at this time was to deal with guests, and he'd have taken Vika with him now, if he'd not feared that 'twas too soon for her to make such a journey. For, aye, tho' he knew she'd lied the night before about her aching head in order to keep from confessing her deceit, he also knew, from speaking at length to Wife Deirdre, that Vika was still suffering from her injuries.

He'd send a missive to his mother, with a passage in

it to his daughter, telling them that he and Vika would be home by the end of *haust*, if the winds of fortune blew no ill. Otherwise, 'twould be closer to *í móti vetri*.

With a sigh of resignation at the battle he'd have ahead of him, he kicked his steed into a canter and rode west, the morn still young, and the sun at his back.

* * *

Not long later, nearing the bells of terce, Robert was just taking the steps up to the door of the keep when Wife Deirdre called to him from behind.

"Laird!" she wheezed out.

His brows slammed together as he made a half-turn on the step to look back at her. "Why are you not attending my wife?"

Still moving toward him, she held her hand to the center of her chest, heaving in loud breaths as she said, "Yer wife is sleepin' soundly, and wi' one o' me daughters there ta tend 'er should she 'waken. I've been lookin' fer ya, Laird, as I've a need ta speak wi' ya."

Tho' his stomach twisted with worry, he managed to keep an outer calm. Lifting a brow, he said, "Aye? Is my wife ill?"

She shook her head and the tight knot in Robert's neck relaxed. He watched as she trudged the last several feet to stand at the bottom of the steps. After taking another moment to inhale a deep breath and, with the back of her gnarled hand, move the stray lock of gray hair that had come loose of her wimple and fallen o'er her forehead, she said at last, "I've discover'd somethin' dreadful, Laird. Aboot why our Lady lost 'er babe th's night past."

His heart thumped wildly in his chest and it was all Robert could do to keep his knees from bending. "Because"—he cleared his throat—"Because I did not call for you earlier?"

"Nay, 'twas naugh' ta do wi' tha' " She looked around, clearly worried that others might hear her. Even tho' she found the bailey all but empty, she still leaned toward him and said in a near whisper, " 'Tis somethin'—some*one*—else, an' no' fer others' ears, Laird."

In a flash he recalled his suspicions regarding Vika's fall, and rage replaced fear. The muscles in Robert's cheek vibrated. His hands formed fists at his side. With a growl and a palm out to assist her, he bade the healer come inside the great hall to give him the full of the tale.

Once he had the aged woman settled on a bench, with a cup of water to soothe her parched throat, he said, "What have you learned, Wife Deirdre?"

She pressed the back of her hand to her lips as she swallowed the cool liquid, then said at last, "Praise be tha' our lady refused th' sleepin' draught 'er maid tried ta ferce upon 'er after...after losin' yer babe this nigh' past, fer I fear I wud no' 'ave noticed th' diff'rence in smell standin' 'way from it as I was then. But, this morn, efter I made sure our lady ate at least 'alf th' bread an' cheese I give 'er ta break 'er fast, I pressed 'er to take th' draught, told 'er she needed ta rest ta heal an' regain 'er strength."

When the healer took another long swallow of water and didn't take up the tale again immediately upon setting the cup down on the table, Robert growled, "Aye? Speak!" His heart nearly beat through his ribcage. When her mouth dropped open, but no words came forth, he slammed his fist down onto the table and yelled, "By God's bones, woman, tell me what you found!"

" 'Tw-'twas fer a mech long'r sleep, wha' I foond. A death draught, i' was, tha' I smelt in tha' vial, Laird."

Robert stormed toward the armory. "I will kill who e'er dared do this."

"Then ye'll be killin' yer wife's maid!" the old woman cried out.

He skidded to a halt and whipped around to find her not more than a pace or two behind him. Narrowing his eyes at her he said, "Speak."

Clearly winded again by her exertion, she sucked in several breaths before answering. "I come ta yer chamber this day past ta check on our lady an' learn'f she required any more sleepin' draught, or any other herbs I migh' offer. 'Twas then tha' I saw th' maid tyin' th' string back 'round th' coverin' o'er th' top o' th' vial."

Robert's brows slammed together even further as he gave a short shake of his head. "And, because you saw her maid with this vial, you would accuse her of attempting to *murder* my wife?"

The healer straightened her shoulders and thrust her ample chest forward, lifting her nose in the air. Her chin quivered, but held belligerence as well, as she said, "Aye, tha', *an'* she knew weel the scent o' th' true tincture, fer she smelt it 'erself when first I offer'd i' ta yer lady, askin' me wha' herbs I put in it, sayin' she 'erself knew th' 'ealing arts." She paused, and Robert gave her a short nod, prompting her to continue. "As weel, she waited 'til I'd left th' chamber ta fetch me sewin' las' eve, ta try ta ferce th' tincture dow' yer wife's throat, an' all th' time, our lady pushin' her 'way an' refusin' th' use o' it. 'Twas only efter I opened th' door an' foond them thus, an' efter I tol' th' woman ta leave our lady be, tha' she heeded either o' us an' placed th' vial back on th' table. If *I* whiffed it, why then di' she no'?"

"Is it there now?" Robert asked in some alarm.

"Nay, Laird. 'Tis wi' me." She brought the draught out of the pouch at her waist and handed it to him.

Robert wrapped his hands around it and lifted the cloth that covered the top, then took in a small whiff. Aye, it had a much stronger scent than the sleeping draught. But, clearly, Morgana had not noticed, for she'd taken the stuff sometime this day past. He must find a way to question her without upsetting her. And was it truly possible that the kind, gentle servant he'd brought with them back from court, the servant who'd only barely veiled her chastisement of his bumbling actions with regard to Morgana, was in fact trying to kill her? Had it been a well-played ruse? Was she somehow connected to the perpetrators of that long-ago deed that left his wife's mother and father dead—left her mute? Had this woman, this maid, been the person to push Vika down the stairs as well? If the answer was aye, then he'd not make the same mistake in hesitating as he'd done this night past, nor as he'd done all those years watching his father near destroy this clan. Nay, he'd take action, as he should have done before. But, he'd have to find justice in some way other than the one planned.

Striding back to the table, he slumped down on the bench. "Nay, I cannot battle a woman, even a murderess." He looked up then and caught the healer's eye. "*If* she be a murderess." Turning his gaze to the hearth, he said, "This will take much more thought and planning." He stood abruptly and settled his hand on the aged woman's back, guiding her out. "Go back to my wife, and I will look for Modron. Until I learn whether the maid is truly the culprit, she will not be allowed near my wife." When the woman nodded and made to turn, he drew her back around with a hand on her shoulder. "And I am placing a guard outside the chamber as well, so make sure my wife is well covered, as he'll scout the interior prior to taking up his post."

"Aye, Laird."

"Only you and your daughters are allowed entrance there, until further notice. As for the food and drink." He shook his head. "You watch Cook prepare Morgana's meal, or you will prepare it yourself. As for the sleeping draught...if my wife has need of such, then only give her what you've kept safe in the vial in your pouch."

"Aye, Laird. I'll no' let harm come ta our lady."

He gave her a solemn nod. "Tell Morgana that I will be up to see her in a while."

"Aye, Laird."

Robert watched the aged woman turn and wobble

out the entrance to the hall before he took the back doorway out that led to the portion of the fortress where the weavers worked, stopping only long enough to send one of his most trusted soldiers, a cousin from his mother's clan, up to guard his wife's door, with strict orders that the man was only to allow Wife Deirdre, or one of her daughters, inside the chamber, and that at all costs, he was to keep Morgana well within his sights, should she depart it for any purpose. When the man questioned him about this cryptic command, Robert said only that there was a plot afoot, and that they must safeguard his wife.

That settled, he continued his trek to the weavers' chamber. At this time of day, he had little doubt, he'd find the woman there, o'erseeing the women as she had been doing along with his wife these past moons.

* * *

Gwynlyan knew instantly upon seeing Robert's grim visage as he came through the doorway of the weavers' chamber that something was terribly amiss. She rushed over to him, meeting him more than halfway and said low: "Is my lady ill? I must go to her," as she scurried past him and hurried out the door and into the courtyard.

She was no more than a pace or two from the weavers' chamber when she heard Robert call to her to halt with the unmistakable sound of booted feet pounding up behind her. Swinging around, she said, "My lady is well then?"

Her heartbeat accelerated and a ball of fear lodged like a river stone in her throat when his only reply was a tip of his head in the direction of the keep; the pressure of his great hand on her back between her shoulder blades, prodding her onward in a quick step ahead of him; and two harshly spoken words, "Great hall."

What has happened to my daughter! Gwynlyan wanted to screech the words at the man, beat her fists against his broad chest, force him to tell her what had happened, but she could not. She could not divulge her true identity. And acting in any manner other than the way she had thus far, would surely cause him to suspect she was not all she claimed. Nay, she must somehow contain her panic until she was certain that 'twas her daughter's demise he was set to speak with her about. She knew, she could *feel* the heat of his anger, and until she discovered whether 'twas directed at God, the Fates, herself, or someone else entirely, she must continue to keep her own counsel.

Several long, silent moments later, she was settled on a stool by the hearth in the great hall, craning her neck to keep her eyes solidly fixed on Robert's thunderous face as he stood, not more than a pace away from her, with his arms crossed over his chest, his feet spread, his nostrils flared, and his silver-gray eyes piercing through her skull.

All at once he whipped a familiar vial he'd evidently been holding all this time in front of her face and said, "I should watch you drink this down myself before the sheriff arrives. 'Twill save him the trouble of a public hanging."

Gwynlyan's head flinched back.

"Who are you? Why do you want my wife dead?"

Dead? With brows furrowed, her eyes still narrowed on the vial, she opened her mouth to speak, but could not form a single word on her tongue.

"Speak!"

"I—Bu—I—" She reached for the vial and he swung it out of reach. " 'Tis only a mild sleeping draught," she said, blinking. In a flash, her mind cleared and dread gripped her like cold steel talons around her throat. Without thinking, she leapt to her feet and grabbed again for the vial, saying in a loud voice, "Are you saying that 'tis *not?*"

"SIT!" her son-in-law bellowed.

'Twas, in a way she would ne'er be able to explain to herself or anyone else, the precise spark she needed to gain her composure. "Are you saying that 'tis not?" she repeated in a much more even tone.

Robert's eyes narrowed as they did a scan of her frame from head to foot. Clearly, he did not like what he saw, for his upper lip twitched as he tried unsuccessfully to control a sneer. When his gaze resettled once again on her countenance, he said, "You are better than most of the traveling players I've seen. But, you will not fool me again. The sheriff will be here soon, and you will be taken into his custody. You will hang on the morrow."

Fear ripped at Gwynlyan's insides, clutched her chest, closed her throat. Only after forcing down a swallow, did she manage to say just above a whisper, "I did not do this thing you accuse me of. I swear it."

"Why should I believe you?"

"Why should you doubt me?" she rejoined. "You

accuse me, yet you have given no proof, nor even a reason as to why you believe such."

He swung around and strode to the hearth, turned back to face her, positioned his body as before: Arms crossed, feet spread, and said, "Then I shall tell you…."

As Gwynlyan listened to the accusations Wife Deirdre had made against her, to her reasons for Robert's believing Gwynlyan the culprit in the crime, to Robert's own suspicion that Vika's tumble down the stairs had been a push by someone at this very keep, Gwynlyan realized two things: The first being that her worst fears had come to pass, and her daughter was now a target to Donnach and his minions; and the second being that if Gwynlyan held any hope of surviving long enough to warn Morgunn, to save her daughter's life, and to possibly gain aid from Robert in that pursuit as well, she must confess the truth of her identity to him without delay.

Just then, a trump sounded, indicating a visitor of some importance had arrived at the gate and Gwynlyan's heart leapt into her throat at the same time she leapt from her stool, saying in a rush of words, "I am Gwynlyan of *Aerariae secturae*. Morgana is my daughter. I love her more than my own life. You must believe me, and you must help me protect her before 'tis too late!"

* * *

Robert's jaw dropped open. Everything within him revolted, as he took in the grayed and ashen-faced woman before him. In the seconds before his mind began functioning fully again, he looked for any indication of the beauty that belonged to his wife. Where his wife was of middle height, this woman was petite, where Morgana owned eyes of the bluest hue, this woman's eyes were brown. This woman—this *Gwynlyan of Aerariae secturae*, if she was to be believed—would have been nearing her middle years when she went to childbed with Morgana. Yet—

The older woman took two steps toward him and, wringing her hands, said, "I beg you, send the sheriff away, and I will tell all. Morgana's father lives, too, and this"—she swept an arm in an arc—"danger she is in will not be eased with my death."

The decision was more a feeling than a thought and he gave her a sharp nod, saying, "Go through the back entrance. Return to the weavers' chamber and I will come for you later, after I have sent the sheriff on his way."

Before the woman was at the doorway, his steward arrived to tell him of the sheriff's arrival. Quickly, he set the man to follow the maid, realizing that she would no doubt try to meet with her husband, if she were truly Gwynlyan of *Aerariae secturae*, or with her accomplices, if she were truly a murderer, telling him that she was not to be detained unless she tried to go further than the boundary to the MacVie land.

***

Gwynlyan did not go to the weavers' chamber, as Robert bade her, instead scurrying with much stealth out the back gate and then onward to the place where she and Morgunn met in secret each fortnight. They'd decided 'twas too dangerous to meet more often, as, at any time, someone might grow suspicious and follow her. So, they'd decided on a code of sorts. A means of communicating when one of them had tidings, or needed to see the other. This time, she would leave under the stone the copper ring with the round ruby center he'd given her when they wed, which told him something of dire import had occurred and to meet her that night after the chimes of midnight.

She'd already determined, in the early hours of the morn after their daughter lost her babe, to signal for him to meet her this eve, but she'd planned to do it later in the day, during the time that all were taking their evening meal, when there was little likelihood of discovery. But now, worried that if she waited, she might not get another chance to at least put Morgunn on guard that all was not right here, and knowing with certainty that her daughter was once again being targeted for murder by her uncle and his cohorts, and also feeling even more pressure to reassure herself of Morgunn's continued safety, she would not delay.

Morgunn had told her that he usually traveled past this place each day nearing compline on his way back from the goatherd's hut some five miles away, where he'd gotten work.

Her heart thudded against her rib cage when she thought of Morgunn's reaction to her breaking her vow—breaking her silence—and telling Robert of Morgunn's existence as well. But what else could she have done? If she had not revealed her relation to Morgana, she would, even now, be on her way to the sheriff's gaol, where she'd eat her last portion of bread, swallow her last drink of water before the dawn broke, and the noose tightened around her throat, cutting off her breath, ending her life, taking away any chance she had of saving her daughter's life, and curtailing all chance of e'er obtaining for herself, and her family, that thing she wanted most: Justice.

* * *

Hours later, after sending the sheriff off, Robert spoke with Wife Deirdre, not telling her what he'd learned, but telling her that, after questioning Modron, he was convinced she was not the one who'd filled the vial with the death draught, and that Wife Deirdre was to keep his counsel, speak to no one but himself about the incident until he'd routed the evildoer, else they might flee. Robert then made his way back to the weavers' chamber to gain the answers he needed from this maid, this professed mother, of his wife. He'd still not been up to his bedchamber to see Morgana. Even if time had allowed, which it had not, he was not yet prepared to see the lingering heartache in her eyes, to be the brave and sturdy one while inside himself, he felt weak and impotent. Nor was he yet prepared to do as he must, and keep this new malignance in their midst a secret until she had recovered more from the devastation of the previous night.

With effort, he turned his thoughts back to the task at hand. His steward had relayed to him that the maid had not gone directly to where the weavers did their work, but, instead, had fled to the dammed portion of the burn and left something under a stone—he knew not what—then had scurried back to the keep, and gone to o'ersee the weaving, where she'd been e'er since.

He shook his head. Aye, and alas. Tho' 'twas not settled as fact in his mind, still, and yet, he did not feel that the woman had done the deed she'd been accused of, and if she was who she claimed to be—and if 'twas truth that Morgana's father had survived that attack as well—then the attempt on his wife's life, and on Vika's, made much more sense to him.

Except.

'Twas clear the maid had left a directive for someone there at the burn. But for whom? An accomplice in this death plot? Or, mayhap, this Morgunn, this supposed-dead, long-lost father of his wife's? Either way, he'd know by dawn. And justice would be swift, if he found that the woman had lied to him.

However, he realized now, if 'twere the case that she had lied, 'twas a boon he'd not sent her along with the sheriff earlier, for he doubted not that the other player in this scheme was a man, and thus, that man would not be given over to the sheriff. Nay, he'd instead feel the sharp edge, the piercing weight through his gut, of Robert's steel.

* * *

'Twas nearing the chimes of midnight when Robert followed Gwynlyan at a slow distance on her trek to the burn to meet with Morgunn.

Upon hearing the full of her tale earlier in the day, he'd at last been convinced—almost—that she told the truth. After all these moons, all his queries into Morgana's past, he'd finally gotten the answers he'd sought. At least, as many as Gwynlyan herself knew, or had surmised o'er the years. The fact that Donnach Cambel was behind this deadly scheme sent a rush of blood lust through his veins. For, if Gwynlyan's tale proved true—and the final proof would be Morgunn Cambel—the *accident* in the old keep involving Vika was, in fact, a botched first attempt on his wife's life, not Donnach's daughter's.

So, now, the plan was set: Gwynlyan, who had left her wedding ring under the stone earlier in the day to give Morgunn the cue that something was amiss, that he should wait for her there tonight, would leave the keep first, and Robert would follow not long after. This would give her time—not a lot—to tell Morgunn all that had happened, and that he was now about to meet his son-in-law, at which point, Robert would then show himself.

* * *

Morgunn tore off a chunk of day-old bread with his teeth and began to chew before he took a long pull on the skin of ale he'd purchased from the alewife on his way through the small village that lay between this holding and the Norman's, where the herder's plot was located and the goats Morgunn helped to tend grazed. 'Twas his first meal since noontime, and his insides yawned with hunger, even at the same time they twisted with dread.

Why had she summoned him?

Something dire was in the offing, his gut told him, tho' he sent a silent prayer of thanks to God that his wife was not whisked away from him again, or worse, dead. *But what of Morgana?*

Pressing the back of his hand to his mouth as he took the last chew before swallowing it down, he looked up through the canopy of trees, and into the night sky. The moon was high in the heavens, and he knew the time for their meeting was drawing nigh.

Just then, he heard the snap of a twig, the whip of a leaved branch as it shot back in place, and suddenly, she was there, standing before him, and even through the dim of night, the silvered sheen of starlight, he could see that her bright amber hair was still dulled with ash, her pale, pink skin, still dusted with the stuff as well, and her frame, that he knew from his unobserved viewing of her midnight bath in the burn was more woolen padding than female form, still well-concealed. Aye, he'd seen the scars as well, and knew what they meant, who had given them her, and the thought of those marks ne'er ceased to buttress e'er more his determination to destroy those that had perpetrated these vile deeds upon his family. The corners of her lush mouth tipped in a shy smile and his heart fluttered. *Someday....* Someday, he would at last melt her reserve and they would once again lay together as man and wife. *Someday....*

Without realizing he was doing it, he rose to his feet, facing her fully, and extended his hand.

She took the last two steps to him and settled her palm o'er his, which he immediately secured in his grasp with the curl of his long fingers around her own as he pulled her into his embrace, opening his mouth o'er hers and tugging her head back with his free hand gripping her plaited hair.

She remained rigid in his arms and, squealing low in her throat, pushed against his chest until he released his hold. Immediately, she sent a furtive look behind her, into the darkness of the night forest, and said, "Nay, no more of that." Swinging her gaze back to his, she urged him further into the light near the water's edge. "I only have a moment or two to tell you all."

He gave a sharp nod of his head, indicating both acquiescence and understanding, and then waited in silence for her next words.

* * *

When Gwynlyan moved the man into the moonlight, Robert bit back a gasp. *Morgana's looks are his.* Even with the knowledge that he would be meeting her father this night, it had still not prepared him for the strength of the resemblance between the two. Any kernel of doubt he'd yet harbored as to whether Gwynlyan was actually leading him to a foe, had now been completely destroyed as well. And, he admitted also, that even were the resemblance not so apparent, he'd already come to the same conclusion regarding the identity of this man, upon witnessing the strong passion he held for Morgana's mother. It made Robert e'er more curious to see the woman as she truly looked, completely undisguised.

He waited another moment longer, waited until the two heads, now bent together in murmured speech, lifted once more, waited even one short moment longer for Gwynlyan to turn her gaze in his direction, tho' he had little doubt that she could see him where he stood in this lightless nook of shrub and wood, before he at last stepped from the shroud of darkness and into the patch of starlight in front of him.

It boded well, Robert thought in that instant, that when Morgunn saw the unknown intruder, his arm shot around Gwynlyan's waist, sending her behind his large frame. However, with his next words, it also became clear that Robert had not waited long enough to show himself.

"—Who goes there?" Morgunn said, sliding his dirk from his belt.

"—Nay! 'Tis Robert!" Gwynlyan said.

"—I am Robert MacVie, Morgana's husband." The last hung in the air between them, weighted in the moment, pregnant with portent.

Finally, the spell of stunned silence was broken by Morgunn when he said to Gwynlyan, tho' his sharp gaze remained fully upon Robert, "You were not so unwitting of his following you here, I trow, my love. Why is that? Did you break your oath to me, then?"

Robert didn't give Gwynlyan time to answer him, instead saying, "The small hours are upon us. Our time to plan is short. Let us leave the whys and wherefores for later. For now, know only this: Morgana's life is in peril, and, with the exception of my trusted healer, and the men attempting the deed, we three are the only ones who know it and can aid her."

Gwynlyan gripped Morgunn's shoulder, lifted up on her toes and said close to his ear, tho' loudly enough for Robert to ken her words, "They slipped a death draught to our lass. 'Tis why she lost her babe, I'm sure, and what I would have told you next, except...."

Morgunn's eyes narrowed on Robert and he gave her a curt nod. "Aye, except my son-in-law has more brawn than stealth."

If 'twere anyone else other than his wife's father who uttered such a challenge, Robert would have thrashed him where he stood. Instead, he sucked his cheeks between his teeth and kept silent. He did position himself in his best warrior stance, however, crossing his arms over his chest, spreading his feet apart and glaring back at him.

Morgunn stepped toward him and it didn't pass Robert's notice that he had a swagger in his step as he did so. "You've lost too much of your Highland instincts, I trow. You've been too long at court, playing at war, instead of living it."

"Not so long I couldn't vanquish an old man like you, if I wanted."

"Enough!"

Both men whipped their gazes to Gwynlyan. She moved from around Morgunn and stood between the two. "We've plans to make, and not more than an hour's time to do it." She took hold of her husband's arm and pressed him to move closer to Robert, then motioned for them both to follow her to a place under a tree where they could all sit.

Within that hour, and by the next dawn, their plans were set in motion.

PART FOUR

―――――✥―――――

A Belief Erroneous

"*L*ove looks not with the eyes, but with the mind,
And therefore is winged Cupid painted blind.*"*

A Midsummer Night's Dream (Act I, Scene i)

"*F*or *love is blind and may noght se*
Forthi may no certeinete
Be set upon his jugement"

Confessio Amantis
(Incipit Liber Primus, 1.47 – 1.49)

CHAPTER 14

ROBERT CREPT INTO his bedchamber, the bedchamber he'd abandoned one night past to give Morgana the solitude she needed to rest and regain her strength, and made short, silent work of doffing his clothes before sliding into bed beside his sleeping wife.

Within mere moments, the clean, womanly scent of fresh flowers and sunshine invaded his nostrils, intoxicated his mind, swept across his heart, and made his loins tense with need. She'd bathed and washed her hair, and every muscle in his body screamed for him to pull her to him, wrap her silken limbs around his hard, scarred frame, and take her, fill her up with his seed, give her another son to grow there in her womb.

Yet, he could not.

Fear screeched through his middle, making his pulse pound.

He'd nearly lost her.

And, it had only been two days.

And he could not have her heavy with his child again while the uncle and his minions plotted against them.

He'd not risk it.

Rolling to his side, he stuffed a pillow behind his back as barrier between him and the temptation resting next to him. If 'twere not for the other danger to Morgana, for which he must keep her in his sights, he'd quit the chamber, find his rest in another part of the keep.

Closing his eyes and taking in long, slow breaths, Robert at last began to drift into a restless sleep.

* * *

Morgana bit down hard on her trembling lip. Tears trickled from the corner of her eyes and she squeezed her lids shut, pushing the moisture free, then surreptitiously used the edge of the linen sheet to dry her cheeks.

He'd not even touched her. Not a peck on the cheek, not a gentle brush of the fingertips to her hair, not a stroke of the palm o'er her hip. Naught. And what new agony was this that he was so repulsed by her that he had to place a barrier between them to sleep?

Did he hate her now? Mean to punish her? She hadn't thought so earlier, but now she wondered if 'twas truth. Was that why she'd been hurried back to their bedchamber earlier in the day, prisoned here with a stoic, stern-faced guard at her door, and refused the request to have Modron brought in to her, to comfort her, to give her more of the words of solace she craved, more answers to the questions she still had regarding

Modron's loss of her own unborn babes?

She heard more than felt the slide of his foot against the linen sheet and it snatched her breath as hope surged. But when naught more than a bleak quiet enshrouded their marriage bed once more, with a valley of cold air between them too wide to cross, Morgana covered her face with both hands and silently sobbed into her pillow.

Aye, it must be so. For, he'd not visited her all day. Not once. Not since she'd told him she'd lost his son, and he'd offered to give her another to replace him.

Aye, 'twas truth, that at the time he'd proposed the notion, she'd been hurt by the seeming callousness of his response to the loss of their babe. But now, after hours of doing naught but thinking about that short time during and after the grievous blow they'd taken, she knew that 'twas merely Robert's own manly need to fix what was wrong or broken that made him proffer such.

And even tho' she had little to no desire to make another babe with him this soon after the loss of the other—assuming she could even carry one to childbed without her body expelling it again much too soon, the thought of which brought on a new terror and turmoil in her chest—still she craved his arms about her, the comfort of his muscular chest beneath her cheek, the warmth of his skin, the bristle of his unshaven chin upon her forehead.

Where had he been so late into the night? *With Vika?* The thought came unbidden, but once it came, it took hold of her imagination like a hungry wolf to the neck of its prey and would not let go. She knew—she'd heard—that Vika was feeling well enough again to leave her chamber and take some air out in the garden, that she'd even come down to break her fast this very morn. *Had Robert joined her?* A spike of jealousy pierced her heart, followed by anger, followed by hurt.

Morgana bit down hard on the side of her finger. Had Vika been told that Morgana had lost Robert's babe? Tho' she loved her cousin dearly for all the care, the guidance, the liberal acceptance she'd given her at court—and even for the gift of Robert she'd given her—Morgana still could not stem the worry that, now that Vika was heavy with Robert's babe, *and now that Morgana was not*, Vika would begin to see the benefit of a wedded alliance with the man. Especially, as he no longer needed her fortune for his clan.

And there was no doubt—*no doubt*—that Robert and Vika shared a passion for the other. Mayhap, even stronger than that which, until by the proof of this long day, and this long lonely night, Morgana and Robert had shared.

In that moment, Morgana made a decision: From this day forth, she would watch very closely the two of them. She would watch the two of them, and she would also test Robert's desire for her, his wife. *And if my fears prove right?* She stifled a moan. She would fight for him, then! Surely, what they'd shared before...before...they would find again! And, she would remind him of just that, with her body, and with her loving care of him. *But what if the madness returns? What if this thing that is wrong with you also means you cannot bear his bairns? What then?*

Will you force him to foreswear the begetting of legitimate sons? Will you pay no heed to his begetting of bastard sons with another, even if he does return to bedding you, even if he does not? She recalled the night of her wedding, recalled her thoughts, recalled her promise to herself that she would meekly allow Robert's faithlessness to her, meekly allow his bedding another, but that was before, before the bond had grown too strong to break so easily. Morgana buried her face in the pillow, clenching her fist around the cushioned edge and silently sobbed. The words of Ma dame Aliénor floated through her mind: *"Love is not jealous, or proud, Morgana, 'tis generous and kind."*

Rolling onto her back and resting her hands, one atop of the other, under her breasts, she took in a ragged breath. Aye, love was generous, love was kind. And she loved Robert. She would not covet what she could not have. So, if her fears were proved right, if Robert spurned her, but desired the company and attentions of her cousin, Vika, then she would try—she *would!*—to not stand in the way of their happiness, nor their ability to wed before Vika's babe was born, thus making it a legitimate bairn to the Laird of the MacVie clan.

With that troubling, yet noble resolution made, Morgana swept in a deep, calming breath, allowed her swollen lids to droop o'er her stinging eyes, and, on the slow exhale, drifted into an uneasy slumber tinged with heartache.

* * *

"Pater noster, qui es in caelis..."

Robert jerked awake, eyes wide, but unfocused on

the pitch dark of night surrounding him.

"*...Sanctificetur nomen tuum—*"

He rolled over and faced his wife, her shadowy form upright, and listened to the lovely sounds of her singing. It both enchanted and worried him.

"*Et ne nos inducas*—Mama! Mama!" Her voice was high, that of a bairn. She extended her hand in the darkness.

Robert sprung up and reached for her, but she lurched away.

"Do not hurt her!" She covered her face with her hands. "Nay!"

Robert would not, could not, let her be. He wrapped his arms around her and she surprised him when, instead of further combat, she curled into his body, as a bairn would, with her damp cheek against his chest.

"Papa, where did you go? You must save Mama from that evil man!" She pressed her nose into the center of his chest and dug her nails into his forearm. "He hurt her, Papa! He made her lip bleed and he—he got on top of her! She made me cover my eyes and...," Morgana yawned, and the next word Robert barely caught, "...sing...." His wife went limp in his embrace and after a moment, he gently settled her head on the pillow once more.

'Twas several more hours, not long before dawn, that Robert's mind at last quieted and he was able to again close his eyes and get a short bit more sleep.

* * *

Later that morn, Morgana woke to find Robert sitting on the edge of the bed beside her, staring down at her with drawn brows and silver-grey eyes that had lost their sheen. Her pulse sped as she rolled to her back and gazed up at him, waiting for what e'er he might impart. For, 'twas evident that something of grave import weighed heavy on his mind.

"You slept well?" he said at last.

She nodded. *Why does he grip his hands? Can he not bear to touch me?*

"You sang in your sleep again."

Something close to panic rose in her breast, nearly choking her. She gave a jerky nod.

"Morgana—" He reached out a hand as if he would take hers, then evidently thought better of it, for instead, it descended to grip his other one once again. She watched his eyes move o'er her face in the long pause that followed before he at last continued, saying, "Morgana, you spoke. This night past, you spoke. You spoke, I believe, about what happened to you, to your mother and father that day."

Morgana's gorge shot up into her throat and she pushed him away, scrambled from the bed, barely made it to the bowl on the washstand before the bile in her empty stomach spewed forth. When she lifted up again, she was startled to find Robert directly behind her, so close her backside pressed into his groin, her shoulders grazed his warm chest. His heavily muscled forearm came into her peripheral view and a dry towel gently swiped across her mouth and cheeks, while his other hand poured some water into the pewter cup on the stand. 'Twas the closest to a comforting embrace she'd received from him since the night she lost their babe.

After she rinsed the sour taste from her mouth, after she'd swallowed down a small portion of the water to ease the sting in her throat, and after he'd walked with her back to the bed and settled her there once more, he said, "So, you do recall what happened that day?"

The same vague images that had attempted to force themselves into her mind that first day of Vika's arrival tried to lodge there again, but the clawing dread the images caused made her gasp for air, and they quickly fled again.

Somewhere on the edge of her consciousness, she knew Robert had leapt to his feet, had called her name, had taken hold of her shoulders, but all she could do was paw at her throat, at her gaping mouth, in an attempt to draw in a breath. Hot tears stung her cheeks, but 'twas not until his strong arm braced her back, until a cool cloth touched her forehead and face that the inner turmoil calmed and she was once again able to suck air into her lungs.

Sometime in the midst of the panic, Robert had poured a bit of wine into a cup for her. Clearly, he'd been frantic, for the red color stained the front of his tunic and dripped off the back of his hand as he gave it to her, saying, "Drink. 'Twill calm you."

The wine did calm her and after a moment she placed the empty cup on the table next to the bed. As she did so, he said, "I had hoped, mayhap, that the return of your voice this night past, the memory of what happened, was some proof that you were healing, but I see now, that 'twas not the case. We'll not speak of it again." He reached out and patted her hand rather awkwardly and Morgana once again worried that he'd ne'er touch her with passion or tender regard again. *He says it not, but he thinks it.* She was more a bane than a boon to him, with her strange spells of memory or madness, and no voice.

He rose from the bed and walked over to gaze out the window with his hands clasped behind his back. He stood there, silent, for such long moments, that Morgana began to wonder if he was through speaking with her and was now making mental plans for the remainder of his day.

After another fretful moment, she began to rise, thinking she'd wash and dress, break her fast. What e'er she did, however, 'twould not include ruminating more on what Robert had revealed to her earlier. If she was to stay in control of her mind, of her senses, and not be a burden to her husband, she had to keep those visions well at bay.

She had only taken a step or two toward the washstand when Robert turned to her and said, "You need your rest, Morgana. I'll have someone bring fresh water for you to bathe, as well as something to break your fast. Get back in bed."

She truly did not want to do so, but she could not bring herself to defy her husband either, so, like the good convent-bred lass she was, she quietly climbed back onto the mattress and tucked the linen sheet and blanket around her.

She thought surely he'd leave her now, but instead he came and sat on the edge of the bed next to her once more.

He took her hand and stared down at it for a long moment, then lifted his gaze to her face. He looked at her so long without saying anything that if Morgana had had the ability, she would have begun to speak in nervous chatter just to break the heavy silence between them.

Finally, he said, "Other than this night past, you've rested well? Had no troubles sleeping?"

Her brows drew together in confusion, but she shook her head in agreement.

"But you did have some trouble, as I recall, two nights past."

The memory of how cheerfully hopeful her world had been that night, with their babe still snug in her womb, flashed in her mind, but in the next second, anguish pierced her heart and was released through her tear ducts. Swallowing past the lump in her throat, she managed to nod her head.

Robert looked away. After a moment, he cleared his throat and said, "I believe, that night, you used a bit of the sleeping draught given you?"

Her brows drew together, but she nodded. *Why is he asking me this?* She sat up, tucking the pillow behind her back, but the doom settled in her breast, for she feared she knew.

"And, I believe, 'twas that next day that you were not feeling well."

She couldn't breathe. *He blames me! He thinks I killed our babe. Mayhap I did! Mayhap I did! I should not have taken the draught!* She twisted her fists into the sheet. The room spun.

"Morgana!" he said, grasping her forearms, "You've lost all color."

He fled to the washstand and brought back a cup of cool water, which he forced her to drink, tho' it choked her. She began to cough and rolled to her side, facing away from him. She felt the warmth of his hand hover o'er her arm, but not alight upon it, before it fell away again.

"I'll call for Wife Deirdre. My pardon. I-I should not have bothered you with such foolish talk." He pressed his lips to her arm and murmured against it. "Rest. You must rest. My pardon." Then he left her, went out the door, and in a few long moments, Wife Deirdre took his place on the edge of the bed beside her.

God, why do you do this to me? Am I not to be allowed even a small portion of joy? She turned her face into the pillow and wept.

* * *

Robert leaned into the table top in the great hall, bent at the waist, and put his weight on his knuckles. He was still finding it hard to take in a good breath. He'd held such hope this morn that he'd at last hear his wife speak, that she'd somehow been healed, and could begin to heal more quickly from the loss of their babe as well. But, 'twas e'er more clear now than it had been before that she was not near to that place yet. Furthermore, there were still unanswered questions, and so he'd tried to garner some further clue that she might be able to impart, even in her innocence, even in her ignorance of all that had been planned against her.

Squeezing his eyes shut and gritting his teeth, he

growled low in his throat. He should not have mentioned the sleeping draught to her, he could see that now. It only made her feel worse about their loss. Why had he not kenned before he opened his gob that 'twould seem to her that he was blaming her for taking the sleeping draught?

But, the only way he could see to convince her otherwise, was to reveal the death plot to her, and truly, he did not see that she was strong enough in mind to deal with the fright 'twould cause her. Not to mention, the blow of learning that her mother and father still lived. What if her mind could not take such a shock, even if the revelation was a pleasant one? Her state was fragile, and he must not forget again. 'Twas best to protect her, keep her safe and quiet, and allow her the rest she needed.

* * *

Morgunn stood beside the tinker's cart he'd gotten off the gnarled man in the next shire using the coin Robert had given him, and gladly took the ladle of water proffered by the old cook. As he drank most of it down, he watched her pick through his store of wares, listening only vaguely to her carping tongue as she curled a lip at one, put it aside, shook her head at another, put it aside, then rattled and knocked her knuckles against another, before turning to him with a nod and saying, "Ah'll take this wun. Coom wit' me, and ah'll fayd and ply yow wit' some of me best ale while I git yow th' pan tha' naids a new 'andle."

"I'll be grateful fer a place ta lay m' head, as well," he said, turning his cap in his hand and keeping his head bent as he walked a bit behind her, "if ya c'n find i' in yer heart, Cook."

"Aye, thar's plentee of ruum for yow and yowr cart in th' stables, if yow don' moind a bed o' hay."

"Tha' be very generous, Cook. M'thanks."

As he, his wife, and his son-in-law had decided in the small hours of the night before, he had breached the holding by disguising himself as a traveling mender and seller of tin pots and pans, using this vantage as a means of wandering the interior of the fortress, specifically looking for Donnach's accomplices, since Gwynlyan had ne'er been exposed to all of Donnach's fighting men, specifically the mercenary soldiers he kept in his service, in the years prior to the ambush.

Over the last moons, he'd allowed his beard to grow, tho' he'd continued to keep his hair cropped short. However, with this new disguise, it now held snarls and knots, and was dusted with ash as well. The tattered clothes he wore, and the patch o'er his left eye were left for him at the burn by Gwynlyan.

It had taken him near to all of the day to travel to the next shire, make the purchase, and travel back here before sunset, but he'd managed it—barely—and was now well entrenched behind the fortress walls, and well placed as well to scout the premises for the whoresons behind the death plot on his family.

* * *

Morgana pushed herself up to a sitting position in bed, using her knuckles to lift and reposition herself so that the pillows pressed comfortably into the small of her back, and watched with pounding pulse Robert before the fire, shed first his boots, then his tunic and shirt, then his braies and hose.

In the darkened chamber, the flames of the hearthfire licked orange and gold light o'er his skin, bronzing his well-thewn naked form, like a statue of some ancient god, and Morgana's lungs seized. Lord, she did not want to give him up. *Please. Please love me. Forgive me.*

Her gaze ne'er left him as he came to his side of the bed, flipped back the covering, lay down, propped himself on an elbow, curled his large, calloused hand around the back of her head, pressed it forward, placed a chaste, indifferent kiss on her forehead, said "G'night," rolled over with his back to her, *again*, punched the pillow a few times, then lay his head upon it and, she assumed, went directly to sleep.

Even tho' the healer had said she should wait at least another sennight more to do so, Morgana, tho' her heart was still torn in two, felt that her body was well enough to take him into her. If he still wanted her. And that, she was determined to discover this very night. So, instead of curling on her side and weeping out her sorrow as she'd done the last two nights, Morgana pressed her naked form to his, kissed his shoulder, stroked her hand o'er his chest, down his taught abdomen, lightly ran her nails through the springy hair of his groin. She felt his muscles tense, heard him rasp in a breath, and knew that he was fully awake to her brazen caresses. Hope and fear surged inside her, for 'twas more she needed from him than his body's initial response. She needed his heart, his mind, as well. Bold with purpose and need, she brushed her palm o'er his raging manhood and he flung her hand away as if burned.

If that weren't torment enough—and answer, as well—he heaved himself from their bed, stood glaring at her with fists clenched at his sides, tendons drawn along his arms and chest. But only long enough to suck two heaving breaths into his lungs before he stormed over to his clothing, grabbed them up, and strode out the door.

Where had he gone? Would he relieve his desire with another? With Vika?

* * *

Early the next morn, Vika rushed to catch up to Robert, for, she was determined, she would release him this very day from the lie she'd given. Grímr was right, and keeping it a secret, especially after Robert and Morgana's loss, seemed more cruel now, than it had at the time she'd originally given it.

Oh, aye, 'twould possibly be yet another sad blow for him to find he'd not sired her babe, but it seemed crueler still to have him find out later, after he'd had even more time to plan for its arrival, for its life.

So, she'd not wait a moment longer to release him from his sworn duties to her and her babe. She had little doubt that he'd draw the truth of its true begetter from her as well, but as Grímr had yet again found her trace, discovered her here, and as he'd only force her to comply with her promise to reveal the truth upon his return of the fact that 'twas his seed, and not Robert's which had taken root in her, she had decided she'd rather it be without Grímr's arrogant, intrusive presence hovering o'er her as she did so.

She was near enough now to call his name where he might hear it, and she did so. When he stopped and turned, gave her a quizzical look, but waited, she quickened her step and held out her hand to him. As he took hold of it, she said, "Robert, I could not let another day pass without telling you how sorrowful I am for the loss you and my poor cousin have borne."

The somewhat stiff smile he'd given her upon seeing her, froze in place as she watched a shadow cross his countenance, saw his eyes grow moist before he blinked and looked away.

"My thanks," he said finally and returned his gaze to hers.

Unable to look him in the eye, she dropped her own gaze to the center of his chest. "I...I must tell you something...." *'Twill no doubt be a relief to learn....* Nay. *'Tis, mayhap, a balm to your....* Nay. *I hope you will not....* Nay. Best not to relinquish power. *You are not....* Aye. That would do. Tho' twas a bit too brief, 'twas also to the point. She opened her mouth, but when she noted the dark circles under his eyes, the lines of worry around his eye and mouth, the words lodged in her throat. Nay, she could not do it.

* * *

After a restless, lonely night spent in worry, rather than sleep, Morgana stood by her window and gazed down at the courtyard below.

"Ye et no' one whit o' th' meat yer husban' had sen' oop jes' fer ye this morn, m'lady," Wife Deirdre chastened in a gentle, but firm tone from somewhere behind her. "D'ye 'ave a bad stomach agin?

Morgana glanced around and, finding Wife Deirdre's worried gaze leveled on her, shook her head and forced a small smile on her lips before turning back to her musings, back to looking for any sign of Robert from the window where she stood.

After a moment, Wife Deirdre, evidently deciding that she'd not have success with any further urging on her part in getting Morgana to eat more, nodded, gave a brief sigh, picked up the tray, and took it back down to the kitchens, leaving Morgana gratefully alone with her thoughts.

Finally, after what seemed to the fretting and despondent Morgana to be much too long a time, she at last saw Robert crossing the courtyard toward the outer bailey, where the work was still proceeding on the furbishing. With a sigh, and a piercing spike of joy in her breast, she lifted her palm to the pane and leaned against it, enjoying the sight of him: The long, purposeful strides; the powerful, broad shoulders; the large, calloused hands, the proud jut of his strong jaw. *Robert.* Her heart pined for him so. *If only....* Again, and for at least the hundredth time since she'd lost her babe, she pressed her palm to her barren belly and a soft whimper escaped her throat. She didn't hear it, however, for her eyes were blurred with tears and her tortured thoughts were on naught else but the remembered pain of his rejection the night before.

Until she saw Vika hurrying toward him. Then Morgana's tears dried. Then the hand on the pane curled into a fist. Then the pining in her heart turned to jealousy and ire as she watched Robert stop, turn toward her cousin, furrow his brow at her, then lift one side of his mouth in a half-smile, nod, and take the hand she held out to him. Morgana might have been able to convince herself that 'twas only Vika, not Robert as well, who played and teased, until she saw Robert lift and hold Vika's other hand as well.

Was it to her he went this night past?

Morgana dropped her face into her hands.

I hate her!

She brought her head up, blinked the tears away.

Nay. To hate was a sin. Besides, 'twould do only harm, and little good, if 'twas Vika he found comfort with, if 'twas Vika he wanted, if 'twas Vika who would bear his babe. It seemed wrong, somehow, for Morgana to keep them apart. For, she loved Robert with all her being, yet if he did not, or could not return that love—and he had yet to e'er say the words to her, tho' she had thought, had hoped, before, when she still carried his babe, that he might—then she would do what she must so that Robert would find the joy and content he deserved. After all, was not that what Ma dame Aliénor would tell her was the most right, the most generous, the most holy thing to do?

But weren't the vows you spoke a holy covenant? Aye, they were! *And, I want to be his wife!*

With a loud sniffle, she roughly scrubbed the damp from her cheeks, and walked to the stand that held the basin, poured water into it from the ewer, then, after swirling the cloth in its cool, liquid depths for a moment, lifted it to her heated cheeks and puffy eyes. Fighting back another bout of tears, she squeezed her lids shut and told herself she'd go to the chapel and pray for guidance.

* * *

"Aye?" Robert prompted Vika, and lifted her other hand in his, giving both a squeeze. "Have you a memory of what preceded your fall, at last?"

With relief at the less perilous subject he'd offered up to her, she pulled from his grasp, turned and began to walk in the direction he'd been going before she'd come upon him several moments earlier. As he fell in line beside her, she said, "Aye. Tho', 'tis not a memory, 'tis more of a feeling. A feeling that mayhap someone was on the landing, that they caused me to fall. E-e-except, who would do such?" She shook her head. "Nay, each time I feel that rising dread again when I think of those moments, and feel that *feeling* that someone might have been there, I always come back to the fact that I cannot fathom *who* it might have been."

" 'Twas—" Robert looked as if he wanted to tell her something, but the glimmer, the fleet moment passed, as he continued, "—Aye, well, 'tis no doubt only part of the recalled panic at the moment of your tumble that brings forth the other."

* * *

'Twas nearing mid-morn by the time Morgana at last saw Wife Deirdre's daughter nod her head in slumber. Her hands worked another stitch before they, too, settled to rest in the older woman's lap. Still, Morgana remained motionless, holding her breath, until at last she heard the first snore that signified a deeper sleep. Then, as quietly as she was able, she slipped from the bed, took one of her work gowns from its peg, and slipped it on o'er her head, not bothering to tie its side lacing until after she'd opened the door a crack, peeked out, and asked with broad hand movements her husband's cousin to fetch a chest from the next room and bring it in to her. While he was occupied with that task, she slipped from the chamber and hurried down the stairs, through the door, across the open covered walk that connected the kitchens and larder to the main keep, and toward the largest of the several storage chambers, with the intent to find Modron, whom she'd not as yet had more than a few words with since the night Morgana's babe had flushed from her womb.

On this day, Morgana knew, Modron would be busy with the larderers, o'erseeing and answering queries regarding the household's plans and needs, as Morgana herself should be doing as well, tho' she had no heart for the duty. But she would attempt it this day, with Modron's help, and mayhap, as they worked together, Morgana could get some few advices from her, some few words that would make the ache in her heart lessen by some small degree.

When she stepped into the larder through its outside entry, she stumbled to a halt upon finding Vika in full command of the proceedings, with no Modron in sight, and with all of Robert's larderers fetching and carrying and scurrying about in obvious awe and deference to Vika's regal dictates. Morgana had ne'er yet found her ease with such duties and 'twas clear that her cousin did such with little effort and with much relish. In fact, to Morgana's eye, the larderers looked much-relieved to have a lady of birth whom they could easily comprehend at their helm. Morgana took a step back, ready to exit the chamber to continue her search for Modron, when her maid appeared through the entry that led from the kitchens, beaming a smile in Vika's direction and holding out to her the book containing the lists and recipes of Robert's favorite foods and flavors that Morgana had meticulously begun keeping upon her arrival here as his new wife.

For a long, painful moment, Morgana remained in the shadowed doorway watching as Vika took hold of Morgana's book and began turning pages and giving further instruction to the women, before Morgana whirled and blindly fled.

* * *

"Why are you not abed, resting?" came a booming, all-too familiar male voice from behind her a few minutes later.

Morgana started, dropping the length of splintered wood and whirling around. She'd needed a bit of solace, a quiet moment to soothe her sore pride, her aching heart, and her feet had unwittingly led her here. To the place, less than a sennight past, that had vitalized her, had given her purpose, had been yet another way to show her love and commitment to Robert, to their marriage. Robert's silver-gray eyes were darkened to the hue of thunderclouds. Before.... *Before*, she would have given her answer with ease, soothing his ire with a soft smile, a gentle touch, using the gestures and mouth movements the two of them had established together o'er the past moons, but now, still suffering from the blow she'd taken earlier in the larder, and again, only moments past, when she'd come upon the destruction that was the remains of the old keep, she could not bring forth the effort it required, the courage it took.

He had known of her desire to use the old keep. Had he destroyed it in a fit of rage at her upon her loss of his son? Seeing the anger, the cold regard, he displayed so freely toward her now, she could do naught else but believe 'twas so.

When she made no move to reply, he took hold of her hand, not in the way of a lover, but in the way of a father leading a self-willed bairn, and pulled her back toward the entrance to the keep, saying, "My cousin told me you'd slipped past his and the nurse's care of you. You need your rest. Wife Deirdre has said that you are to stay abed for at least a fortnight."

A fortnight! Even tho' she had no knowledge of the usual and expected duration of recovery for a mother after the loss of her unborn babe, she found that length to be extreme. Why, she felt quite well enough to walk, to continue, if not all, then most of her duties as castelaine of this keep. If only she were able to have more time with her maid, Modron. Then she would have such questions answered from the woman who'd not only suffered the same loss herself, but aided her these past moons—and had become a dear and trusted friend in that time as well. And mayhap she'd know what Morgana might do to bring the warm regard back into Robert's gaze when he looked upon her. But, she was not able to do so, for Modron (and, from what she had spied earlier, Vika, too, it seemed) was being kept busy now with the duties that Morgana should be about herself.

And now, she wondered again if Robert meant to punish her for her weakness, for her use of the tincture that may have killed their babe. And, as well, if 'twas to do with Robert's not wanting her about. Not only so that he might more easily tryst with her cousin, but also, because, Morgana no doubt reminded him, when e'er he saw her, of his bad fortune in being forced to wed a woman incapable of speech, incapable of governing a household without the aid of her maid, and incapable— or so she daily feared—of keeping a babe in her womb to childbed. And, for certain, there was the other thing—the swoons and visions—which must plague him with thoughts that he'd wed a madwoman.

When compared, as he must be doing, with her cousin's hale constitution, her loveliness, and the MacVie babe she carried, 'twas no surprise that Morgana would be found lacking in his eye.

Which only underscored, yet again, the urgency she felt to do the right, the holy, thing; to step aside; to release Robert from his ill-fated vow. For, hadn't Guy de Burgh told her once, when she'd asked him how he was able to win so often at joust, that a good fighter knew when to retreat, and when to advance? 'Twas more and more evident to Morgana that this just might be a time for retreat.

* * *

That eve, Morgana, Vika and Robert were having a

quiet supper together when all at once Vika took in a sharp breath and her hand flew to her belly.

"What is it—is it the babe?" Robert asked, with a thread of gentleness overlaying the worry in his voice, Morgana could not help but notice.

The knife of desolation she'd had thrust in her heart at the tender scene, performed a vicious twist when Robert's hand went toward Vika's belly, stopped short of touching it as his eyes, filled with guilt, flicked to Morgana's face, before the hand was caught up by Vika and placed there herself. Robert did not pull it back, however. Instead, he smiled—chuckled low (a rare and beautiful thing that Morgana infinitely craved earning from him as well)—and said, "Aye, he's a strong, bold one, is he. A fine MacVie."

Vika blushed—a thing that was even more rare to see than Robert's smile—and a shadow of guilt traveled o'er her countenance as well, which only Morgana saw, as Robert's gaze was still fixed on his growing son. Was it some belated remorse at giving herself to Morgana's husband this night past? But then, as quickly as the look arrived, it flew away again, replaced once more by sparkling eyes and a teasing grin. "Aye. Strong and bold he is for certain, like his sire."

Morgana had gone to the chapel after the nooning meal and prayed for an hour for some answers as to what to do next. Should she continue to hope that she and Robert would overcome this crisis in their lives, would eventually find their way back to that loving bond they'd shared prior to Vika's arrival, prior to losing their babe, or, should she begin making arrangements to quit this place for good, quit her marriage to Robert, thus giving him and Vika the chance to build their own family through the legitimate connection of marriage? The answer had not come. But, now, seeing the tender exchange between her husband and her cousin, the jubilation he felt for his unborn babe, she was sure 'twas the sign she'd asked for, and had now received. 'Twas clear—as clear as a crystalline drop of melting snow off a pine needle at *Pasche*—that the bond Vika and Robert shared, their bairn, as well as the attraction that burned between them, must not be forced to remain secret, but be celebrated, rejoiced in, and allowed to flourish.

She would write to King William, explain all to him, and ask that he do what e'er he must to arrange things with the Bishop for an annulment of her marriage to Robert. If her muteness and strange fits of swooning were not enough to gain that end, then she'd admit to anything—even telling of Robert's and Vika's amorous affair, and the babe that was the result—if 'twould allow the breaking of the legal bond between them.

And then.... She straightened in her chair. And then, she would return to the nunnery. Aye, to the nunnery she would go. 'Twas where she belonged. The place where she could mend her broken heart, her tattered hopes. They loved her there—or, at least, loved her cooking—and if these fits of hers continued, the nuns would not abandon her. They would care for her, keep her safe. Aye, 'twas what she'd do.

With that settled in her mind, she broke off a portion of mutton and placed it on her tongue. The quivering in her belly rose up to settle in her jaw as she attempted to chew and, feeling the sting in her eyes, the urgent pressure in her throat to let out a wail, she choked down the half-chewed mass, rose to her feet and quietly excused herself with a brush of her hand to her forehead, indicating a sick head before she scurried toward the exit. Robert's brows had merely drawn together—in concern, or ire, she knew not which—before he'd given her a nod, then tucked back into his meal, with nary a word.

* * *

"My wife is still not strong enough to be told of all we've learned these past days," Robert told Gwynlyan the next day. "Only last eve, she fled from the table not a quarter-hour into our meal. She gestured something about a sick head, but I could see that she was about to begin another fit of tears o'er our lost son." He swung away from her, scrubbed his hands o'er his tired face and eyes, then looked, unseeing, out the window of the solar, where they'd agreed to meet once they were certain that Morgana was back in bed, resting. "I am of no use to her—to any woman—when she is in such a state. She turns from me, only shakes her head when I speak."

"She will revive, regain her vigor in time, worry not. But, aye, I cannot think of giving her yet another blow while she is in such a fragile state. We must continue to do this work in privy."

" 'Tis only in her sleep that she seems to turn to me for comfort, but, I confess, 'tis too great a temptation then for me to do more with her, and I cannot risk getting her with child again when there are men who would see her dead."

"Aye, you do the right thing, for restraint is the only true means of preventing such."

Aye, as Vika's childing has borne out. He almost spoke the thought aloud, but thought better of it. Best to keep to the problem at hand. Taking in a deep breath, Robert nodded and turned back to Gwynlyan, saying instead, "What of Vika? I've yet to give her any warning of the peril caused by her own father that we find ourselves in. 'Tis truth, I cannot decide whether 'tis best to send her back to her manor, or to keep her close, in case I am wrong in my reasoning, and 'twas no mistake made that day she was pushed down the stairs."

"I will tell her. Once she knows 'tis me, her aunt, she will believe me. And, nay, I do not think it wise to send her back to her manor. 'Twill be best to keep her close, especially as the knock she took to her pate still brings an ache in her head some days, tho' the pain has lessened, so says Wife Deirdre."

* * *

While his mother-in-law was above stairs speaking to Vika, Robert went in search of Morgunn. His father-in-law was standing just under the wooden eave that extended o'er the blacksmith's wide doorway, speaking to the blacksmith and his round, red-cheeked wife. 'Twas clear immediately that, while Morgunn spent this time in innocuous conversation, he had also placed himself in a prime position with which to be privy to much of the ebb and flow of all those that worked within the walls of the keep. Specifically, Robert noted, the men who completed the furbishing.

When Robert passed by the three, he gave them a brief nod and greeting, meeting Morgunn's eye and giving an almost imperceptible jerk of his head in the direction of the enclosed garden without e'er breaking stride. Hopefully, Morgunn caught the gesture and would follow shortly.

He was not in the garden long before his father-in-law slipped through the gate Robert had purposely left open, then quickly, and quietly, shut it behind him before sweeping the area with his gaze, moving with some speed to stand behind a large oak in one corner of the garden, and summoning Robert over to a bench that sat beneath its shaded boughs with a wave of his hand.

When Robert was settled on the bench, he heard Morgunn say, just above a whisper: "I've as yet not found any who have the look of those who attacked our caravan, tho' there are still some I have yet to gain a good view of."

Robert pounded his fist against his thigh, answering harshly, but in the same low tone, "I wish they would show themselves—fight like men, out in the open—but this sly, crooked, *cowardly* stealth is driving me to madness."

"Aye, but if we are to win this deathly game, we must use reason and cunning ourselves—and ne'er reveal our intent."

"Gwynlyan is with Vika now. She tells her of her father's plot."

There was a long, silent pause before Robert heard

his father-in-law speak again, saying, "Aye, 'tis no longer right to keep her from the truth of his deceit. And, knowing his nature, as I do now, I will also say this: She must not remain here while we attempt to bring his treachery to full light and justice, else he will have little scruple in putting an end to her life as well."

"Except...she still suffers from the injury to her head."

"She will suf—A maid arrives!"

Robert leapt to his feet and walked a few paces away, pretending interest in a large planting of some kind of white flowers with yellow centers. After a moment, he looked o'er his shoulder, saw that the maid had returned to the kitchens, and went back to settle on the bench again, saying, "Vika still suffers injuries from her fall. She cannot make a journey now."

"She must," Morgunn replied, "for she'll suffer more, should she be an inconvenience to her father's plot. Nay, she must go. And soon."

Robert let out a heavy sigh. "Aye, I will find a way." *But how?* He rose from the bench and stretched his arms over his head, emitting a loud yawn, as he took a last look around the garden, as if he were finished with some much-needed rest, and said, "I will meet you here again before the chimes of midnight. I hope by then you will have found the devil's disciple of Donnach's that 'bides within these walls." He strode out of the garden, knowing Morgunn would creep out later, when no eyes would see.

* * *

"My father? My father was behind...?" Knees

atremble, Vika reached blindly beside her for the stool and, finding it, settled upon it. "I-I believe it not.... I knew he was.... But, this...?" She gave a slow shake of her head. "Surely not...."

Her mind whirred. She barely noticed when Gwynlyan took the stool next to hers and covered Vika's hand with her own. "Your father wanted what he believed to be his birthright—*Aerariae secturae*—both the holding, and the copper mined there."

Vika blinked at her, trying to focus on her words, to see past the disguise to the woman she'd known long ago. Finally, she said, "All these years...believing you dead.... 'Tis more than I can comprehend."

Gwynlyan patted her hand. "I fear there's yet another blow I must give to you." She straightened, took in a deep breath then said, "Your tumble, my daughter's loss of her unborn babe, were in fact attempts on my daughter's life." Vika opened her mouth to protest, but before she could say a word, her aunt rose, stood gazing down at her with a stern expression upon her countenance, and continued, "Or, 'tis what we believe, as we can find no good reason for your father to want to end your life—unless.... You are sure he has no knowledge of the babe you carry?"

Her heart thudded against her breastbone. She had to swallow before she could answer, tho' there was little moisture that remained, as her mouth had grown parched. "I—" She blinked and looked around blindly, stood up without realizing she was doing so, took a step toward the hearth, twisted the onyx ring on her finger Grímr had given her on the day their daughter was born.

"I can see no way he could have learned of such. I told no one, not even my maid. Tho'...I suppose 'tis possible she might have guessed...." Vika shook her head, turned, and rested her gaze once more on Gwynlyan. "But even if she had, she would ne'er reveal such to my father, unless forced to do so. And, unless my father had some suspicion himself beforehand, he would ne'er visit the manor, nor think to question my maid." Having thus worked this out in her mind, and flooded with relief, Vika was able to once again take in a long breath.

Gwynlyan inhaled visibly, clasped her hands before her and, with a renewed look of purpose gracing her countenance, said, "Then 'tis as we believed: 'Tis only my daughter's life they mean to end."

CHAPTER 15

$\mathcal{Y}$ET ANOTHER NIGHT had passed with Morgana fretting and unable to sleep. She'd hoped to await the response from the nunnery where she'd been raised as to whether they would allow a visit, but had decided 'twas better to simply arrive, beg entrance, and well-entrench herself behind the safety and sanctity of the holy place prior to petitioning the King for aid in ending her marriage to Robert.

For, she felt sure that if the King did not (or, even if he did) agree with her desires, he'd inform Robert of Morgana's wishes and plans and, even tho' Robert might secretly desire the same conclusion to this alliance, he would feel honor-bound to keep his vows with her, would more easily foil the proceedings, and that would simply not do.

She had a bit more than another sennight remaining to this forced *rest* as Robert called it, and with little to keep her hands and mind occupied, and with Robert growing e'er more distant—e'er more irritable—when e'er he came to their chamber at night, keeping to a small portion of his side of the bed, or striding out to, she feared, share Vika's bed—or mayhap even some other's—Morgana was near to tearing out her hair by its roots to stop the somber thoughts and worries from invading. For, even if he was not sharing another's bed now, his withholding of his affection, his passion, from her did not, *could* not bode well for their union.

With a soft sigh, she tossed the woolen blanket off her lap and rose from the chair Robert's cousin had placed by the window for her a few days ago.

And this last eve, Robert had discontinued even pretending he'd abide beside her in their bed and had merely walked with her to their bedchamber after supper to wish her a good rest before departing again. There was much strain around his eyes and mouth, and she could only surmise 'twas due to the added burden she presented, now that she'd proven to him with her midnight visions and tearful fits that he'd bound himself with a woman who was not well in the head. Morgana pushed her fingers against her eyelids to stem the flow of tears that were e'er on the verge of gushing forth these days and took in a deep, ragged breath. After a moment, she regained a modicum of composure and was able to lift her head.

Tho' 'twas still more dark than dawn, Wife Deirdre had departed the chamber not a quarter-hour past to care for and redress a wound that one of Robert's soldiers had acquired on the training field the morn before, and Morgana felt restless. Turning with her arms folded over her chest, she gazed down at the courtyard, idly watching (and envying as well) the folk as they hurried about, fulfilling their daily tasks for the clan and the keep. One of the kitchen maids scurried across the courtyard toward the well with an ewer in her hand and Morgana smiled when she saw that one of the apprentices, a big man of some height and weight, with hair the color of spring carrots, and a beard to match, was already there, and clearly awaiting her arrival, for the maid's countenance brightened and her tread quickened when the man smiled at her.

There was a young wedded pair of pilgrims who'd arrived late this day past and were granted a place to lay their heads for the night with the blacksmith's family. They were already preparing to depart, she noticed. O'er the last days, as her body had grown stronger, Wife Deirdre and her daughter sat with her less and less, only coming in to check on her a few times a day to ask if she required a sleeping draught, or if she required them to bring her meal to her or if she would be taking it with her husband. This would make it easier for what she had planned.

Hurrying now, she rushed to the washstand and took up the pot of ink and small painting brush she'd gathered last eve on her way back up to her bedchamber after supper. Dipping it in the dark liquid, she swirled it around until 'twas drenched, then brought it up to her hairline and began stroking it up and o'er the white strands. It worked as she already knew 'twould as she'd tried it on the base of her braid this night past after Robert left her alone in their chamber, turning her hair a deep russet.

'Twas a precaution, along with the worn and ragged brown gown made of rough wool and the plain dingy cotton chemise and *napron* she'd purloined from their pegs in one of the small storage chambers off the kitchen and put on after Wife Deirdre's departure earlier.

As the ink almost immediately dried, she secured her braid in a coronet around her head, then twined a drab square of cloth o'er that, tying the ends and tucking them in. Taking only another brief moment to study the results as best she could in the silvered glass, she turned her head from side to side and was pleased to see that the effect was as she'd hoped. If she were very careful to hold her head down as she left the keep, she believed no one would recognize her.

As quickly as she could, she stoppled the pot of ink, wrapped it in a long, thick length of dark wool, then tucked it inside a small pouch before tucking that into the woven basket that held the coin she'd offer the pilgrims, the owner of the vessel she'd travel o'er the water in, as well as to the nuns when she arrived, with only a penny or two left for the unforeseen. There was also a good amount of cheese, some bread, dried meat, and for later in the journey, bannocks.

Afterward, she placed a scrolled parchment on Robert's pillow. 'Twas a short, and she thought, plain explanation to Robert for her departure, that was not marred by too much feeling.

Then, with a last sweep of her gaze, she took in the chamber that until recently had been the haven for the most joyful moments of her life thus far. With a shaky sigh, she turned and stared at the door. Now, to deal with Robert's cousin.

* * *

She'd had to cover her head with a dark veil and slip one of her better gowns o'er her head before opening the door to query her guard. It had not been easy to roust him from his place by the door. She knew Robert kept him there for her use while she was confined to her chamber, but she found it odd that he would balk so oft at leaving her when Wife Deirdre, or her daughter, were not in the chamber with her, and the fact that he was as a shadow to her when e'er she took a turn out in the garden, or out of the keep at all, had only made e'er more evident to her Robert's worry regarding her odd spells. So, she'd had to deceive him into believing that Wife Deirdre's daughter had spent the entire night in her chamber and was now asleep next to the hearth. She'd placed a fur there and made a pile of clothes, then covered it all with one of the patterned woolen blankets Wife Deirdre had brought and left on a stool for her and her daughter's use. In order to convince the man fully, Morgana had opened the door just enough for him to peek around it and see the lump she'd made. The Fates were with her, praise be, because her guard did not notice that there were no loud snores coming from the lump, as would have been the case were the woman truly slumbering within.

She'd had to be cunning because she did not want any to follow her—if they would—until she was well away from here, so that she'd have the best chance of making it to the abbey and finding sanctuary there before her flight could be stopped.

While one of the pilgrims she would be traveling with—the husband—made an exchange of a slightly bent, heart-shaped pewter brooch for casks of both ale and well water that the ale wife assured would last them the journey, were they careful of it, Morgana gave a furtive look left and right before tucking herself, unnoticed by any who knew her, under the coarse blanket of heavy cloth that covered the bales of wool. The bales were going as far as *Inverleith*, where the Holyrood Abbey was to have a fair and Lammas day feast. Morgana had taken it as a sign from the Almighty that 'twas time to act. For, these pilgrims arrived late last eve, begging for a place to lay their heads for the night, and told Vika, whom they'd assumed to be the mistress of the keep, that they were headed to the very port where Morgana had arrived all those moons ago.

The loss of her place here, tho' it pained her still, was also a boon. For, because of the pilgrims' misbelief, she was free to set forth with her plan with little question or suspicion from them. And, as Robert had proven with his e'er-growing distance these past days that she had become more a hardship than a helpmeet, it seemed the quickest and cleanest way of severing their bond.

She brought with her only the small pouch of coin and the other larger and heavier one filled with meat, bread and cheese to share with her hosts, who'd agreed to her request of transport to the holy place, understanding that she hoped for healing there.

The pilgrims—Cormac and Gruach—would be here in another moment or two. She'd conveyed to them that she was feeling a bit tired from her late night preparing for her departure, and would take an hour's rest in the wain with the bales of wool.

* * *

Morgunn had come around the corner of his own cart after hitching his ox to it, and was about to leave on yet another search of the outlying land to see what traces, if any, he might find with regard to where the minions were hiding themselves when he saw a flash of pale hose-covered leg and feminine-shoed foot sweep up under the blanket in the young pilgrims' wain. Prickles of alarm traveled up his spine. *A messenger for Donnach working within the keep?* He'd follow them. Capturing her would be the first step in bringing the entire plan to an abrupt end. He was about to turn and go to the door to the nearby weavers' chamber to find Gwynlyan, whom he'd taken to openly wooing these past days, so that he might tell her of his discovery and that she should find Robert and have him follow, when the pilgrim's cart began to move toward the gate. Immediately, his plan changed. He swung up on the seat of the wain, took the reins, and trailed them out. He soon discovered he'd be pushing his ox to keep up with them, for the couple were not poor and had the means to afford two oxen to pull their load.

In the hour that followed, with no sign of the hider slipping from beneath her covering, Morgunn developed his plan of action.

* * *

'Twas nearing terce that same day when Grímr at last returned from his journey.

As Robert stood in the courtyard waiting for his guest to dismount and come toward him, he pondered all that had been discovered since Grímr's departure. There was much to be decided between them, now that Robert knew of Vika's father's connection to the attack on Morgana, her mother, and her father all those years ago, as well as the current plot to destroy her. And, as Morgunn had told him, and as he'd come to be e'er more convinced of as well the longer he'd ruminated on it, Donnach would have little pang in slaughtering his own flesh as well, should her presence here, or even her mere existence, become inconvenient to his purposes.

* * *

As Grímr came further into the courtyard and saw that Robert awaited him, he could see by the dark cloud shadowing the man's countenance that he had something dire to impart, and his pulse sped. Had he been wrong in his belief that Vika pretended illness the last eve of his stay here? Had she perished while he went about his plans to force her to his will? 'Twas well known that injuries to the head could be strange in their healing, hard to remedy.

Without waiting for his mount to halt, he leapt from its back and all but ran to meet his host. When he was still several feet from him, he called out. "Where is Vika—is she dead?"

The look of surprised confusion that passed o'er Robert's countenance told Grímr that his worry was misguided, and his heart—his very soul—took flight even before he heard Robert tell him nay. Finally able to begin breathing normally again, he said, "What more dread tidings do you have for me, friend?"

Robert turned toward the entrance to the keep, and Grímr followed. His host said naught further as they walked, and Grímr kept his silence as well. 'Twas clear, what e'er he had to impart to him was for his ears alone, and the worry, so fleetingly gone, returned. If Vika was not dead, had her illness grown worse? Yet, if 'twas the case—why the secrecy? Nay. It must be some other dire thing. *Á vegginum Ásgarðr.* He prayed 'twas not Robert's own wife who'd perished. Yet...it seemed more likely the case, for he would not want to speak about his loss with so many eyes and ears about.

Sverð af Óðinn! He did not know what he would say to him, if his fears proved right. And, Robert would no doubt be asking that Grímr find other lodgings during this time of grief, as well. What would he do then? He could not force himself upon an unwilling host. Yet. He could not leave without Vika, either. His hands curled into fists at his sides. Blast the woman! Well, if it came to that, then he'd simply have to ferret his way back in someway and steal her away, if Robert would not see reason and give her o'er to him freely once he confessed his true purpose for having come here.

'Twas not until Robert had cleared the great hall of everyone, leaving only the two of them seated by the hearth that he again spoke directly to Grímr, saying, "Someone slipped poison in my wife's sleeping draught."

Grímr's head jerked back.

" 'Twas why she lost our babe. And, 'tis plain to me now, 'twas my wife who was the true target that day on the stairs in the old keep, not Vika, as first we thought."

Grímr sat forward. "Who—"

"The earl. Vika's father, Donnach Cambel."

Donnach Cambel! His shoulders struck the back of the chair, causing the air to leave his lungs in an audible *whoosh!* "*Bǫllr of Óðinn!*" he murmured, blinking. After only the briefest of moments, his gaze returned to Robert's, and he sat forward again. "What do you need from me, friend? I've fighting men waiting at the docks on the coast. I will send for them." He made to rise, but Robert gripped his forearm, forestalling the motion.

"I cannot reveal more, but know that I've the King behind me, and have no need of your men. But...Vika cannot remain at my holding. I know you've not concluded the dealings that brought you here, but—"

"Aye, aye. I shall away with her forthwith."

Robert's eyes narrowed on him. "Even tho' she grows heavy with my bairn? You will protect it and keep it from harm, as if 'twere your very own?" He sat back with his elbows resting on the arms of his chair and folded his hands together, allowing them to settle o'er his solar plexus.

Grímr bit back a growl. As he'd suspected would be the case, she'd not confessed her treachery while he was away. *Vika! You will pay dearly for this!* "The babe she carries is mine. She lied to you to gain her own ends—and she alone knows what they might be."

* * *

Robert shot forward. He opened his mouth to refute

Grímr's claim but closed it again, quashing his initial impulse in favor of a more temperate response. He sat back slowly and crossed his arms over his chest. "How know you that 'tis not to you she has lied?" Relief and sorrow dueled for prominence within him as he studied his guest's visage and awaited his answer. He did not have long to wait.

Grímr sat forward, resting his forearms on his thighs. He loosely twined his fingers in front of him as he met Robert's gaze with a penetrating pale-blue one of his own. "A couple of reasons." He began steepling the fingers of each hand together as he rendered his list. "The foremost being that the date of my *free* and *unhindered* encounter"—he paused and his look sharpened even more in that instant it took Robert to nod his understanding—" is in close accord with Vika's adjudged date of conception." He took in a deep breath, continuing on the exhale, "And the second being that, at least by Vika's words, you and she had used more care *and* had not lain together in the sennight or so before, or after, the time she conceived."

'Twas more a verification of a question that had niggled the back of his mind these past days, than any true revelation, but still Robert allowed himself to mourn the second loss a moment, tho' he ne'er revealed such to Grímr as he said, "Aye, you've proved your belief. I am assured."

Robert did not miss the shadow of relief that crossed o'er Grímr's countenance before Grímr stood and said, "I think it not best for us to delay even another night."

Robert stood as well. "Aye, you are right."

"I must gather Vika and we must fly."

"I will send a small contingent of guards with you, but you must start in the direction of Vika's manor, else Donnach's accomplices may grow suspicious," Robert said as he started toward the entrance to the great hall with Grímr in step beside him.

"Aye, I see the verity in that. We shall do as you say, fear not."

"All is settled then. You shall find her with the weavers."

After arranging for Vika's belongings to be brought from her chamber and placed in a covered horse-drawn cart so that she might travel with some comfort, Robert walked with Grímr as far as the base of the steps outside the entrance to the keep. For only a mere moment before he strode to the training field on a mission to collect five of his best guards for the journey, Robert watched Grímr go as far as the doorway to the weavers' chambers. With good fortune, and continued good weather, they'd be safely out of Donnach's view and concern within a day's time. And then all of his efforts and attention could be applied to capturing the miscreants and saving his wife's life.

* * *

Grímr stepped out of the sunlight and into the dimness of the interior to the large, cool, low-ceilinged chamber where the women toiled busily with long skeins of colored wool or silk on multiple wooden looms or long boards. The clack and clatter of the devices along with the low buzz of the women's voices as they worked created a harmony of sound both pleasant and calming. His eyes adjusted quickly and he found Vika near the other open doorway, which led into yet another chamber and looked to be populated with a group of spinners.

As if she felt his gaze upon her, she looked in his direction. For a fleet moment their eyes locked and he saw a glimmer of dread that was quickly replaced by ire before she twirled around and headed into the other chamber.

He followed, and his strides were long. As he moved past the women one-by-one, their looms went silent, and so also did their mouths. He felt more than saw their curious stares upon him, but his quarry was fast escaping toward yet another door and he could not allow that. He picked up his speed and managed to catch her 'round the waist and drag her full against him before her hand reached the handle. The assault of desire that the contact caused made the air push from their lungs in unison. Although...he was not so full of vanity that he could not admit that for her, at least, it might have been the pressure from his arm on her middle that caused her to respond in such a manner. He touched his lips to the delicate shell of her ear and murmured, " 'Tis time," knowing from long experience that the fluttering caress would make her wet, make her burn, make her easy to manage.

Except he was wrong.

Instead of going limp in his embrace, she turned into a she-devil, kicking, clawing and even trying to bite his arm, if she could have reached it.

He heaved her into his arms. 'Twas the safest way to deal with her, and even tho' she continued fighting him with her waspish tongue and with pounding fists to his shoulders, he knew she'd not fight so hard that she'd cause harm to their babe. As for his own injuries, tho' his shin and toes burned, as did the scratches on his arm, they were as naught compared to any he'd received in battle, so he cleanly ignored them.

* * *

"I will ne'er be able to lift my eyes to those women again! You have mortified me for the final time, Grímr! I am not your property!" Vika said the last just before ripping a satisfying fistful of pale yellow hair from Grímr's scalp. Unfortunately, the only response he gave was a low grunt and yet another squeeze to her bent knees, which were positioned perfectly in the crook of his beefy arm. The surprise came when he had the brazen boldness to run his calloused thumb o'er the hardened (from anger, not desire!) peak of her breast. Her body went slack, but her pulse went wild.

"Your body says otherwise, *svanfríðr*."

She stiffened in his embrace and folded her arms over her breasts. She would not let him do this to her! Not again. *Never* again. And she wasn't going with him back to *Leòdhas*, either, tho' 'twas plain, by the grim look on Robert's countenance and his arrogant stance where he stood near the cart Grímr unswervingly carried her toward that he'd not be a confederate to her in this. She must bear the humiliation until she was away from this keep and able to ply her wiles on either an unsuspecting guard or, mayhap, a village alewife somewhere along the journey before they reached the shore.

Grímr settled her on the carter's bench with his arm slung around her middle to keep her in place and turned to Robert, saying, "My thanks, friend, for the use of the cart, and for your generous hospitality as well."

Vika snorted and dug her nails into his arm.

Robert's gaze didn't waver from Grímr's countenance, which vexed her even more, so she said (even tho' she was almost certain Grímr had revealed otherwise), " 'Tis no more than I'd expect from you, Robert MacVie, handing off your bastard to be raised by another man."

Robert did look at her then, but 'twas more of a sweep of the eye with one brow lifted, before he turned his attention back on Grímr. "You are sure you do not need a carter?" he asked him.

"Nay, I shall drive it myself. 'Twill be...safer, I trow."

Vika narrowed her eyes at him. She knew all too well what he meant: Safer for *his* purposes, not hers. For, she'd not have the freedom to alight quite so easily with him sitting beside her.

Or, so he thought.

An intent look passed between the two warriors, which Vika took as more proof of their conspiracy against her, before Robert gave a nod and said, "Aye."

Grímr clamped his hand on Robert's shoulder and Robert returned the gesture before Grímr hauled himself up on the seat beside her, took up the reins, whistled to the horses and signaled to the men with a lift of his hand that they should all begin moving toward the gate.

A quarter-hour later, Vika, her heart thudding in her chest, twisted around with her hand unknowingly levered on Grímr's hard thigh, and sent one long, last look in the direction of the MacVie holding as it grew smaller and smaller in her vision. *Before God and all his angels, I say this true: I shall not again set so much as a foot down upon* Leòdhas.

PART FIVE

───✦───

A Madman's Lair

"*Fetter strong madness in a silken thread,
Charm ache with air and agony with words.*"

Much Ado About Nothing (Act V, scene i)

"*Things bad begun make strong themselves by ill.*"

Macbeth (Act III, scene ii)

CHAPTER 16

"WHY ARE YOU not inside the fortress, doing your day's work?" Alaric growled at Symon, who stood in the doorway of the abandoned cot in a small wooded copse on the outer border of the de Burgh land that Alaric had been living in these past moons.

"Because I've news that could not wait. The kitchen maid put her ear to the door this morn and has learned that Robert MacVie knows of the plot against his wife, and has the support of the King in doing what e'er is necessary to bring us to justice."

"God's Bl—!"

"Wait," Symon said, lifting his hand, "there's more. Donnach's daughter has fled with that warrior from the far North who has been staying at the MacVie holding."

Alaric swung around and took two long strides to the hearth.

Symon followed and shut the door behind him.

" 'Tis too dangerous to remain here now, that much is clear," Alaric said after a moment. "And Donnach would agree. We must abort this plot, as they've still no notion of who it is that aids him. We will wait a time, start again with another method." He turned back to Symon. "But, we cannot allow his daughter to be taken away by that warrior. She is too valuable to her father. He's been trying for another alliance which would benefit him as well as the one he made with the aged raider of that island."

"What do you propose?"

"We must follow them and take her back with us. For, 'tis truth, I fear Donnach's wrath more even than I do the King's."

"Aye, me as well. I confess, I foresaw such, and did what was needed before I departed."

Alaric's eyes narrowed on Symon. "The maid?"

"Aye. She is dead, so will tell no tales."

"And the body?"

"Let us simply say, 'tis well with*in* the keep's walls."

Alaric turned, stroking the beginnings of a beard on his chin. "Good. But we must hasten from here, and hope that none follow."

"No one will."

Alaric swung 'round to face Symon once more, his gaze sharp. "Tell me."

Simon grinned. "You will be pleased, I think, to learn that I've arranged a bit of a distraction, which will force all within the fortress—and without as well—to turn their full attention to. In fact, there may even be a chance that the mute will not survive it."

"You will tell me what you've done on the way. For now, we must flee."

* * *

Morgunn didn't have to wait more than another half-hour for the lass to show herself, and when she did, his heart shot into his throat. *Morgana!*

In that moment, all his previous plans crumbled into dust and he acted without thought, leaping off the slow-moving wain and running forward. When Morgana's head whipped around and her eyes went wide in what he saw to be terrible fear, he knew instantly he'd made a grave error. 'Twas likely she recognized him from the keep, but clearly she thought he'd turned to freebooting by the manner in which he'd approached, and no doubt his eyepatch and look of worry, which Gwynlyan oft had told him was more grim than troubled, seemed sinister and even malignant.

Morgunn skidded to a halt, holding up both hands to show them empty, and was about to yell to the occupants requesting they stay their cart a moment, but by this time, the young man driving it had heard the clomp of Morgunn's boots and had turned around and seen him. The pilgrim pulled on the reins and, after a few more feet, the conveyance came to a stuttering stop.

Fortunately, oxen were easily led and his was prone to idleness, so had already stalled his own motion and pulled to the side of the well-worn path that served as the road to graze on the vegetation growing there.

"Know ya tha' ya 'ave the lady Morgana, Laird MacVie's wife, on yer wain?"

The pilgrim blinked twice then turned a perplexed gaze on Morgunn's daughter. "Nay, she is not that lady. This is but a mute who hopes for healing at Holyrood Abbey."

Morgunn stepped closer. Close enough that he could see the pulse fluttering in his daughter's neck. With his eye still on her as he continued to speak to the pilgrim, he said, "Aye, she be mute, but again, she be the wife o' Robert MacVie. I think he wull like i' no' tha' ya 'ave hied her away wi' ya, and ya wull surely find tha' his gen'rosity o' this nigh' past wull turn more ta a gen'rous wielding o' righ'ful joostice 'pon discov'rin' sech."

* * *

"Are you in truth the MacVie chieftain's wife?" the pilgrim, Cormac, said, at last dismounting from his seat and coming around to the back of the cart where Morgana sat wringing her hands. Morgana nodded.

What dire misfortune was upon her that this man—this tinker—had chosen to depart behind them, to take the same path! Now she had no choice but to return to Robert's holding. *And if he has read the scroll already?* What to do then? For, he'd know her plan and, with her still in place as his wife, she knew he'd think it his duty to keep her, to bring to an end any further attempt to step aside so that he might wed with her cousin.

"We must turn this wain around then and take you back forthwith," Cormac said before leveling his gaze once more on the other man. "Tinker, will you pull your cart off the path while I do such?"

"Nay, no need. I had only joost discover' tha' I'd no' loaded some o' m'wares back on m'cart after doin' a count o' them las' night when I saw the lady coom oop froom 'neath th' cov'rins. I wull be pleased ta return her ta her keep fer ya." He came up to the wain then and offered his hand to her. "I feel sure the Laird wull no' coom after ya, once his dear bride be back safe 'neath his roof."

Seeing the keen spark of intelligence and determination in the tinker's dark-fringed blue eye, a wave of something akin to recognition swept through her center, but 'twas too brief to capture or study. So, having no other choice but to return from whence she'd so recently fled, and with a mental sigh of resignation, Morgana reluctantly took his rough, gloved hand and allowed him to aid her to the ground.

* * *

It took a bit of physical maneuvering, as well as gentle coaxing of his ox to get his wain turned around on the narrow path, as 'twas heavily loaded with metal, and a few wooden wares, but, after almost a half-hour, and a small crack in the axle, Morgunn at last managed it, and he and his daughter were at last plodding back toward the MacVie holding. If he was careful, and if good fortune held, they'd make it at least to the gates before they lost a wheel.

He wanted desperately to ask why she'd left her husband, but knew he'd already o'erstepped his place by taking charge of her and forcing her to return with him. Unless, of course, he told her who he truly was, which he'd not do. At least, not until he'd returned her to safety. He realized 'twas time to reveal all to her, otherwise, she might risk her life again without realizing.

Just as she'd done this day.

"She suffers...." His wife's words came back to him and this time, he kenned the true depth of what Gwynlyan had tried so hard to relay that night. Aye, when they were secure within the walls of the keep once more, he'd tell his daughter the truth.

They were nearing the fork in the path, one veering west, one veering east, when Morgunn felt a jolt on his side of the cart. He pulled on the reins and whipped his head around, saying aloud to no one, "What's this?" The ox hadn't even fully stopped, and Morgunn's glance hadn't yet reached the back end of the conveyance when all at once a loud crack rent the air and the wain leaned. The ox let out a sharp bellow, as its cumbersome burden tilted almost completely onto its side, while pots clanged and clattered onto the path. Morgunn was flung out as well, with his daughter's weight aiding the descent to the ground. Instinctively, he secured her in his embrace so that his frame took the impact. With his vision still spinning from the knock he'd taken to the back of the head, they both lay there stunned and still for an extended moment, until he heard the ox scream again and start to pull forward, trying to get free of the harness that was choking him.

With a quick look at his daughter to make sure she was uninjured, he scrambled to his feet and ran to the distressed animal, then quickly released it from its cumbrance. The ox staggered back a few steps, then turned, as if naught was amiss, and began to graze again at the side of the road.

When he shifted back around, he was surprised to

find his daughter busily gathering up the stray pots and other wares from the ground and making a neat stack of them near the tipping cart. Without saying a word, he squatted next to it, craned his neck to look at the underside, and saw what he'd expected to see: A broken axle.

There was naught for it. They'd have to walk the remainder of the way back to the holding. And, if fortune shone on them, his son-in-law would have discovered his wife's disappearance and would meet them on their way. He only prayed Donnach's cohorts were not about. A chill of trepidation ran down his spine. He liked it not, being so open to attack, with only a meager dirk, and no sword for protection.

* * *

Symon mounted his steed, saying, " 'Tis glad I am to be out of those workman's weeds and back in finer cloth again."

" 'Tis a boon that they travel in a covered cart, for with the added load, they will not have got as far," Alaric said, hoisting himself into his saddle. "We shall cross the heath to where the path forks. 'Tis, I think, the shortest distance to our goal."

Symon nodded. "Lead the way."

* * *

With Grímr and Vika well on their way, and the brief discussion with his mother-in-law relaying all that had been decided, as well as his need for her to take full control of his wife's duties as castelaine for the time being accomplished, Robert turned and began climbing the stairs leading to his bedchamber.

Wife Deirdre had told him early this morn that Morgana had grown restless in her seclusion and wanted to return to her daily tasks. In fact, his wife was becoming more difficult to keep confined to her chamber without force, and he could not allow that. Tho' if it came to choosing between imprisoning her against her will or telling her that someone had tried to kill her—and had succeeded in killing their unborn babe—he didn't know which he'd choose. For, either option would no doubt send her into an even worse state than she was in already. Mayhap, one from which she'd ne'er recover.

Nay, he must somehow soothe her, keep her believing 'twas the right thing to do, the best thing for her to do.

He was several steps from the landing when his steward called to him from below, saying Guy de Burgh awaited him in the great hall.

Robert pivoted and trotted back down the steps, saying, "My thanks. Have some ale brought in."

* * *

Morgana grabbed hold of the tinker's outstretched elbow for leverage as she slid her foot from one of her low leather shoes and shook from it the pebble that had lodged there. She was just slipping the covering back in place when she heard the sound of horses' hooves pounding o'er the heath to her right. Startled, she whipped her head around and quickly stood, fear spiking inside her that 'twas her husband she'd see galloping toward her.

Vaguely, she became aware that her traveling companion

had gone rigid beside her as well, and from her periphery she saw a spark of steel flash in his hand. "Keep your eyes down, what e'er you do," he murmured gruffly, then pushed her behind him. She saw then that he'd slit the back of his tunic and tucked the dirk inside a leather sheath strapped to his waist there. Who did he fear these men to be? *Freebooters?* Her heart lurched in her chest and began to speed. *Surely not.* But who else then? With hands that trembled, she folded the gap in the slit closed more fully and pressed her chin to her chest.

All at once, the men were upon them, waiting until they were near to trampling them before pulling sharply on their reins, causing dirt and gravel to fly up. A pebble hit Morgana on the cheek and before she realized what she was doing, she'd jerked her head up and lifted her hand to her bloodied cheek. The tinker lunged forward with a guttural cry in the same moment that Morgana's eyes landed on her uncle's priest. She staggered back and her heel landed on the side of a hole in the path. Her ankle twisted painfully and she fell backwards onto her elbows and her backside, making the covering on her head fly off.

" 'Tis the mute! Get her!" the priest yelled to the other man and when he did so, Morgana's horrified gaze shifted to him. *The apprentice at the well!* She struggled to gain her feet, but her ankle gave way when she tried to put weight on it, and she fell back again just as the large red-bearded man gripped her by the waist and flung her o'er his shoulder. "What fortune!" he said to the priest. The hard shoulder pushing into her chest made it impossible to take in more than a scant bit of air.

"Make haste!" she heard the priest say.

Her heart thudded against her breastbone. *What is happening?* She blinked the floating lights from her eyes, then switched her gaze to the tinker. The priest had somehow gagged him and tied his hands behind his back while she was being captured. She lifted her eye to his and, for yet another time that day, a *frisson* of recognition passed through her as he conveyed to her with only a look that all was not lost and she must not fret.

Her effort toward calm only lasted another moment, however, for, with the priest's next words, she knew all was lost.

"We'll hang him o'er there, in that stand of trees," the priest said, pointing. "And I've taken his purse, so any who find him will think 'twas thieves who did the deed."

Morgana's heart raced so hard that it ached. She lifted her eye again to the tinker, and found his countenance stolid. How could he remain so unmoved? In the next instant, she was hauled onto the priest's mount, and when he slithered up behind her, her skin crawled.

Squeezing her eyes shut, she swallowed back the bile. The horse began to move and, once again, she swung her gaze around to the tinker. He was now seated on the other man's horse, with that man riding in front of him, and with a rope around his and his captor's waist securing him there. Before she had time to form another thought, they were flying toward the grove of oak, and 'twas all she could do to keep from hurtling off her seat. Her heart sank into her stomach. *I am to blame for this.* If she'd not fled this morn, the tinker would now be about his daily tasks, not here, riding toward his own hanging. And she...well, what e'er became of her, she surely deserved. For, she'd clearly not done God's will. Yet...she'd been so sure that God had brought those pilgrims for her.

But, she'd been wrong, and now her sin was so grave, she'd no doubt burn in hell.

* * *

"He is a good King," Guy explained, "but his coffers are low, and he must, as he duly pricked my memory, be e'er-vigilant of John of England." He dropped his gaze to his tankard and idly twisted it to and fro where it rested on the table. "He has ne'er forgotten Alnwick, nor what he was forced to do at Falaise."

Robert, arms crossed on the wooden surface, drummed his fingers against his elbow. "Aye, 'tis more than understandable, yet.... *Aargh!*" Swinging to his feet, he strode several paces away with his arms firmly akimbo. After a moment, he turned back to his guest, continuing, "Exceedingly vexing, as well."

One corner of Guy's mouth lifted as he leaned forward. "Aye, and that, I am sure, is why he also wanted your memory well-stirred that he would not have given his consent for you to wed with Morgana, no matter her uncle's wishes, if 'twere not for the coin I offered in your stead."

Robert grinned, in spite of his ire, and opened his mouth to give a biting retort, when a loud scuffle came from beyond the door of the great hall, followed by the anxious, low tones of men's voices. The thought fled as he bolted toward the entry. *Morgana!*

He flung the door wide and was met with two sets of eyes, round in either astonishment, or fear, he knew not which. "Speak," he said to his cousin. In his periphery, he saw the door guard step away several paces and resume his post.

"The lady Morgana is not in her chamber, and some of her ladies' things are missing. Sh—"

Robert shoved past him and tore up the stairs, bellowing as he went, "Where is Wife Deirdre?"

"She is awaiting you in your bedchamber, Laird," his cousin replied from not far behind him.

"How long?"

"From my guess, since dawn."

They'd made the landing and were now jogging toward his chamber door. " 'Tis nigh on five hours then," Robert said. "She could be anywhere, she could be..." *dead.*

"My pardon, Laird. I-I do not—"

"Nay. Later. I must find my wife." With a yank of the handle, Robert threw the door wide. His gaze landed immediately on the distraught healer.

"She fled, Laird," the healer told him. "She was no' taken."

"We cannot know that for sure," Robert said with force. Crossing the room in two strides, he studied first the washstand, stained with smears of what looked to be dark ink, yet empty of her brush and comb, then scanned the rest of the chamber, noting the odd bulging mass under a blanket by the hearth. "She may have been wiled."

"She left ye a letter, Laird. Or, someone did." Wife Deirdre handed him the scroll.

As Robert unfurled the small square of parchment, his cousin said, "She made me believe that lump there," pointing to the blanket, "was Wife Deirdre's daughter, then bade me to do a task for her. I ne'er would hav—"

Robert held up his hand and said, "Enough," as he began to read. A vise of both anguish and fear gripped his insides. 'Twas true: She'd left him. He strode toward the door. "If I am to retrieve her and return before night falls, I must leave forthwith."

* * *

"Here," the priest said to the red-beard as he reigned in his mount and looked up into the boughs of a large oak. "This one has a good-sized branch. Just there." He pointed. "It should hold him."

This man was no priest, that much Morgana had at long last perceived. In the past moments, as they traveled toward the grove, she'd also gathered that she was their true quarry, and evidently had been for quite some time. They spoke freely between themselves, as if, because she was mute, they believed her to be deaf as well.

Or, mayhap—and this was even more chilling—they simply realized that she was no match for their strength and would not escape their plans for her, no matter if she attempted such or nay.

The red-beard slid from his horse then yanked the tinker off as well, throwing him to the ground.

"Ow! Ya deevl's spawn!"

"Whist!" the false priest yelled, kicking the tinker in the chest.

Whist...whist.... Whist, while I lay claim to my prize. The words spun in Morgana's head and her vision tunneled as she watched the tinker's face land in the dry sticks and other fallen plant debris that littered the area under the canopy of branches and leaves.

The tinker lifted his blue gaze to hers and in that suspended moment, a flood of memories flashed in her mind. *Papa!* Her vision cleared. She flung herself from the back of the horse and knelt down, shielding him with her body. She'd scarcely gotten her arms around him before she was wrenched back up.

"Tie her hands and feet," the false priest told the red-beard.

Manacles of flesh, sinew, calluses and bone gripped her wrists, but she twisted and turned, pulled and kicked. He snatched her head back with a fist in her hair and shook her, growling, "Be still!"

"No!!" she bellowed back, slamming her elbow into his solar plexus and grinding the heel of her uninjured foot into his instep.

"She's got her voice back, it seems," the red-beard said in a strained voice as he grabbed her around the waist and lifted her off her feet. She tried to elbow him again, but the blows found no purchase.

"Be still, m'lady!" she heard the tinker, her father, say and she swung her gaze to his. His look—it held a message, but she knew not what. "Be still," he said again, this time with less force, but with more surety. "Do no' figh' them becooz o' me."

The false priest stepped toward her and lifted a lock of her hair, caressing it between thumb and forefinger. "He speaks rightly, my dove. Be a peaceable little bird, and you may yet live to see another dawn."

She gathered a pool of spit in her mouth, but before she let it fly, she glanced at her father and he shook his head. Then, almost imperceptibly, he tilted his head at the false priest, indicating she should do as the man said, so she went slack and allowed the red-beard to drop her to her feet and continue trussing her wrists. The red-beard went down on one knee and was about to tie her ankles when the false priest said, "Nay. Just the wrists for now, I've changed my mind."

"Are you sure? She seems awfully attached to this peddler. She may give us trouble again when we put the rope on him."

"Aye, just the wrists. She's a sore ankle for now, she'd not get far." Almost as an afterthought, he added, "And muffle her, as well."

The red-beard shrugged and returned to a standing position.

Her gaze ne'er left her father while she was forced to silence anew, then settled on the back of the false priest's mount once more. Again, she wondered how her father could be so calm in the face of his imminent death. Yet, now that she'd had another moment to think on why he'd been so keen to stop her from fighting her captors, she realized that he wanted her to have a chance at rescue, and if they killed her here and now, there would be none.

* * *

"Make haste," the false priest told the red-beard a time later as he swung one end of the rope o'er a broad tree limb, "but be thorough, 'twill not be good for us if the rope fails."

"Aye...*argh*...he's a heavy one," the red-beard said as he hoisted Morgana's father up, using the long-tail of the rope that was coiled around his neck and o'er the branch. "We must be miles away, and quickly, else we shall hang beside him, I trow." Her father hadn't said another word since speaking to her earlier, and now he seemed resigned to his fate, his eyes downcast, his frame loose, his hands and feet, fettered.

Her father was still no longer. His body jerked and twisted, his face turned red, then blue. A shuffling noise, not too far off, came to them, and the two men panicked. The false priest pushed the red-beard toward his mount, saying between his teeth, "Go! Make haste! Make haste!" then stabbed her father in the chest with a dirk that seemed to come from nowhere.

"Papa!" she screamed, tho' the sound was muffled by the oiled cloth they'd used to silence her, but her father made no sound or movement.

The false priest leapt upon his steed behind her, and her two captives ran their horses at break-neck speed, not back to the road, as Morgana had expected, but in the opposite direction.

Her body shook, her heart ached, her mouth dried. *All is lost...all is lost...all is lost.* Nay. Nay. She would pray.

Heavenly Father, if it be your will, lend me your strength and courage to escape these terrible men.

With her wrists bound behind her, she was having difficulty staying seated, and if 'twere not for the false priest's arms at her front and back holding her in place, she would have fallen off the racing animal already. Her stomach would not be still, it roiled and turned with every pounding beat of the horse's hooves across the great expanse of earth. Where were they taking her? She tried to remember every word they'd spoken since she'd been seized by them, but naught made sense. They'd talked of a place, but not by name, that they'd used before, but it gave her no clue of how far they would be traveling. Nor had they given her any indication of their plans for her. A flash-memory of the violence against her mother sent a chill down her spine, and her gorge up.

She gagged and coughed.

"If you spew, you'll choke. And if it lands on me, I'll slap you so hard, your ears will ring," the false priest hissed.

She nodded and swallowed, afraid to look at him, lest he take that as an offense and slap her despite her submission to his will.

The false priest reined in his mount, and the red-beard did the same.

"We're far enough away now to drive our beasts at a slower pace," the false priest said.

It had been at least a quarter-hour, by Morgana's estimation, since they'd fled the site where her father had been hanged. *Please let him have died quickly.* The thought of him suffering there, still alive, yet tormented with pain, made her vision blur with tears. The knife wound had not spurted blood; it had gone in clean, so she believed 'twould not have immediately ended his life. And she had no knowledge of hanging death; how long it took for the person to find his eternal peace. Was it mere moments, or longer still?

She tried to determine their current location, but she did not recognize the area. However, she did know they'd fled further south, which meant they were on, or near, the de Burgh holding. *If only Guy was not at court!* But, nay, even then, he'd surely not be wandering about this far from his fortress.

And Robert? Had he found the scroll yet? And if he had, had he rushed to find her, or had he been relieved that she'd taken the burden of their marriage off him so easily and willingly? She didn't know which she wished for. Nay. She did. She knew what these men—well, this *man*—was capable of, for she remembered it all now. What he'd said to her mother when she'd asked where her husband was: *"He is dead, my dove, clove through, then dropped into the loch. And now, Donnach will get his lands, and I will get my prize as well."* She also knew that this man—this false priest—was the devil who'd forced himself upon her mother, with her small daughter as terrified witness; that he was the man that haunted her dreams, whether waking or slumbering; that he was the *Ankou* who'd carried the limp, lifeless corpse of her mother from the cot that night, demanding silence from Morgana, else she would be next.

He'd left her alone in that dark, dank, abandoned

cot, with the fire set to her family's covered cart licking, angry and hot, just outside the door. The flames, she knew, were meant to engulf the cabin as well, but rains had come, hard and fierce, and blessedly, they had not. She'd spent the remainder of that black, lonely night shivering and weeping in the cold corner she'd been forced into, not allowing a single sound to emerge lest the man return, and too terrified to venture forth, lest wolves be on the hunt for their next meal.

Sometime in that night, she'd drifted into a deep, Cimmerian sleep, until, come the dawn, a stranger, another minion of her uncle's, had arrived. He'd been angry to find that the dwelling still stood, that she still lived, and had moved toward her with hands outstretched, as if to strangle her, but when she'd cowered and covered her head, unable now to utter a sound, he'd halted. After a moment, she'd heard him mutter that he'd not the stomach to kill an innocent bairn, then yanked her up, hoisted her onto his horse, and flew with her to the coast, where he'd given her o'er to this man—this devil—once more. It hadn't taken him long to realize she'd lost her voice, and sometime in the night, her memory and the black pigment to her hair, as well. He'd paid a sour-faced stout-bosomed woman to sail away with her to the nunnery in Brittany, where Morgana had been left for years and years without voice or memory of her life prior. She'd gone mute and stoic, and 'twas only through the years of loving kindness she'd received from the nuns that she'd later warmed to them and accepted that what e'er had happened to her had been the Lord's will, was part of his plan for her, and must ne'er be questioned.

Another thought struck, and her heart plummeted. Did Vika know of her father's betrayal of his own blood? And if she did? If she did, then Morgana had put Robert in grave danger! For, her uncle, 'twas clear, was capable of any low deed to gain his own ends, and if Vika was an accomplice, even simply by keeping her silence, then one must assume that she was capable of such evil as well.

'Twas another quarter-hour before either of the men spoke again.

"All right. Our mounts are breathing easier now. We will run them again, traveling another four or five miles in this direction, then we'll cut back to the road leading east."

"To the burial site?"

"Aye, to the burial site."

CHAPTER 17

'TWAS AS ROBERT took the last step down the stairs into the antechamber of the great hall that he was reminded of the guest he'd left so suddenly nearly a half-hour past.

"Is there aught amiss with your lady Morgana?" Guy asked, striding toward him.

Robert halted.

Guy's eyes did a quick sweep of him, then met his once more, a glint of alarm added to the worry shining in their depths. "You're in your mail. Is there danger?"

"Aye—aye. I've little time," he said, and strode to the door of the armory, taking long strides.

His guest followed.

"Morgana has fled with some pilgrims."

"How long ago?"

Robert took up sword and shield then hurried back across the antechamber, out the door of the keep and into the courtyard, with Guy on his heels. Motioning for one of the stablemen to bring him his steed, he said at last, "Dawn."

"They've not got far, I'm sure, as they are no doubt traveling by ox and cart. You'll get to her in a trice." There was a brief pause in which Robert felt his guest's hard gaze on him before Guy continued, "But why the battle weapons, then? Surely, there is little peril from a few devout pilgrims?"

Robert turned to his guest and hesitated, but finally said in low tones, so that only he would hear, "There is more: Her uncle has sent men to murder her, but she knows naught of the plot."

Two stablemen brought both their horses to them and Guy swung up onto his saying, "I'll go with you, then. In case there is need for another well-trained sword hand."

"My thanks." Robert turned to one of the stablemen and said, "Where is the tinker that I've seen about the past few days?"

"He left this morn, Laird. Early. Behind that family of pilgrims."

With a nod, Robert mounted the courser. "We must fly."

After they were out of the gate, with several of Robert's guards riding a small distance behind, Guy said to him, "So you believe the tinker is in on the plot?"

Robert took a quick glance behind him and saw that the men were far enough back not to hear him, if he spoke quietly. "Nay. 'Tis Morgana's father in disguise."

"Her father!" Guy said in like tones. "But, I thought—"

"Aye, as did we all—and, more importantly, as did Donnach Cambel, and does *still*, which is why we've kept it hidden from all but a chosen few. We've been attempting to find and capture the men he sent here to harm Morgana, then lay a trap for him."

"Does King William know of this? Surely, he would—"

"Aye, he knows, and has been doing what he can to locate any who might betray Donnach for coin or position, but he has yet to be successful."

"In which direction do we travel?"

"East. Unless we discover something amiss."

"They can't have gone more than ten to twelve miles at the most by my estimation, so we should reach them in not more than three hours—two hours, if we push our mounts."

"Aye. I confess, I've a dread in my gut, and 'tis telling me to speed to her, but if aught is amiss, 'twill work against me—us—if we ruin our animals in doing so."

"You are right. And we might miss something we need to see, if we fly past too swiftly."

* * *

Morgunn lay curled on his side, the dirk he'd used to free himself on the ground only inches from his still-twitching body. 'Twas an agony he'd not expected, this prickling and shooting pain exploding through his frame, all the way to the tips of his fingers and toes, with the rush of blood and vigor that pushed anew through his veins.

He'd swooned once he'd dropped to the ground,

and he had no notion of how long he'd lain here afterward. He only knew he would not be able to rise until this suffering lessened. He'd gambled and won, for that he sent a prayer of thanks to heaven. And now he knew the face of his daughter's enemies, as well as what direction they were headed with her. All that was required of him was to survive long enough to relay as much to Robert. This time, his brother would pay. Not only with the loss of land and power, but with his life. There would be no reprieve; there would be no mercy.

He'd landed in a crumpled mass on his side. With a grunt and sharp intake of breath, he managed to reach for, and capture, the dirk in his fist once more. Reaching down, he awkwardly, and painfully, sawed at the loosened rope that bound his ankles. The effort made flashpoints of light swim in his vision, and the blessed blackness of an imminent swoon beckoned, but he fought hard against it, and finally got the rope off.

'Twas several more moments before he felt he could try to stand. It took all the strength he could muster to roll o'er onto his stomach and rise to his hands and knees. The strenuous attempt brought a murky fog to the periphery of his vision and he had to rest without motion with his head dangling between his shoulders and his lids closed for a bit of time.

The dirk wound stung now that the sharp tingling had lessened, and he opened his eyes again to view the dark round stain and the clean slice in his tunic, where the knife had entered. Alaric's panic had either given him bad aim, or he had little knowledge of the exact location of lung or heart in a man's chest. Either way,

Morgunn praised heaven for that bit of unexpected good fortune, for it too easily might have gone another, much more dire, direction. Nay, this wound was not fatal, and he'd survived worse, so he ignored the petty annoyance and focused once more on gaining his feet.

He found he could not do it alone, no matter the strong desire, nor the chiding voice in his brain telling his body to follow its orders. So, in desperation, as he felt the time for successful action slipping away, he gripped the dirk in his hand and crawled to the trunk of the same tree from which he'd been strung, and girding it with his arms, used it for leverage as he at last, and finally, came up into a standing position.

His legs did not want to hold him, and his knees bent, but he gripped the trunk as if he were a drowning man on a sinking ship, until his limbs stopped quaking beneath him. His breath blew harsh from his lungs and out his mouth, causing the ache in his throat to worsen, but still he would not give in to it.

After a short while, he felt steady enough to attempt to walk, and was grateful when he was able to take several staggering steps without falling on his face. Standing, swaying in place after each set of steps he took, 'twas not more than another quarter-hour before he at last made it to the edge of the grove.

At this slow rate of pace, he knew that 'twould be past sext, and possibly nearing nones by the time he made it within the walls of the MacVie fortress once more. *And if Robert has already gone in false pursuit of the pilgrim wain?* Then he would fly to their side. *In the state you are in? You'll not make it to the crossroads.* Aye—aye, he would. Or die in the attempt. *But, I shall also send a missive to the King, for the sake of my daughter's safety.*

* * *

They were nearing the crossroads when Robert happened to glance toward the grove of oaks up ahead and saw a man holding his palm to his side and stumbling forward. "There!" he said to Guy, then spurred his horse from a trot into a gallop. 'Twas not until he was several yards away that he recognized that the man was Morgunn.

Robert reined in his mount and leapt from its back with the animal still in motion, the force of which gave him the added speed needed to reach his father-in-law in a mere twinkling. However, 'twas still too late to catch him up before he crumpled to the ground, wheezing in shallow breaths.

"Can you sit a horse?" Robert asked him.

For answer, Morgunn gave him a nod.

Robert saw the red and swollen rope marks around his father-in-law's neck, as well as the patch of blood that stained his tunic, and knew instantly what they portended. "Donnach's minions?"

Morgunn nodded. "They...," he rasped, "...have...have my daughter."

Guy arrived then. "Her father?" he asked Robert.

Robert nodded, lifting his father-in-law up using a shoulder under the man's arm, and an arm around his back. "Know you in which direction they have fled?"

"Aye," Morgunn croaked. "South."

"South?"

"You—*argh!*—will find their tracks there," Morgunn

pointed to an area behind the grove. " 'Tis been a while, but I've lost time, so I cannot say for sure." He sucked air in and out of his lungs for several heartbeats, then continued in a stronger voice, "They are headed for an ancient ritual site, but I know not which." Morgunn gripped Robert's arm. "Find my daughter. Find her before he defiles her, before he does to her what he did to my Gwynlyan."

Robert's heart sped. "Aye, I will." In all this time, he'd only thought of the minions' goal to murder, ne'er that they'd ravage her first. His hands, clammy with sweat, fisted at his sides. *If she's been used for their base pleasure, I shall castrate them, stuff their tarses in their gobs, sew their lips shut,* then *I shall kill them.*

Even more anxious now to continue on, and seeing that the strain of speaking was diminishing Morgunn's strength, Robert questioned him no further. In twenty more struggling steps, they reached the group of guards. Robert said to the first, "This man fought to save my wife's life from freebooters. Take him directly to my wife's maid, Modron. Tell her he is to be given a chamber inside the keep, along with what e'er care Wife Deirdre decrees."

"Aye, Laird."

After hoisting him up on his guard's horse and taking a moment to watch the pair ride off so that he might confirm that Morgunn would, indeed, stay mounted, Robert swung back up onto his courser again, saying, "We must fly."

They'd traveled some distance before Guy asked, so that only Robert would hear, "Why did you not tell the guard that the man with whom he was entrusted was your father-in-law?"

"I know not if they left someone behind to continue spying, and Morgunn is an even greater prize to Donnach than is my wife."

* * *

A half-hour and a quarter later, Robert, Guy and the remaining guards stopped at a small trickling burn to water their horses. Yet again, his hand slid o'er the pouch at his side that held Morgana's letter, itching to bring it out and read it another time, but more slowly, with hope of finding some unwritten reason, other than the one declared, for leaving him without a word, without one inkling of her worry, of her intent to do so. He looked behind him and as he did, something odd, some design on the horizon, unnatural in color and placement, and in the direction of his own holding, caught his attention. He blinked, then focused with more precision. His mind and body went on full alert. "Guy," he said, gripping the other man's arm without realizing.

Guy whipped his attention from the stream where his horse was drinking deeply and turned it to Robert. "Aye?"

"Tell me that is not smoke coming from my holding."

Guy followed the line of Robert's gaze with his own. "Holy Mother of God. Aye. Aye, 'tis yours."

The cogs in Robert's mind whirred. "I must continue on to save my wife." He swung his sights on Guy. "Will you go back with the guards and do all you can to get those within the keep to safety—forget not that Morgana's mother and father are within the walls as well—then do what you can to put the fire out?"

"Of course." Guy said naught else, simply mounted his steed and began to fly back in the direction he'd come, not awaiting the guards.

"Rally our neighbors, if need be!" He called to Guy's back, satisfied when the man lifted his hand in recognition and accord as he galloped away.

Robert ran towards his men, who were several yards down stream from him. "Make haste! Go with Guy de Burgh!" he commanded. "Our keep is afire!"

A chorus of agitated "Ayes" filled the air as the men swung their horrified gazes in the direction of the MacVie land and scrambled onto their horses.

"Follow Guy de Burgh's command, for he acts as my proxy. Do what you must to save our people, then do what you can to save our fortress!"

* * *

Alone now, Robert hurriedly finished watering his horse, took several handfuls to drink himself, then mounted and quickly picked up the trail of his quarry once more. As he flew across the glen, it took everything within him to maintain the single-minded focus needed to the goal most paramount and to stifle the worry and ill-boding that threatened to rise up within him at any moment with regard to the welfare of his keep and clan.

* * *

Sunset came late this time of year, and tho' the two men had ridden at a slower pace once they'd gained the road east once more, Morgana battled fatigue. Hypnos poured out sleep upon her, enticing her to succumb to the divine torpor he offered, making her lids heavy and her mind muddled. She struggled mightily to stay awake, to shed the fog that crept slowly in, to concentrate on the direction in which the men were moving, on what they were saying to each other, on any small chance she might have to escape them, and to push away the waking dreams of violence and fire that crowded in uninvited.

A piercing pain at the tip of her breast yanked her back from the edge of oblivion and she cried out, wrenching away. In a fog, she tried lifting her hand to cover the pained region, but met the resistance of the cord that still bound her wrists. 'Twas in that moment that she became aware of the false priest's thumb stroking o'er the same stinging nipple. "Nay!" she shrieked, and tried to twist out of his hold. The maneuver was both a success and a failure, for tho' he released possession of her breast, he gripped her waist with a violent passion that frightened her even more.

A low rumble of angry laughter came from him then. "You are as well-formed as your mother," he murmured against her ear. "You shall make a fine replacement for my games I'll wager. Very fine indeed."

Her pulse pounded in her ears. She said the first thing that came to mind. "Nay, I'll not. For my husband will catch and kill you first."

The red-beard had evidently heard her words, for he burst into laughter as well. The false priest met his eye and grinned. "Nay, dove. *He'll* not," he answered, his gaze ne'er turning to her.

Panic sent her stomach into her throat. "What have you done?" A terrible foreboding squeezed at her heart.

"Only a few strategically placed vats of animal fat, and Symon's own recipe for Greek fire, my dove."

Her ears rung. "Wh—what do you mean?"

He threw his head back and chortled.

Symon answered. "Fire. Fire is what."

Robert! Modron! My clan! She bucked and lurched, bit and clawed her way out of his embrace and off the horse, landing hard on her hip and thigh, and skinning her cheek on the graveled road before she managed to roll and rise to her knees and then to her feet. She only made it ten to twelve running paces before he caught her by the arm and yanked her up against him, gripping so tight, she couldn't take air into her lungs.

"Nay, dove," the false priest murmured against her cheek, his hot, moist breath wetting her skin, making it crawl. "You are mine...at least, until you *are* no longer." He gripped her breast in a painful squeeze, sinking his teeth into the tender flesh at the base of her neck at the same time.

She elbowed him in the ribs, letting go a roar of fury, but it only whetted his appetite for her more, as his other lecherous hand clamped her between her legs, fondling her roughly there, and pushing her left hip and buttock against his grinding, engorged manhood. "Aye, there's fire in you, just like your mother."

Her racing heart tripped. A fleet thought: Was her mother dead, or alive? Nay, she had no time to ponder it now, as 'twas plain he'd take her with violence here on the ground, and in front of the red-beard, if she didn't manage to stop him. It demanded more will than she e'er believed she had, but she went slack in his brutal embrace, forcing her eyes to rest impassively upon the far distance, making sure to give him no sign that this attack on her frightened, pained, or affected her in any small way. And in that extended moment, she prayed that this new tack would dash his depraved desires, not ignite them even more.

* * *

Somewhere to Robert's left, an owl screeched, then flapped its wings into flight, making the tree's leaves, where it had so recently perched, shiver and shake. The dark shadow up ahead in the distance, which Robert had thought to be a river boulder stone, suddenly moved, became distinct, and he halted his tread, went still. The roe deer lifted his head, met his gaze briefly, then twisted and bolted into the stand of trees that graced the bank of *Garbh Uisge*.

He'd been leading his horse on foot, and by the puny light of a small torch fire, since darkness fell two hours past, as the road was uneven, and his horse needed a rest from his weight. He'd have to stop and allow the animal, and himself, a rest, but not yet. Nay, not yet. For his gut was telling him 'twas too soon, that if he kept moving, he'd gain on his prey. If not this night, then on the morrow, surely, and before they had an inkling of his presence. As well, there was the fear that gnawed and clawed like angry lions at his middle. The fear that if he ceased moving, if he rested the night, his wife would not be alive by the morn. As if a charm against evil, or a tangible connection to his wife, Robert ran the rough pads of his fingers o'er the rolled parchment in his pouch once more. *I'll let no harm come to you, Morgana. This I vow.*

He'd traveled another hour down the dark road that skirted the north bank of the river when he heard the low murmur of voices. He stilled, tensed and primed to strike, his eyes and ears honed. But as the sound became more distinct, he relaxed. 'Twas merely some canonical chanting. There must be a cloister near. Perhaps they had some well water, and some grain for his courser—and a bit of bread and meat for him as well. He'd not stay long, but he knew 'twas time to give his horse another rest, and if fortune shined on him, perhaps the clerics might have seen his wife with the two men, might be able to tell him that she still lived, might be able to say, for sure, how long ago they'd passed through.

He began to jog, moving toward the sound, and 'twas not long before he saw, twinkling in the blackness, several dark figures carrying tapers, and walking in a line. He slowed and stayed several paces behind them until they led him to the low stone gate that surrounded the court of a small chapel. As he watched them entering one-by-one through the door of the church, he tethered his horse to an iron ring in the gate, jogged over to the well and doused the torch in a bucket of water, then somberly, and quietly, followed the last of them inside.

Pushing the hood of his mail back from his head, he went down on one knee and bowed his head, awaiting the completion of the monks' service, and an indication from the abbot that he would be allowed an audience. After another quarter-hour, the abbot ended the service and came over to stand before Robert's kneeling form.

"I am Abbot Alasdair. By what name are you known, sire knight?"

"I am Robert MacVie, Laird and Chieftain to the MacVie's of Awe."

"Rise, Robert MacVie, and tell us what brings you to our humble church in the dark of night. Is aught amiss?"

Robert came to his feet, only recognizing then how short of stature the corpulent man of God truly was, as, for a brief moment, Robert only saw the crown of the abbot's shining tonsure before he stepped back a pace and craned his neck to meet Robert's gaze.

"I hunt the men who have snatched my wife." The abbot's eyes grew round. "There are two of them, and they are traveling with a woman—my wife. I believe she is dressed in plain wool, as a poor pilgrim." Robert swept his gaze o'er all in the chamber. "Have they passed by here?"

The abbot made a half-turn to include his brothers and said, "Nay, we've had no others rest here for many moons. Since Lenten last. Is that not so, Prior Fearghus?"

A tall, gaunt, white-caterpillar-browed monk answered, "Aye, that is so, Father Abbot."

A youth, not more than sixteen summers, with black hair and pale eyes took two steps forward, saying, "I saw three travelers on the road not long before sunset, Father, when I was crossing the south glen in search of the two missing ewes."

"Were they on horseback?" Robert asked, moving around the abbot.

"Aye, sire, they were, tho' I was not close enough to see their garb, or their faces, clearly. Two rode on one horse, a man in black cloth—possibly a priest's robe, but I cannot say for sure—and...and...aye, it could have been a lass riding with him, but the hood of her mantle hid her hair from view."

The priest! Of course! Why had he ne'er put that together before? "Aye, that would be them. I'm sure of it. And the other one? What of him?"

The youth's brows furrowed in thought. "As I said, I did not see their visages, but the second horseman was large, with red hair." His eyes brightened. "And red beard!" he said, his voice lifted in excitement.

The description sent Robert's heart into his stomach. *The apprentice!* What a fool he'd been! Donnach's minion had been directly under Robert's nose all these moons, and he'd failed to uncover the man's true purpose; failed to block the man from executing Donnach's murderous plan; failed to keep Morgana safe; and, now that Robert's suspicions regarding how the fire was set were confirmed, failed his clan as well.

"They were traveling east?" Robert finally managed.

"Aye, sire. East. 'Twas nigh on four—nay, five hours past."

Robert turned and addressed Abbot Alasdair. "I cannot tarry long here, but would beg a meal for both my horse and myself, and an hour or two to rest him as well before I begin my hunt once more."

The abbot nodded and, with a comforting pat on Robert's shoulder, led him through a short corridor off the nave and into the small chamber that was clearly being used as their refectory. He was given a pottage of venison and root vegetables within moments of being seated, along with a tankard of ale. Robert made short work of downing the meal, then asked again that he might beg some grain for his horse as well.

A half-hour later, he and his courser shared a stall filled with fresh hay, and at long last, he allowed himself to doze.

* * *

'Twas still dark when Robert woke with a start, his heart hammering in his chest. His body had betrayed his will and he'd fallen into a deep, dreamless sleep. *But for how long?* Pushing to his feet, he took precious moments to groom, feed, and water his courser before tacking it up again. Once out in the stable yard, he was able to gauge the time by the setting moon. He'd dawdled here at least two hours, 'twas clear, but he had every belief that the two men who held Morgana captive had stopped for the night somewhere as well.

Learning that his wife was still with the men late last eve had calmed Robert's worry, if only by a small degree. For, they'd had more than ample time to kill her and dispose of her body this day past, if that had been their intention. Nay, 'twas becoming plain to Robert that the men, Donnach's minions, had some other plan in mind for Morgana—at least before they snuffed the life from her—which would give him the blessed time he needed to catch and kill them first. Donnach, he'd leave for his King—and Morgunn—to deal with.

There were already a few lay monks and brothers moving about the small court, readying for their day's labors when Robert passed through leading his steed. One of them, the youth from the night before, waved to him, then jogged over.

"There is a small village, some few miles from here, where your lady and her captors may have taken their rest. 'Tis not directly on the road, but off a bit to the north. There is a footpath to it, just look for an old, gnarled oak that sports a wooden sign on its trunk with 'Ale' scribed on it, and an arrow pointing to the path."

Robert gave him a grim nod. "My thanks. Here,"—he counted out 12 pence from his pouch and handed them to the lad—" give these to Abbot Alasdair, along with my thanks."

"Bless you, sire. I shall pray for your lady, and your victory."

Robert gave him another grim nod, then hoisted himself onto his mount and walked the courser out the gate.

The sun began to rise as he traveled down the east road, the horizon ablaze in a shimmering gossamer veil of orange and yellow light. 'Twas not long until he at last saw the oak the youth had spoken of and, as he came closer, the path as well. He veered to his left and maneuvered his courser along the well-worn, and somewhat o'ergrown trail. He'd traveled nearing a quarter-hour when, beyond a rise, he beheld in the distance a cluster of wooden, as well as wattle and daub buildings. The largest stood, with smoke rising in curls and twists from the center of its roof, on the east side of the path that continued on through the village.

Allowing his horse to pick its way down the path's incline, Robert took that time to study again the flattened grass; the infrequent clods of turned-up soil; the fresh horse tracks in both directions, indicating riders carrying some load had recently passed there. He was almost certain they were made by the mounts of the men he hunted, but he would know with certainty once he spoke to the alewife. And, mayhap, he might learn if the men let slip their exact destination once their tongues were loosed by drink.

* * *

By Morgana's estimation, they'd traveled at least twelve miles o'er these three hours past, and she had little doubt they would have traveled further, had the darkness and pots in the road not slowed their mounts. She strained to remain forward, upright, and with always some small distance between her frame and that of her captor's on the mount she'd been forced to share with him these long, unending hours since her capture.

Thanks be to heaven that her ploy had worked, at least the once, and the false priest had let her be, had molested her no further, but she did not know if 'twould be as successful, should she be forced to employ the ruse again.

The time she'd spent bound to the gnarled oak this night past, not long after her attempt to fight and flee, had been the only rest Morgana had been able to attain. Her captors had left her there while they went into the village, down the rough-hewn path off the east road that led to an alehouse, so they might engage in a drunken revel, and find provender for them and their horses. It had surprised her, not an hour after the two men had left her there, when the red-beard returned for her and, after threatening to slice out her tongue if she uttered even one sound, had taken her back to the village with him, where she'd been put into service pouring ale out for all the patrons at the house.

Aye, but it had proved more of a boon to Morgana than she'd hoped, for she'd managed to steal a blade from off one of the tables. Her conscience was sore, and she'd given an oath to herself that if God allowed her to survive, she'd return the knife to the yeoman she'd stolen it from, for she knew the price to replace such a worthy tool would feed the man for near a moon.

She had no notion of when she might be able to put the weapon to use, but the having of it bolstered her lagging courage ne'ertheless. *Do any come for me? Does Robert?* She wanted desperately to crane her neck around and search the land behind them, but 'twould only draw the false priest's attention, and no doubt his libidinous wrath as well. Nay, she'd not take that chance.

'Twas growing e'er more evident to her that, if she wanted to remain alive, she was going to have to save herself. She would look for any opportunity to gain her freedom, and she'd not hesitate to fight, if that was what was needed. In spite of the red-beard's words of the night before, she'd gone into the village with a clear intention of begging refuge there from someone of import, of revealing that she was being held captive by men who intended to murder her. Unfortunately, she'd soon seen her intention would not be possible. For, there were only the alewife;—a hard, sharp-eyed woman who had naught to say to anyone if it did not pertain to fattening her coffers—drunken louts; ill-mannered boors; poor yeomen and tradesmen passing an hour there; and a serving maid that Morgana soon saw was serving up more than ale to the men when the brazen lass had gone out the back, hanging on the arm of a man, returning not a quarter-hour later, disheveled, red-cheeked, and limpid-eyed. Nay, Morgana had known then, in such vulgar company she'd find no protector.

* * *

"Aye, th' three of 'em passed time 'ere durin' th' night, but leeft agin 'fore th' cock's crow, soom three hours past," the buxom, black-haired serving wench said, stepping nearer, so close to him now that he had an unhindered view of the tops of her creamy-white breasts. "But th' priest said th' lass was to be a maid to th' red-haired merchant's betrothed."

There was a time, before Morgana, Robert would have easily and gladly accepted the invitation, but now it served only to grind at his patience. With effort, he held back the rebuke that formed on his tongue and said instead, "She—the maid—She was in good health? No wounds or marks upon her?"

"Nay, she was sound. Weel, 'cept fer a scratch on her cheek. An' th' merchant e'en give 'er o'er to me ma to help serve th' drinkers their ale."

A scratch? Anger boiled in his gut. He'd flay them, then beat them, then kill them.

The wench's look grew shrewd. "Is she yers then? Has she 'scaped yer bed 'fore ye were doon wit' 'er?" Her long-lashed, glimmering brown eyes scanned with some avarice down to his groin, tho' 'twas well hidden by his tunic and mail "If ye've an itch, pleased I'd be to scratch it, if ye want." Her gaze slid to the pouch of coin Robert held loosely in his hand at his side. " 'Tis eight pence a tickle I commonly ask, but fer ye, 'tis naught."

Again, he bit back a sharp retort. " 'Tis a generous and tempting offer you give, lass, but I cannot tarry. I thank you for sharing what tidings you could regarding the lass I seek." Robert fished six pence from his pouch and handed it to her. "Take this as recompense." As she avidly counted the coins, he said, "Tell me, lass, know you where they were heading?"

She looked up and blinked at him, then answered, "Aye. Aye, they were goin' to th' ol' burial site some miles distant. Joost follow th' road east, then look fer th' ol' tumbled well, and a few miles past tha', there be a path to th' south. Take tha', and 'twill lead ye to th' place."

With a nod, Robert swung around and mounted his courser. Once astride, he settled his gaze on the upturned visage of the wench once more. "My thanks," he said, and with a dip of his head, turned and led the horse back toward the east road. He'd traveled only a few paces when he heard at his back, "Coom back to see me, if ye should want, and I'll nay charge ye!"

Robert smiled, in spite of his worry and his grim mood, and lifted his hand in salute.

CHAPTER 18

'TWAS IN THE gloaming by the time Morgana's captors stopped at the base of a hillock. This second day of travel, the two men had been less anxious, had stopped more often to rest their horses, had not even ridden them hard, which told Morgana that no one had followed.

For some miles now, a strong sense of recognition had pervaded her being, and now, seeing the ancient stones standing tall against the night sky, and the slab that lay askew atop what she knew to be a hidden underground chamber, her fragmented memories of this place coalesced. 'Twas her and the other clan children's secret fortress. A place they'd come to play, to look for fey folk, and to hold their pretend faery court. A distant cousin, she recalled, always insisted on being king.

But, why had they stopped here? Was this the burial site of which they'd spoken this day past? Her heart tripped, then escalated in meter. She'd had it in her head that 'twould be closed graves they'd bring her to, not here, where the ancients had held their pagan sacrificial rites.

"They'll ne'er think to look for her in this forsaken place," the false priest said, pulling a flask of water from his satchel and taking a long swallow before continuing, "But it grows late, and as we've seen no sign of any who follow, I think it safe to bide the night here before we flee."

"Where is the load of copper bullion we were promised at Lenten to do this deed? He will not yet have got the missive we gave coin to the lad to deliver to him in the last village we passed through, so he still knows not our plan."

" 'Tis on a ship, harboured at *Inverleith*, and awaiting our arrival. But we'll not get our hands on it until he's sure his niece is dead, and no one has traced the vanishing back to him."

"But if he does not pay...?"

"He'll pay. He filled my coffers well with the first of his schemes, and then you reaped the benefit of that payment to me as well. He shall honor his debt to us, this I vow." The false priest pointed to the slab that covered the underground chambers at the top of the mound. "Move the stone and prepare the place. I'll bring her up in a moment."

The red-beard gave a nod, slid from his horse, walked it several paces away to one of the standing stones, tied it there, then lumbered up the incline.

After his cohort was out of earshot, the false priest

slid from his mount, then yanked her by one of her bound arms, making her topple in an awkward fall forward from the horse, twisting her still tender ankle yet again, and nearly spraining it as she plummeted into his rough embrace.

Without mercy, he dragged her with him to the stone and tied his own mount there as well, then bent down and pressed his cheek to hers. "I thought to share you with Symon," he hissed in her ear, "before we end this 'venture, but I think now...not." He gripped her buttocks until they stung, and pressed her mons into his repulsive arousal. Her gorge threatened to come up and she shook her head.

His hot serpent's tongue slashed o'er her earlobe. "I'll send him off on an errand later, so that we can be alone," he hissed in a whisper.

"Nay! Never!" She tried to twist from his hold, a squeal of exertion exploding from her throat. When he only laughed and squeezed her tighter—so tight, it cut off her wind—and then clamped his wet, acrid mouth to hers, she bit down hard on his lip until she tasted blood.

"Ow-w—You shrew!" He flung her from him and she fell onto her side at the base of the grass-covered hillock, scraping again the same cheek as the night before, making it sting and, no doubt, bleed afresh. Thankfully, her skirts had not risen enough to reveal the purloined weapon she'd strapped to her calf. Tho' her wrists were still bound behind her, she struggled to rise. The effort nearly put her shoulder out of joint, but she finally made it to a sitting position. She'd barely caught her breath before he hauled her to her feet, wrenched her around and pushed her, making her stumble but not fall, as she was forced to walk up to her grave.

* * *

Robert tied his horse to a tree a half-mile from the place he'd seen his quarry turn off the path they'd been on for o'er an hour. 'Twas not more than a quarter-hour more before he saw in the growing darkness the licking orange flame of a torch positioned on a knoll up ahead. *This must be the burial site.* He stealthily made his way closer, crouching as he moved forward and doing all he could to seem part of the shadowed land.

He'd pushed his mount hard to catch up to the three, and had at last been successful some five hours past, tho' he'd remained far enough behind them that he would not be detected, or suspected. 'Twas during that time, he began to ponder the best strategy for freeing his wife; killing the priest, who Robert knew from past experience would have been the one responsible for his wife's chafed cheek; and capturing the apprentice as proof against the uncle.

Several yards from the base of the rise he spied the horses tethered to a tall standing stone. *God be praised!* The men had made the first tactic in his plan easy. He went down on his belly and crawled closer to the stone until the men's horses served to hide him from view. Using some of the rope he'd brought with him, he hobbled the animals' legs, intermittently soothing and murmuring to each when it snorted or balked.

Next, he moved in a hunched run around the base

of the hillock until he reached the side that was not visible from the underground burial chamber, due to the position of the slab o'er its opening. From his close proximity, he could now hear the raised voice of the priest. He was telling his confederate to unsaddle the horses for the night and take them down to the burn that flowed a quarter-mile away to let them drink and feed on the grass. In spite of all that was at stake, Robert grinned, mentally rubbing his hands together in anticipation of the coming battle.

Crouching down as low as he could go, he prepared to pounce.

* * *

Morgana surreptitiously slid the blade from its leather sheath as she watched the priest help the red-beard awkwardly maneuver himself on all fours through the small opening of the carn. It had been necessary to unbind her wrists in order to get her inside, and the false priest had yet to rebind them. 'Twas clear this was the best, and only, chance she'd have of escape, and she intended to take it—with zeal. Even if it meant committing a mortal sin, even if it went against all her teachings at the convent, and even if she was not successful and she was killed in spite of her endeavor not to be.

For this man, this false priest, had led the brigade of bandits who'd attacked her family and had later defiled her mother multiple times, and in front of a bairn of a mere five summers. And now, he intended to defile her as well, before ending her life and leaving her remains to rot in this forgotten tomb of the ancients.

***

The apprentice heaved himself into a standing position with a grunt, then worked a knot out of his neck with his fingers, grumbling under his breath the entire time. Robert fisted the grass under his hands to keep from rushing the man there and then, but he knew his best chance at a clean capture would be once his quarry was by the restless animals. So, Robert held his breath and waited until the man was halfway to the tree where they'd tethered their beasts before he began a silent crab-walk around the slope toward his prey. When the apprentice was but two paces from the animals, Robert sprang forward, flung the noose around the man's neck, and yanked him to the ground. As Robert had planned, the rope cut off the man's wind, and his quarry made no more than a puling, strangled sound.

Robert fell upon him with a right to his jaw, sending the man into a swoon, to keep him still long enough to bind his hands, so that he could loose the noose to allow him breath again. Tho' he'd like naught more than to slice his gullet clear through, he'd not forgot that the villainous vermin was worth more to him alive than dead, so he suppressed the urge and forced his focus back on the task at hand.

***

"Your mother learned quick enough," the false priest said, sliding the rope through his hand and walking on his knees toward her, " 'twas best to obey me than to defy me."

Morgana gripped the hilt of the blade, hidden in the

folds of her gown, in her clammy fist, ready to strike. Her heart raced so, she feared it might seize. In the quiet of the cold, dim tomb, she could hear the *whish* of her ragged breath as she sucked in, then blew out again.

"Aye, she learned that lesson early on." He paused in his motion, dropping his gaze to the rope and continuing in a musing voice, " 'Twas a shame, what happened." He blinked, as if coming out of a dream and focused on Morgana once more. "But, alas, it could not be helped."

Morgana sat forward. Somehow, she found the courage to ask, "What mean you? Did you ki— is my mother dead?"

The false priest's visage tightened, grew stern. He sat back on his heels, resting his hands and the rope on his thighs. "The foolish whore tried to fight me, and caught her gown on fire. She was burned, scarred." He let out a hallow laugh. "I thought surely 'twould douse the flame of my desire for her, but I found it only kindled it higher."

But does she live?! Morgana wanted to scream the words, and would have, except the man took up his knee-walk toward her once more and she swallowed them back. *Go directly into the groin or neck.* The heart or lungs would be good, too, but if she missed or hit bone, it might not lay him low long enough for her to make her escape. She sent a grateful thanks to the bloodthirsty ladies she'd met at court who had avidly watched the men on the tourney field and eagerly spoken of all the quick-kill maneuvers a knight might employ in a real battle to the death.

"If I enjoy you as well as I did your mother, I might just keep you." The false priest reached out and gripped her chin between his thumb and forefinger. "You'd prefer that, would you not, to burial alive? Give me your wrists."

Strike! Morgana straightened, tense, but kept her gaze locked on that of her captor's. *Strike!* Her heart raced. Her frame shook. *Strike!* Fanning her fingers, she clenched tight the hilt once more. *Strike now!* She lunged forward and swung the blade.

"Wha—?" The false priest grabbed hold of her wrist and twisted until her numb hand let loose the weapon and it fell to the earthen floor.

God in heaven! She'd missed.

"I'll beat you raw for this!" he said, clamping his hand o'er the bleeding wound in his shoulder.

"I think not," came an all-too-welcome and familiar male voice as she watched him leap to the ground behind the false priest. In the same movement, he kicked out, hitting her captor from behind and propelling him face-first into the wall next to her.

The false priest whirled around and, bellowing, plowed into her husband's middle with his shoulder, but thankfully Robert's larger girth kept him firmly on his feet.

"Hurry! Flee! *Now!*" Robert said to her as he yanked the priest's head back by the hair then punched him in the jaw, sending him sprawling onto his arse.

Morgana rushed to obey. As she skirted the two men to gain the exit, the false priest struggled to his feet, swayed a moment, then barreled forward with the same crude blade in his hand Morgana had used on him moments before, aimed right at Robert's face.

"Robert!" she cried out in warning, frozen in place behind her husband.

Robert grabbed the man's wrist in an iron fist to deflect the blow, then pressed the blade, still in the false priest's hand, against the man's throat.

Just then, a calloused, beefy palm snaked from behind Morgana and clamped o'er her mouth and nose, impeding her ability to breathe. She clawed and stomped, tried to fight, but could not break the man's grip.

"You make this too easy," Robert said to the false priest through gritted teeth.

"Aye, you do," the red-beard said, tossing her away from him onto the cold, stone floor.

The false priest grinned.

"Blood of Christ!" Robert gritted out, swinging his head around just as a *thud!* rent the air.

Morgana watched in terror, Robert's head loll, his eyes roll back, and his frame crumple to the floor of the carn.

"What took you so long?" the false priest said, tucking the dirk in his belt and sliding her husband's sword from its sheath, then kicking it so that it landed at the red-beard's feet. While he listened to his confederate's reply, he lifted the rope he'd dropped earlier and restrained Robert with it, binding his arms against his chest, and his ankles together.

"He ambushed me and tied me up outside, but he didn't know of my ability to slip from such bonds by moving my bones from their sockets." The red-beard let the stone clatter to the floor, then lifted the rope tied 'round his neck and let it slither through his palm as he hissed, " 'Tis clear we've been found out, so I say let's kill them here and now, barricade the entry, and get to that ship that holds our copper and then on to our own holdings without further delay."

The false priest's eyes narrowed on her. "Nay, I've got a bit of unfinished business with the mute." He reached out his hand to the red-beard. "Hand me that...and give me an hour, then, aye, we'll make haste from this hole."

Morgana's heart sped. *Oh-God-Oh-God.*

The red-beard growled. "Nay! We must leave forthwith!"

"Aye, and we will. In an hour. The rope."

The red-beard grudgingly handed it over, but protested, "We know not how close behind are his men, for 'tis sure there will be more."

"I believe he is but one, and that is why we've seen no others yet."

"He'd not have undertaken this on his own."

"An hour more, or I take the mute with me."

"Are you mad? Do you want to hang?"

As the two men continued to argue, Morgana's gaze tripped from her captors to her husband. A trickle of blood ran o'er his forehead, across the bridge of his nose, and dripped into the dark red puddle that had formed near his cheek. She waited with breath held and eyes keen until she at last saw a slight rise and fall in his back and shoulders. *He lives!* Praise be.

Now. How to save them both. She took a look

around. From playing here as a bairn, she knew that there were two other chambers off this one, but none held another opening to the outside. So, her only option was to somehow o'erpower her captors and gain the exit. But how? *How?*

In the next moment, the false priest yanked her up with a vicious grip 'round the tender flesh of her upper arm, whirled, kicked Robert in the side, and said, "Wake up!", then told his confederate to gather their belongings and wait for him by the horses.

* * *

Robert battled his initial instinct to pound his fist into the priest's face until all that remained was an oozing mass of blood, flesh and broken bone, for daring to touch Morgana in such a manner. Instead, he listened to the other that told him to continue the ruse, which he'd begun moments before when he'd first awakened, that he slumbered still, in hopes that his captors would become careless, and he would then be able to implement the remainder of his original plan.

He'd been trying to find a way to divide the two so that he could vanquish them one at a time, when the priest had told the apprentice to leave him with Morgana for an hour. Tho' Robert had nearly come out of his skin, so great had been his thirst to pulverize the lascivious priest, the realization that, yet again, the two men were making this venture easy for him, as well as the fact that the priest would ne'er have a chance to implement his lechery, had served to temper the need.

From behind his lashes, Robert watched the apprentice, clearly annoyed, but submitting to the priest's wishes, grumble under his breath and reach for his leather satchel, then trudge toward the false priest's to do the same with his. He left Robert's sword where it lay on the ground, either from dull-wittedness or rebellion, Robert knew not which. 'Twas a tight squeeze, just as it had been for Robert, but the apprentice at last managed to wiggle and worm his way back through the opening of the carn.

Robert had already managed to slide the hidden dirk from its sheath. Thanks again to the bumbling of which e'er man had tied him, his work had been made simple, for the manner in which he'd been bound had left him access to his weapon. He began surreptitiously sawing at his bonds, but they were proving harder to cut through than he'd expected. Swallowing a growl of frustration, he doubled his effort, hoping against hope that the priest would not see the added movement. He must get free, and before the priest could do his will on Morgana.

In the next moment, when he heard the distinct sound of cloth ripping, Robert knew he'd not been fast enough. Swinging his gaze to his wife, he was met with the smooth, white flesh of her breast on display and her dainty white hands fighting the angular, yellow-nailed, blue-veined ones to keep from being bound with rope. With a vociferous roar and the crazed furor of a demon, Robert raged openly against his bonds. "Lay so much as a finger on her again, and you'll beg for the bliss of death before I'm done with you!" he told the priest.

"Ah, good. You are awake," the priest answered

without looking at him, clearly set on his purpose, and confident in his belief Robert was securely bound and of no real threat to him any longer. " 'Twill be much more enjoyable with you as unwilling witness." Finally managing to capture Morgana's wrists, he said to her, "I like a good tussle, sweeting...so, pray, continue," and yanked her forward until her exposed breast was only a mere quarter-inch from his chest.

Recognizing the gruffness in the priest's voice for what it was: Lust for flesh, Robert bellowed, "Touch her and die!" just as the last stubborn fragment of rope broke loose and his wife began to sing.

Morgana's pure, sweet voice, raised in song, sent spikes of dread through his heart. He caught her gaze. 'Twas bright. Too bright. If he didn't get them both out of here now, her mind, already fragile, would surely break.

But first... he must... he... must... shake... must... shake... this-s-s ...leth...argy. Against his will, his lids dropped o'er his eyes and he was transported to a glen, greener than any he'd e'er seen, surrounded by mountains and a wood, and with beams of sunlight and a faery queen's enchanting song swirling and swirling all about him.

* * *

The answer to how she could save herself and her husband had come with a flash of memory, like an answered prayer, and now Morgana fervently hoped the effect of her song inside this underground chamber would work its magic as swiftly upon her captor as it had done the members of the pretend faery court she'd held here as a bairn.

When her eyes had shifted for at least the hundredth time to her wounded husband a moment past and her gaze had, at last, been snared in the hot liquid silver of his, hope had filled her heart and trilled e'er higher from her throat in joyous sound.

"Shut...*huh*...." The priest's eyelids drooped. He swayed on his feet. "...your gob, w-*huh*-wench!"

Ah. 'Twas working. *Praise be to heaven.* Zealous now in her pursuit, Morgana lifted her voice louder in song, and, in the next instant, when the priest reached out for her, she found victory, for his eyes closed, his head drooped, and his frame teetered, before collapsing to the floor. Again, she sent a silent prayer of praise to God.

Galvanized into action, she captured the rope that had fallen in a slithery coil next to the false priest and tied his wrists and his ankles together behind him, as she'd seen done by the sheriff when she was a lass of twelve summers. The official and his men had captured a criminal in the wood and had brought him to hang in the town square near the nunnery.

Next, she went to kneel at her husband's side. He'd fallen under the mystical spell woven by her song reverberating within the walls of the carn as well. Leaning down, she brushed her lips o'er his, then whispered his name in his ear. When that didn't rouse him, she nibbled his earlobe. At last, she heard a low rumble come from his chest, and his arms enfolded her, taking her with him as he rolled onto his back.

He swept her up in a savage kiss, squeezing her so

tight within his strong embrace, that she thought her ribs would crack. She cared not. For that lost, glorious moment, the world around them receded, and there were only the two of them. She answered his passion with the heat and need of her own. Aye, for that spare, wonderful moment, all her worry, all the reasons she'd given herself for fleeing him, were diminished, and all that existed between them was their mutual desire.

Robert broke the kiss first. "Where—" He blinked and craned his neck to look in the direction of the false priest. "Ah, I see. You'll tell me later how you managed it, for now, I must take care of the other one." He rolled her off him, and sat up, but swayed, dropping his head in his hands. "Blood of Christ!"

"Robert!" Morgana exclaimed, folding her arm around his shoulder. "Are—"

"—I didn't think the blow to my head that red devil gave me so fierce that 'twould render me weak as a lass, but my pate must not be as hard as I thought, for I fell into another swoon a moment ago, and into a strange dream as well, and now all about me spins."

If she could lure the red-beard in here, she could weave the spell of the song and the carn on him as well. She started to rise. "Rob—"

Her husband startled her mid-rise by grasping her hand and pulling her back down. "Nay," he told her, "stay here, but well away from the priest. For, tho' he is well-bound, I will not risk your safety another time." He maneuvered himself to his feet, taking up his sword where it had been flung by the man earlier as he did so, and continued, "When you hear the clash of steel, then flee. I will somehow loose a horse for you. Take it and get back on the road to *Sruighlea*. Go directly to the King's castle, and I will meet you there—or, if fortune holds, on the road. You will give me then, in *Sruighlea*, the truth of why you left me." He dropped his gaze to hers, seeming to take the briefest of moments to memorize the contours of her visage as he stroked his fingers o'er her cheek. When his silver gaze settled once more on her own, she saw the steel behind the look, heard the steel in the tone, when he said, "Stay." Then, as she watched, pulse pounding, and nerves rioting, he squirmed his way out of the small opening to the carn, sword-first, and balanced in an iron-fisted hand.

When he was gone, her eyes tripped briefly to the still-dozing false priest. He'd not remain so for long, and she would not have him divine her ploy and use it against her, so she defied the first of her husband's edicts and scooted over to her slumbering captor. Using her purloined dirk, which he'd tucked in his belt earlier, to cut away a strip from her linen chemise, she then muzzled him with the cloth. In the midst of doing so, his eyes shot wide, and Morgana was met with a look of venomous hatred just before the unmistakable sound of clashing swords and raised voices bounded in to them from outside.

Next, and once more defying her husband's orders, she crawled far enough out of the opening of the underground chamber to get a view of what transpired outside it. She did this with the thought, again, that, if need be, she'd lure the red-beard into the carn and thrall him with her song, as she'd done so easily to the priest. She'd not leave Robert here, no matter his order to do so, not when she had such a weapon—and certainly not without knowing whether he would vanquish the other man. In most instances, she'd ne'er question, but with the strike to the head Robert had received—and the ensuing slumber it had caused—her surety was shaken.

Crouching low in the shadowed recesses next to the carn's opening, Morgana swept the surroundings with her gaze, instantly noting that, as Robert had promised, one of the men's horses looked to have bolted into the grasses some distance away, and now grazed there, fully tacked up and packed with his master's burdens.

If not for the torch, the only light she'd have would be from the full moon and its neighboring stars. But thanks to the flame, she could see the battle that ensued between her husband and the red-beard very well. From behind her, she heard the muffled grunts and gyrations of the false priest as he fought to free himself, but couldn't, and a small smile of satisfaction bloomed on her lips.

Taking in a deep breath to bolster her courage beforehand, she then began the slow, creeping, low-crouching movement down the side of the carn. Not toward the horse, as her husband had decreed, but toward the two fighting men, as her heart demanded.

CHAPTER 19

"*I* SHOULD GUT you now," Robert growled as steel sparked against steel.

"Try it and die."

Robert chuckled. "Nay, you are worth more to me"—with a swift twist of his wrist, he nicked the apprentice's neck with the edge of his blade—"alive."

"*Ahhh*. And—And—you are worth more to me...*huh*...dead."

Robert grinned. As he circled his opponent, he caught a flash of moonspun hair behind the man's shoulder, and taunted him no further. With a bloodthirsty cry, he hefted his sword o'er his head and came down hard with the broad side of his blade to the red devil's skull, just as the man executed a strike of his own. 'Twould have sliced Robert through from shoulder to hip, if not for the wild, star-kissed virago, who leapt on the man's back with a voracious yell, sending the killing blow careening off mark. His opponent staggered back, a look of stunned disbelief on his face. He swayed, glass-eyed and gape-mouthed, dropped slowly to one knee with Morgana still clinging, clenching him in a stranglehold about his neck, then succumbed to Morpheus' irresistible lure, crashing face-first to the ground like a great fallen oak.

In the short stretch of stunned silence that followed, his wife lay motionless, sprawled atop her would-be murderer, and Robert's temper flared. Pulling her up by her waist, he said only, "Go and stand with your mount."

'Twas not until after he'd gotten the man bound that Robert felt his pulse begin to slow, and the eviscerating fear his wife's antics had caused him begin to lessen. The ire at her rash daring, however, had grown.

* * *

From the corner of Morgana's eye, she saw her husband approaching. She knew he was angry with her for not obeying him, but she'd not cringe from his anger. Morgana bit her lip. *Much.* She did not look his way, instead continuing her affectionate strokes to the horse's mane.

When he was not more than a yard from where she stood, he rumbled, "You should be a mile up the road by now."

She nodded, was about to explain, when he startled her by unceremoniously hoisting her up onto the back of the mount.

"You could have been killed—by *my blow*—you could have been killed."

She leaned down and touched her hand to his shoulder

and he flinched.

"Ro—"

"Nay. Later. After." He led the animal back over to where the other was still tethered, then left her there with the bound red-beard and disappeared back inside the carn.

Many long minutes later, and with Morgana—and now the awakened red-beard—as audible witness to the sound of raised voices and battling bodies, Robert at last emerged from the underground chamber, grim-faced, blood-spattered, and gripping the false priest's bonds in his hand. Tellingly, he was alone.

"Wh-what did you do?" she said, frantic. "Did you kill him?"

He did not answer, did not even meet her eye when he passed by her, heaved the red-beard to his feet, then adjusted the ropes around the man's ankles. Afterward he untied the reins of the other horse, led it toward her, took hold of her reins as well, then shoved the red-beard in the direction of the path that led back to the road saying, "Walk."

As Robert marched them away from the carn, Morgana's alarm grew. Despite all inner voices screaming for her not to do so, she looked behind her, struggling to gain one more glimpse of the carn where she'd played as a bairn, where she'd nearly lost her life, and where she'd left the false priest shackled...and still alive. But, the torch had been doused, and she was met with only deep purple shadows. *Robert killed him.* The false priest was a threat to her no longer. Twin waves of nausea and relief swept her being. After a moment, she sent a small prayer heavenward for the man's soul, then resolutely turned to face forward once more.

* * *

Some time later, once they were well on the road to the King's court, and after Robert had hobbled the apprentice's horse, tethered himself to the man by the waist, mounted his own courser, then granted the man a seat upon the fettered horse, he at last allowed his thoughts to shift back to his wife.

She'd attacked the apprentice with the fervor of a rabid beast, as a mother protects her young. Despite Robert's ire at her reckless attack, now that 'twas past, and she'd survived it,—and his pulse had at last slowed to its normal meter—he could permit the warm glow of gratitude and pride for her demonstration of loyalty to seep into his bones and bind his heart in gossamer ribands once more. He'd worried her fond regard for him had lessened, that 'twas the true reason she'd so easily left him, no matter the words she'd writ. And her show of bravery, no matter how perilous to her own safety, made his chest expand with pride. His hands gripped the reins. Aye, the same chest that would have borne a fatal blow, if not for that rash action she'd taken. She'd saved his life.

His gaze drifted to her gently-cut profile and his heart tripped. *Beautiful.*

Yet. There was tension there as well, for her brows were furrowed and she worried her lip with her teeth. Her words when he'd come from the carn floated across his mind. *Wh-what did you do? Did you kill him?* Aye, she liked it not that he'd fought the priest to the death. But he'd done what needed to be done, and he'd not defend it. He'd given the priest a fair fight, and the man had lost. 'Twas the way of battle—and the way of the world.

Wait.

Thunderstruck, Robert could do naught more than stare at Morgana, heart pounding, blood rushing. "You are mute no more."

His wife laughed, and he was enchanted. 'Twas the sound of tinkling faery bells. It wove a spell 'round his being, tighter—and softer—than any man-made bonds he'd e'er known. It made him giddy.

"Aye, and my memory has returned as well," she told him, darting a worried glance past him to the apprentice, before settling her sparkling blue eyes and radiant smile on Robert at last.

The reminder that they were not alone, as well as the reminder of his true purpose, brought him back to himself and he gave a short nod, then turned his attention back to the road. "We'll arrive in *Sruighlea* sometime after nones"

From the corner of his eye, he saw his wife's shoulders droop as she said, "So long? I thought—I remembered—*Sruighlea* being closer than that."

Robert lifted a brow. Clearly, she had some familiarity with this area. Something else he'd have to wait to glean from her when this business was concluded. She was weary, that much was plain. "I shall inveigle the sheriff there to aid in the transport of my prisoner to where the King is holding court in Scone. While I do so, you will have a bed—and a bath—if it please you."

Again she turned her delightful smile upon him. "Aye, 'twill please me well."

* * *

Robert had not been wrong. They'd arrived in *Sruighlea* not long after nones, and Morgana, after first washing the ink from her hair, was now avidly standing at the basin scrubbing the palpable grime, and the impalpable horror, from her quickly pinkening skin. The proprietor of the thriving inn had given her his own chamber to rest and bathe in, and the overstuffed mattress and soft bedding was calling to her. She'd not slept more than a few winks in the past two nights and now that the immediate danger was past, she could barely keep her lids open.

How her husband, who'd likely had as little sleep as she these past days, and had in addition sustained a blow to the head, still managed to remain sensate, she could not ken. She supposed 'twas due to his long years of training for war, and warrioring as well, that gave him the power to endure and remain alert in such deprived circumstances.

The sound of the door handle rattling startled her from her thoughts and she jumped, flinging the wet cloth and her arms across her breasts and calling out o'er her shoulder, "I need naught more, my thanks!"

* * *

Robert stepped o'er the threshold saying "I've—" He stopped short, the remaining words dying on his lips as his eyes hungrily devoured the blessed sight before him. He'd not been witness to the lush, glowing flesh of her in far too long, and now every muscle, every tendon, in his frame went rigid with desire. His heart raced. *Bed. No. She is not wanting to bear again yet. Seed wool, then bed. Nay, fool! You've still Donnach to deal with.* Flaming hunger turned swiftly to leaden disappointment and he said brusquely, "I see all is well. I shall be keeping watch on the prisoner throughout the night. Be ready to leave at sunrise." He dipped his head in quick salute saying, "Sleep well," then took a step backward into the corridor once more, closing the door firmly as he did so. He stood there a full minute blindly staring at the wood portal and trying to catch his breath. Finally, and resolutely, he marched back to the sheriff's garrison to spend the night outside the cell of his prisoner.

* * *

Morgana slowly slid her arms down and dropped the now-cold cloth into the basin of soapy water. Robert's visage had been so harsh, so stern, and his tone the same. Would he ne'er forgive her for hurtling herself into the fray between him and the red-beard? Or was his anger more centered on her attempted desertion of her marriage vows? A small sigh escaped her throat, and she abandoned her bath, stepping over to her chemise and wiggling into it, before settling despondently curled on her side on top of the mattress.

Clearly, naught had changed between them. Tho' Morgana admitted to herself, she *had* held some hope that his rush to find her, that his ensuing battle with her captors, and that the passionate kiss he'd given her, proved that he held some depth of feeling for her. But mayhap not.

Had his pursuit of her been driven more by his sense of duty and honor, and not by affection, as she'd so desperately hoped? And *had* the kiss been more a reaction to his relief that the priest had not slain her while he was still in the grip of his dark swoon, rather than actual passion and desire for her?

Aye. Mayhap.

For, there was still Vika. Still the unborn bairn.

Naught had changed. And when she arrived at court on the morrow, she'd beg a privy word with the King to request his aid in dissolving her and Robert's union.

* * *

An hour before daybreak Robert coiled the woolen blanket he'd dozed on all night outside the apprentice's cell into a tight roll and worked the stiffness from his shoulder.

"The cart is ready for your prisoner, Laird MacVie," the sheriff said, striding down the corridor toward him. He was young for his office, Robert had noted that immediately upon meeting him. But he was ardent in his pursuit to fulfill his duties, which Robert found admirable. Tall and wiry, with more lean than fat on his bones, and with more down than bristle on his chin, he met Robert's eye unflinchingly as he came nearer.

"Good. Let us secure him, then I shall fetch my wife and we can depart forthwith."

Over the next half-hour, Robert oversaw the chaining of his captive inside the locked cage attached to the bed of the cart. He'd thoroughly questioned the man this day past, and even spoken again to him late in the night. After no small amount of brute persuasion, the apprentice had at last yielded, telling Robert all he knew of Donnach's plot against both Morgana and her mother and father. Telling him also of the young kitchen maid he'd brought into the deadly deceit. He'd also given Robert the location of the ship which held the apprentice's pay for his part in Donnach's plot. That would go a long way in implicating Donnach, because the copper bullion could be traced directly back to the mines he'd been bequeathed after Morgunn's supposed death.

* * *

As she was led toward her mount with the assured pressure of Robert's large hand in the small of her back, Morgana could not help but to glance at the prisoner when she passed by the caged cart. The brawny redbeard looked defeated, and resigned. Shackled as he was, and safe behind iron bars, he'd lost all his fearsome demeanor and now, with the threat he presented to her life quelled, she found herself feeling pity for him—pity for the fate he was to meet once they arrived at the King's court.

In spite of her weariness, she'd not managed more than a few hours of fitful slumber the night before. Disappointment, dread, and a sense of finality weighed upon her heart and mind, keeping her just outside the misty portal to Hypnos' realm.

" 'Tis not too late to acquire a covered cart," Robert said to her as he was about to aid her ascent onto the back of her mount.

A memory flashed in her mind of her as a bairn inside such a cart, clinging to her mother's breast, with the sounds of bloody battle outside it, and the fearful thought drumming through her young mind, *Where have they taken my papa?*

Her lungs seized.

"Morgana!" Robert said, lifting her into his arms, "You are unwell. You there! Make haste! A covered cart for my lady."

Morgana wiggled, trying to drop her feet back to the ground, saying, "Nay. Nay, I am well."

His gaze, steel in hue and intent, dropped back to hers. "You've lost all color. You will ride in the cart and rest. I'll brook no argument."

Placing her hand on his arm, she implored, "I beg you, do not force me do this. I—I've a memory of the attack on our caravan when I was a bairn. It...it makes me uneasy, unable to take in breath."

Robert studied her countenance a moment, then met her eye. "Halt!" he called out to the guard who'd taken on the task and was striding toward the stables where several conveyances were unhitched and awaiting their owner's return, "No need. Return to your post."

Giving a barely audible sigh of relief and a shy smile to Robert, Morgana landed back on her feet with his strong hands about her waist. She turned in his hold and allowed him to assist her to mount. Once settled, she gave him a nod of assurance that she was fit and, after squeezing her knee, he turned and mounted his own beast.

"We'll make as few stops to rest our animals as we are able, my lady," the young sheriff told her, "For tho' 'tis arduous to travel thus, we want you safe in the

King's care as soon as is possible." He would be traveling on one side of her, and Robert on the other, with guards in front and behind. "We will rest the night in the town of *Uachdar Àrdair*. If the weather and the fates permit, we should arrive at Scone two days hence."

"Which is the reason I want you in a covered cart," Robert said. "To rest."

"I am fit, and rested enough, my lord, I swear it. I beg you, do not fret so."

Robert's only response was an intent look and a raised brow, before giving the sheriff a short nod and kneeing his courser into motion.

* * *

"You have not asked me how I regained my memory—my voice," Morgana said in a rush that eve in her chamber at the inn, as Robert turned to depart after peremptorily depositing her there not more than a moment before. *Please. Stay. Talk to me.*

Robert stopped short, but did not turn, instead keeping his back to her as he said the same words he'd said to her by the carn, "Later. After."

"Will you tell me at least if my cousin was part of this? Did she want me dead as well?"

Briefly, almost so briefly she'd near not caught the reaction, his visage lit up with surprise, but then his shoulders visibly relaxed, the strain around his mouth softened. "Nay. She knew naught of this villainous plot."

Relieved, yet wondering at the gentling in his demeanor when Vika was mentioned, she took a step forward. "Bu—"

Song of the Highlands

He held up his hand. "Later. After." There was a brief, weighted pause, as if he wanted to say more, but when he spoke again, he said only, "I'll come for you at dawn. Be ready," before he strode out and left her there, hanging in a state of anticipation, as if waiting for the final blow in a trial to the death.

There was a time—was it truly only two moons before? It seemed an age now—that he'd been avid to hear her speak, to learn her history. Now, he seemed to want naught more than to flee from her presence, to expedite this task, to return to his home. Where Vika still abided.

With their arrival at the King's court growing e'er more imminent, with Morgana's heart and soul aflame with hope (the hope she'd fought, but had finally allowed to blossom in her breast), *and* with the profound love she still felt for her coldly distant husband biding there as well, she had thought to give him another chance to change her mind about petitioning the King for aid in gaining an annulment.

But this final rebuff in his renewed, and continual, brusque behavior since the plot to kill her had been foiled, proved to her his actions were motivated more by duty than devotion, and she would not be that selfish. If 'twas Vika he wanted, then Vika he would have.

* * *

The orange, yellow, and purple hues of sunset washed the abbey in a shimmering amber glow as Morgana, her guards, and the caged cart holding the red-beard made their way up the road toward it. They'd be inside its gates soon, and after that... Well, after that, before the King. She'd been rehearsing her speech in her head these past hours as they traveled, and still her heart pounded with dread—and ached with sorrow.

Darting a quick glance Robert's direction before turning her gaze once again forward, she made note of the grim, hard line of his mouth, the tension that gave his profile a sharp contour. His thoughts were on the coming meeting as well, 'twas plain. What would be his reaction when he heard her plea to the King? *Nay, heart, becalm yourself.* His sense of moral obligation would no doubt compel him to argue against such an end, but she must remain firm in her resolve.

"I see no reason for you to face the King, unless he requests it of you later, so you shall go directly to the chamber provided you and take your ease there, awaiting my return," Robert said.

"Nay."

His head swung around, his gaze so sharp, it seemed to penetrate her skull. "What did you say?"

A flutter of misgiving made her heart skip a beat. Still she did not bend, saying, "I said nay. I *want* an audience with my King."

Robert's eyes narrowed. "Why?"

Morgana shot a glance in the sheriff's direction, then turned it back on Robert. "You shall see."

Robert's gaze left hers and settled briefly on the sheriff as well before resting once more on her. He lifted a brow, gave a brief nod, then returned his gaze forward.

For an extended moment, Morgana's gaze remained

on Robert's profile. *So strong...so brave...so...* Her bones went liquid. *...manly-fair.*

But, Vika fires his desire, bears his babe. With a sigh, she forcefully closed her eyes, breaking Robert's momentary and unwitting spell on her.

"We are almost arrived. You will sleep," Robert said, misinterpreting her body's response to him as weariness.

She'd not argue the matter again with him. He'd learn soon enough that she'd not be daunted by his fierce demeanor into doing what e'er he demanded.

A half-hour later, and in spite of Robert's continued pressure for her to do his bidding and go to the chamber given her, she and Robert stood before the dais that bore the King's throne in the chamber inside the abbey where he held his court.

* * *

"I think it best that you leave after you've said your piece to the King. I'd prefer a privy word with him," Morgana said softly without looking Robert's way.

"Nay."

"Aye."

Robert could not ken why Morgana was so determined to have an audience—nay, a *privy* audience—with King William, but the sense of foreboding had been spreading in his gut these past moments since being shown into the King's court chamber. His wife had become e'er more still, her visage e'er more grim, as they stood there together, silent, and waiting. But now, with this newest decree, the apprehension had grown immense.

What did she fear him hearing? Had the priest done more to her than Robert had originally believed? Had the apprentice? His fists clenched at his side, his blood raced with the desire for violence—for vengeance, sure and swift—if 'twere so. The thought of either that puling, corpsish priest, or that lumbering, foul-smelling red-devil defiling his woman made his skin crawl, made his gut wrench, made his temper explode.

"Aught that pertains to you is my business as well. I'll not leave."

* * *

Morgana opened her mouth to argue, but just then the doors to the chamber came open and they both turned to look. *"Guy!"* she cried, hurrying toward him. "I forgot you were at court!"

He dashed a sharp glance behind her to Robert, then settled his gaze back on her. Taking her outstretched hand as she dipped a quick courtesy, he said, "You've found your voice," he said with some surprise. " 'Tis as an angel's."

Morgana felt herself blush.

"And, nay, Lady Morgana, I've only just returned." He bowed, released her hand, and walked toward Robert, saying, "I arrived here only this morn. The fire set by the men is extinguished. There is damage to the new portion of the wall, and there were a number of casualties among the men fighting the blaze."

"A fire!" Morgana exclaimed, rushing forward. "At your keep?"

"Nay, at ours," Robert said.

"At ours!" Morgana gripped Guy's arm. "My maid—Modron—is she well?"

"*All* who stayed inside the keep are well," he

answered her, but a look passed between him and her husband, and she knew—in her gut she knew—what the look meant.

"My cousin is well then, also?" *Stop this jealousy. Did you* want *her and her babe to perish?*

Guy looked confused. "I—"

Just then, the sound of shuffling footsteps and muffled voices came from the hall behind the King's throne, and they all turned.

In the next moment, King William's arrival was announced and the three of them bowed in deference.

"You've routed Donnach's minions?" the King said to Robert once he was settled in his chair.

"Aye, my lord King," he answered.

"Come, up with you—and you—and you, as well, sweet lady. Robert MacVie, come forward, for I would speak with you first."

Morgana straightened, lifting her head, as did Robert and Guy.

Robert complied, taking a step toward the King. "But only one survived the fray, sire," Robert told him. "He is prisoned in the dungeon here and needs trying."

"Donnach is not at court. He is at *Ràthtref*, one of his lesser holdings near the abbey at Dunkeld."

"But sire, he is the instigator. The one we truly seek—"

"Aye. Be still," the King said, waving his hand at Robert in a gesture to settle him down. "I will have a warrant writ for his arrest and capture, and will strip him of his title forthwith."

"My thanks, sire. For he *is* the man behind the murderous scheme against my wife, there is no doubt.

The prisoner has confessed as much. What is more, there is a shipload of copper bullion—from Donnach's own mine—awaiting our prisoner at *Inverleith*."

A glint entered the King's eye. "A load of copper bullion, say you?" He rubbed the side of his finger against his lip. " 'Twill bear Donnach's mark. Aye, definitive proof. And being that 'twas to be used as payment for unlawful ends, 'twill become the property of the crown. I'll send one of my captains with his men to seize it." He sucked in a breath and pounded his palms on the arms of his chair. "Good. Good."

"I would beg your leave to go to *Ràthtref* to deliver the warrant and bring him here to you myself," Robert said.

Nay! 'Tis too dangerous! Morgana wanted to scream, but dared not, as she'd not been given leave to speak.

The King's eyes narrowed on Robert, evidently pondering the request. Finally, he said, "Nay, you shall remain at court. I want him brought here alive, and there is too much enmity between your house and his for me to trust that outcome if I allowed such." There was a short pause before he continued, saying, "I'll need Morgunn here. I want him present at the trial of both his half-brother, and the minion."

Morgana's breath caught. *He knows my father survived the ambush!* How? 'Twas a battle, but again, she anxiously held her tongue.

"That may prove difficult, sire. He was maimed in his attempt to rescue his daughter from their clutches before I learned of her capture."

He survived the hanging! Praise be. But on the cusp of

those thoughts, trotted another set. She glared at Robert. "You know my father lives?" she said, unable to stop herself from speaking this time.

"Aye," Robert whispered o'er his shoulder, with a finger o'er his lips indicating she should not speak.

Suspicion gripped her insides, making her heart race, and she could not obey. "For how long? And why did you not tell me?"

As if from a league away, she heard the King exclaim, "She's found her tongue!" just as Robert replied in a stern, chiding tone, "Later. After." It sent Morgana's temper soaring.

She flew at him with all the anger, betrayal, and shock she felt. "Nay! Now! You shall tell-me-*now!*"

Robert caught her arms before she was able to barrel into him and try to tumble him to the ground. "You are fevered. You must rest," he said, grunting as he tousled with her. He was clearly trying to be gentle in his domination of her, and his gaze held worry, but she would not be still—she was much too vexed.

"Sire, you can see my wife's humors are much expended. I must take her to her chamber forthwith. I shall return in a trice."

"Aye, but quickly, quickly. I've others who wish an audience."

Morgana went still. If she was to voice her request, 'twould have to be now. Looking deeply into Robert's eyes, she said to the King, "I no longer wish to be wed to Robert MacVie. I beg your aid in annulling my marriage contract." The moment the words were out, her anger fled, and in its place settled a cloak of despair.

As if outside herself, she watched Robert's pupils contract. Watched his jaw tighten. Watched his warm, gentle grasp on her arms fall away. Watched him step back a pace and turn to face his King once more.

"If it be her wish, then...'tis my wish as well, sire," he said.

"I will have her, my lord King, if Robert will not," Guy said, stepping forward.

Morgana could only blink at him.

"I'll see you dead first," Robert growled.

A calculating gleam appeared in the King's gaze, and his eyes narrowed on first Robert, then on her. "If all ends as is planned—and I see no reason why it should not—then you will be a very wealthy heiress, indeed. I—and your father, of course—will benefit mightily from a better alliance."

"I knew it! I *knew* you wanted her for your own," Robert said to Guy, as if the King had not spoken. Nose to nose, the two men glared into each other's eyes, lungs blowing.

"Aye, she's a tasty morsel. And clearly, you were not man enough for her."

In a lighting flash, Robert punched him in the gut. Guy staggered back a step, bent over and wheezing.

"Meet me on the tourney field, and we shall see which of us is the man, and which the lad," Robert snarled.

Guy lifted up, virile anger darkening his countenance, and bumped chests with Robert, saying, " 'Twill be my pleasure...*lass*."

Robert roared, gripping the front of Guy's tunic in

his fists. "Or, I could end you now."

Guy gave a humorless laugh. "Or I you."

"Nay, you'll not! Either of you!" Morgana said, wriggling herself between the two. Guy stepped back. Robert did not. Where e'er her body touched his—her breasts, her belly, her thighs—went up in flames.

"A tourney! Excellent idea!" the King interjected, breaking the spell, and Morgana stumbled back.

Robert struggled to break eye contact, or so it seemed to Morgana, but when he did, he turned his hot glare on Guy, growling, "I should ne'er have trusted you!" He dug inside his pouch and lifted out a very familiar scroll.

Morgana's heart leapt into her throat.

Shoving it toward her, he jabbed his finger in Guy's direction, accusing, "*He* is who you were running to, not back to your nunnery! Admit it!" He dropped his head and muttered under his breath, "Fool. Such a fool!" Then, without bowing to his lord King, without another glance, another word, he stormed out of the chamber, in direct defiance of protocol.

Morgana whirled around to face the King. "Please, sire, I beg you, do not punish my husband for his actions just now. He is angry at me, and would ne'er slight you thus otherwise, I know this, and I swear to it upon my life."

"Be still, sweet lady," the King answered, his calculating gaze remaining on the door through which Robert had just departed. When he turned it to her again, it held a knowing look that she could not ken. "I have no desire to punish, only to profit." He leaned forward. "Tell me," he said, in a conspiratorial tone, "what was writ on that scroll your husband brandished?" His eyes narrowed on Guy a moment then swung back to penetrate her own. "*Were* you conspiring to leave him for this knight before me?"

"Nay, sire. I... 'Twas a letter to him telling him I was on my way back to the nunnery."

He sat back. "The nunnery? Why e'er would you desire such? Has he been cruel? Has your life with him been so disagreeable?"

Morgana blushed, bowed her head. "Nay, sire."

"Then why do you wish to make void your alliance?"

Tears welled in her eyes and she fought mightily the urge to give in to them. The effort, and the remembered hurt, made her tremble. "Be-Because he loves my cousin, has fathered a babe with her, my lord King. As I have not produced an heir for him, and she has, I do not wish to stand in the way of his duty to his clan, nor to her and their bairn."

The King sat back, took in a deep breath, then said finally, "I see."

"And my petition," Guy blurted into the charged silence, "to wed with the lady Morgana, my lord King? Will you consider it?"

Morgana whirled to face Guy, "Nay! Surely, you were not in earnest. I—"

"Aye. If Morgunn agrees, and if you offer the right bride price, I will consider your suit. *If* I decide to aid this lady in her cause." He turned his gaze on Morgana and studied her for a long, charged moment. Finally, he said, "Aye. I will aid you in this pursuit to nullify your vows."

Morgana's heart dropped into her stomach, and it began to churn. She'd done what she came to do. 'Twas over—or near to. So why did everything within her revolt? From somewhere far away, she realized the King was still speaking to her, and she gave herself a mental shake, struggling to listen.

"...others to see this day. A guard awaits your exit," the King said brusquely, "just outside these doors, he will escort you to your chamber." He leaned forward once again, giving her a stern look and wagging a beringed finger at her. "And you will stay within it until I send for you."

Morgana wanted naught more than to argue, to tell him she'd been wrong, to tell him she did not wish to have her bonds to Robert broken after all, but recalling the childing Vika, and the joyful words Robert had spoken the eve he'd felt beneath his palm his babe move within Vika's womb: *"Aye, he's a strong, bold one, is he. A fine MacVie,"* she forcefully refrained, instead bowing, giving reverent assent.

* * *

Robert slammed the door of his bedchamber, stormed first to his satchel, yanked the skin of *uisge beatha* from it, took several long pulls on it, swiped the back of his hand across his mouth, then dropped the half-full skin to the table next to the bed and stomped over to the window, crossed his arms over his chest, and glared out at the courtyard below. A brief period of time passed with him standing there, stoic, his mind blank, his heart in shreds, before he unfolded his arms and stared at the crushed scroll in his sweaty fist. With hands that shook with pent-up anger and heartache, he unfurled the parchment. At first, the words swam before him in a tangle of fragmented curves and lines, but after a moment of vigorous effort, he was again able to put meaning to symbol.

Finally, he looked up, thoughts racing. *The first thing to do would be to... no, that will not work... but after... aye, then....*

CHAPTER 20

THE NIGHT WAS warm, and there was a full moon gleaming silver-bright through the window. Morgana stripped herself bare for sleep—a thing she'd not done since losing her babe—and pulled the fur blanket from the bed, then climbed atop the mattress and curled on her side, away from the shining moonglow.

The linen sheet beneath her cooled her skin, and it brought, unbidden, a memory of the second painful night after the loss of their babe, when she'd failed in her attempt to seduce her husband. 'Twas the last time she'd lain in bed thus, and after he'd bolted, she'd attempted to assuage her humiliation and grief by turning back to the remembered ritual she'd lived so long with at the convent—and that she'd gleefully (and rebelliously) ignored from her first night at King William's court—of covering her body with a chemise. As if it had only just happened, again the shame, the hurt, pummeled her heart, clogging her throat with unshed tears.

Without realizing she was doing so, she bit the side of her finger, her thoughts, a chaotic tumble. She had made the right decision. Or...mayhap she hadn't. For Robert had been so angered, seemed to have felt at least some twinge of jealousy, at Guy's petition to wed with her. *Was* she making the right decision? Again, an image of the childing Vika swam to the forepart of her mind, and she thought resignedly, *Aye, I am.*

A jagged sigh slipped from her throat, followed by a lone tear burning a long trail o'er her cheek, and she closed her eyes tight against more. *I must turn my thoughts on something*—anything—*else.*

She began to sing:

"Nay, young rascal, fondle me not!
Fer I'll not share yer lowly cot—"

Argh! She sat up and beat her fists into the mattress. *He* will not *leave my thoughts!* She dropped her head into her hands and sat there breathing deeply for several prolonged moments. Finally, with renewed determination, she lay down on her back, closed her eyes, and mentally began to recite the third psalm by rote...

"Et erit tamquam lignum quod...."

Feeling drowsy at last, Morgana rolled onto her side again, softly translating,

Song of the Highlands

"And he shall be like a tree which...,"

...as she drifted off to sleep.

* * *

His soft kiss brushed her lips, then turned greedy as, with a virile groan of pleasure, his tongue plundered her mouth. The taste, so familiar, so longed for, brought his name forth in a whisper. Suddenly, warm, calloused hands cupped her face, tangled in her hair. One grasped the back of her head, urging her into a deeper embrace, as the other trailed down her frame, gliding o'er her breast in a feather-like touch, then o'er her belly, o'er her hip, o'er her thigh. She whimpered, lifting her hands to clutch at his shoulders, to cling in his hair, and brought her hips off the mattress in a quest to give his hand purchase where she most craved.

* * *

Robert breathed deep the intoxicating scent of her hair, of her pliant flesh. Her hips rose up, bringing her mons under his hand, and he slid his fingers o'er her labia, then pressed one, then two, deep inside the warm, wet, throbbing cushion of her womb. He broke the kiss. "What do you want, Morgana? Say it."

"I want you! I want you, Robert!"

His tarse, already turgid, grew another inch. The sound of his own hammering pulse beat in his ears. "Then you shall have me," he said, and devoured her mouth once more.

It had been too long since last he touched her thus. Since last he'd heard the passion in her voice as his name tripped from her tongue. He wedged a knee between her limbs as he positioned himself above her, and she spread herself wide for him. The head of his cock found her center. "I am going to love you until you swoon," he rumbled next to her ear as he prepared to plunge.

"Laird MacVie!"

From somewhere far off, the sound of a fist pounding on a door jarred Robert, turned his mind from the woman in his arms.

"Nay! Answer him not," she murmured.

"Aye," he growled, bending down to drop another kiss on her lips as he began pressing forward again. "*Ahhh!* Christ's Bones, I've missed this."

"Laird MacVie! Are you in there? My pardon, but the King requests your presence forthwith!"

This time, the pounding became louder, more urgent, and again, Robert's thoughts were yanked from the sensual to the mundane, and with it, Morgana, his lover beneath him, shifted from earthly to ethereal. *Not now! Not now!* He tried holding her to him, but 'twas as impossible as embracing the mist on the moor.

Nay! A tide of despair washed o'er him, and the searing pain of unfulfilled passion gripped his groin in a vise.

"Laird MacVie?"

Robert struggled to swim up from the warm splendor of his dream into the cold temporal world that waited him.

The pounding continued, followed again by a disembodied voice coming through the heavy wood door.

"Laird MacVie?"

"Aye," he managed to croak, rolling into a sitting position and dropping his head into his hands. As he rubbed the sleep from his eyes with the base of his palms, he called out, "Enter!"

* * *

Morgana's eyes shot open. Her heart pounded in her chest, and an unbearable yearning throbbed in her womb. Blinking, she rolled her head on the pillow and scanned the chamber. She'd not closed the heavy drape o'er the bedframe the night before, and she could see much of the area in front of the hearth and window. The chamber, praise be, was empty. There were none to hold witness to her vocalized pleasure in her phantom lover's caresses, no court gossip would be spouted of her fleshly dreaming.

On a desolate sigh, she rolled out of bed. She'd allow herself no more naked slumbering in future, for it clearly brought on sensual longings for the man she could not have.

If only...

Another sigh escaped her lips as she tugged a clean chemise o'er her head from the chest of borrowed clothes given her upon her arrival this day past, and walked to the washstand to do her ablutions of the morn. She needed to speak to Guy. If she could not speak to Robert about his false belief—and she could not will herself into doing so, no matter the desire to part ways without rancor—she at least needed to inveigle Guy to do so. And if the two were earnest in their threats to battle the other on the tourney field, then she hoped to quell that as well.

They'd not faced the other before, at least not as far as she knew, and Morgana had little doubt that Robert would be victorious, tho' she'd seen Guy win more than he lost, and 'twould be a close match, she knew. But Robert needed Guy as an ally, for they were neighbors, and Guy's forces were strong, so this malice between them needed quashing. It meant defying the King's edict, and she prayed his wrath, if he learned of it, would be mutable, even allayed, once she explained her reasons for such uncommon rebellion.

In another quarter-hour, she slipped from her chamber without being spied, and went in search of Guy de Burgh.

* * *

"This is truly your wish as well?" the King asked Robert later that morn as they walked side-by-side around the edge of the apothecary's herb garden, his hands behind his back, his eyes perusing the landscape as they moved.

" 'Tis what Morgana craves, and I will not stand in her way, if she wishes to return to the nunnery."

The King gave him a sidelong glance. "I thought you were set on believing she plotted to cuckold you with your neighbor, Guy de Burgh."

" 'Twas a fleet idea. I know now, could not be true."

"Why e'er not? He is a strong and powerful warrior, holds titles in both Alba and England, is well-liked by the ladies, and has a considerable fortune as well."

Robert's shoulders tightened. "Aye, and even so, they had no opportunity to plan such an end."

"But he wants her now. Has petitioned me twice for her hand. And, I confess, 'twould be a beneficial alliance for me as well, as the marriage of one of my Norman subjects to a native Gael would more strongly tie him to my will."

"She will not wed him."

"You are so certain?" the King said, turning away from him and bending down to smell the purple blossoms on the cluster of lavender next to the path.

"Aye. I am. She will return to the nun..."—Robert glanced to his left, and a lightning bolt of need near eviscerated him—"...ery...." There she was. Frozen in place, as a doe facing an arrow, staring at him. Their eyes met, and he felt his cheeks flush. A look flashed in her eye, and her visage went up in flame as well. Then she blinked, whirled, and fled.

His palms dampened, his brow moistened. His heart would not stop racing. 'Twas as if she'd known of his carnal dream. Nay. Nay. 'Twas impossible. A wish his heart made, that would ne'er be fulfilled. Slowly, he surfaced from his thoughts and realized the King was speaking again.

"...the marriage was not, at first, desired by you, but I did believe 'twas a good match."

"Aye, I believed so as well, sire."

"But still, you do not love her."

For some reason, the King's certainty bothered Robert. Vexed him. "Aye, sire, I do." And, on the chance that King William was still not clear of Robert's meaning, he added. "Love her."

The King grinned, and Robert squirmed inside.

"Your wife believes 'tis her cousin you crave."

"Nay, sire. 'Tis Morgana. Only Morgana."

"Yet you tupped her cousin, even still, and made a babe with her?"

"Wha?—Nay. Nay, I did not."

"But 'tis what your wife believes. She seemed quite certain."

Robert's heart began to *glub, glub, glub* in his chest. *God's Bones!* 'Twas the reason for her flight. He was a true buffoon, a prime idiot. Even tho' it had been at Morgana's urging that Vika stay, 'twas before...and he should have known....

"Nay, 'tis not my babe her cousin carries. 'Tis Grímr Thorfinnsson's. What is more: She has left with him to return to the isle of *Leòdhas*."

"But your wife knows not of this?"

"Nay, sire. For Vika left the same day Morgana was taken by Donnach's minions."

"And you have not told her this."

"Nay, there has been no time."

"Grímr Thorfinnsson, you say? The husband's nephew?"

"Aye."

"Hmm. I must think on this...."

In a rush of renewed conviction, Robert stated, "I will not allow this annulment."

The King lifted his gaze to Robert's. "You no longer wish to grant her what she desires?"

"Nay, I'll not."

"Even tho' by our laws you are no longer wed, now that you have both stated before me your desire to end your marriage? 'Tis only the matter of the gaining the church's agreement now, and Richard was a clerk of mine before he rose to the Bishopric of Dunkeld. I have little worry that he will speed the matter for me, if I wish it so."

"Aye, but if I contest the annulment, and I will, and 'tis delayed, then 'tis only a matter of the both of us stating the opposite again, by those same laws."

The King grinned at him again. "Excellent!" He clapped him on the shoulder. "Even tho' she's worth more to me without the cumbrance of marriage vows to you, I am pleased to hear it. For, I'd not have given her back to the church, no matter her wish."

"Then that makes me doubly eager to curtail the annulment proceedings."

"Good. Good." The King resumed his previous posture, folding his arms behind his back once more. The two walked without speaking several paces more, until the King broke the silence saying, "You've not told Morgana your true feelings for her? That you love her above all others?"

The skin on the back of Robert's neck crawled, traveling o'er his scalp. "Nay. But... She knows." *Or knew....*

"I'm old now, but in my day.... Heed me well, young warrior knight: Speak the words, and often, else you'll face this again another time."

"Aye, sire, I will." And he would, as soon as he was released from this meeting, he would.

The King inhaled, gazing up at the cloudless blue sky as they continued to amble down the garden path.

"Aye, pleased I am indeed. 'Twould also do you well to not delay the telling that you are not the sire of her cousin's babe."

"Aye, I had that very thought as well, my liege."

"I've a few other matters to discuss with you, then you are free to seek out your lady."

Inside, Robert chafed, but he dipped his head, saying gravely, "Aye, my lord King."

* * *

"I will not wed with you, Guy de Burgh," Morgana hissed not long later as the two swept through the doorway leading out of the great hall together, after at last finding her quarry breaking his fast in that chamber. "I am for the nunnery as soon as I am released to do so by my King."

"You will ne'er be allowed to do so now; you are worth too much to the King to be given o'er to the church." He sighed. "In any case, I only petitioned for your hand to vex Robert enough to fight for you." He stopped walking, and she stopped as well. "However, if you and he do succeed in having your marriage contract annulled, then I—as I did before in the dungeon of this very abbey—humbly give you my troth." He pulled in a deep breath and reached for her hand, but evidently thought better of it when he glanced past her, and seeing others passing near, dropped his arm back to his side. "Know this: You *will* be bartered off in marriage, and if you continue in your quest to end the one you have with Robert, then 'twill be better for you to wed with me, your friend, than some other who may only want you for what wealth and power a connection to your family and the King may bring him."

She felt her cheeks heat with embarrassment, but knew she must speak the truth. Darting a look around her, she stepped closer to Guy and whispered, "I may be barren—or, at least unable to bear a babe to childbed. Robert's babe flushed from my"—her eyes welled with tears again, her throat closed, but still she continued—"w-womb n-near to two sennights past. My pardon," she said, sniffling and turning her face away. With quivering fingers, she brushed the tears from her cheeks.

Guy took hold of her hand. "I am sorry for your loss, dear lady. I did not know."

She nodded, gulped back another fit of weeping, and managed to say thickly, "So you see why I do not wish to wed again."

" 'Tis not uncommon, or so I have heard told. You will bear again, and well, I am sure."

"And if I do not? Would you wed a woman who could not give you an heir?"

"Aye, I would. But only if that woman were you."

Morgana lifted her gaze to his and gaped at him. "You—Are you saying you love me?"

"Aye,"—Morgana's heart fluttered in dread—"and nay. I will not deny the deep affection I hold for you, but nay, 'tis not the passionate love of which I believe you are speaking."

Morgana nodded, dropping her gaze to their twined hands, before slipping hers from his grasp and stepping back.

There was a long, weighted pause, as if Guy was

battling a decision to tell her something, before he said at last, "You asked me before about Vika. She was not at your holding when I arrived to o'ersee the dousing of the fires set by your uncle's men."

Morgana's head jerked up.

"I was told by your mo—maid that she left the same morn as you, with her lover—the father of her unborn babe—a man by the name of Grímr Thorfinnsson, and that Robert was made aware of this before she left."

"Grímr? Grímr is her babe's father? Bu-But she said...." Morgana whirled and took several steps, then swung back around. "Aye, I believe it! The way the two of them behaved together. 'Twas plain they were attracted. And he arrived at our holding only a sennight past Vika's own arrival. He must have been hunting her! Oh, aye. Oh, aye." She rushed over to Guy and gripped his hands in hers. "Do you know what this means?" she said, looking glowingly into Guy's dark-fringed blue eyes. "It means that Robert does not pine for Vika!"

"Aye, that is what it means, my dear lady. Tho' I did not think it best these tidings should come from me, but from your husband. Still, if I have lightened your heart with this knowledge, then I am well pleased in doing so."

Morgana's jaw tightened. "Aye. My husband should have told me." Again, she whirled around and stormed several paces away, saying, "*Why did he not?* Truly, I cannot ken it."

"My dear lady," Guy began in a gently chiding voice, "he has been otherwise occupied with the—and I'm sure you will agree with this—*much* more urgent need to

Song of the Highlands

save your life."

She hurrumphed. Crossing her arms, she said, "Aye, but 'tis his stubborn silence *after* that which irks me so."

Guy took a step toward her. "Mayhap...." He took another step. "Mayhap, he only wanted to wait until all was settled, until he could relax his guard on you and enjoy your time together without worry or dread."

Morgana dipped her head and bit her lip. "Well, why did he not say thus?" She swung back around. "I must halt this annulment!" Her eyes went wide and she beamed a grin Guy's direction. "And I know just how to do it! Come," she said, turning and striding with purpose toward the chapel. I'll need your aid, and we have much to plan."

* * *

As Robert rushed toward the other doorway that led to the stairs, on his way to Morgana's chamber, passing visitors and courtiers taking their meals at trestle tables in the great hall while he went, he was intercepted by a messenger holding a small scroll of vellum tied with a blue silk riband. Robert thanked him and unfurled the missive. Instantly, the familiar fresh floral scent of *her*, of Morgana, invaded his being, and his blood rushed. Quickly, he scanned the words. *Meet me in the chapel in a half-hour*, it read. Aye, 'twas Morgana's signature, Morgana's seal. His heart danced. Mayhap she, too, regretted so rashly breaking ties. In which case, 'twould make their reconciliation all the more simple.

The weight of worry lifted, he strode out the doors and went in the direction of the chapel.

'Twas not until he'd knelt in prayer that it struck him

what had transpired after the last time he'd met her thus, and his hopes soared all the more. It also gave him an idea for how best to convince her to take him back as husband. And with that thought came a rare grin. Aye, before the sun was set, they'd again be where they belonged—together, and in bed.

* * *

"All is in readiness, you are certain?" Morgana asked as she stepped into the corridor and closed the door to her chamber behind her. She'd been granted leave by the King to remove from her chamber, as long as a guard gave her escort, but she could truly see no reason for such continued care. Donnach was not at court, and the men who'd worked for him were no longer a danger to her.

"Aye, my lady," one of Guy's men-at-arms responded.

"My thanks. And the others? They are within the chapel already?"

"Aye, my lady, they are."

"And your liege lord? He is awaiting us near the cart?"

"Aye, he is, my lady. I only just left him there to come for you."

"No need to escort me, I prefer to meet my husband alone."

"Please, my lady, I must take you as far as the chapel door, at least, else I am sure to be punished severely by my lord."

"Very well," Morgana said with vexed resignation.

They'd gone no more than ten steps down the curving stairway, when several men, masked in black cloth, and bearing daggers and short swords, o'ertook them from behind and front.

"Nay!" she cried, twisting and kicking in a fruitless effort to free herself from the steel embrace of the one who'd captured her. She let out a blood-curdling scream, but before more than a note or two had been lifted into the air, a leather-gloved hand closed o'er her mouth and nose, stifling it, and cutting off her wind.

Guy's man-at-arms fought valiantly the blows and attempted blows of his assailants, and at one point, just before Morgana lost consciousness, he managed to use one of them as a shield, and the man was impaled on his own comrade's sword. After that, all faded to black.

* * *

From just outside the heavy wooden doors of the chapel, came a violent commotion of sound and fury. Robert jerked around, leapt to his feet, ran toward the fray with sword at the ready, blood pounding in his veins. If the abbey was under attack, it meant a war against the King. He had to find Morgana, get her to safety.

He was a scant yard from the entry when one of the doors flew open and a guard, wearing the de Burgh colors and with newly-let blood staining the front of his tunic, fell through the opening and landed face-down on the stone floor, leaving a freshly-slain hooded soldier in plain garb and bearing no cognizance sprawled on the ground behind him.

Robert rushed to kneel beside him, turning him o'er onto his back as he did so. The man's face was battered and bruised, his eyes, tho' glazed, were open and his lips, split and swollen, moved as if he spoke, but Robert heard no words coming forth. He leaned down so that his ear was only a breath away from the man's mouth.

"Your lady, Morgana...attack...stair...taken...could...not...ss...ssstop...." The last trailed off as the man's eyes closed and his head rolled to the side.

Donnach! 'Twas Donnach. Robert seethed. He should have been more insistent with the King this morn. He should have gone in pursuit of Donnach himself, instead of allowing others to do the deed, for he would *not* have failed. Robert quickly checked the guard's pulse and found none, then sprang to his feet ready to rush to the stables to go in chase of Morgana and her captors before the trail grew cold. When he looked up, three more of Guy's men stood before him, but within the chapel, not near the door. Fleetingly, he wondered how they'd gotten there, but said instead, "He is dead, and my lady Morgana has been captured. Where is your lord?"

"In the courtya—"

"—I am here," Guy said, lungs heaving. His gaze dipped to his slain man-at-arms, and he swiftly, yet somberly, made the sign of the cross. Using his hand to leverage his weight against the door for balance as he caught his breath, he spoke, saying, "I know in which direction they are headed. Hurry, we must fly!"

* * *

When Morgana began to revive, she thought 'twas night. 'Twas only when she attempted to open her eyes, and realized a blind had been secured o'er them, that she knew it had not been so long since her capture on the stairs. For a fleet moment, hope sprang in her heart that 'twas Robert turning her own plan for him 'round about on her, but when she heard the all-too-familiar, all-too-distressing voice of her uncle, she knew her fate had turned utterly grim.

Where does he take me? she thought, and on the tail of that: *Why did he not simply kill me, as had been his plan?* For some reason, the fact that he had not done so produced an even denser, more painful, burning knot of dread in her gut.

For several long hours more, Morgana lay bound and blind on the hard bed of the wooden cart, as it bumped and creaked along an unknown path. Finally, she felt the cart shift, as if climbing higher, and she thought they might be on a mountain path. Could her uncle be taking her to that same hunter's cot where he'd found her and Robert this winter past? The same cot where she'd planned only this morn for a privy—and amorous—renewal of her and Robert's bonds?

But for what purpose would her uncle sequester her there? Again, her gut clenched with the fire of dread. What could be her uncle's plan? Was she a lure for her husband? Her *father*? What e'er it might be, she'd not make it easy for him to accomplish. If she could, and she prayed heartily she could, she would thwart him. *But how?*

The cart came to a lurching stop, and Morgana rolled with great force, the weight of her movement casting her onto her face, jamming her nose and making it sting and throb, making her eyes water with tears.

* * *

Robert ripped the vellum sheet and ice-blue riband from the nail that attached it to the tree and, his hand trembling with repressed anger, the snorting and shifting of the score of men's horses behind him a vague backdrop, scanned the script as he held the silk strand to his nose. As he'd feared, it held the scent of Morgana's tresses.

If you are reading this, you are on the wrong path, just as I had planned. Bring to me my half-brother at the place we two first met, and I will forfeit your bride. Else, I shall see you in hell.

There was no salutation, no signature, no seal, yet the tremor in his gut told him he was not in error. The missive was meant for him, and Donnach Cambel was its author. ...*the place we two first met*... The hunter's cot! *Nithing! Caitiff!* He would play Robert's weakness against him.

"What is writ there?" Guy asked from above him, still astride his mount.

Robert crumpled the vellum in his fist. "Donnach. He's got her at the hunter's cot where we...where he first found Morgana and I together."

"I believe it not. Let me see."

Without looking up, Robert thrust the vellum at Guy.

Guy kneed his mount foreword and took it. There was a tense silence while Guy read.

"Blood of Christ! *Tricked.* The cur!" He looked up. "Morgunn will be on his way to court, even now. Do we wait, or do we ride?"

Robert mounted his courser, saying in a growl, "We ride."

Guy gave a sharp nod. "I'll send one of my men back to inform the King we know where he's lodged with your wife."

Wheeling his steed around, Robert said only, "Aye," then moved to the head of the rank and wasted no more time there, simply spurred his mount into a canter down the road they'd just been traveling for nigh on three hours.

Tho' he knew that Morgunn would relish the chance to face his half-brother, Robert also knew that his wife would ne'er forgive him if her father was maimed or, worse, killed—a very likely outcome, in Robert's opinion, as Morgunn was not young, and so would still be recovering from the injuries he sustained five days past.

And there was also the fact that Robert held no doubt that Donnach lied, that he would kill Morgana—may already have done so—even were Robert to bring Morgunn to him. Which was why his gut was, and had been, telling him to hie himself to her side without delay. *You are on the wrong path, just as I had planned.* The words chafed, made spikes of bile that pierced the insides of his stomach. *If he's killed her, I shall kill him.*

Guy rode up next to him then. Robert felt the weight of his stare, but refused to bend in this contest of wills.

Finally, Guy said, "I know what you are thinking."

Robert shrugged.

"The King's warning to you in the bailey before we departed was clear: He wants Donnach brought to him alive."

Again, Robert shrugged.

"You'll hang."

Robert said naught. The silence thrummed between them. Finally, Guy shook his head and turned his gaze back to the road.

* * *

Several hours later, Robert, Guy, and his force were at last on the steady incline of the path that would lead them through the wood to the cot. All was quiet, except the sound of horses' hooves clomping as they stepped and shifted up the slope. The hairs on the back of his neck stood at attention. Robert scanned the area. Sunlight dappled the ground, gilded the trees in gold light, and from every direction came to him the lush scent of green leaves, earth, and woodland flowers. Fleetingly, Robert recalled the winter snow that had weighed upon the brown branches and blanketed the earth beneath on his last journey up to the cot, but swiftly forced his mind back to his purpose. 'Twas too quiet, too still.

Yet. He saw no one. Even so, he moved his hand to the hilt of his sword, saying to Guy sotto voce, "I full believe we shall find a contingent of Donnach's mercenaries surrounding the cot. There may even be some that will meet us here on the path. I've a feeling in my gut. Warn your men."

CHAPTER 21

GUY PIVOTED IN his saddle and lifted his arm, giving the signal to his soldiers to be on guard. Just as he was turning back around, the boughs of the trees came alive. Men with daggers raised fell from the skies onto them, dropping their shrubby shields as they went, and making short work of stabbing as many as they could in their eyes or throat when they came down on top of them, before fleeing with their victims' mounts through the trees, like cowardly robbers.

In little more time than 'twould have taken to utter the Lord's Prayer, 'twas finished, and six of Guy's men lay slain. Still more—by a quick count, four—lay moaning and writhing, blinded and bleeding.

"Follow them!" Guy yelled to two of his soldiers nearest the place off the path the cowards had taken, but Robert gripped his arm and bellowed to them, "Nay! Stay where you are!" then to Guy, he said, " 'Tis what Donnach wants. To delay us, mayhap even to trap us with not enough men to fight. Did you not see that we two were left unscathed—were not the goal, in fact. He hopes to weaken our force before we e'er reach the cot."

With a nod, Guy tossed his reins to Robert and swung down from his steed, calling orders to those men closest to the injured to make haste to bind the maimed soldiers' wounds, then drag them off the path to a more protected area while those remaining completed the operation.

As Guy was o'erseeing that task, Robert walked his courser over to two other of the de Burgh guards and said, "We need a new scout, for 'tis clear the first has been captured or killed." Tho' he spoke to both, his sights were fixed on the older, better thewed, and better tried of the two. As he expected, the knight did not hesitate, simply said, "Aye. I'll go," and kneed his mount into a trot down the path that would eventually end at the hunter's cot.

For the remainder of the journey, the men rode with swords drawn, but there were no more attacks, which put Robert even more on edge. Tho' they had placed a guard to ride on either side of the path, about twenty feet into the wood, but still close enough to see and hear, so that they might spy for mercenary movement, the guards had found naught. However, something was not right, he could feel it in his gut, but he could not ken what it might be. And by the tick in Guy's jaw, he could see that his neighbor was of much the same mind as he.

* * *

Song of the Highlands

As the yellow-orange orb of the sun sank behind the trees, and the wood became naught more than dusky shadows, Robert scanned the perimeter for those who might be lying in wait for them. Restless and agitated that his gut was telling him what his eyes did not, he gripped the hilt of his sword tighter and looked behind him. All was as it should be—or so it seemed. The animals of the forest were preparing to settle in for the night, and all about them could be heard the rustling and snuffling sounds of the creatures as they made their beds or searched for their meals. In the far distance, the *hoo-hoo-hoo* of an owl on some towering tree branch announced his presence, as the pleasant *chirp-chirp-chirp*ing of the last rush of bird flocks found their perches in the dense profusion of leaves high above Robert's head.

"It grows dark," he said to Guy.

"Aye," Guy said, and Robert heard the same tension he, himself, was feeling echoed in his neighbor's voice.

" 'Tis time to light the torches."

"Aye." Guy twisted around and called out the command.

A guard—the same youth that had been traveling beside the more seasoned man that Robert had earlier commissioned to scout the path ahead—came forward bearing a torch to light the way for Robert and Guy. As he did so, the scout came trotting toward them from the area up ahead.

"I've been as far as the cot, and have seen no sign of those who attacked us." The scout's mouth opened, but no words came forth. He shot a glance to his right, then settled his gaze once more on Robert and Guy. "John

Gault, the first scout, is dead—hanged by his feet and gutted like a swine."

"Blood of Christ!" Guy growled. " 'Tis worse than I thought," he said to Robert.

Robert only gave a solemn nod, then asked the scout, "What else?"

"There are two guards outside the cot, but I saw no others, which I thought odd."

Robert and Guy fired grim glances at each other, and Robert said, "Aye. Odd."

"But," the guard said, "I will tell you that once, when the door was opened, I happened a glimpse of your wife. She lives."

The tight bands of dread that had been constricting his chest for all these hours loosened and Robert was at last able to take a full breath.

"Praise be," Guy said, expressing in words the same overwhelming relief that Robert was feeling.

"He must have been told by now that you travel with another knight and believes that 'tis Morgunn," Guy said to Robert.

"Aye. These men that ambushed us were mercenaries, felons not of his clan, so would not know your colors. But only two guards? What is his plan?"

"I know not." Guy scanned the trees, scanned the wood, tho' the torchlight did not penetrate the dark by very far. "Another attack, no doubt."

"Aye. No doubt." Robert scanned the wood as well, his fist yet again gripping the hilt of his sword. He growled low. "Argh! He plays us like pawns in his cheater's game of chess! *Nithing!*"

"Aye, that he is, and much more. Or is it less? Either way, I'll be there to cheer when he hangs."

"Well, staying here doing naught is pointless, and I'll not turn back—not now. For, no matter the current case, my wife is still in grave peril for her life." He paused, but only briefly. "However, I shall feel no ill-will toward you if you and your men decide instead to go no further, to await the King's contingent, when e'er they may at last arrive."

"Nay," Guy said, "we continue on. For, as you say, your wife's life is still in danger."

Robert gave a sharp nod. "On guard!" he barked to the men, then, with the scout, and the stripling soldier who held the torch, riding vanguard, the force, now down to ten men, set out once again for the cot.

They had continued on up the path no more than another quarter-hour when a clamor of raised voices and neighing, panicked horses broke out at the back of the rank, followed on its heels by the shouted warning, "Attack! Fire!"

Robert, Guy, and the two in their vanguard reeled around in time to see a barrage of flaming arrows fly from every direction—except one: Theirs.

The shafts that did not topple the men from their mounts, landed at their horses' feet, which sent the beasts up on their hind legs screaming in panic, stalling the men where they were, unable to move out of the line of fire.

"I'm going to kill them with my bare hands!" Robert roared, then kneed his courser and charged into the wood to rout their unseen foes. Guy and the two guards followed instantly on his heels. In the next moment, they were upon them: A band of archers crouched on the ground, firing their flaming missiles with lightning speed and precision.

But they were no match for raging steel. Within a mere whisper of time, Robert had toppled the heads of three of them before they had even turned to view him. Guy and the scout took their cues from Robert and began doing the same, making swift work of annihilating their attackers, while the young de Burgh guard sped up to Robert's side, lifted his sword to an archer who had rolled to his back and lay screaming, "Nay! Nay!" with his arms o'er his face, and hesitated, unable to finish the deed.

"Get back!" Robert thundered at him, then slashed his sword in a heaving arc, quickly severing the archer's head from his torso.

In only moments, 'twas completed. Twelve archers, total, lay dead on the ground, and by Robert's reckoning, that was all of them. But to be sure, Robert and Guy, after taking a bow and quiver of arrows from four of the dead for each of them, went further into the cavernous blackness to look for stragglers, and found no sign of any more. Eventually, they turned back to the path.

* * *

"I am to blame," Robert said to Guy later, when they broke through the copse of trees back onto the open path and stood stunned looking at the carnage the archers had left. "We should have destroyed them earlier, as was your plan."

Guy clamped his hand on Robert's shoulder. "Nay, 'twas the right decision. We might have lost hours—lost your wife—if we'd spent that precious time in pursuit of the cowards instead of moving ahead to save the lady Morgana." He inhaled a deep breath. "Donnach, the craven cur dog. *He* is to blame, no one else."

The stench of burning flesh and fresh blood invaded Robert's nostrils and he bit back a roar of rage. Not a man nor beast was left standing, and at least two horses had arrows, still flaming, protruding from their eye sockets. Lit torches scattered the well-worn path where they'd been dropped to the ground. Only one lay close enough to the underbrush that it might catch the wood on fire, and Robert leapt off his mount and lifted it up, then doused the other flames using the dry earth of the path.

As he walked back to his courser, he took stock of their situation. They were down to a force of four—three and a half, in Robert's estimation, as the stripling was surely as green in experience as the flesh on his cheeks had been in the moment past when he'd hurled the contents of his stomach o'er the side of his mount and onto his boot.

"There was not a sign of them, I swear, when I searched the area earlier, Laird MacVie," the scout told him, breaking the silence.

"Nay, there wouldn't have been," Robert replied. "The sniveling whoresons waited until we passed, then attacked from behind, like the puling cowards they are."

"And left us unscathed, yet again, while we watched the slaughter unfold," Guy added, a thread of anger and disgust woven through his tone.

"All right. We dally here no more," Robert said. "Let us speed to the cot." *And kill Donnach Cambel.*

* * *

Morgana, seated on a stool, leaned against the wall of the cot. Her wrists tied securely in her lap, her ankles bound, and her mouth muzzled, she allowed her gaze to follow the frantic movements of her uncle as he paced the twenty steps it took to go from one end of the chamber to the other, mumbling and gesticulating as he went.

'Twas only in the past hour that he'd risen up from what e'er dark hole his thoughts had prisoned him and loosed her bindings again to allow her to move and rub her limbs long enough to work the cramping and tingling out, before he once again bound her with the rope.

Her uncle swung toward her suddenly and paced to the window above her head. He'd done this many times in the last hours, but this instance was different. This instance showed more madness. More fever. More fire. More wrath.

"He should have arrived by now."

By *he* she knew he was speaking of Morgunn, her father, not Robert, her husband.

"If he does not come within the next hour... Let us just say, 'twill not be well for you." He blinked down at her with Vika's dark-fringed amber eyes, and it set Morgana's world off kilter. *How can one so evil own such a comely gaze?* Just as quickly, he turned his vision back to what e'er he was beholding outside, and she let her lids drop to force her world back to center.

He turned and resumed his agitated pacing. After several passes to and fro, her heart settled back into a regular *thud-thud-thud*, but now her head pounded to the same rhythm, so she rested it back on the wall behind her.

"You shall be my bait, niece," he said into the rabid silence, and for the third time that day. Still pacing, he wiped the spittle off the corner of his mouth with the back of his hand. "Aye...aye. He'll not want that pretty neck of yours sliced, that I'd wager my earldom on—if 'twas still mine to wager! Aye, you for him, that will be my demand." His head bent, he began to mumble to himself once more, and Morgana only caught fragments of what he said. *"...he'll not have it...get what he deserves...not let him win...even tho' I hang...."*

Once again, he flung himself toward the window, this time leaning his palms on the sill, and stared out. Coming from directly above her as it was, his labored breathing sounded even louder, harsher, wetter. Glancing up, she saw the sheen of sweat on his brow, the beads of it that had collected above his mouth. Was it worry...or madness?

"Where is that bastard brother of mine! The archers—"

Morgana's breath caught. *Archers?*

"—should have weakened their convoy by now, and he and your libidinous husband should even now be straggling up the path."

Was Robert injured? Dead? Morgana had not allowed the thought to take root in these past hours, tho' it had crept into her mind unannounced and unwanted every so often, but now she could not push it back. For the first time, she fully considered the fact that this day might truly be her last.

Thus far, she'd not found a way to escape with her life. She'd had some small bit of opportunity to bash her uncle o'er the head earlier, but then she'd worried he'd recover and kill her then and there. Or, if her aim were true, she wouldn't be able to get past the two guards at the door. For, even if they did not hear the sounds of the scuffle coming from within, one of them had been checking in with her uncle every hour or so, and she did not want to take the chance that they would fell her with no further thought, if they found that she'd slain her captor. Nay, she'd thought 'twas best to take her chances that her uncle would do as he'd planned. That he would release her when her father came. That Robert and her father would vanquish her uncle and his minions. So, she'd determined 'twas best to wait for some sign that Robert and her father were arrived before she joined the fray.

All at once, her uncle pushed himself away from the window, startling her out of her thoughts. Pivoting and taking several steps toward the hearth, he continued raging to himself, saying, "Did the arrows fell them also? Or, is this some ploy to get me out in the open so that he might slay me before I can do the deed to him?"

He whipped around again and stormed over to her, then yanked her from her stool onto her knees, saying, "Pray!" as he pulled the gag from her mouth. "Pray for my victory, and pray for your soul before 'tis too late!"

Song of the Highlands

* * *

When the four warriors drew near their destination, but still far enough out that the men guarding the dwelling could not hear or see their approach, Robert signaled 'twas time to leave their horses behind and move into position so they might swiftly dispatch the guards in silence, with Donnach ne'er the wiser 'til 'twas too late.

They tied their mounts to trees, doused the one torch they'd permitted themselves, took several precious moments to allow their vision to adjust to the pitch darkness, then took the bend in the path.

When the cot came into view, Robert made the signal, and the scout, whom he'd learned was known by Hubert du Valognes, and his son Richard, the stripling, crouched low and, making a wide arc off the path and around either side of the cot, ran without sound to take up their bow target positions. When they were well in place, Guy made the sneezing sound, as planned, in hopes to draw one, or both, of the guards from his post and out into the darkness where they would eliminate him.

The ploy worked. From where they stood, they could hear the low, rumbling voices of the two men, evidently deciding which of them would be the one to find the source of the noise, and in the next moment, the taller, stockier, of the two came striding with a lit torch into the dark toward them.

As the guard approached, Robert moved into position, and as he did so, he let his gaze track for a heartbeat to the light coming from the window of the lodge, to the shadowy figure that moved within, and sent up an unuttered prayer that Morgana was still alive, and unharmed.

He waited until Guy was almost within the circle of light the torch provided, then he pounced from behind, covering the man's mouth with his hand and rending his throat with his dagger at the same time, sending him to the bowels of hell before he could make a sound, before he could even ken his own demise. Quietly, Robert lowered him to the ground.

Robert remained in that crouched position, using the sleeve of his foe's shirt to rid the blood from his blade, as he gave a nod to Guy.

Guy returned the nod, took the torch from him, then walked toward the cabin with his dagger drawn and the light away from his face so that the man guarding the door would believe 'twas his confederate returning.

In the meantime, Robert moved further into the shadows, then made his way as well closer to the cot. Blood pumping more with anticipation than dread for the coming conflict, it took all his will to keep from rushing the moment to its final conclusion.

* * *

Positioned as she was below the window, Morgana could hear the infrequent murmurings of the two men that guarded the door. The one speaking now sounded uneasy. She strained to discern the words... something... something about a noise they'd heard. Her pulse pounded. Could it be Robert, here at last? *Had* he brought with him her father, as per her uncle's orders? 'Twas truth, she knew not which she hoped for more: That he'd obeyed his demand, or defied it.

She'd prayed aloud, as her uncle had demanded, for she'd had no choice, tho' asking for his victory in this had been a bitter tincture on her tongue, and she could only find solace in the knowledge that the Heavenly Father knew what was truly held in her heart, no matter the words spoken.

Everything went deathly quiet outside.

Her uncle stopped his pacing and looked toward the window.

He took a step toward it.

Morgana screamed.

The door flew open.

Robert burst through the door, sword raised.

Her uncle's steel flashed, sang when he freed it from its sheath, but still he staggered back.

A tumult of men's horses came from outside the cot.

Robert maneuvered, slowly, deliberately, to the side so that he still faced her uncle, but had the view through the opened doorway in his sights as well.

Her father barreled through the door.

"How—?" Robert said.

Her father's eye ne'er leaving her uncle, he said, "We were summoned to court. We met the King and his men on the road. He told me all." He took a menacing step toward her uncle. "Get her out of here, I'll handle my brother."

Robert hesitated, but only briefly, then stepped over to Morgana, lifted her from her stool into his arms.

"Nay!" her uncle bellowed. "This was not how 'twas

to be!" He moved with menace toward Robert, but her father stepped into his path.

Her uncle raised his sword as if to strike, but Morgana saw the terror in his eyes, and realized that he would only do so if pressed for his life.

Robert swung her around and strode from the cot. Briefly, and only from the corner of her eye, she saw the dark, crumpled shape of one of the guards, on his haunches, slumped against the exterior wall with his head forward, as if asleep. Morgana knew otherwise. He was dead. Dead as her uncle would surely be in the next moment or so. She also knew, that if 'twas not night, she'd see the blood that soaked the guard's skin and clothing as well. A shudder ran through her, and she turned her head into Robert's neck, pressing her lids into the stubbled skin under his chin. His arms tightened around her back and knees, his hand gripped tighter her arm, but still he said naught, only moved inexorably down the path toward the shadowed group in the distance.

Someone ran up to them and when he spoke, she recognized the voice.

"She lives?" Guy said.

"Aye."

"Praise be. The King insists Donnach Cambel be brought to him alive. Where is Morgunn?"

"Battling him even now, I expect," Robert replied, and with little concern in his voice.

"Will you stop him, or will I?"

"I hope the deed's done."

Morgana heard Guy's retreating footsteps as he pounded up the path toward the cot. Robert continued his journey forward.

* * *

Guy skidded to a halt in the doorway of the cot. Morgunn had Donnach pinned on the floor, the point of his sword pressing into the man's tunic, directly o'er his heart. A pace from Donnach's hand lay a dirk, and by the scatter of hunting blades fallen to the floor, 'twas evident that there had been an abortive struggle for one of them. There was blood running from Donnach's ear and nose, a consequence of a beating got from the broad side of Morgunn's blade, as the streaks and dabs of wet, vivid red upon it proved.

"This.... This, you puling, fetid coward, is for letting that Armoric swine rape and scar my wife!" In the blink of an eye, he hefted the sword with the intent to impale.

"Nay!" Guy shouted, and flew forward, crashing into Morgunn, making Morgunn lose his balance and his aim on his victim's frame.

Morgunn turned a feral gaze on Guy. "Stay!" he bellowed, pressing the weight of his booted foot down on Donnach when Donnach tried to roll out of range. Tho' his eyes remained on Guy, Guy knew the words were meant for Donnach. Morgunn's next words, however, were clearly for him. "There is no mercy to be found here. Leave me to it, or I swear by my sword, I will cut you down as well."

Guy took a step back, put some distance between himself and Morgunn, but said, "The King demands

Donnach be brought to him alive. You know this. You must."

Guy saw the doubt that flickered in Morgunn's eyes, and he pressed on, saying, " 'Twill be a much better, a much more deserved punishment to have Donnach withstand the shame of being publicly tried and hanged for his crimes. Surely, you see I speak the truth."

Morgunn did not move. Guy could see the tension in the man, manifested in the pulse point in his jaw, in the flaring of his nostrils, in the flexing of his fist on the hilt of his sword, in the rapid movement of his chest and shoulders as he inhaled and exhaled.

"What good is done if your daughter loses her father a second time—and to disgrace and dishonor as well?"

Finally—and after such a prolonged moment that Guy had begun to believe he would have to battle Morgunn for his sword—Morgunn stepped away from his quarry. Guy went immediately into action. He bound Donnach's wrists behind his back, bound his ankles as well, then called out the door for aid from one of his guard to get the man onto the cart. For he held little faith that Morgunn's assent would hold if Guy solicited his help with their felon.

He followed his men out, walking toward the gathering of soldiers, toward the King, and 'twas not long before he heard the crunch of Morgunn Cambel's bootsteps coming from behind him as well. *Good.* He would leave to him all explanations required by King William.

As he stood with arms akimbo watching his men

load the trussed Donnach Cambel onto the cart, the low rumble of Robert's words to Morgana came to him from somewhere behind: " 'Tis done. At last, you are safe."

PART SIX

———◆❈◆———

A Song Well Sung

*"I like this place,
And willingly could waste my time in it."*

As You Like It (Act II, scene iv)

*"All's well that ends well, still the fine's the Crowne;
What ere the course, the end is the renowne."*

All's Well That Ends Well (Act IV, scene iv)

CHAPTER 22

AN HOUR LATER, with Morgana resting on the bed inside the cot, and with the contingent of soldiers, the King, and the cart that held his wife's uncle gone back down the path, his father-in-law turned to Robert and said, "I crave to hold my wee lass in my arms again, to speak with her, but 'tis not the time. I shall wait until she is back at the abbey, when both I and her mother can meet her together."

" 'Tis a good plan."

"You will tell her all then, in the next hours?"

"Aye."

"Are you sure you will not make camp with us this night? If there are any of Donnach's minions still about, they might strike once we are gone."

"Fret not. We vanquished them all, I am certain."

"But, if they were not, I—"

"I will guard your daughter well."

Morgunn's brow lifted and his gaze sharpened. "As

you did five days past?"

Robert swung 'round and stalked several paces away, then turned back to his father-in-law with the letter she'd written him gripped in his fist. He moved back to stand near Morgunn and, so that the soldier guarding the cot would not hear, said in a gruff whisper, "She bolted. If she'd not done so, by my vow, she'd ne'er have been captured."

After a brief pause, his father-in-law gave a nod, saying, "Aye. Aye. I have no worry on that score."

"And this night, I will learn why, and turn what e'er is causing her desire to forsake me into naught."

Morgunn clamped his hand on Robert's shoulder, saying, "I wish I could advise you on this, but I fear I ken as little of the workings of a woman's mind as do you. All I will say is, have a care, and I wish you well."

* * *

When Robert entered the cabin a time later, he found Morgana deep in slumber, lying on her side facing him, with her palm under her cheek. A sharp pang of tenderness pierced his heart, stopped his breath. In repose, in the firelight, with locks the color of starlight still damp and curling about her gentle countenance, and the bit of skin not covered by the linen sheet pink from the warmth of the bath (or fire, he knew not which), she looked as innocent as she had been the first time e'er he'd seen her. Her lithe, woman's form moving in unison with her cousin's as they'd entered the great hall of the abbey her first night at court.

With effort he turned his gaze from her, allowed it

to scan the chamber, allowed his mind to turn to the scent of rabbit stew in the pot o'er the hearthfire, to the sound of its bubbling juices, to the gnawing hunger in his belly, and took a step toward it, but stopped short when he realized she'd left the bath as well, along with a kettle of hot water to heat it up again. Aye. Aye. A bath, then a meal, then...*bed*. A hunger of a different sort set his groin to throbbing and he closed his eyes, closed his fists against it. *Nay*. Not yet. Not until he'd got his answers, got her oath that she'd not leave him. *Then*. Then. Aye, then.

* * *

Robert stood naked in the small wooden tub, his back to the bed. He would not test his mettle by giving his eyes easy access to Morgana's form, not without at least one of them full-clothed. He scrubbed away the grime, scrubbed away the dried blood, scrubbed away the ache in his muscles from long hours of worry and riding, scrubbed away the feral desire for her until his skin was so fiery red it stung.

A hand landed as light as a dove's feather on his back, and a lightning bolt charge thrilled through his being, making him start. The touch—the connection—broke away, and he said hoarsely, "Nay!" as he turned and captured her arms, pulled her a step closer again. He reached over and lifted another washing cloth from the table, ne'er taking his gaze from hers, and handed it to her. "My back," he said, tho' it seemed as far off as the sea, with the sound of his blood pumping, his accelerated breathing, filling his ears instead. "Do you mind? I can't reach."

Her cheeks flamed, and he could not ken why, but her soft lips tipped up in a gentle smile and she took the cloth from him, dipped it in the warm water in the basin on the table, lathered it with soap, while he turned so that she could do as he'd asked.

Why did you leave me? His heart raced. "Wh—" He cleared his throat, waiting until she'd taken the first stroke down his skin before beginning again, "Wh—" He couldn't. He just couldn't.

"Aye?"

"The—" He cleared his throat again. "The song you sang in the carn. What was it?"

" 'Twas one my mother sang to me as a wee lass. 'Tis a song of the ancients—or so she told me. She learned it from her mother, who learned it from her mother, who learned it from her mother, and so on. And when 'tis sung in that carn, I discovered when I played there as a bairn, it works some magic on others, and brings on the sleep of Morpheus."

Robert swung around, eyes wide. "That expl—" The cloth that had, only a moment before, been sliding across his back, now stroked his stomach, just a hair's breadth, or so it seemed, from his groin. Blood filled him there, made him heavy, made his need for her rage. "Morgana," he murmured, his voice rough. Without conscious thought, his desire became manifest when his arms went around her, lifted her to him, brought his mouth down upon her own, sent his tongue into the recesses there, to taste, to be fulfilled.

* * *

Morgana returned the kiss, stroke for stroke, pressure

for pressure, rising up on her toes, sliding her arms about his neck, drawing him closer into her, drawing into him so tight that her breasts, her belly, her groin met answering points upon his frame.

Desire, long smoldering, burst into flame. Of its own accord, her body writhed against his, her mons taunted and teased the underside of his raging manhood.

When he swung her up into his arms without breaking the kiss, stepped from the tub, took a long stride toward the bed, she dug her nails into his shoulders and redoubled her kiss. Through her mind ran the words, o'er and o'er again: *At last! At last!*

* * *

When Robert reached the bedside, he turned and fell on his back upon it, taking the weight of Morgana's lush form on him with unholy pleasure. Her long silken skeins of moonspun hair caressed his arms, his chest, his cheeks, as each of them continued to ravage the other's mouth. Finally, his hands trembling with need, he combed his fingers through the mass, brought it away from her neck, and brushed his lips along the warm column of her throat, whispering hoarsely, " 'Tis been too long. Take me, for I fear I'll maul and savage you otherwise."

She shook her head and whispered in his ear.

His heart tripped, then pounded. "Are you sure?"

She grinned against his neck and nodded.

Drawing a stray strand of hair away from her face again, yet keeping his palm, his fingertips lightly touching her cheek and ear, he said against her mouth,

"Next time. For now I want no bedposts between us. 'Tis been too long since I held you, felt your body move against mine, enjoyed you."

Morgana surprised him then. She captured his mouth in a violent storm of a kiss, pushing her own hands through his hair as she did so, and stroking her naked torso o'er his own. His thighs went up in flames; his tarse lengthened, throbbed; his ballocks drew up high into their sack; his heart raced; and his urge to mate with her grew ten-fold. Still somehow, he managed not to fling her to her back and impale her with force and roughness his body screamed for him to do.

He wanted gentleness for her, he wanted tenderness, he wanted to show her with his body how deeply he loved her, craved her for wife, not just for spending his passion upon. He'd nearly lost her, and meeting her, being wedded to her, was the best thing—the absolute *best* thing—that had e'er happened to him. Knowing that, realizing that, he would do aught he must to keep her bound to him with the strong, eternal bonds that, not merely desire, but love, could engender.

Finally, blessedly, *finally*, she lifted up, encircled his tarse with her delicate hand and positioned the head of it at her portal, then in a slow glide, took him inside her.

The intensity of the pleasure near eviscerated him. His body was in her full power, no longer his own. It arched, he cried out, his hands gripped her lush bottom and he erupted inside her on an extended, growling, body-bucking, moan.

His head spun, but the pleasure continued to expand

as she started to move on him. The slick, hot, tight grip of her kept him hard, kept him there with her. He raised his head, and brought her breast down to his mouth with a hand on the back of her neck and began to ravenously suckle, showing her with his mouth how much he needed the sustenance only she could provide him.

She cried out her passion as if 'twould rend her apart, moved upon him with e'er increasing strain and tempo, until they both were soaked with the sweat of their exertions, until at last her spine arched, her head went back, her cries turned to long, lovely moans, and he felt the walls of her canal undulate, gripping and releasing in rapid succession.

He held tight to her nipple, licking, stroking, suckling, as she rose e'er higher on that crest, until he, himself, once more, and just as nearly always was the case with her, felt the high, chaotic waves of pleasure take him o'er again as well. In the next instant, they both stiffened, both yelled out the other's name, both flew apart into millions of tiny bits of starlight, then both collapsed where they were into a deep, restful sleep.

When he awoke some small time later, he looked at her, a mangle of emotion beating in his chest and placed a soft kiss on her brow. As he stroked his hand through her hair, he smiled. This time, they'd not only found heaven together, they'd found oblivion together as well. Another first.

After a quiet, peaceful while, he finally let her go, rolling her gently off him, then rising from the bed. He went to the bucket, that now held tepid water and brought back a damp cloth, then cleansed her love-swollen folds with it before cleansing himself as well. Tossing the cloth toward the bucket, and satisfied when it landed directly inside it, he turned his attention once more to his wife's comfort. He moved to the side of the bed, lifted her up and scooted her closer to the wall. In her sleep, she turned on her side and placed one hand under her cheek.

He lay down on his back beside her, a portion of his large frame hanging o'er the edge of the narrow mattress, and tucked his arms under his head. *Had he planted another babe in her?* If he had…. No. Wife Deirdre had told him that Morgana was fit, was ripe for bearing his son. That same image he'd had, of her holding their babe in her arms, not long after their first time together flitted across his memory and a funny little soaring feeling entered his heart. Aye, 'twas truth, he desperately wanted another babe with her. More than one, in fact.

Morgana stirred beside him, then rolled over to face him and he instinctively shifted into a more secure position on the bed and brought her closer against his side. She settled her hand on his chest and began to caress it, which made him look down at her. Slumberous and satiated, her blue eyes met his gaze.

"What has your brow so furrowed after such a loving, I wonder? Surely, you were not left unsatisfied?" she asked, tho' there was more humor than worry in her tone.

With a growl he wrapped an arm around her and

rolled on top of her. "Nay, tho' 'twas not I who swooned," he lied, and for the life of him, he couldn't say why. Unable to resist, he pushed his fingers into her silky, silver-moon hair, dragged her head back so that her neck was fully exposed, then clamped his mouth o'er the tender, sweet-salty flesh and gave it a long, sucking bite. He felt his tarse thicken, and evidently so did she, for she moaned and rotated her pelvis so that it pressed into his, teasing the proof of his desire for her with her dark curls.

* * *

As Robert's mouth toyed with her neck, Morgana stroked her palm o'er his manhood and moaned deep in her throat. 'Twas not until she heard the rush of her own shortened breaths that some semblance of reason returned, and she dragged her hand from him, pushed against his shoulders, saying, "Nay, not again. First you must restore your vigor with a bit of supper."

He startled her with a short chuckle and a grin. "What, pray, in this past hour, has given you the notion that my vigor is waning?" He moved again to capture her neck with his teeth, gripping her wrist and pulling it back toward his manhood, but she rolled away, taking her hand with her.

"Nay. First food," she said, "then loving, for I want some answers now."

Robert stiffened. His jaw went rigid, and so did his gaze. "Aye," he said and left the bed, "as do I."

Morgana's heart fluttered with alarm. Aye, 'twas time, as well, for her to give to him the reasons she'd forsworn her vows to him. As they moved toward the table where she'd left a trencher for him to fill with stew, she opened her mouth and almost began to tell him all. *Nay.* She clamped her lips together. First, he would give her the answers she needed. She'd waited long enough, and asked, then begged, then demanded and been denied far too often. He must prove to her his willingness to respond with more than a brusque, "Later. After," then she'd tell him what he desired to know.

Once they'd both cleaned and clothed themselves in shirt or chemise, once they were settled on the bench, once she'd ladled a portion of the stew into the trencher, once she'd poured some ale into a cup for him, and once she'd watched him devour near all the trencher-full in no more than three bites (thus proving, in her own mind at least, that she'd been right about his need for sustenance), she said, "For how long did you know my father lives, and why did you not tell me?"

His gaze met hers. From her periphery, she watched him finish chewing, watched his throat flex as he swallowed, watched him wipe his mouth on the cloth she'd provided, and waited, refusing to utter the words again.

His eyes narrowed and he lifted his cup, taking in a long swallow, then slowly set it back atop the table. Finally, he said, "I've known since the day our babe flushed from your womb."

Anger boiled in her gut. "That long?"

"I did not tell you because I feared you were not well, neither in the mind, or in the body."

Morgana would have loved to refute him, but knew

all too well that he spoke the truth, so she said naught.

"And later?"

He scrubbed his hand o'er his chin. "Later...well, later...." He turned to more fully face her. "Morgana, 'tis not only your father that survived that attack, your mother did as well. You know her as Modron, your lady's maid."

Morgana gasped and leapt to her feet, taking several paces away from him. For long moments, she stood with her arms folded over her chest and stared blankly at the array of hunting knives that graced the wall of the cot. She felt cold inside. "She misled me," she said at last.

From behind her, she heard Robert rise from the bench and move toward her. "Only because"—She took another step away, needing to keep the distance between them—"she knew her only chance to succeed in finding evidence against your uncle, so that he could be punished for his crimes against your family, was to allow him to believe she'd perished in her attempt to escape Alaric Albinus' clutches."

"And my father? Does she know he lives, or did you keep that knowledge from her as well?"

She heard him clear his throat. "She was the one that revealed it to me."

Morgana shivered. *Betrayed.*

"But, by then we knew that Donnach wanted you dead, and our best means of exposing his crimes was to keep you safe in your chamber, and keep the fact of your mother and father's surviving the attack a well-guarded secret."

She'd stopped listening. *Betrayed.* The word kept repeating in her head. Her mother, her father, her cousin, her uncle, her *husband.* They'd all betrayed her. From far off came the sound of Robert's voice. He was saying her name and it brought her from her thoughts.

"...there was a plot against your life. Morgana... *Blood of Christ, Morgana*, they poisoned you, killed our babe! I should have protected you. I failed."

Poisoned. Killed our babe. She felt lightheaded and took in a sustaining breath to keep from swooning. She swiveled and strode past him back to the bench. He followed.

In silence, she poured another cupful of ale for him, filled his trencher with more stew. As he ate, she pondered all she'd learned. Her uncle's minions—the ones that had seized her—were the cause of her losing her babe. 'Twas not her fault, as she'd feared. And 'twas not Robert's either, tho' clearly he felt he was to blame. Lifting her eye to his profile, she recalled his words, and listened with new ears to the reasons he'd given her for his betrayal of her trust. After losing her babe, she *had* been heartsick, she *had* had spells. If it had been he who was in such a state, would *she* have told him of the danger? Taunted fortune, and revealed Modrun and the tinker's true identities? Nay, she knew she would not have done so.

"They killed our babe, Robert." She pounded her fist down on the table. "I hate my uncle! I hate those men!" She flung herself up from the stool and stormed toward the wall of knives, her arms folded tight over her chest, her eyes blindly staring into the distance.

"I know, love, I hate them too."

Her head bent, her eyes filled with anguished tears. "I didn't before," she murmured, "but I do now." Her shoulders quaked and she covered her face with her hands. "God will punish me for such a sin, but truly, I cannot help it."

A warm wall of comfort spread behind her and strong hands settled on her shoulders.

"Nay, he will not," Robert soothed. "I cannot—I will not—believe it. They are the devil's minions, and you—you and our babe—are the innocents."

She turned in his arms and he held her close. After a quiet moment, he led her back to the table and he resumed his meal.

"Why did you not tell me that Grímr is the father of Vika's babe?" she asked into the silence.

He looked up at her, his eyes skimming her countenance. Evidently deciding she'd recovered enough from the earlier blow, he said plainly, and with a thread of accusation running through his tone, "Because I discovered the truth *after* you'd bolted."

Morgana remained still, but inside she squirmed. "I...see." She dropped her gaze to the trencher. "Finish your meal, it grows cold."

Robert surprised her then, reaching out and covering her hand with his. "How could you e'er believe I love Vika?"

"Because you believed—I believed—I was mad." She peeked up at him, but then dropped her gaze once more, unable to retain the courage. "But I am not mad. I thought I was, but...once my memory returned I realized my swoons, my visions, were merely antecedents to my remembrance of my past and all that happened."

"Aye, I know. You are far from mad. And you are not as fragile as I once believed you to be, either."

Her spine straightened and her chin went up. "Aye, I am not. 'Tis glad I am that you have at last realized such."

With a grin, he tucked a lock of hair behind her ear. He leaned in and dropped a soft kiss on her lips then drew back a fraction, enough to capture her gaze, and murmured, "Know this: 'Tis you, and you alone, who holds my heart. I love you, Morgana."

Humiliatingly, her eyes misted. "Truly?"

She wanted so desperately to release her burgeoning joy in a flood of tears, but she fought them back. Still, her nose grew damp, and she was forced to sniffle. Robert wrapped his arm around her shoulder, drew her into his side, settled his cheek on the crown of her head, and pressed the cloth to her nose, saying, "Blow," and as she obeyed, she felt the weight of his lips on her forehead, and knew, no matter what else might be revealed this night, their hearts and lives were irrevocably bound for e'er more.

EPILOGUE
The Highlands, Scotland
The MacVie Holding, Yule 1207

THE SMALL MACVIE chapel was cast in a citrine glow that eve by the flickering of a hundred taper flames. Finely made tapers of beeswax, with a series of swirls and fleurons upon their bases that framed an illumined gold leaf letter *C*, had been sent as a gift from King William for the couple, and had arrived only this day past. The sweet honeyed scent of them pervaded the chamber, brought a smile to Morgana's lips.

The couple kneeled at the altar, heads bowed, hands clasped in front of them in prayer, as the priest began to recite, *"Concede, quaesumus, omnipotens Deus...."* Through the bride's lilac-hued gossamer veil, Morgana surreptitiously admired the unbound golden brown hair that fell past the lady's waist. Even now, five moons later, she could not fathom how easily guiled she'd been by her lovely, still youthful, mother's disguise.

She and her family had been through so much these past moons since Morgana's capture and subsequent rescue. They'd only been given leave by the King to return to the MacVie holding five sennights past, after having been obliged to stay as his guests at his castle at *Sruighlea* until her uncle's trial and punishment were concluded. But now, with Donnach's hanging witnessed, and well in the past; the furbishing and additional construction to the keep all but completed; and with the feasts for both the Yule and for this joyous occasion of the renewal of her mother and father's vows planned o'er the next days before they at last would return to their own forsaken home, *Aerariae secturae*, Morgana finally could let all her sadness, her bitterness, her anger fly away, and simply enjoy the moment.

The prayer concluded, the priest invited the guests to rise from their kneeling stools and take their seats on the benches behind them. Robert aided her to rise then continued holding her hand as they settled together on their seats.

"Et ait faciamus hominem ad imaginem...," the Priest intoned, beginning the first reading from the Book of Genesis.

A sudden fluttering movement beneath her breast made Morgana gasp aloud before she could restrain it, and she pressed her palm to the side of her belly.

"Is it the babe? Are you well?" Robert said anxiously, placing his own hand o'er hers.

The priest continued to read, but sent a stern glance in their direction, so Morgana shushed her husband and straightened on the bench, giving Robert a nod and a whispered, "I am well," in answer. From a bit further down the bench, she caught a barely audible chuckle coming from Guy, and Robert made a distinctly unholy hand gesture at him low enough so the priest could not see, which caused Guy to snort, then pretend to cough behind his hand, which, of course, made him the next target for the priest's baleful gaze, which then, again of course, made her husband sit back with his arms folded and with a satisfied grin upon his visage. Robert's nine-year-old nephew, David, who was seated on Robert's other side, leaned forward and grinned at both his uncle and their Norman neighbor, and Morgana pressed a finger to her lips, indicating he should be still and quiet. The smile dissolved and he settled back again. *Lads!* They were naught more than unruly lads. But they were hers, and she loved them all. Quietly, she slid her hand onto Robert's thigh and was set aglow when he took it in his and twined their fingers together. It took everything within her not to sigh and settle her head on his shoulder.

Thankfully, the remainder of the wedding service held the solemnity it deserved, and when 'twas over, they rose from their seats and proceeded from the chapel behind the couple. Once her mother and father were seated in their places at the long table upon the dais in the great hall, and the wine had been poured into all of the cups, Robert raised his high and said, "The clan MacVie has much to be thankful for, but let us this night lift our cups to Morgunn and Gwynlyan!" and all about them shouted "Aye!" then drained their vessels in one long pull. Morgana could not help but smile in absolute pride. Aye, another man might have said much more, but for Robert, that public address was a true accomplishment. Recalling how ill at ease he had been at their own wedding feast, she, at least, could see the transformation in him, and knew the toll such a change was taking on him as well.

In fact, when he sat down, she could see clearly the sheen of sweat on his brow and upper lip, and was struck again with pride for him. She leaned in and placed a kiss on his cheek, saying, "Well done, my love, well done."

He shrugged self-consciously, and dug into the trencher, spearing a large piece of venison with his knife, then shoveling it into his mouth.

Her heart fluttered and she swallowed a sigh. He was just so wonderful. Truly, she felt so blessed. She sent a silent *thank you* for about the millionth time to her absent cousin Vika for giving her the chance to be with Robert that first time.

"I love you." She only realized she'd said it aloud when Robert stopped chewing and turned his warm silver gaze upon her. She watched his throat work as he swallowed, saw his expression gentle, heard him murmur gruffly, "I love you, too," before he leaned over and settled upon her mouth a not-so-chaste kiss. As his tongue caressed hers, her blood heated, and, held captive by his virile will, she could do naught but delight in the heated embrace. After a long moment, and from what seemed a thousand miles away, came the shouts and slamming down of flagons on tabletops by their guests. From closer still, came her father's familiar voice saying, "This is *our* feast, remember you that?"

Morgana grinned and so did Robert, but he kept kissing her anyway, which seemed to cause much mirth in David, for she heard the bell-like laddish giggles begin behind Robert's broad shoulders. Finally, she broke away, breathless, but with her spirits floating above her. The only thing that would make this feast even more perfect would be to have Vika and Grímr, and their newborn son, Hildrgrímr, here with them as well. Why had Vika not sent her the letter herself? Why had Grímr sent the letter to Robert, and not her? The letter they'd received a few days past had been brief, with naught more than the tidings of the recent birth; that the babe had the look of Grímr, with pale-hair, blue-eye, and was hearty and hale; and that Vika was doing well within its text. Men were so vexing! Did they not know that ladies craved a full account of such things? She had already begun a long letter to Vika herself, and Morgana would beg for an answer to all her questions quickly, and in return.

A commotion was heard near the entry to the great hall, and a wash of pleasure went through her as she looked with anticipation toward the doorway. She felt Robert move beside her, then the warm, calloused comfort of his hand on hers.

"Is this the thing you were telling me of?" he asked low.

"Aye," she said through her smile, never taking her gaze from the entry.

As was expected, the lyre player began the soft, ceremonial

tune, and she soon saw the line of spinners, dyers and weavers come into the chamber one at a time, dressed in the fine colored cloth Morgana's new trade had afforded. The last two carried in front of them bolts of fine wool. One, the color of copper, meticulously spun, then woven, then died to match her mother's aspect, and the other the blue of the midnight sky, to complement her father's eyes.

When they were positioned as Morgana had requested, she gave a nod to the head spinner and head weaver, and they each took one of the colored bolts from the two others' arms and presented them to the wedded pair. As rehearsed, the head weaver said, "This fine cloth from our Lady's own looms is her gift to you on this, your wedding day."

Murmurs of approval traveled through the room, as the guests looked with delight upon the brightly colored gifts. Her mother and father leaned forward and saluted her with a smile and mouthed praise.

She felt her cheeks heat with pleasure and dipped her head in a sudden spell of shyness.

Robert's arm came around her and he pulled her into his side, giving her a squeeze and whispering in her ear, " 'Tis lovely, Morgana."

"My thanks," she said softly.

All at once, she felt more than saw a presence in front of their section of the table and lifted her gaze. Again, a wash of pleasure went through her and she smiled, a question in her countenance, at the group of spinners, dyers and weavers, and now even the larderers, the maids, and a host of the other women who worked at the keep, had made a mass congregation before her.

"This, my lady," the head spinner said, stepping forward with yet another bolt of dark lavender colored samite, "is from us to you, and is the first and best bolt from our new silk weaving looms. You've aided our Laird and aided our clan. You've helped to bring prosperity back to us here, and for this, we give you our thanks."

When she'd first arrived home, after so many moons away, she'd worried that her place with the women—already precarious, or so she had felt—would be even more so. But she'd been wrong. The women of the clan, the women of the keep had welcomed, and even pampered her. And o'er the past sennights, she had found the added space, as well as a means of beginning the cloth trade she'd hoped to establish all those moons ago. In fact, there was now a store room filling with bolts upon bolts of the MacVie wool and silk to be sold the next holy day and fair.

Morgana reached out and ran her hand o'er the slick cloth, saying, " 'Tis the loveliest cloth I've e'er seen! My thanks."

The women dipped in courtesy, then took all three of the bolts of cloth out of the feasting hall so that they would not get stained, and Morgana could not take her eyes from them as they left the chamber, so proud was she of them, so humbled, and awed as well.

Robert lifted the chalice of wine and offered it to her, and she gratefully took a sip of the cool liquid. With a sigh, she sat back in her chair and allowed the images of all the coins they'd garner from selling all that cloth in not too long a time to whirl through her thoughts.

The pipers began to play a familiar melody, and it brought Morgana from her thoughts. The musician moved in graceful, dance-like steps toward her, and when he was just below her place at the raised table, he beckoned her with a wave of his hand. Robert nudged her, leaning down to whisper in her ear, "Sing for us, Morgana. Sing this for your mother and father."

Her face flamed and she started to shake her head, but then her gaze traveled to her mother's and she saw the longing in her eyes, so she gave a nod and rose to her feet. Once off the dais, she moved to the area that had been cleared for the musicians and, after the lyre player and piper were in their positions as well, she began to softly, hesitantly, sing the song, in the ancient tongue, that her mother had sung to her so oft when Morgana was but a wee lass:

Upon th' misty moor did I
Go tha' fateful morn . . .

She allowed her gaze to drift from her mother's gleaming one to her father's. His was filled with the same pride and love for her that her mother's held, and it gave her courage to lift her voice higher for the next verse:

And lay me down upon the ground
To 'wait me fey tribe's horn . . .

Song of the Highlands

And on she went, singing all ten of the verses. It seemed as if a sennight had past by the time she sang the last note, and the dampness in her palms no doubt matched that on her brow. Still, she exulted in the clamorous show of approval she received from all the guests once the song ended. She let her gaze fall on her husband, and her spirits soared higher still when she caught his broad smile and tender look. He motioned to her to return to him, and she dipped a swift courtesy to the crowd, then quickly, and gratefully, obeyed.

When she was seated once more at his side, he murmured against her ear, "I shall ne'er tire of your voice, Morgana. Will you sing to me again later, when I am inside you?"

Her cheeks turned hotter still and she darted a glance around him to David, who thankfully had his attention upon his trencher and had not heard, before answering, "Aye, always, if you wish it." She felt the now-familiar fluttering of her babe, like butterfly wings, inside her womb, and said with a hand on her belly, "I think he likes my song as well. He dances."

Robert's marvelous grin lit his visage once more and he settled his palm on the small mound of her belly as well. "He's a strong one."

Her heart constricted. "Aye. You said the same of our first."

He didn't respond immediately, instead his eyes scanned her countenance, then met her eyes. Finally he said, "We would not have lost him had you not been poisoned, Morgana. You must believe that." He paused again, but only in the time it took to blink an eye. "*I must believe that.*"

A hand settled on her shoulder and she started. 'Twas her mother.

"The babe is hale, and so are you, daughter. I know these things. Besides, Wife Deirdre says the same, so do not forget."

A calm settled upon Morgana. She lifted her countenance to her mother's and gave her a wide smile. "Aye, you are right."

"May I go to my bedchamber now, Uncle?" David said to Robert.

"Aye." After only a small pause, he said, "Are you missing Callum and Branwenn and the feast at the Maclean holding this year?"

He swiped a fallen lock of sandy blond hair off his brow "Aye, I miss them, but...." He looked up at the rafters, a pensive look upon his visage. In that moment she saw a trace of Robert there and her heart melted even more for the young orphaned lad.

Morgana held her breath and without realizing it, placed her hand o'er the one her mother still had resting on Morgana's shoulder.

Finally, David continued, saying, "But I'm glad I came to stay with you this Yule. Your lady wife is pretty and she lets my dog sleep in my bed with me."

Robert turned to her with one brow lifted and said, "Truly? Hmmm."

Morgana felt her cheeks heat, but she said, "Jasper's

a good dog—I could not see the harm."

One side of Robert's mouth lifted and he stroked her cheek with the back of his fingers, then turned back to David, saying, "Off with you then, and take a meaty bone up for the hound—but he must gnaw it by the hearth, *not* in your bed."

"Aye, Uncle," David said with renewed energy.

While David went to gather a bone for Jasper, Morgana turned back to her mother and said, "Are you ready to go to your bride's bed now?"

Her mother returned the smile. "Aye—and so is your father." She'd barely spoken the last syllable when Morgunn strode up behind them as well and placed a proprietary hand on the small of her mother's back, saying to Morgana, "You've the voice of an angel, daughter. I'd forgot that song until you sang it just now." He didn't wait for an answer, but turned to her mother and said, "Let us be off to our chamber, my love, for I'll not wait another moment to finally have you again in my bed, where you belong."

Her mother's cheeks turned crimson, and Morgana could have sworn she saw worry, doubt, or even a small amount of fear flash in her eyes as well, but 'twas gone so quickly, she decided she'd imagined it when Gwynlyan took Morgunn's arm and they both departed the dais with a bit of a skip in their stride.

As Morgana watched the swaying backs of the couple move across the great hall and out the door, Robert touched her cheek and whispered, "Take me to bed, wife."

"Aye," she answered.

And she did.

~ THE END ~

*Don't miss the bonus material that follows:
The additional chapter of Gwynlyan and Morgunn's wedding night and their love story's resolution that could not be fitted within the scope of Robert and Morgana's tale, but beckoned that it be told nevertheless.*

K.E. SAXON

Of Us That Trade in Love

Morgunn & Gwynlyan

Postquel to Song of the Highlands

Of Us That Trade in Love

Morgunn & Gwynlyan

Postquel to Song of the Highlands

K.E. SAXON

OF US THAT TRADE IN LOVE
(Morgunn & Gwynlyan)

Copyright © 2014 by K.E. Saxon
http://www.kesaxon.com

All rights reserved. No part of this book may be used or reproduced by any means, graphic, electronic, or mechanical including photocopying, recording, taping, or by any information storage retrieval system without the written permission of the author K.E. Saxon, the copyright owner and publisher of this book, except in the case of brief quotations embodied in critical articles or reviews.

This is a work of fiction. Names, characters, places, brands, media, and incidents either are the product of the author's imagination or are used fictitiously. Any resemblance to actual events, locales, organizations, or persons, living or dead, is entirely coincidental and beyond the intent of the publisher. The author acknowledges the trademarked status and trademark owners of various products referenced in its work of fiction, which have been used without permission. The publication/use of these trademarks is not authorized, associated with, or sponsored by the trademark owners.

Cover image obtained from Jenn LeBlanc / Illustrated Romance
Cover Design by K.E. Saxon

Of Us That Trade in Love
(Morgunn & Gwynlyan)

AS MORGUNN ALL but dragged her by the hand from the great hall, Gwynlyan pasted what she hoped would be perceived as a smile of anticipatory joy on her lips, very much aware of the friendly and amused gazes of all their well-wishers watching them as they made their way out of the feasting chamber to go to her bride's bed for the night.

"At last, at last, my Gwynlyan, I'll have you thrashing and moaning 'neath me again in mere moments," Morgunn said, a little too loud for Gwynlyan's liking, and she darted a glance to the nearest table of guests. She didn't know why she'd bothered, as the snorts of mirth would have told her just the same: Aye, they'd heard him. "Truly, Morgunn. Must you be so lewd?" she said sotto voce.

"You used to like it when I spoke in that way to you," he said in like tones.

She felt her cheeks flame and his eyes twinkled at her before he tossed his head back and gave forth a great belly laugh. Even that did not slow his stride.

In another moment, they were alone together on the stairs, away from all prying eyes, and Gwynlyan allowed her guard down, but only slightly. For, the true trial was only just beginning. In a matter of moments, he'd have her in their chamber and expect her to strip bare for him, as she'd intimated, but not promised in words, she'd finally do once the obligation for the ceremony and feast were concluded.

Aye, she'd give him her body, as he was so clearly determined to have. She owed him that. She only hoped she'd not give herself away, give the extent of her experience with other men away. She must remain on her guard. Try to recall how it had been with them before, how innocent and pure, and try to mimic it the best she could. She.... Her brain stopped the thought. Nay, she could not tell him of that time, for she knew him so well. He'd push and prod and not let her be until she'd spilled every vile deed she'd done, she'd had done to her. And truly, she could not bear to speak of it. Not to him, not even to herself. See only how her mind would not form the remainder of the thought just now? That was how 'twas with her, and she wanted it to remain thus.

Aye, the key was to tell him their relationship had changed, it had had to change, because of all that had happened o'er the years. But that did not mean they could not build a new, a different, mayhap not better, but certainly a companionable, good relationship from

Of Us That Trade in Love

the ashes of their past. Could they not? And, aye, eventually, she *would* show him the scars, and, *mayhap*, years from now, she might even find that she could tell him of all that had happened to her. But not now. She simply was not ready.

* * *

'Twas wonderful and strange how much this wedding night felt like the first, Morgunn thought. Gwynlyan was just as skittish, just as shy. 'Twas making him feel a bit of the same. He'd attempted to amuse her a moment past, calm her a bit by reminding her of the easy way they'd had between them years before by giving her one of his lusty jests that would, in that time past, have sent her into titters of guilty glee. When she'd not reacted as he'd expected, he'd o'ercome his own embarassment with a laugh. She no doubt thought him course.

He'd need to take things slower than he'd afore expected. Be more the gentle knight, not the libidinous warrior lover. The habit had grown rusty, as he'd only been with whores these past years since his recovery from his head wound. Women who served as mere vessels to receive his urges, his wasted seed, then sent on their way with ne'er more than five words exchanged between them in the short time they were together. Could he remember how to woo a virgin? For, that was clearly, or at least, nearly what she was for him at this point. He'd best, if he wanted her 'neath him this night.

Oh, aye, she'd given him her promise to do just that, after their wedding ceremony. A ceremony insisted upon by King William in order to strengthen the weakened, and now questionable, vows of marriage they'd taken twenty years past, and in so doing, make the transfer of, not only *Aerariae secturae*, but the vaster holdings that had been Donnach's as the first son of Comgeall Mór, and as one of the King's earls, less dubious. And a renewal of wedding vows that left no weak link, no question of lineage for future offspring, so that another might more easily claim and win right to it. Aye, she'd delayed the bedding. And he'd complied, knowing that she feared his seeing the mars on her skin, left by that beast Alaric. For, she still had no notion that he'd seen them on one of their meetings when he'd come upon her at the burn while she still bathed, and he could not find the courage within himself to tell what he'd done, what he'd seen. It seemed as if it might make matters worse between them, rather than better. It seemed as if it might be best for her to willingly reveal them to him instead.

He had little doubt she would comply, would fulfill her vow, to him as well. But would she do so grudgingly? That would ne'er do. Not for him, not for Gwynlyan, and not for the health of their union. "We're here," he said to her, opening the door to their chamber wide and, with a bit of slight pressure to the small of her back, invited her entrance first.

* * *

Gwynlyan's heart was pounding so, she had trouble getting enough air. 'Twas making her lightheaded, and she could not afford to swoon. The humiliation would simply be too great. She must remain strong. She must remain fully present. She must remain calm.

And give to him what he expected.

Of Us That Trade In Love

Quickly, she decided in that instant. Aye. Get the thing o'er and done, and then she might finally find a bit of rest, a bit of peace in her breast. And knowing she'd done her duty to her husband, and had hopefully pleased him, would be all the gratification she would need this night, or ever.

"The chamber's still a bit chilled," she said to him. "I suppose the maids thought we'd stay at our wedding feast a bit longer."

Morgunn's gaze settled on the hearthfire. He walked toward it, saying, "All it needs is a bit more peat, I think. I'll take care of it. Do you need help with the gown?" He said the last without looking in her direction, which she was more than grateful for. "I can get a maid, if—"

"—Nay, I can manage. My thanks."

Her fingers trembled so, she twisted the laces in her hurry and fear. One of them got a knot in it and would not come through the hole. A tight ball of anger at herself, at...herself, and at the lace itself brought on a show of temper and she began to tug and pull on it, determined to rip the thing out of its place. 'Twould not come, and as she continued to try to force it, her vision began to swim. She blinked the tears away, but still more came. Her throat throbbed with the unuttered shout she craved to emit. Her nose began to drip, so she swung around, allowing herself a barely audible sniffle before she took in a deep, calming breath and wiped her eyes and flushed cheeks with the hem of her gown. *You will not master me!* With one last, vicious yank, she at last got it free. Then, more determined than ever to get this thing, this duty, o'er with, she slid out of the gown, tossed it o'er the trunk at the end of the bed, then turned.

Her heart leapt into her throat. Morgunn was not more than three paces from her now, and he simply stood there, with a brooding, helpless look upon his countenance, his arms limp at his sides, as if he knew not what to do with them where she was concerned.

"I am ready for you now," she said, and climbed up on the mattress, scooted into place at the far side of the bed, then patted the space next to her in, she hoped, a coy, but clearly willing, invitation for him to join her there.

"I want you bared to me, Gwynlyan, as before...."

She swallowed the terror that rose up in her throat, but there was still a quaver in her voice when she said, "I cannot."

* * *

Morgunn bit back his first instinctive response, which was to tell her aye, she could, and she would, reminding himself instead of his vow to himself only a small time past that he'd treat her with gentle care. So, instead he said, "All right," and he knew he'd said the exact right thing when he saw her visibly relax, saw a small glimmer of a warm glow return to her hazel eyes as she gazed upon him.

He'd not remain thus, however, and in moments he was bereft of clothes, standing before her with not a barrier, not a defense between them—except, of course, her own.

"My scars are many. More, and more terrible, than

Of Us That Trade in Love

last we shared our bodies," he said, hoping that the sight of the wide, raised white slash across his chest and abdomen, as well as the newest, smaller, yet still blueish red in color, from the stab wound he'd received at Alaric's hand a few moons past, would make her more easy in revealing to him her own.

But, he was mistaken, for all she said in reply was, "So I see."

Did she find them repulsive? He'd not spent time worrying about what her reaction to them might be these past moons, but now he had to wonder.

"I'll wear my shirt, I think," he said, stepping o'er to where he'd laid it atop her gown on her clothing chest.

"Nay!"

She startled him with the vehemence behind the word and his movements halted.

"Stay as you are, if it please you." Her head dipped, but not before he saw a wash of color o'er her cheeks. "I...I like you well that way," she murmured.

She liked him well? His chest swelled with both pride and relief, and he dared not utter more, instead going with steady, quiet, purposeful steps toward the bed. His goal: her body. His ultimate purpose: to get their lives, their marriage back to that place it had been before the ambush. To forget the horrors of their past and embrace only what had been beautiful.

He settled on his side on the mattress and immediately pulled her toward him. She did not resist, but she did not melt into him either. A worry, but he dismissed it, thinking he'd soon have her trembling with need, all her fears forgotten for the moment.

His own hand shook as he lifted it to comb back the silken mass of amber hair that had fallen o'er her shoulder and hid from him half of her lovely countenance. He dipped his head and placed a gentle kiss on her soft mouth. His heart raced when she returned it with some of the fire he was used to receiving from her. After a moment, he broke away, his breath coming in more rapid spurts than before, and said, "You are so beautiful, my love. More so, even, I think, than you were when first we wed."

She stiffened in his embrace, and he could see in her eye that she thought he lied to her, yet still she remained rooted where she was, allowing him what e'er touch he craved to give, what e'er brush of his lips he craved to bestow.

In the next moment, she lifted her hand to the back of his head and, as she brought his lips down to meet hers again, said, "I am ready for you, Morgunn. Do not make me wait more."

His blood rushed and, as their lips met in a fiery kiss, he hauled the hems of both their garments up to their waists. Gratification doubled as she spread her thighs for him, gripping his hips and helping him to unerringly find the center of her.

She'd not lied. She was slick and warm and he easily slid the full length inside her. A warning bell clanged in the back of his brain, some odd, cold feeling threatened the edges of his heart, but the need for her was too great, and those things were quickly ignored as waves of ecstasy rolled o'er him.

" 'Tis just like before, aye, my love?" he said, less as

a question for her than a statement of reassurance for himself, yet she grew still beneath him, and after a blink of time responded with: "Aye, just as before."

* * *

What was it that you did—and did not—do before? 'Twas best to keep it simple, she decided. Let him lead. But the feel of him moving inside her was near more than she could bear. She wanted to move as well, rip at her clothes, force his mouth to her breast. She wanted to cry out her delight, she wanted to scrape her nails down his back, she wanted to push him deeper inside her. She'd not expected to ever feel such thrills of desire again, and certainly not to this degree. Not with the burden of her guilt, not after the trove of men she'd been forced to pleasure, whom she'd barely been able to stomach, yet who'd sometimes still managed to bring her to completion. She simply could not bear for him to know of it. So, she must somehow please him in the way he expected. As a bride who'd e'er had but one lover: him. But, God in Heaven, how was that? She could not remember. So, she erred on the side of caution and remained pliant (she hoped) beneath him, keeping her responses soft, and to the minimum, and prayed he thought 'twas her years of near chastity and shyness that were the reasons for such a demeanor.

On the cusp of that thought, Morgunn rolled his hips a certain way and began a swifter gliding motion that stroked a place in her womb, making it throb, making her unable to control her reaction, making her strain and buck beneath him, making her cry out, "Aye, fuck me like that, just like that!", making her claw at his back, making it hard to take in a breath, making her see black spots behind her eyes.

All at once, she was lighter. Her body was bereft of his warm, straining weight, and in its place, cold air wafted o'er her hot skin, making it tingle. She gave a shudder and opened her eyes, searching for the lover that had only a second before been working her and himself toward the ultimate bliss. 'Twas not a long trek her gaze took to find him. He stood, lungs heaving, beside the bed. For as long as she lived, and until she took her very last breath, she would ne'er forget the look she found upon his countenance. 'Twas the exact look she'd hoped, prayed ne'er to see. 'Twas accusation. Pure, and simple, and brutal in its scope.

"How many?"

She knew what he meant by the question and struggled to swallow back the cry of crushing heartbreak it engendered. Slowly, she raised herself up to a sitting position, resting her back against the headboard, and pulling the linen sheet up to her chin at the same time (although, why she felt it necessary to do so, she did not know, as her chemise covered the worst of her). 'Twas an even graver betrayal that her sex still throbbed with the need for completion, the need for the completion only he could truly provide. But he didn't know that.

"More, no doubt, than you," she said. It hadn't been what she'd planned to say, but somehow, when she'd opened her mouth to speak, the venom came forth instead.

* * *

Morgunn stormed over to his shirt, threw it on, and

Of Us That Trade in Love

then swung around and stormed as far away from her as he could go in the chamber, which was not far enough. Only about sixteen paces, only to the area beside the hearth. He stood in a turmoil of anger, wrath, and intensely painful heartbreak. His arms crossed over his chest, he fumed in silence. Tho' his gaze was upon the licking flames, his mind ran a riot of lewd, perverse images of his wife across his imagination. A wife whom he'd first thought dead, then hoped against hope lived, then prayed was safe in Alaric's tower dungeon, living as the man's captive and, aye, possibly concubine, he'd admit at least that, and then, once found, believed had been maimed because of that man's perverse urge toward violence against women, which Morgunn had long heard of in the years prior to the ambush.

Not once, however, had he e'er conceived that she would have been giving her body to a host of men. Whether of her own consent, or against it, at this very moment, in his heart—in his soul—it mattered little the difference.

From what seemed a sea away, came the sweet timbre of her voice, this time gentle, this time soothing. "I thought you were dead, and inside myself, I felt the same. Aye, I breathed—and God knows I tried hard not to do even that, but it proved a greater force than I could win against. And so, I breathed. And so, I took my mind somewhere else—back to the time with you, the time with my daughter, the time when naught filled our heads but our youth and what next bit of enjoyment, what next journey, might fill our days. I did this and more, what e'er I might, just...just gave up my body to what e'er Alaric wanted of it, or who e'er Alaric wanted to give it.

Morgunn's hands fisted under his arms, his wrath grew until he shook with it. Without knowing he was going to do it, he swung to his side and, with a ferocious snarl, hurled one of the chairs against the door of the chamber. For a breath of time he stood staring at his work, sucking in deep lungfuls of air. Until, and again, as if from some great distance, came her voice again.

"Our relationship has changed, it had to, do you not see? Because of all that happened—to both of us—o'er the years. But it does not mean we can not build a new, a different life together from the ashes of our past."

Everything within him balked and he was about to say so, when a knock came on the door. A low rumble of frustration exploded from his throat, but he stormed over to the portal and opened it a crack. When he saw 'twas his daughter on the other side, he forced an blithe smile to his lips and said, "Aye, daughter? What brings you to your mother and my nuptial chamber at this late hour?"

His daughter's brows were furrowed with worry, and her eyes moved past him, and he knew she was straining to see within. "I heard a crash. Is aught amiss?"

Morgunn put on his best grin and said, "Nay. 'Tis just a bit of.... Well, let us just say, 'tis of no care of yours, shall we?" and he moved his eyebrows in a way that let her know 'twas the result of the more amorous pursuits he and Gwynlyan were engaged in. He opened

Of Us That Trade in Love

the door a bit more, allowing her to see Gwynlyan in bed with the sheet covering her, so it seemed as if she were naked beneath, and said to Gwynlyan, "Is that not right, my love?"

Gwynlyan gave him a shy smile and nodded.

The ploy worked, for his daughter's cheeks went up in flames and she said in a rush, "Well, I bid you a good night then," and swung around and headed on swift feet back in the direction of her own bedchamber door.

When she was well away, well out of earshot, Morgunn quietly shut the door and moved back to the hearthfire. This time he sat down on the remaining chair, sat forward with his head down, and twined his fingers together.

"Tell me how many others, tell me their names, tell me what they did to you, tell me what you did to them, tell me if you enjoyed it, tell me if they enjoyed it. Tell me."

* * *

Gwynlyan's lungs seized as terror gripped her. The desperate need for air finally forced her to suck in a breath, but she could no longer face him and she could no longer remain as a lamb to the slaughter, lying there helpless and weak in the bed he'd abandoned her in. She rose to her feet and walked to the washstand. She knew, she could feel, the wall of impatience behind her, yet she refused to answer immediately, nor would she answer the specific questions at all, not until she'd soothed her heated cheeks, washed the dried tears from her face, cooled her swollen eyes.

When she at last turned to face him, he'd stood up and had walked back to brood at the hearth once more.

But he'd evidently sensed her eyes on him, for he turned and looked at her, waiting for her to speak, and breaking her heart with the pain she saw reflected there.

"I am not able to tell you of those times. Mayhap, if our marriage lasts, someday I will be able to, but not now. I cannot bear to think of it myself, much less share it with you."

"I have to know."

She turned to the side, and rubbed her hand across the corner of the washstand, focusing her attention there as she said, "Then I am truly sorry for you, for it is something I am unable to give."

She heard him take a step forward and rumble, "Gwynl—"

Her heart quivered in her breast, threatening to crack in two as she let go the glimmer of a dream she'd had that they might just make it. Understanding now the only possible thing that could work for them, she said, "I know 'tis of utter import that we two seem happily bound in marriage, but I also know that you feel betrayed by me. A thing that is, in your estimation, worse than any other sin between man and wife. So, here is my proposal: We live apart." Her voice cracked on the last word.

"Nay!" he bellowed, taking two steps toward her, but stopped short again, and she knew 'twas because he could not stand to be too close to her now. "I'll nn—"

She swung her gaze to his and lifted her chin to show that she would not let him coerce her into changing her mind. "Aye, we shall. I shall live at one of the smaller manor houses you'll be gaining from Donnach's estate now that we've wed, and you shall stay where e'er your business takes you, and you shall keep a leman, and I shall remain chaste, and you shall have no worries of me, and I shall not pine for you or begrudge the enjoyment you receive from your lover, and to all eyes, when e'er we must be seen together, we will display to them the view of a blissfully wed couple. The perfect pairing."

* * *

Morgunn didn't know what scared and angered him more, the unrevealed, and numerous, carnal encounters his wife had had with an unnumbered variety of men, or the fact that she could so easily toss him away, like so much refuse, with no more than a blink of an eye.

"I love you Gwynlyan. Do you still love me?" The words slipped out, had been less than a thought, but had somehow made their way into the space between them, and he felt them settle there, bare and unarmed. Would she flay them, or would she nurture and hold them close?

Her answer was not in words, but in her eyes. They filled with tears as she gazed at him with a longing he'd thought ne'er to see from her again. He took a step toward him, and she took two toward him. Her chin quivered, her throat worked. And 'twas only then that he realized his own eyes, his own chin, his own throat was reacting the same.

When they were no more than five paces from the other, she stopped. "I do love you, Morgunn. I ne'er stopped. I thought, when first I saw you again all those moons ago at the burn that aye, mayhap the love I'd felt for you had gone. Gone with my innocence, gone with my youth. But then you kissed me, you held me close, and the love, the connection to you all came clear once more, there where I'd left it buried, deep in my heart."

Morgunn's own heart swelled and he smiled for the first time in what felt like ages, but was no more than an hour, surely. He took another step forward, reaching out his arms to her, but she stopped him with a raised hand, saying, "I cannot now tell you all that you asked about that time, but I will give you one last thing, one thing at least that I can, a thing that is a proof, a small proof, that even with all that I was forced into, I did not willingly forsake you."

She took him by surprise when she lifted her chemise o'er her head in a single sweep and dropped it to the floor beside her feet. His heart recoiled, not at the horror of the sight, but at the brutal, instinctive and gut deep recognition of the pain she'd suffered. These were not stripes from a crop, as the dark moonlit night had seemed to reveal, but pale red and white scarring from burns.

He went to her and settled a gentle hand on her waist, sliding it o'er the top of her hip, where the scarring showed most. Then he turned her and she willingly went, and he stared (he could not help but to do so) at the largest damage there on the curve of her back. "If he were not dead already, I'd torture him first, then kill him slowly and painfully," he said at last.

"I thought you were dead," she said so softly, he barely heard. "I thought: My husband is dead, and so is my soul. My daughter is safe in a nunnery, and of no further worry to Donnach. What matter it if I do this thing? If it kill me, fine; if it make me so hideous that Alaric no longer use me, allow his comrades to use me, that is fine as well.

Morgunn's stomach lurched. His breathing turned erratic. Beads of sweat dripped from his brow. "You—" the word came out more as a *whoosh* of air, so he tried again. "You did this to yourself?"

She didn't answer directly, simply continued on as if the confession might free her from what e'er ethereal prison had her still in its bonds. "It worked. For after that, he left me alone. Sent no healer, just let me lie there in my misery. I wanted to die, but it did not come to pass. When later, my body had healed itself enough for me to dress, I found I was left to myself most days and only when Alaric was in one of his rages did I see him again to receive his beatings, but 'twas better than the other, and I found I could bear it well enough, for I was ne'er again made to pleasure any man in my bed."

Again the tears clogged Morgunn's throat, made it ache, again the frustrated anger, the absolute violent need to harm, maim, destroy, kill the man responsible for this traveled through him.

She turned and looked at him, saying, "Aye. And I know what you are thinking, but don't. Think of this instead: If Alaric had done what Donnach had wanted, I'd be dead now. Instead, he took me, prisoned me, and *aye*, used me in ways I sometimes thought I would not be able to bear. But I did. I did bear them, and now here we are. Together—again." Her hands gripped his arms, her nails dug into his flesh. "And we've won,

Morgunn! Donnach is dead, Alaric is dead, the king, and the Cambel clan have given o'er to you the land and the power Donnach wielded. Let us only think on that, and from this moment forward, begin anew."

"Aye, begin anew," he said, and because he could no longer keep from doing so, he leaned down and settled his mouth on hers, trying with that kiss to show how deeply, how eternally, he loved her.

After a moment—a very splendid moment—she pushed him away and, looking him directly in his eyes, said, "We cannot go back. We ne'er can. That man and woman, the man and woman we were before, we are no longer them. We are who we are now, and I believe, if we are to make this work between us, build another strong, tho' different, bond between us, we must agree to that before all else." She paused, but only briefly, before saying with more force, "Can you accept me for who I am now, what I've done?" Her head turned so that she no longer looked directly at him. "For, if you cannot, say it now, and we will go on as I suggested before." Her gaze lifted to his again, and there was a definite spark of purpose there as she said, "And 'twill work, 'twill work for us just fine. You shall see."

"Never," he said, "I'll ne'er be satisfied to have you only in name," and swept her up in his embrace and took her to their marriage bed once more to prove just that. "You are mine. For e'ermore. For always, and a day. I will have no others, for you are my perfection. My only true mate."

Her smile faltered and she looked away. "Perfection. Nay, you go too far—the scars—"

Of Us That Trade in Love

"—Are beautiful. Are the scars received in a deadly battle. You are my warrior princess. You fought for yourself, and you fought for our love. Again, I say: They are beautiful. *You*, my love, my dearest, dearest love, are *beautiful*." He tossed his shirt to the floor and climbed on top of her, pulling her arms o'er her head, so she could not escape, murmuring near her ear, "Now, now I will do to you all the things I have been dreaming of doing to you all these moons since first I saw you again." He lifted his head and grinned down at her. "And this time, if you tell me I'm fucking you properly, I promise not to stop, all right?"

* * *

Gwynlyan's heart raced with both dread and anticipation. "All right," she said, closing her eyes. She was determined not to cringe from any touch Morgunn bestowed, but the effort made her muscles taut to the point that she knew he knew her fear. Yet, clearly, he was bent on seduction, for he said not a word, simply dropped his head down to run his tongue along the column of her throat until cold thrills ran up the length of her raised arms, rippled 'round her nipples, and shot down to the core of her, leaving it in tingling, throbbing need.

Next she felt his large, calloused hand capture her breast and mold it in his palm, before the long-remembered, long-yearned for feel of his hot humid mouth took possession there as well. As he began to suckle and tug, stretching taut the strings of her desire until neither her will, nor her body, were her own any longer, she opened for him like the petals of a wild rose blossom, and he greedily took all that she offered, trailing his other hand o'er first one thigh then the other, before he pressed the heel of it o'er her mons and began tracing the outer lips of her cleft with his blunt fingers, prying them open, teasing her there with light strokes, using the moist proof of her desire for him to ready her even further.

He swirled the pad of his finger o'er her clitoris and her thighs quivered. White spots of light bounced beneath her lids. A ragged groan escaped her throat. Still, she would not open her eyes, for she could not bear to see him ministering so lovingly to her grotesque form. For long moments more he continued to work on her, stringing her tight as a bow, one moment, then swiftly retreating, until his touch was so light, her body strained toward it. It made her skin mist with the exertion he put it through. Then, when his mouth left her breast to rise up and nibble upon her ear, before leaving her ear to tickle and twirl his tongue about her navel, her eyes flew open and a gasp of surprised desire ushered up from her throat, for she knew too well where next he'd land. She arched beneath him and he pressed his palms to her hips, forcing them back to the bed.

He touched his tongue to his fingers, damp with the dew of her arousal. "Your desire for me tastes as sweet as I've dreamed 'twould all these lost years," he rumbled, and the vibration of his breath and voice tickled her belly, making it quiver. "Let us see if I can make you come completely apart, love, for 'tis truth, I'll not stop until I do."

Gwynlyan shut her eyes tight again, but with her blood so fired for him now, 'twas beyond her to protest his purpose. For she wanted what he offered, wanted it with a need that clawed at her insides.

'Twas not long before the feel of his bristled cheek abraded the tender skin of her inner thigh, before his fingers widened her further still, before his silken tongue began that torrid, carnal dance upon her sensitive flesh she'd known was his intent. He found the spot unerringly and her head went back with a guttural growl of intense pleasure. Her frame stiffened, her womb convulsed, and multiple starbursts, one after the other, erupted behind her eyelids.

The stars were still falling down all about her, leaving a silver-light glow within and without her in their wake, when he came up o'er her again and slid to the hilt into her still throbbing, still contracting sex. He rotated his hips at the same time he began to move inside her and it made her nerve endings tingle, made her canal grip him tight.

He thrust his hands through her hair, and plowed his tongue into her mouth as he took her with a force of need she'd not expected, yet made her burn for him even more.

"Yes," she ground out, breaking the kiss to arch into him, "like that."

But instead, he slowed the pace. She could feel his gaze on her, but still she could not find the courage to open her eyes. "Only if you look at me, love."

She whimpered. Shook her head. "Nay. I cannot."

He stopped altogether, making his earlier promise a

lie, and she cried out, "Nay, please!" bucking beneath him.

But he only brushed the hair away from her forehead and placed a soft kiss there. She felt the touch of his own brow upon hers as he said, "I love you, do you love me?"

"Aye, I love you so very much, Morgunn." At least that she could give him freely and without fear. "I need you. Please."

"Aye, in time." His lips brushed hers, his rough hands cupped her face. "What is more," he continued, "I've given you my trust again. 'Twas, I confess, seeing and knowing what you did to save your honor, save the purity of our love, that made me able to do so as quickly as I did. Otherwise—and mayhap you will not believe me on this, but 'tis a truth that I know from the very center of my soul—it may have taken a small bit more time, a day, mayhap two, mayhap even a sennight, but soon after I would have done the same, whether you'd fought your captor's wishes or nay. For you were just that, his captive, and I know you had no choice, and I know if you had not, 'tis possible he might have killed you for the pleasure and the spite of it. And I cannot bear to think of a life without you in it, Gwynlyan. I cannot. For you are all that makes my life bearable, all that makes it whole. I cannot live without you. This. This I know for certain."

Her heart thrummed in her chest with the riot of love she felt for him, with the joy and excitement of new beginnings. She gave him a smile and a nod.

"And you? Do you trust me, my love?"

Of Us That Trade In Love

Trust. How could he ask her that? After she'd bared her deepest shame to him, handed herself, her heart, her soul o'er to him? A fist of fiery anger settled in her middle. She did open her eyes then and pushed him off her. Flinging herself up into a sitting position, she covered herself without thinking, and said, "This has naught to do with trust, Morgunn. For if 'twas a matter of trust, then I'd say we are near to even, for I wonder where you learned these new things you've tried with me just now? Did the woman who nursed you teach you such?"

* * *

Morgunn's mind balked. He settled himself in bed much as his wife, tho' with much less fire in his movements than she'd expressed, and much more outward calm, resting his back to the headboard while he thought how best to answer. Finally, he said, " 'Twas not with the nurse that I gained that knowledge, for I was much too weak, and still learning to reason and think well again while I was under her care." He heaved a sigh and combed fingers through the short hairs on the side of his head. "But, aye, later. When I knew not for certain, but only hoped, that you'd somehow survived, I did succumb to my body's urges. I did lay with whores. But when I discovered you still lived, I ne'er again broke our covenant."

"So, you lay with whores to satisfy your urges, much as the men did with me?" There was venom laced in her tone.

He cringed inside. " 'Tis not the same, and you know it. The women were more than willing. I've ne'er forced myself on a woman. Never. And I ne'er will, either. I know. I *know* you know this."

She gave him a grudging nod. It served to both answer him and prompt him to continue.

"Gwynlyan," he growled in frustration. "Do you truly need to know more than that?"

She sat forward, clearly in a huff, and said on an almost yell, "Aye! Aye, I find that I do," and beat her fist into the portion of mattress between them.

He growled on the exhale of yet another heavy sigh, but told her, "There were a few whores I had who'd learned their trade in the holy land, and had brought those skills with them. One—I forget her name now, but she was gentler in nature than the others—managed, with a bit more *uisge beatha* than I should have drunk, to pry some of the story of my heartache from me, but only just a bit, a small fraction, for even in my cups I knew 'twas dangerous to reveal too much. I said only that I'd lost you and was looking for you. She misunderstood. Thought you'd fled our marriage. Said she knew just the trick to keep you in my bed, and crave no other's. She was the one that taught it to me. I confess, I practiced it each time I took another whore clean enough, for I wanted, if e'er I was fortunate enough to find you living, to have you in my arms again, to give that gift to you. To bring you to rapture with only the touch of my tongue."

"It worked well, all this practice," she said into the yawning silence that followed. Blessedly, he heard a thread of humor running through her words.

He brought his gaze to hers and found mirth

dancing in her lovely hazel eyes as well. A flood of relief crashed o'er him and he reached out, drawing her into his embrace. After settling a kiss on her brow, he murmured, "So, if 'tis not a matter of trust, then why can you not look at me while I enjoy you?"

* * *

Gwynlyan tensed. She must answer him honestly, for he'd been so candid with her, she dared be naught less with him. *Because I am too hideous to look upon.* The words formed, then clogged in her throat, created a small whimper instead.

"Gwynlyan?" he prompted on a pained whisper. "Tell me, I beg you."

She tore out of his embrace and rolled to her side away from him, not able to face him when she said low, "I hate what I look like now. I hate that my body is no longer lovely, as once it was. I hate looking upon it, so I close my eyes against its ugliness, not.... Not against you. Ne'er against you. For you are handsome, and strong, and oh so appealing to me. You could have any woman you wanted. Why you still chose me, I cannot fathom. For, I know 'twas my looks, the beauty of my frame, that drew you to me all those years ago."

"Gwynlyan," she heard him say, and there was a chastening tone in his voice when he said it. "Turn around and look at me." Not waiting for her to comply, he dropped his hand on her shoulder and rolled her onto her back. She settled her gaze on his darkly handsome countenance and waited for what e'er lie he'd tell her now.

"We were bairns. Or just past it. Of course, I was

drawn to your beauty, as many, many others were as well. And you, my love, were just as drawn to mine. You will at least admit that, will you not?"

She didn't know where he was going with this, but she willingly admitted with a brief nod to her own initial reaction to him.

"And that, of course, is why you still crave me in your bed, love me, want to make a life with me? Because of my aspect?"

"Nay, 'tis because you are the best man I've e'er known. 'Tis because, when I am with you, I am happy. I am home."

He grinned. "Good. Because, if the other were true, I'd begin to worry how you will feel when I am another twenty years older, grey-haired, and not so fit."

She grinned then, too and lifted her hand to brush a lock of hair off his forehead. "Oh, I'd wager I'll be wanting you to pleasure me as much then as now."

He dropped a kiss on her nose, startled her by ripping the sheet off her body, and said, "Exactly how I feel about you."

"Morg—!"

"Look at yourself. Right now. Look."

Gwynlyan shook her head and grabbed for the covering but it was out of reach. She squeezed her eyes shut. "Nay. I can't. Don't make me do this, I beg you."

He brushed his lips o'er her lids and murmured low, "Let's save our begging for later, when you're riding me like a warrior princess upon her stallion."

That image alone made her want to shrivel inside. "Nay, Morgunn. I cannot."

"Do it, or I'll tickle you until you pee," he said, and then his evil fingers began to do just that.

She laughed out loud and tried to twist from his hold, screaming out, "Nay! Stop! You—*ha! ha!*—know my weakness—*aaaii!*—and used it against me!"

"Do you give in?"

"Aye, aye! *Ha! Ha!* Just stop!"

"Open your eyes first."

"You're evil. *Aack!*"

He chuckled. "Aye. I know."

"All right. *Eep!*"

"Do it."

She opened her eyes and found his own directly above her. His mad hands went still and for a suspended moment, the only sound in the chamber was the blowing of both their breaths. Her mirthful smile turned gentle and she lifted her hand to his cheek. "I truly do hate you at this moment. I hope the next time you pee it burns."

He grinned. "I love it when you talk mean. Do it again."

"Nay. I'm out of the mood."

He chuckled and rolled a bit to the side. "Okay, coward, then 'tis time to take a long look at yourself and see yourself with truth. Look now."

It took every ounce of courage within her, but for him, she did this thing that made her want to retch. When her eyes found the scars, immediately the urge to shut them tight again near o'erwhelmed her, but she fought it hard, and won against it. Forced herself to gaze unwaveringly at the proof of her ugliness.

"These scars," Morgunn said into the silence, running his fingers o'er them, "are truly not as horrid as you think. And believe me when I say this, they have not taken from the lushness of those gorgeous full breasts, nor the tempting curve of your waist, nor the beautiful bend of your hip, nor the enticing handful of your rounded buttock, nor the strong, straight line of your limbs. In short, even if I were to see you for the first time, have met you only a short time past, still I would want to mate with you. Often, and with avid enjoyment."

For a long moment—a very long moment—she just stared at them. Trying hard to see them in the same way that Morgunn did. Finally, something began to change within her. Some shift in her perspective took place. It seemed to have to do with—she knew not what, exactly—something, she thought, with simply looking at them, getting to know them, getting used to them as something that was part of her now, and all right to be there. Some proof, as Morgunn said, of the battle she'd fought and won. It settled and calmed her. It made her able to let go of that young woman she'd been, and embrace the stronger, mayhap even better, woman she was now.

Finally she looked up into his eyes again and said, "So, you want to be ridden do you?"

He grinned and gave a brief nod.

"All right, stallion, take me for a ride," she said, shoving him to his back and settling atop him.

His manhood sprung up between them like a jack-in-the-box, and 'twas only then that she remembered he'd ne'er found completion yet this night. And that, she thought, was a very bad thing for a new bride to do to her new husband. She leaned forward, grasping his phallus in her hand, said to him, "Get ready for the ride of your life," then took him full into her on a slow glide.

As she began the ancient rhythm, he caressed her breasts, tweaked the peaks of them with his fingers, moved his own hips beneath hers, groaned her name o'er and o'er. 'Twas not long before her own cries of pleasure mingled with his. She found the exact rhythm, the exact motion that brought on a wave of such intense pleasure, she could do naught but continue, work her hips harder in a bid to reach that pinnacle that was just there, but still out of reach.

As she did moved with more force, he answered in kind, gripping her hips and pushing her down even further as he rose up to meet her, until the head of his shaft pounded the mouth of her womb. All at once, he arched beneath her, pressed his head into the pillow, and yelled, "Aye, like that. Fuck me just like that." And she did. She did until he went rigid beneath her and pumped his seed high within her. All at once, she was there as well, giving out a ragged cry when her inner muscles convulsed around him, when her world exploded into waves of rapture.

A long time later, the two of them lay twined together, naked, and though 'twas a cold night, uncovered on their marriage bed. She felt Morgunn's breath as it fluttered a stray lock of her hair o'er her cheek and snuggled even tighter into his side.

"That, my love, was even better than we'd had before—and before was more than marvelous," he said into the silence. "Aye, I can definitely avow that our future may just be magnificent. Do you agree?"

She felt his chin move off her pate, so she knew he was looking down at her now. She tipped her head and returned the look. "Aye. I do," she answered with a giddy smile.

He gave a snort that turned into a belly laugh and she used his chest as leverage when she raised up. "What? What makes you laugh so?"

"Our daughter. I could see that she was not utterly assured that all was well within our bridal chamber, but she had not the daring to put her nose too far into my and your affairs."

Gwynlyan smiled as well, but nibbled her lip, too. "I do hope she isn't fretting even now about it. She needs her rest."

Gwynlyan made to rise, but Morgunn brought her back down to him with a strong grip about her waist.

"Nay, 'tis not long now until sunrise. We can see her then. For, if she sleeps, then we will awaken her, and if she does not, she will grow even more suspicious if you go to her and declare all is well, when we told her that already before."

"Aye," Gwynlyan said on a sigh, and settled more comfortably once again into her husband's side.

They lay there in companionable silence for quite a time more, until finally, and blissfully, they, too, found their rest.

* * *

Of Us That Trade in Love

Gwynlyan bit her lip in concentration as she carefully made the final flourish to her signature. After her capture by Alaric, she'd not been given the means by which to write, so her skill had grown weak with disuse, but in the past five moons since her renewal of vows to Morgunn, and their subsequent return to their holding, *Aerariae secturae*, she'd exchanged several letters with her daughter and the skill had slowly begun to return, become easier.

A hand landed on her shoulder and she started, but calmed when she heard the dulcet murmur of Morgunn close to her cheek.

"Another letter to Morgana, is it?"

"Aye," Gwynlyan replied, carefully setting the quill down away from the vellum she'd been scribing upon and turning her head up to meet her husband's eye. "Their son's well whelped, our daughter is hale, and she craves a visit from us."

"And by what name will my grandson go by?"

"Robert the Younger—Morgana insisted."

Morgunn lifted a brow at her, giving her a sardonic smile. "Knowing my daughter as I do now, this surprises me not."

Gwynlyan smiled, though she too lifted her brow. "You held no such loathing in doing near the same with the naming of our daughter, I will remind."

He tweaked her nose, dropped a quick kiss on her lips, then, making her eyes want to cross, said close to her face, "Aye, but mine holds more dignity, my love."

She grinned and rolled her eyes as she looked down again at her letter. "Aye, and I'm sure Robert would say much the same of his in any comparison to yours." Shaking her head with a sigh, she continued, "You know you like him well, why can you not admit it?"

She'd expected a witty rejoinder and instead received a small pause, a thoughtful reply.

"Because he is the man that took my place in my daughter's esteem."

This made Gwynlyan swing around and stare at him. "Morgunn! Your daughter adores you. What an odd thing to say."

His brows furrowed and the corners of his mouth turned down. "Aye, but not in the same worshipful way she did as a lass." His voice had a tinge of bitterness in it when he said, "Nay, that she reserves for her husband now."

Gwynlyan reached out and took hold of Morgunn's hand. "Do you not think that is as it should be, my love?"

He looked down at the floor, shrugged, and said with a bit of a pout. "Mayhap."

"You would not have liked it had I not transferred my worshipful regard of my own father to you, my husband, once we wed. I know you would not have."

"Aye, but you are my wife. She is my daughter. 'Tis different."

Gwynlyan sighed. "And as such, 'tis natural to feel the loss, I suppose. I'll say naught more of it. However, I will at least get that confession from you that you like well your daughter's husband."

'Twas Morgunn's turn to roll his eyes. He heaved a heavy sigh, but finally said, "Aye, I like him well. I

Of Us That Trade in Love

confess, 'tis hard not to do so."

Gwynlyan grinned up at him and he returned it, giving her hand a squeeze as well.

"How are you feeling this morn?" he asked her.

By habit, her hand went to her rounding belly. "Fit. Well. Joyous. Content. Eager. Well."

"You already said *well*."

"Aye, but 'twas worth repeating."

He glanced at the letter she'd written, tipping his head at it. "And did you at last tell her the reason you've been delaying a journey there these past few moons?"

Gwynlyan gave him a giddy smile. "Aye, I did. Now that her babe is born, and now that I've carried this one"—she glanced down at her belly—"until past its quickening, I feel more ease in doing so. Tho' I do still worry what her feeling will be to having a new brother or sister when she, herself, is old enough to bear."

"Knowing my Morgana, she will plan a feast and dance a reel. She will be as pleased about our babe as we are, fret no more on that score, my love." He leaned down and kissed her again. As he broke the kiss, he said, "Mayhap she will visit us instead. For, I would like to meet this grandson of mine, this Robert *the Younger*." Bringing her to her feet, he continued, "Leave that for now, let us walk in the glen, enjoy the sun, enjoy the flowers, *enjoy* each other.

A shiver of anticipation traveled through her. "Aye, let's."

* * * * *

Thank you for reading
Song of the Highlands

If you enjoyed Song of the Highlands, I would appreciate it if you would help others enjoy this book, too.

Lend it. This e-book is lending-enabled, so please, share it with a friend.

Recommend it. Please help other readers find this book by recommending it to friends, readers' groups and discussion boards.

Review it. Please tell other readers why you liked this book by reviewing it.

Author updates can be found at
http://www.kesaxon.com

Connect with K.E. at:
http://www.facebook.com/kesaxonauthorpage

DON'T MISS THE FIRST THREE BOOKS IN THE MEDIEVAL HIGHLANDERS SERIES:

THE HIGHLANDS TRILOGY: The Macleans

Highland Vengeance
Book One

Highland Grace
Book Two

Highland Magic
Book Three

MORE BOOKS BY K.E. SAXON

Sensual Contemporary Romance
Love Is The Drug
A Stranger's Kiss (novella)
A Heart Is A Home: Christmas in Texas (novella)

Sensual Romantic Comedy/Fantasy Romance
Diamonds and Toads: A Modern Fairy Tale

ABOUT THE AUTHOR

K.E. Saxon is a third-generation Texan and has been a lover of romance fiction since her first (sneaked) read of her older sister's copy of *The Flame and the Flower* by Kathleen E. Woodiwiss. She has two cats, a 26-year-old cockatiel, and a funny, supportive husband. When she isn't in her writer's cave writing, you can find her puttering in her organic vegetable garden or in her kitchen trying out a new recipe. An animal (and bug) lover since before she could speak, she made pets of all kinds of critters when she was a kid growing up. Her mother even swears that she made a pet of a cockroach one time (but K.E. doesn't believe her). She likes to write humorous, sexy romances.

* * * *

Made in the USA
Lexington, KY
22 July 2015